The Idea of Perfection

KATE GRENVILLE was born in Sydney in 1950 and is one of Australia's best-known writers. Her novels include *Lilian's Story*, which won the Vogel/*Australian* award, and its companion piece *Dark Places*, winner of the Victorian Premier's Prize, as well as *Joan Makes History* and *Dreamhouse*. Two of her books have been made into successful feature films, and all have been published to critical acclaim in the US and the UK.

Kate Grenville's experience as a teacher of creative writing led to the publication of *The Writing Book, a Manual for Fiction Writers*, and she collaborated with Sue Woolfe on *Making Stories: How Ten Australian Novels were Written*.

She lives in Sydney with her husband, son and daughter.

Kate Grenville has a website at:
    http://www.alm.aust.com/~kategren/index.html

KATE
GRENVILLE

The Idea of Perfection

PICADOR
Pan Macmillan Australia

First published 1999 in Picador by Pan Macmillan Australia Pty Limited
This 2000 edition published in Picador by Pan Macmillan Australia Pty Limited
St Martins Tower, 31 Market Street, Sydney

Reprinted 2000 (twice), 2001(five times), 2002, 2003

National Library of Australia
Cataloguing-in-Publication data:

Grenville, Kate, 1950– .
The idea of perfection.

ISBN 0 330 36206 2.

1. Bridges – Australia – Fiction. 2. Country life – Australia – Fiction. I. Title.

A823.3

Typeset by Post Pre-press Group, Brisbane, Queensland
Printed in Australia by McPherson's Printing Group

Cover design by Ruth Grüner

Thanks

Even more than most, this book is a kind of collaboration. I did a great deal of research, and even though not much of it appears directly in the book now, the writing would not have been possible without it. At all stages of the research and the writing I depended on the generosity, knowledge and goodwill of many people.

For information and inspiration on the subject of quilts and other arts I'm indebted to Margot Child, Dianne Finnegan, Jim Logan, Jane Peek, Margaret Rolfe, Lindie Ward, Vara Whale, the women of the Tumbarumba Pioneer Women's Hut, Jennifer Isaac's book *The Gentle Arts*, and above all to Wendy Holland.

On the subject of bridges, concrete, and all matters of engineering I wouldn't have known where to start without the enthusiasm and erudition of Chris Amet, Terry Doolan, Maggie Kortes, Geoff Skinner, Mark Stiles, Peter Wellings, and especially Elizabeth English. Any howlers are, however, all my own.

The Idea of Perfection would not be the book it is now without the contributions of many readers at draft stage. I owe a huge debt of gratitude to Nikki Christer, Suzanne Falkiner, Gabriel Fleming, Ivor Indyk, Sue Kucharova, Judith Lukin-Amundsen, Drusilla Modjeska, Julie Rigg and Lyn Tranter for their thoughtful and honest responses.

Many others showed their interest and support in various ways, great and small, and I thank you: Don Anderson, Alison Klein,

Sandy Gorman, Peter Mills, Adrian Mitchell, Ross Petty, Susan Robbins, Garry Shead, John Tranter and Susan Wyndham.

Thank you, David Rawlinson, for letting us use your wonderful photo on the cover.

Joan Symington had a particular and powerful effect on this book, for which I'm deeply appreciative.

On a practical level I'd like to thank the people in the Department of English at the University of Sydney who provided me with a room in which to write. On the most practical level of all, I'd like to express my very great appreciation to the Australia Council for awarding the fellowship that supported me during the writing of this book.

My family was always supportive and warmly encouraging, even when I was full of doubts. Thank you Isobel, Ken, Sam, Joe, Anna, Julie, Tom, Alice and, most especially, Bruce.

FOR TOM

AND

FOR ALICE

WITH LOVE

"An arch is two weaknesses
which together make a strength."

LEONARDO DA VINCI

CHAPTER 1

IN HIS EX-WIFE'S clever decorating magazines Douglas Cheeseman had seen mattress ticking being *amusing*. Marjorie had explained that it was amusing to use mattress ticking for curtains the same way it was amusing to use an old treadle Singer as a table for your maidenhair ferns. But he did not think the amusing aspect of mattress ticking being used as a curtain had made it as far as the Caledonian Hotel in Karakarook, NSW, pop 1374. He could feel the cold dust in the fabric as he held it back to look out the window.

Over the top of the corrugated iron roof next door, he could see nearly all of Karakarook. It looked as if it had just slid down into the bottom of the valley, either side of the river, and stayed there. Where the houses finished straggling up the sides of the hills there were bald curves of paddocks and, further up, the hilltops were dark with bush. Above that was the huge pale sky, bleached with the heat.

From the window he could see part of Parnassus Road, wide and empty as an airport runway, lying stunned under the afternoon sun. Along the strip of shops a few cars were parked diagonally into the gutters like tadpoles nosing up to a rock. A dog lay stretched out lifeless across the doorway of an empty shop. The awnings over the shops made jagged blocks of black shadow and the great radiance of the sun pressed down out of the sky.

A ute so dusty he could not tell what colour it was drove slowly in and angled itself into the gutter. Out of it got a man with a big round belly straining at a blue shirt, who disappeared under the awning of the shops opposite the Caledonian. Douglas could hear the squeak as a door was pushed open, and the thump as it closed again. GENERAL STORE EST 1905, it said on the facade above the awning, but the shiny awning said MINI-MART.

He went on watching, but nothing else moved. Standing at the window, holding the frame, he could feel the heat of the sun beat back up from the grey corrugated iron roof of the shop below him.

After a long period of stillness an old brown car appeared small at the end of the street, came slowly along and pointed itself tentatively into the gutter outside the General Store. A woman got out and stood looking up and down the street with her hands on her hips. She did not seem to be worried by doing nothing more than standing and looking. She seemed pleased, in a stern way, and interested, as if Parnassus Road, Karakarook, was a diorama in a display provided especially for her pleasure.

She was a big rawboned plain person, tall and unlikely, with a ragged haircut and a white tee-shirt coming unstitched along the shoulder. It was a long time since she'd been young and it was unlikely that she'd ever been lovely. She stood like a man, square-on. Her breasts pushed out the old tee-shirt, but it was clear from the way she stood that she'd forgotten about breasts being sexy. Her breasts made bulges in her shirt the same way her knees made bulges in her black track pants, that was all.

She was not *accessorised.* The tee-shirt hung off her shoulders and came straight up to her neck. There was no collar, no scarf, no beads, no earrings. Her head just came up out of the tee-shirt saying, *Here I am, and who do you think you are?*

Douglas stood with the curtain in his hand, watching her as she looked at Parnassus Road exposed under the sky. A salt of the earth type.

Salt of the earth: that was one of Marjorie's expressions. What she meant by that was, badly dressed.

The way the woman stood with her hands on her hips, looking down the road as if she owned it, he could imagine her life, a proper life anchored solid to the ground. There would be a big cheerful husband, uncomplicated children, fat red-cheeked grandchildren calling her Nanna. He could imagine the kitchen out on the farm, with the radio going on the bench, the big basket of eggs with the chook-poop still on them, the fridge door covered with magnets that said things like *Bless this Mess.*

A dog came along from somewhere and barked at her, making pigeons puff up in a scatter from the awning. She glanced at it, and he saw a frown darken her face.

He let the curtain fall and stepped back from the window. Then he stood in the dim room wondering why he had done that.

He glanced at his watch but it did not tell him anything useful. He sat down on the bed, pulled off his boots. Considered, pulled them on again. He wanted to have another look out the window, but he would not like anyone to catch him. It was only a kind of hunger, but it could be misunderstood.

*

Douglas Cheeseman was a man no one would look at twice. His eyes were no particular colour, and too close together. His lips and cheeks were made of the same fabric and his nose was big and freckled, even with the caps he always wore. In summer he could always be picked out on the site by the zinc cream. The younger ones laughed. He knew they laughed. On every job there were a couple of young blokes, only there for the week, pick up a bit of cash, move on. They laughed at the engineer standing solemnly with his roll of plans: they tossed bricks to each other and laughed from their brown faces at him, anxious in his zinc cream.

He was fifty-five, but he could have been ten years either side of that. Thin sandy hair, a big awkward mouth. Bad teeth, crooked and dark when he smiled, jug-handle ears. As a self-conscious boy he'd tried different things with those ears. He'd made an elasticised band with elaborate leather flaps to flatten his ears while he slept. He'd tried his hair short. He'd tried it long. He'd tried all kinds of hats. Eventually he'd grown the moustache as a kind of diversionary tactic, and he'd kept it.

Now he'd forgotten about his ears. He'd stopped bothering to wish they were smaller, his hair thicker, his mouth nicer.

He could see now that Room 8 was on the wrong side of the building, where it got the full force of the afternoon sun and the heat bouncing up from the roof of the shop below. It gleamed with lino and sticky yellow furniture and smelled of beer and dust. The bed sagged under its dim chenille cover. Three slow flies circled through the heat in the centre of the room.

He knew he should ask for a different room, but knew he would not.

In spite of its mattress-ticking curtain, the Caledonian was not an amusing hotel. It was just a pub of the old-fashioned kind, the kind that was praised as being *authentic* by city folk. He had seen on the blackboard downstairs that the Set Dinner was *Corned Beef With White Sauce & Three Veg*, and to follow *Jam Roll and Custard*. It was *authentic* country food, food from his childhood, still going strong out here in the bush, but it was not going to be especially amusing actually eating it.

From other Caledonians in other country towns he knew just what the bathroom down the hall would be like: the cream tiles, the unsympathetic fluorescent lights, the green stains under the tap, the cistern that trickled, the shower with the water saver so you hardly got wet.

There was a drought on. He sympathised. Just the same, a decent shower was a comfort in the heat.

Another sort of man, he knew, would be able to make the best of the Caledonian. Another sort of man would nip down to the public bar for a beer, where it would be cooler. He would read the paper, watch the trots on the telly. Would get a conversation going with the man next to him at the bar about the way the country was going to the pack.

He wished he could be such a man.

He got up from the bed. The structure groaned and a spring twanged as if in mockery.

Harley had seen him looking, the man holding back the curtain, with the D of the word CALEDONIAN hanging upside-down from a screw above his head. She had seen him drop the curtain and move back from the window, but she knew he was still there, perhaps still watching her, as this dog was that had appeared from nowhere.

She had forgotten how empty a country town could be, how blank-windowed, how you could feel looked-at and large.

As she watched, a woman appeared from somewhere and hesitated on the edge of the footpath, looking up and down Parnassus Road as if a stranger like herself. When she glanced along and saw Harley watching she swapped the basket quickly from one hand to the other, pushed her hair behind her ear, and swiftly, purposefully, crossed the road towards Alfred Chang Superior Meats, in deep shadow under its awning. Harley heard the ping of the bell as she pushed the fly-door open and the slap as it closed. Then it was all silent again.

She wondered if she had imagined the woman with the basket.

Further down the street past the Caledonian she could see the old picture theatre. You could tell what it had been from its shape, tall at the front and falling away steeply at the back. The brackets were still screwed on down the front of the building where the sign must have been, *Odeon* or *Starlight*. Now the whole lot was painted utility grey.

There was a piece of masonite screwed up on the wall, with a sign, hand-lettered, hard to read. She squinted towards it. COBWEBBE CRAFTE SHOPPE, she read. OPEN WED & THUR, and beside it another one left over from the previous month, with a corner broken off, MERRY XMAS PEACE ON EAR.

She laughed without meaning to and the dog barked. Then it stopped as if to let her have a turn.

Get lost, she said.

Its tail began to swing from side to side. Opening its mouth it panted with its tongue hanging out, pulsing. It went on watching her closely, as if she was about to perform a magic trick.

It showed no sign of being about to *get lost*.

The Cobwebbe Crafte Shoppe still had the old ticket window from the picture theatre, and through the glass she could see two quilts competing like plants for the light.

She glanced back at her car. It was not too late to get back in and drive away. No one would know, except this dog, and someone behind a curtain. As she stood hesitating, a rooster crowed lingeringly from somewhere, and a distant car horn went *dah diddidy dah-dah*. Then the silence pressed back in over the sounds.

She straightened her shoulders and cleared her throat.

Get lost, she told the dog again.

It sounded loud and rude in so much quiet.

The dog watched her as she looked right, looked left, looked right again. Nothing at all was moving anywhere along Parnassus Road. It was just her and her shadow, and the dog and the shadow of the dog, as they crossed the road together. Under the awning of the Caledonian their shadows were swallowed in the larger shadow.

Looking along at the Cobwebbe Crafte Shoppe, not at where she was going, she walked straight into a man coming out of the doorway of the Caledonian. When they collided, he staggered backwards and nearly fell. She grabbed at a handful of his forearm, clutching at the fabric and the arm beneath, and he flailed out to steady himself, hitting her on the shoulder. Then they were both standing in the beer-smelling current of cool air from the doorway, apologising.

The man had a look of hysteria around the corners of his mouth. He wanted to blame himself.

My fault, he kept saying. Completely my fault. Stupid.

She had a feeling it was the man who had watched her from the window, but with his hat on it was hard to be sure.

Totally stupid. Not thinking at all.

So clumsy, Harley said. Oh, me, I mean.

She did not look at him, but at the ground, where their shoes were arranged on the footpath like ballroom-dancing instructions. His were elastic-sided bushman's boots that looked brand-new.

Did I hurt you? Hitting you?

She looked at him, surprised.

Hurt me?

He pointed but did not touch.

I hit you, he said, humbly. There.

No, no, she said, although now he had mentioned it, she could feel the place hurting.

She looked at her own hand, large and plain, the one that had clutched at him, and wondered if she should ask whether she had hurt him.

Well, he said, and laughed a meaningless laugh.

A moment extended itself into awkwardness.

Well, he said again, and she said it too at the same moment.

Their voices sounded loud together under the awning. She felt as if the whole of Karakarook, behind its windows, must be watching this event that had burst into their silent afternoon: two bodies hitting together, two people standing apologising.

Sorry, he said again.

He was backing away from her now, making little meaningless movements with his hands. She went on along the footpath, trying to make her mouth less stern, her walk jaunty, casual, as if nothing had happened, but the dog spoilt it, running along beside, looking up anxiously into her face.

She did not want anyone to look up anxiously into her face. She strode out hard, ignoring it.

The same unsteady hand that had done COBWEBBE CRAFTE SHOPPE on masonite had done another just inside the door. SOUVENIRS OF KARAKAROOK — GATEWAY TO THE FOOTHILLS! A long wobbly dribble had slid down from the exclamation mark.

There was a smell of pot-pourri and a dense muffled quality to the air, padded around with shelves piled with soft shapeless fabric things. There was a rocking-chair draped with crocheted blankets, and shelves of jams, and face-washers with KARAKAROOK NSW done by hand in cross-stitch in the corner.

It was much hotter in here than out on the street, and stuffy. A fan laboured away in one corner, turning its big face this way and that without effect.

Over behind a table with a cash register a small middle-aged woman was counting a stack of doilies.

Forty-one, forty-two, forty-three.

She raised her voice so she would not be interrupted.

Forty-four, forty-five.

She flipped the last doily on to the pile and looked up.

Help you at all?

Her eyes took in the unravelling shoulder seam, the big unadorned face.

Harley smiled, then remembered too late that when she smiled broadly her eye-teeth looked like fangs.

Hello, she said, and modified the smile.

Her voice was unnecessarily loud for such a quiet shop.

I'm Harley Savage, she said more quietly. From the Applied Arts Museum. In Sydney. You wrote to us.

She went on smiling, but carefully. There was a pause.

Here for your Heritage Museum.

The woman behind the table cried *Oh!* in a long falling sound that started surprised and ended dismayed.

You're Harley Savage!

There was an awkward little moment. Harley went on smiling, but felt that her smile had congealed. The woman behind the counter was small and sharp like a bird, with red glasses and red lipstick that matched the glasses, and hair that had been dyed so black it was almost purple.

It took her a moment, but then she bustled out from behind the table and it looked as though she was going to make up for staring, and the sound of that disappointed *Oh*, by shaking hands.

I'm Coralie, Coralie Henderson. I'm the one wrote the letter.

She gestured vaguely, and Harley got her hand ready to shake, but she was too late, and in the end they did not touch. The gestures hung like a mistake in the space between them.

We weren't expecting you, Coralie cried, and got her hands out of the way on her hips.

Till later on, type of thing. Round tea-time.

She was shouting, and standing too close, as if proving she was not afraid.

I stopped the night, Harley said. In Badham.

Like an ectoplasm, the thought seemed to form in the air: *where the prison farm is.*

She heard the words come out in a jerk like a cough, too loud again.

I used to have family there, she said impulsively, and wished she had not.

But they're gone now, she added quickly.

The shop woman said *Oh!* again. Then she waited for more. Being so close, and being so short, she had to tilt her face up towards Harley.

She was prepared to wait. She had plenty of time. She was more than willing to wait for a brief version of the life story, and in particular as it impinged on *family*, and *Badham*. She was sorry for the sound of that first *oh*, Harley could tell, and had forgiven her the unravelling tee-shirt. Now she wanted to be friendly. She had a warm attentive look on her face, getting ready to hear all about it.

But Harley did not find it as simple as that. She could see that this Coralie Henderson found other people easy to like, their stories always worth hearing. She was probably a gossip, but that was just a nasty way of saying she found people and their lives interesting.

Harley felt herself tighten against Coralie's warm curiosity. She knew she had gone a hard ugly red that made her eyes look small and desperate.

In the corner the fan changed its tone as if the air had grown thicker. A knitted baby's bonnet suddenly slipped down from a pile on to the floor and Coralie bent down to pick it up again.

Look, she said, like someone beginning a confession.

Lorraine Smart, lovely woman, known her all my life, do anything for you.

She was smoothing away at the bonnet, where one of the ear-flaps kept popping up behind her fingers.

But her place, where you're staying, it's not real flash.

Harley tried to think of something reassuring to say.

That's okay, she said. I don't like things flash.

But Coralie did not seem convinced. She took her glasses off, cleaned them on a doily.

You could have my spare room, you know, she said. Fresh curtains, the lot.

She looked at Harley.

Maybe you'd rather be on your own, though.

Harley could feel her feeling her way. She seemed a kindly woman, this Coralie, and was trying to set her at her ease. It was no fault of hers if Harley Savage was never at ease.

There was another pause.

We've got a lot of interest in the Heritage thing, considering, Coralie said.

She pressed her lips together as if putting on lipstick, thinking.

We've got Leith Cousens, and Glad Fowler and Felicity Porcelline. And then we've got Freddy Chang, and of course little Helen Banks. Bert Cutcliffe from the school. And we've got old Mrs Trimm, she goes right back to well before the War.

She was nodding and smiling as if everyone knew little Helen Banks and old Mrs Trimm.

Harley tried to make an interested noise. It came out a pitch higher than was quite appropriate.

That's good, she said.

She cleared her throat.

Wonderful, really.

Outside somewhere, a crow made a long agonised noise like someone being slowly strangled.

CHAPTER 2

THERE HAD BEGUN to be a little *atmosphere* in the butcher's shop. It had got so that Felicity tended to put off going there. The problem was, the butcher was in love with her.

She hesitated outside the dusty window of the closed Karakarook Bakery. She wished there was something to look at, something to make hesitating look natural, but it seemed to have been a long time since the Karakarook Bakery had been open for business, and there was nothing in the window but a few shelves with a lot of dead flies on them.

From the school behind her, she could hear the distant strains of the National Anthem. *Our land is girt by sea.* As a child, she had had an Aunt Gert, a big woman smelling of face-powder, and for a long time it had been confusing. She had gone through the anthem carefully with William when he had started at school a few years ago, but telling him about Aunt Gert had only seemed to make him more confused.

She glanced up Parnassus Road once more. Sometimes, if she dawdled like this, someone else would come along and she could go into the butcher's shop with them. Fiona, or Christine. Christine's husband the truck driver liked meat three times a day, so she was always in and out of Chang's.

The trouble with a little place like this was, a person

could not dawdle too long on Parnassus Road without becoming conspicuous. You could not window-shop convincingly in Karakarook, unless you were in the market for dead flies. And there was no way you could sit somewhere and be *watching the world go by*. The *world* simply did not *go by* in Parnassus Road, Karakarook.

The butcher's shop had an awning that went out over the footpath, held up by old turned wooden posts. The sign said ALFRED CHANG SUPERIOR MEATS in curly sign-writer's cursive, and higher up there was a wedding-cake effect of thickly painted decorative plaster and *1889* in raised letters that each cast a small black shadow.

The awning made the shop-front very dark. You could not see into the shop at all, but of course the butcher would be able to see out, if he should happen to be standing there, looking out the window. It would look bad, if the butcher glanced out of his window and saw her dawdling, putting off going into his shop.

She brushed away a fly that was circling her face, and shook her arm when it landed there. Then she bent down and brushed her leg, although it had not landed there yet.

Sometimes a person could actually be pleased at the diversion a fly could provide.

Partly it was that the butcher was Chinese. She was no racist, and wanted him to know that she did not count it against him, him being Chinese. The trouble was, not wanting to be thought racist always seemed to make her too friendly. She could hear that her voice was a little too loud and a little too sprightly in the quiet shop. She smiled too much, and did not know how to stop.

She was no racist, but noticed, every time he spoke, how

he spoke exactly the way everyone else did. She was no racist, but listened for something Chinese in the way he talked, the little foreign something. The funny thing was, it was never there. She had tried closing her eyes when he talked, and you would never have guessed. If you happened to find yourself with him in the dark for any reason, you would never know he was Chinese.

In the dark, he would sound just like any other man.

The woman from the craft shop had told her one day that Changs had been here, meaning in Karakarook, *since the year dot.* They had come for the gold in the first place, she said, *but had the sense to see there was more money in food.* She had caught herself thinking *but it's not the same.* Her own family had only been Australian for two generations, but somehow it was different.

She was no racist. She was sure of that. But she never thought of Alfred Chang as *Australian* in the way she herself was *Australian.* He was *Chinese*, no matter how long Changs had been in Karakarook.

The other thing that was the tiniest bit awkward was the business of the bridge. As she crossed the street, she could see the poster, sticky-taped to the window of his shop. Even from here she could read SAVE THE BENT BRIDGE along the top, although the rest of the rubbish about *Heritage* was too small to see from here. From this distance, the photograph of the old bridge curving into its backdrop of bush looked like a question mark.

She had never actually seen the Bent Bridge because it was out of town on a tributary of the river, on a road that did not go anywhere she had ever wanted to go. But it was obvious that it had to be replaced, as the one in town had already been replaced. It was too old. It had become an eye-sore. Also, it was a danger to the public. Hugh had also explained that there was some problem about Shire liability. It was the sort of thing he liked knowing about and he had gone into it in some detail.

Heritage was well and good in its place. She was a great believer in Heritage. Look at the way she was taking care of Great-Grandmother Ferguson's old quilt. Now that was Heritage. She had written away to the Library to find out about the special acid-free tissue-paper to store it in, and everything. But it was not enough for something to be old to be Heritage, and if there was a matter of ratepayers' money, it was important to keep things in perspective.

One way and another, though, it was becoming just the tiniest bit *awkward* in the butcher's shop. There were several subjects she felt she had to be careful not to mention: the bridge, or the Shire Council. Or being Chinese. Or being Australian. Or love.

It would have been perfectly possible to avoid the little *atmosphere* with the butcher by going into Livingstone for the meat. It was only half an hour in the car, and she had the freezer.

But Hugh had insisted that as the manager of the only bank still left in Karakarook, he had to be seen to be sup-porting the town. Actually, the Karakarook branch of the Land & Pastoral would be closing at the end of the year. But no one in town knew, and in Hugh's view that made it even more important to be seen to be involved in local issues like the bridge business, and buy locally.

When the branch was closed they would be transferred back to Sydney, and William would go to a decent school, and they would get a nice place in Lindfield or Strathfield, and get away from the heat and the flies. She was counting the days, quite frankly. Sometimes, though, she wondered if Hugh actually liked it in Karakarook, and would be sorry to have to close the branch and leave. He had said, several times, how closing the branch would be the *death-knell* for the town. Privately she thought that a *death-knell* might be the best thing that could happen to a place like Karakarook, but she had not said so.

The street remained obstinately empty, apart from a scruffy woman further down who seemed to be watching her. She looked to the right, looked to the left, looked to the right again. There was no moving vehicle anywhere, in any direction. She wished the woman further down would stop watching her.

She hooked her thick blonde hair back behind her ear and it fell forward again straight away. She liked the feel of it, swinging against her cheek: smooth and slippery. Something about the way it swung against her cheek made her feel girlish.

She knew she looked, well, *attractive* was the word she used to herself. Looking *attractive* was taking longer these days, and required a fair amount of work with the beauty routine. What had come naturally at twenty had to be worked at when you were forty-one. But she had only just turned forty-one. A month hardly counted. Really, she was still only forty.

So many of the women in Karakarook seemed to let themselves go when they got to a certain age. Overweight, or their grey roots showing, or those terrible stiff perms that were so ageing.

She checked her reflection sideways in the window of the

Karakarook Bakery. She had always had a good bust, and the little blue top set it off well. In the reflection you would never imagine she had just turned forty-one.

The woman standing with her hands on her hips was still looking in her direction. She swapped the basket from hand to hand, pushed her hair back again, and crossed the road.

Hugh had said something this morning before he left for work. She thought she had been listening, but now somehow she could not quite remember. *A nice bit of T-bone*, had it been, or was it, *I fancy a couple of snags*? No, that had been yesterday. Or was it the day before?

The human brain could only remember plus or minus seven things. She had learned that in her last year at school, in the *How the Brain Works* chapter in the science text. She had not forgotten. It had turned out to be one of the plus or minus seven things.

She remembered the days before her marriage quite thoroughly, more thoroughly than she could remember what Hugh had said this morning. She could remember how she had sat on the bus on the way to the *Ladies' Dresses* Department at Honeycutt's, after she'd left school, and carefully embroidered pale green chain-stitch on the pale green blouse she had saved up for. Honeycutt's had only been for the time being, while her modelling career got off the ground. The Palmolive ad had gone all over Australia.

The green blouse had been pure linen, and she had had to save up for weeks to buy it, even with the staff discount. She had not been able to afford the one that was already embroidered, but had done it herself. Hugh had liked it. In fact, he had proposed the first time she had worn it. Not long after that, he had finished his Accountancy, and the Land & Pastoral had sent him out to Campbelltown, and they had got married. The wedding dress had had such a pretty little fitted waist, and a sweetheart neckline that had made the most of her bust.

She had thought she could keep the modelling going, but what with the distance from town, and one thing and another, it had drifted away. Hugh was terribly supportive, but he had pointed out that modelling was an uncertain income, whereas a bank career was dependable, so it made sense that his job should come first. When he did so well at the Land & Pastoral, and he got the first promotion, and they were sent to Dubbo, that was the end of it, really, with the modelling.

Not that she regretted it. Not for a moment. She was perfectly happy, making sure things were all kept nice, and no one could wish for a better husband than Hugh. Then of course there was William, and goodness he kept her busy.

There was absolutely no reason why she should not be as happy as anything.

She turned to the fly-door, waved at the cloud of flies gathered there, and went in on to the sawdust of Superior Meats. Behind her the door slapped back into place and a triumphant fly shot in ahead, up towards the ceiling. Inside the shop it seemed dark after the sunlight and the air was heavy with the thick smell of meat. She glanced up to where the wall of fly-wire that ran from floor to ceiling met the white tongue-and-groove plank ceiling far above. A fan rotated slowly next to a blue insect-light. She could not see the fly that had come in with her, but it would not last long.

On the other side of the fly-wire there was something

human in size and shape. In the dim light it could have been either the butcher or a carcase on a hook. She peered, and the shape moved towards her.

Mrs Porcelline!

He always seemed to enjoy saying her name. Somehow, he made the sibilance more noticeable than most people did.

She could see him now, granular behind the fly-wire, turning away from the chopping block, slipping a knife into the holster on his hip, wiping his hands on his blue and white apron.

He always did everything slowly, as if on stage behind his fly-wire. She supposed they taught them at butcher's school not to hurry, if they wanted to keep their fingers. He finished wiping his hands at last, and came over to the counter. The white laminex between them was cut into two separate benches by the wall of fly-wire coming down from the ceiling. She could see his big bland face, but could not see its expression behind the mesh.

She thought it might be like this, visiting someone in jail. The question was, who was the prisoner? Alfred Chang was at ease in his cage, with a peaceful purple-stamped carcase hanging beside him. It was she herself who felt like the trapped one.

Mrs Porcelline, he said again.

The way he said it, it was a name full of hisses. He stood smiling. She did not know how to break their gaze.

Would he think she was a racist if she looked away?

Her eyes were adjusting so she could see him better now. He was a solid man, brought up on plenty of red meat, though not tall. She could see the black hair, so straight it stuck out stiffly over his collar. She wondered if it would be coarse to the touch, like a dog's hair, or soft.

Hello, Mr Chang, she said. I'll have six short-loin chops, please.

There was something about the word *loin* she did not like. Something slightly suggestive. Especially here with Alfred Chang looking at her that way.

She would have very much preferred Woolies in Livingstone, the meat all tidy in little polystyrene trays. So much more hygienic. Coming to Karakarook had been like stepping back thirty years: cutting the meat up separately for each customer, the sawdust on the floor, carcases hanging up for anyone to see.

It made it all rather personal. There was a kind of intimacy about the butcher knowing exactly what you were having for dinner.

Now he went out through the white-painted wooden door at the back and closed it behind him. The first time she had come here, she had given her order and watched him go out through the little door and had stood, shifting from foot to foot, for so long she wondered if he had forgotten her. She had imagined him going out into the backyard and sitting on a tree stump having a smoke.

Now, twelve months and many short-loins later, she knew that the door took him into the cool-room, and that it was best to sit in one of the chairs thoughtfully provided. But sometimes he was gone so long she wondered if he had died in there, or coagulated.

Today he returned quite quickly with a lump of meat and put it on the block, worn into a curve like a wave.

He stood side-on to her and reached into the big tube full of knives hanging from his belt. He brought out one, unhooked the sharpening steel from his belt, and started to strop with lingering movements. She could see the muscles of his shoulders moving under his shirt as he stroked away deliberately at the blade.

He said something, but his voice was swaddled by fly-wire, the space above him, the dim coolness of the shop, the stirred air from the fan.

It was an awkward place to have a conversation. You could talk through the fly-screen, but you had to talk to a face that was grey and fuzzy, like a film out of focus. Or you could both twist down sideways to talk through the small flap at counter-level, where you handed the money in and he handed you the wrapped-up meat.

I beg your pardon?

He put the knife down deliberately on the block, hooked the steel back on his belt as if sheathing a sword, came over to the gauze.

Ever tried the mutton?

He was close enough for her to see his eyes, dark in his smooth face, but she could not tell what sort of expression he had. She realised you could call this being *inscrutable*.

Oh, no, she said. No, I never have.

Somehow, she'd got the tone wrong. There was more regret in her voice than was warranted by not ever having tried the mutton.

She went on quickly to cover the sound of it.

Bit tough, isn't it?

Too late, she heard how tactless that could sound.

She could feel a blush start in the small of her back.

Alfred Chang smoothed a large hand over his laminex counter and smiled down at it.

Up to the butcher, he said. Butcher it right, mutton's sweet as a nut.

Now he was staring at her through the gauze.

Oh! she said. Yes! I suppose so!

She hated the way she kept on exclaiming and smiling but she did not know what she might do if she stopped. You could hide behind a smile and no one could blame you, or guess what you were thinking. She crinkled up her eyes to show what a lark it all was, but then she remembered that crinkling up your eyes gave you wrinkles.

No one, not even a Chinese butcher, would want her if she had wrinkles.

He had finished wrapping the chops now. She flinched as the hatch flipped up with a bang.

Here you are, Mrs Porcelline.

His eyes dwelt on her, and his voice did a sort of yearning thing. The fly-wire made it hard to be sure, but she thought it was possible that he winked.

The very best there is, Mrs Porcelline. For you.

He hung on to the parcel when she reached into the hatch for it, and for a moment they were joined by the little squashy packet of meat.

It was like holding hands, in a way.

They have a fascination for white women, she thought, and suppressed the thought.

Finally he let go of the packet and bent to get something from under the counter.

Was hoping you'd come in, Mrs Porcelline, he said in his languorous voice.

Been keeping this for you.

It was like a dirty secret when his big hand came out from the hatch holding a brown paper bag towards her.

Oh! Really! What is it?

She heard her exclamations travel through the meaty air, filling the shop. She had a feeling she was shouting.

When she opened the bag, something cool rolled out against her hand and she gave a little cry of fright, snatching her hand back. The thing was cool and damp and bright red. She thought in shock that it was a tiny heart. *They eat dog*, she thought confusedly. *Dogs' hearts.*

She heard herself go *Urgggh!* It was the sort of noise her mother had made when taken by surprise. She had made it herself in the long-ago stale dusty playgrounds of childhood. *Common.* It was a noise she thought she had long since trained herself out of.

And she could see now that the thing was not a dog's heart at all. It was only a strawberry.

From my garden, the butcher said.

She hated the way she could not see him properly.

Picked them myself. Six o'clock this morning.

She smiled at the mesh, where he was a vague square dark shape.

Thank you so very much, she heard herself gush. They're perfectly marvellous.

They were horrible. They were too big, too solid, too meaty looking. Fleshy, solid, like a heart. Revolting.

Ox-heart, the butcher said, and she was startled.

Pardon? I beg your pardon?

She wondered in panic if she had spoken aloud.

What they're called, that kind, he said. Ox-heart.

She felt paralysed. He brought his head down to the flap and inserted his big face sideways into it to look up at her, his eyes skewing sideways.

Ox-heart, he said clearly. Heart of ox.

His head stayed there, sideways in the hatch, watching. The hatch was just the size of his big smooth face. She put her own head sideways too. It seemed only polite. She could feel her smile hanging down on one side. It was like being a huge sparrow, head cocked.

They're so big! she exclaimed. They're enormous! What enormous things!

She felt as if she had got the hang of the conversation now. They were strawberries. They were not dogs' hearts, although they were called ox-hearts. But her brain was going very slowly. She could not think of anything to say apart from how big they were.

She held up one of the strawberries and turned it around and around. It was not really all that interesting.

How do you get them so big? I've never seen them so big! They're incredible! So huge! Marvellous!

Suddenly she thought it sounded as if she was actually exclaiming over and over again at the huge and marvellous size of his – well – *organ*.

She felt herself starting to sweat.

She was certainly not thinking about his – well – *organ*.

And I'm sure they will taste just delicious!

She blushed more and longed for rescue. Where were all those meat-eaters' wives when you needed them?

She flung her husband into the breach.

Hugh will love them, she said. And so will William. They love strawberries.

The butcher's large bland face did not move in the flap but his eyes blinked.

Oh, he said. But I picked them for you.

He was watching her, and she thought he was smiling,

but with his face sideways it was hard to be sure. She wished the face would go away, the eyes stop looking at her. Smiling away hard, she thought of how she could jam her shopping bag up against the hatch. It would be right up against his face. It would be just the right size to block the face out completely.

Oh, but I'm allergic, you see, she said wildly. To strawberries.

She felt herself flood with heat. He was still just watching. It was as if he had unscrewed his head and wedged it in the hatch. The silence, with him watching, was unbearable.

Only strawberries, she shouted. Lucky really, nothing else. Just strawberries.

She went on piling words in front of his face.

They bring me out in a rash. Well, a terrible rash, really. More like a . . . *disease*.

The word came out in a hiss.

She was thinking, *Leprosy*.

His face recoiled and disappeared from the hatch. She had not meant, of course, that Chinese people gave you leprosy.

Sort of a rough rash, she amended. Like pustules.

She had heard the word, but perhaps it was not quite what she meant. She had not exactly meant *pus*.

And itchy, she hurried on. Terribly itchy. Oh, you wouldn't believe.

Behind the wire she could not see if he believed or not. The flap slapped down and she saw his large hands on the counter smoothing the white paper there, pressing down a dog-eared corner.

Well, he said. I wouldn't want to bring you out in a rash.

She could not see if he was smiling.

27

She heard herself giggle explosively.

No, she said, and could not think of what to say next. Certainly not.

I hope Mr Porcelline doesn't come out in a rash too, he said. Or William. Do they, Mrs Porcelline?

She rushed in.

Oh no! Mr Porcelline just *loves* strawberries! So does William!

She hated the way he went on just standing, watching as she laboured to find more words.

She was still smiling hard when she left the shop, and she went on smiling until she was out of sight of his window. The strawberries were cool and damp through the paper of the bag. She went briskly along Parnassus Road holding them casually, smiling at old Mr Anderson standing in the doorway of the Mini-Mart across the road, calling *Hello, how ARE you*, very warmly, to the mother from the school whose name she could never remember, waving to Fiona who was just now, too late to be any use, heading over towards Chang's. She smiled and waved, and held the bag of strawberries as if they were the least significant thing in the world.

The thing was, Hugh would want to know where she had got them. It would seem a little odd to tell him the butcher had given them to her. Why should the butcher give her strawberries? Why strawberries? Why her?

All things considered, it might be a bit *awkward* if he knew.

Taken all round, it might be better for the strawberries simply to disappear.

But in a little place like Karakarook, where nothing went unobserved, getting rid of a paper bag full of strawberries, the unwanted gift of a Chinese butcher, was not as simple as you might think. If she just put them in the bin at home, Hugh might notice. He was strict about the recycling, and had a way of glancing into the rubbish-bin. It would look odd to have thrown away perfectly good strawberries.

It might even make her look guilty.

She was at the end of the shops now, coming up to the park at the corner of Virgil Street. There was a bin in the park, outside the public toilet. She could just pop in through the gateway and drop the bag in the bin, and pop out again, and that would be that.

She glanced around. Outside the Mini-Mart, old Mr Anderson was still standing on the footpath, although it was hard to know if he was watching her. She could not see in, but the Acropolis Cafe across from the park was open, and it would be just her luck that Ellen would be glancing out the window as she dropped the bag in the bin. Greeks were such busybodies. In a little place like this, someone was always watching you. It would look funny, to be throwing something in a public bin. Ellen might be curious enough to go over and look, and everyone in Karakarook would know who grew the ox-heart strawberries. Ellen would pop over to tell Coralie in the Cobwebbe Crafte Shoppe. Australians were busybodies too, really. Before you knew it, everyone in Karakarook would know.

That was the kind of little place it was.

The best thing would be to burn the whole lot in the incinerator at home. They would make a bad smell, burning, but if she went home and did it quickly now, the smell would be gone by the time Hugh came home. She had got the knack of the incinerator now. You would be surprised how often there was something that needed burning, what with one thing and another.

Hugh might smell the smoke in his office at the Land & Pastoral, but he would never guess that it was coming from his own backyard.

Burning was always the best idea. It tidied everything away marvellously. And ash could never create any kind of *awkwardness*.

CHAPTER 3

CORALIE HAD BEEN right that Lorraine Smart's house was *not real flash*. The front gate sagged off a single hinge and a length of gutter slanted across the front porch like a demonstration of something in geometry. Inside, everything was broken, faded, worn-out, improvised: the kitchen window with a length of white cord hanging out of its sash like a rude tongue, the mantelpiece full of glass swans and china horses that had been broken and glued together again, the laundry where the taps were covered by a brown-paper bag with DO NOT USE in big letters.

Harley had dreaded Lorraine Smart's house, imagining matching tea-cups that she would chip, and polished tables that she would scratch, and a Master Bedroom with the private shape of someone else's feet still in the shoes in the wardrobe, and the troughs made by other people's lives still in the mattress.

But she was starting to feel she would probably like Lorraine Smart, whoever she was. She liked the fact that the ornaments had all been broken at least once already, and when the kitchen tap came off in her hand and had to be fitted back on, she felt at home. The fridge door, speckled with rust, as if it had measles, was covered with photos of people lined up, squinting at the camera, smiling. In some of them you could see the shadow of the photographer, stretching out over the grass to meet them.

A space had been cleared among the photos for a note: *Welcome, make yourself at home, Best regards, Lorraine* held on with a pineapple-shaped magnet that said *Greetings from Rockhampton*.

The kitchen window looked out over the backyard, which was *not real flash* either. There was grass as faded and dry as straw from the drought, and a few limp shrubs, and dead sticks where other shrubs had given up. There was a big messy gumtree hung with ragged ribbons of bark, and underneath it, tilting on the hard ground, a Garden Setting in white plastic. There was a Hill's Hoist with a little brick path leading out to it, and a square of pink concrete underneath to stand on while you pegged out the washing. A bare wire archway with a few dead sticks tangled in it had obviously been meant to have roses *rambling* over it.

Harley opened the window and leaned out. The sun was beginning to lower itself down towards the hills and although it was still hot the light was beginning to thicken into gold.

It was another planet out here. The city became merely a dream, or as distant as something you had read about in a book: something you could remember, or not, as you pleased. The country made the city and all its anxieties seem small and silly, and yet when you had been too long in the city, you forgot how the sun moving through its path was a long slow drama, and the way the sky was always there, big and easy-going.

*

When *C. Henderson* in brackets *Mrs*, Hon. Sec. of the Karakarook Heritage Museum Committee, had written to the Sydney Museum of Applied Arts, no one there had been very interested. The setting up of the Karakarook Heritage Museum sounded a worthy project, but small-time, and it looked a long way on the map.

The letter was just a photocopy. You could tell that *C. Henderson* in brackets *Mrs*, had sent it off to the National Trust as well as the Sydney Museum of Applied Arts, and the Historical Association of New South Wales, and anyone else she could think of.

But *C. Henderson* in brackets *Mrs* had applied to the Cultural Affairs Board for a grant to establish the Karakarook Heritage Museum, and the grant included money for an expert to oversee the setting-up.

The *Curator* in brackets *Textiles* at the Museum happened to mention it to the *Consultant* in brackets *Part-Time*. The *Consultant* in brackets *Part-Time* had expressed interest. No one grew rich making artistic patchworks, or being a *Consultant* in brackets *Part-Time*, and there was the matter of some outstanding medical bills.

The grant from the Cultural Affairs Board did not run to accommodation for the hired expert, so *C. Henderson* in brackets *Mrs* had suggested billeting, but the *Consultant* in brackets *Part-Time* would not agree to that. The various complicated baggages that the *Consultant* in brackets *Part-Time* carried around with her took up too much room to be accommodated in someone else's spare room.

For a while that had seemed to be the end of the whole idea. The *Curator* in brackets *Textiles* filed the letters from *C. Henderson* in brackets *Mrs*, and the *Consultant* in brackets

Part-Time put the Road Map of New South Wales back in the glove box.

Then there was another letter from *C. Henderson* in brackets *Mrs*. The daughter of a woman called Lorraine Smart, no brackets, had just had twins, and Lorraine Smart was going up to Sydney to help her out. *Able to offer you the use of a fair-sized house*, the letter said. *And any other assistance we can provide*.

To the *Consultant* in brackets *Part-Time*, the fortuitous arrival of Lorraine Smart's daughter's twins had seemed like a little nudge. *Go on. Go.*

The dog was there, ranging around Lorraine Smart's backyard nosing at the Garden Setting, lifting its leg against the wire archway. She had not invited it to come. While Coralie had stood outside the Cobwebbe Crafte Shoppe giving her directions, tilting her face up earnestly so the lenses of the red glasses flashed – *First right, first left, past the church, left again, you can't miss it* – the dog had got itself into the car, sitting up on the back seat looking out the window like the Queen of England.

It had not seemed the right moment to have an argument with a dog, there and then in the middle of Parnassus Road, with everyone behind their shop windows, watching. She had started the engine, repeating *first right, first left, past the church*, and waved out the window to Coralie, and watched her in the rear-view mirror, waving back.

Now the dog was nosing along the fence and suddenly a shrill voice called *Come here! Come here!* The dog jerked back guiltily and Harley did too.

Johnny? Johnny? Come here!

It was coming from the next backyard. She peered out cautiously and saw a big white cockatoo in a cage beside the fence, hauling itself up by its beak. It stuck its head out between the bars and she could see the crop moving in its beak as it called again: *Johnny? Come here, Johnny!* It was not interested in the human at the window. It was watching the dog.

Harley was no expert on dogs, but this one did not look special in any way. It was biggish, and greyish, blotched all over like camouflage paint, with a big feathery tail. There was a thin white stripe down the centre of its forehead and its eyebrows were picked out neatly in tan.

She thought it would probably go home soon. Her boys had done the same thing as children, wandered off, attached themselves to people, had adventures. The middle one had gone across the road one day with his little suitcase packed with underpants, and told the woman who lived there that he had come to stay. *That's lovely, dear,* the woman had said, and when the catch on the bag had come undone and all the underpants had fallen out she had picked them up and taken him inside for a chocolate biscuit.

Harley had laughed, the way you were supposed to, when the neighbour told her the story. *The look on his dear little face when all the underpants fell out!* But there had been a pang, that he had thought this woman with her chocolate biscuits might be a better bet than she was.

At the end of the day, though, the boys had always come back home, even from the best adventures. After the chocolate biscuits, or the walk to the railway embankment to look at the trains, or the conversation at the bus-stop with the smiling woman with the flowered hat, the boys had always come home and had their dinner.

She thought it was probably much the same for dogs.

Beside the kitchen, along the other half of the back of the house, was a glassed-in verandah that the Smarts probably called *the sunroom,* with a daybed covered with a faded Indian bedspread. A great pale wash of afternoon light fell into the room from the windows. A stripe of warm syrupy sun lay along one wall and sloped across the polished boards of the floor. A tree alongside stroked leaves over the glass with a whisper. It was like being outside, except that it was inside.

The *Livingstone & Shire Weekly Clarion* lay on the daybed showing a big headline: TOWN SPLIT ON BRIDGE. There was a grainy photo of a small river with a timber bridge, and a smaller headline: *Councillors Call for Calm.*

Harley heard herself laugh. It was very loud and abrupt in the silent room. She glanced around and caught sight of someone looking around furtively in a mirror, which she recognised as herself.

It was the only problem with Lorraine Smart's house: the mirrors. She had already startled herself in the living-room, catching herself frowning, and in the kitchen a magnifying mirror had given her a fright, staring at her with a huge close cold eye.

After fifty years of looking into mirrors she felt she had looked enough. She knew all about the big flat face, the meaty cheeks, the naked domed forehead, the thin hair. All her life people had been sure of what she should do about her hair. *Perm it,* they had said and she had permed it. *Grow it out*, they said, and she had grown it out. Whatever she did with her hair it made no difference to the way her face looked.

She knew just how the two deep grooves beside her mouth gave her a stern and unapproachable look. She had put them there, over the years, by making sure her face was stony and unyielding. Some admirer had once told her, *the eyes are the windows of the soul*, and she had put the stoniness there to stop anyone peering in her eyes at her soul.

Now her face stared back at her, truculent, at its reflection. After enough years, the look you put on your face to hide behind became the shape of the person you were.

She approached herself in the reflection until she swallowed herself up in it, and took the mirror in both hands, lifting it down and leaning its face to the wall.

She sat on the daybed, hearing it creak. After a moment she lay down and stretched out with her hands behind her head staring at the white ceiling. The stripe of sunlight angled up from the wall, over the ceiling. Sunlight and shadow lay together in big simple shapes. *Light, dark.*

There was a tremendous emptiness of the air here in the country. She took a deep breath. It was so pure it almost hurt. Silence filled her ears like noise. The big pale simple skin of sky she could see out the window was blank, crossed only with the chirp of a bird darting past.

Wall. Window. Sky. They were simply themselves. No weight of meaning needed to attach itself to them.

She had got ahead of herself, travelling along the freeway. Now she had a space of time before she caught up with herself. For a short time, she could simply be *woman*, looking at *ceiling*, just one more object in Lorraine Smart's house.

Overhead the roof ticked and creaked in the afternoon sun. *Woman with Afternoon Light:* a still life.

Sunset had come and gone, and a big country darkness had absorbed the backyard when she woke up.

She was large and inefficient in Lorraine Smart's roomy kitchen, opening every cupboard to find the tea-bags, then opening them all again to find the jam. She walked backwards and forwards as if pacing out the distance, taking the bread over to the toaster, the tea-bag over to the mug. Her movements were stiff and polite, as if Lorraine Smart, and the family squinting out from their photos on the fridge, might be watching.

Standing at the sink, she could see that the dog was still out there, just within the band of light that fell from the kitchen window, a darker shape against the darkness of the yard. They stared at each other through the glass.

There was no point in thinking it could not see her.

The feathery tail began to wave slowly from side to side as the dog cocked its head on one side, its large ears pricked forward keenly. Its mouth was closed, giving it something of an anxious look. Quickly, like a soldier getting back into step, it shuffled its back feet and settled again. But it was not going to go anywhere. It was certainly not going to pack its little suitcase and go home.

The thing was, even someone who had never owned a dog could see that it was expecting to be fed. It was expecting to be fed, and it was expecting her, the woman in the kitchen, to do it.

All at once, it was not simple any more. It was not

woman and *dog,* tastefully arranged in various poses in the lights and shadows of a country evening.

The trouble was, even as *woman* looked at *dog* and *dog* looked back at *woman, still life* had turned into *life.* There was no escaping the fact that *dog* wanted something from *woman.* Like it or not, *woman* had to make a choice. Already, it was getting complicated.

In fact, it was in danger of turning into a *relationship.*

Her sons had all wanted a dog. One by one, at a certain age, like clockwork, they had asked. She had reluctantly agreed to other animals. They had had a succession of short-lived goldfish, and rabbits, and mice, more of them every time she looked in the cage. They'd had a cat that dribbled when you stroked it, and for a time they'd had a hen out in the back-yard, until it started crowing and they had to pay the butcher to take it away.

Mice and cats were all very well, but what the boys had really wanted was a dog. They had put a collar on the cat and tried to take it for walks, to show how well they would look after a dog. They had tried to teach the mice to sit up and beg.

She had gone on saying no. She had talked about the fleas and the smell and the problems with holidays. She had talked about responsibilities. Three husbands, three sons: it was already too much. With each son, each husband, the argument was stronger.

It was not untrue about the *fleas* or the *smell,* or the *responsibilities,* either, but none of that was why she went on saying no. It was the dogs themselves. It was the way they *adored* you. That was the thing about dogs. Mice did not *adore* you, and nor did chickens. But dogs did.

Husbands *adored* you, too, at least at first.

Being *adored* was something she had come to mistrust.

She felt *adoration* to be a small and lovely-looking bomb that could blow up in your face at any time.

It was not that she disbelieved. Eyes certainly brimmed with tears, voices grew reedy, faces soft.

But it could not be Harley Savage who was being *adored*, because Harley Savage was not *adorable*. She was not even a particularly *nice person*. She was not *generous* or *unselfish*. She was not a *sunny soul*. She was not especially *talented* or *creative*, except in a limited way. She had certainly never been *pretty*, much less *beautiful*.

But they kept on and on, hammering away at her with the words: *I love you. Oh, how much I love you.* Her heart sank when they started in with all the words, and she hated having to look deep into someone's eyes. She was always the first to look away.

After a while the whole thing started to feel like a terrible misunderstanding, or an exam she could never pass. She knew that she herself, Harley Savage, was not the Harley Savage they *adored*. That Harley Savage was someone she could try to be, but in the end it was too difficult.

Someone had once asked her why she had had so many husbands. *Only three*, she had thought in surprise. Then she had found herself saying, *I've got a dangerous streak*, and her mouth had laughed.

I've got a dangerous streak. She had said it lightly, as if it was nothing important.

It had just popped out, surprising her, but it had stuck.

Harley Savage. Watch out, she's got a dangerous streak. It was like a curse.

The first husband had soon found someone else to adore, a pretty little woman with a sweet fluting voice so soft it disappeared into the furniture. It was easy to see he had been after someone as different as possible from big plain Harley Savage, with her abrupt ways.

The second one, the one with the nice smile, had been taunted by Harley's air of cool amusement, her refusal to look deep into his eyes, until he had got his hands around her throat one overheated night. He had been frightened, then, of what he was doing. She had seen it in his eyes, the surprise. *Me, doing this?*

That was when she first saw that she could be dangerous.

She had tried once more, marrying the third husband. He had not taken any of the easy ways out. He had never been interested in other, sweeter, kinds of women. He had not tried to look deep into her eyes, had never allowed her to provoke him out of the calm he carried around with him like a shield.

Until, at last, the calm turned out to be as brittle as the sheet of ice on a puddle, and had snapped. In the end, he had chosen the hardest way out he had been able to think of, and it had taken up residence within her like a living wound.

He had chosen his way out fifteen years ago, and since then she had not let anyone get very far. She did not wait for the familiar words or the looking-deep-into-her-eyes to start. As soon as she felt them coming on, she moved on smartly, and after a while they had stopped being offered. Sometimes it was a little lonely, but it was safe.

*

Her sons were like trophies, a neat set, one from each husband. They were a different thing from husbands. Children adored you, but in their case it was not a test. There was no need to get anxious about not being perfect. No matter how unlovable a mother you were, they still loved you. It was just a biological thing. It had nothing to do with your personality.

She had not had any choice but to love them too. It came naturally. You did not have to look deep into their eyes or talk about it all the time. No matter what they were like, and what kind of people they turned out to be, she would have loved them. She did not need them to be perfect. Her feelings for them went deeper than loving them because they were lovable. Her love for them was just an uncomplicated fact of life, like needing to breathe.

She had been a soft-eyed proud mother who knew how to cherish a necklace made of painted macaroni. She had kept some of the macaroni, and all their primitive drawings and their little letters to her when they were learning to write, that said, *deAR MUm, I LoV yoUo.*

Sometimes, when she needed to remember that she could love, just like anyone else, she got these things out and looked at them. They brought about a kind of swollen feeling in her heart that went on for a long time after she had put them away again carefully in their special box.

There had been times when her love for her sons had been so great it was painful. She had dreaded it then, as another thing that could be dangerous. At times it felt like something separate from herself, a parasite that had her in its grip, something that could turn on her at any moment and destroy her.

You could not leave children behind, the way you could

leave a husband behind. Your children were something you carried around with you for always. You could not push them away, explaining that you *had a dangerous streak*.

But you could hold back your love for them and not let it show. You could pretend it did not really matter very much. So she had not paid as much attention as some of the mothers did. She had not gone to all their little school plays and got teary from how sweet they all were, or helped them with their homework, and had never known where they were after school or who their friends were. She had overheard someone saying that her boys had had to *drag themselves up*.

The youngest, Philip's boy, had got the worst of it, and had spent time out at Badham. But he had met a nice girl on the day-release scheme and was doing all right now with the water-pump business. *Back on the rails* was the expression he used.

They were all grown up now, and in spite of having missed out on a dog, and a motherly kind of mother making sandwiches in the tuck-shop, they had not turned out too badly. They were far from perfect, certainly, but then so was their mother.

It was hard to understand why she had mentioned *family* to Coralie Henderson. She must have been in a strange state from the hours on the freeway. They could have that effect, the freeways, the landscape unreeling, bland, colourless, unconvincing, all those shining shark-shaped cars screaming past in a blast of air, the semi-trailers with flapping tarpaulins grinding alongside until they could tuck themselves in ahead.

You could get yourself into a buzzing unreal frame of mind where you might forget and let anything come unawares out of your mouth to a total stranger. She had not really been thinking about *family* at all.

Perhaps the freeway trance also explained why she had let the dog come along with her in the car. It made no sense. Three sons, three husbands. It was already a long unhappy history.

She was definitely not going to add a dog.

Outside, the night was making many small unfamiliar noises. Lying stiffly on Lorraine Smart's lumpy daybed, she felt her ears straining for the endless soft roar of distant traffic they were used to, up and down Alfred Street, Mount Street, Carlotta Street, and now and then a siren to let you know people were out there, being rescued. Here between Lorraine Smart's unfamiliar sheets she felt the strangeness of this other planet, and herself in it.

Here it was the foreign indifferent sound of the wind in the trees: all those stiff leaves rubbing over each other, making a whispering like a conversation that excluded you. And those hollow ponking noises. She thought they must be frogs because what else could they be? But frogs were supposed to *croak*. This was not so much a *croak* as a sound like someone hitting a cardboard box with a stick at irregular intervals. Sometimes several people with several sticks hit different-sized cardboard boxes all together. It did not sound like frogs, but it must be, unless there were people out there, hitting sticks against cardboard boxes in the darkness.

CHAPTER 4

DOUGLAS CHEESEMAN WAS woken up by a rooster somewhere nearby that seemed to have no faith in itself.
Cock-a-doo! it would go, then try again. *Cock-a-doo!*

In the end he got up, although it was miles too early, and
got dressed. Then the only thing to do, until it was late
enough to go down to breakfast, was to stand at the window
and look – cautiously – at the view.

Across and slightly below him was a grey tin roof and
below that the faded blue paint of a brick wall. Funny how
you could come to the country and still be facing a brick
wall. There was a window in the wall, but a curtain was
drawn over it. The fire escape that ran down beside his own
window passed so close to the window opposite you could
almost step across. Terrible security hazard, but in the country he supposed security was not an issue.

He did not lean out, but over the top of the grey tin roof
he could see along Parnassus Road, heroic in scale, tapering
majestically away to a vanishing point like the exercises in
perspective they had done in Technical Drawing.

You could see that Karakarook had once taken it for
granted that it had a big future. Wool and beef had poured
out of it, along the old highway or down the barges on the

river. The founding fathers who had wanted to show off their classical education would never have guessed that the river would silt up, the new roads leave them marooned, the price of wool make it hardly worth shearing the sheep.

The narrow shops were jammed up along Parnassus Road in an irregular wall. Each one had done something different in plaster: there were swags of flowers, pointed urns, furled brackets, wreaths, pediments. There were little niches and meaningless piercings and fluted columns holding up nothing.

From here you could see how long it was since anything had had any maintenance, except the big shiny Coke sign along the awning of the Mini-Mart. All the fancy decorations were rough with paint that had cracked and weathered into a kind of oatmeal. Something had taken root in the droopy bit of one of the swags of flowers of the closed Karakarook Bakery next to the Mini-Mart, and had even gone so far as to produce small yellow flowers of its own. Grass sprouted all along the gutter, like a fringe that needed cutting, and one of the pointed urn things had fallen off the facade of the shop below him. Standing at the window, he could see where it had rolled down the sloping roof behind the facade and come to rest against a chimney.

In the presence of so much sky, the attempt at grandeur was a mistake. Up beyond the flimsy little shops the hills were very close, very solid. They were a structure of another kind altogether. Up there, dark timeless pelts of bush folded themselves over the curves of the land. Air moved in stately tides. Clouds made large bold gestures in the sky.

*

He seemed to be the only guest at the Caledonian. He pushed at the big wooden door with DINING ROOM in gilt letters with big serifs, like something engraved in Latin on a public monument. A woman was there, putting knives and forks away in a drawer.

Morning, he said.

He felt conspicuous, standing among all the empty tables and chairs. He sat quickly in the first chair that came to hand.

Morning, she called. The Set Breakfast, love?

He nodded, more eagerly than the Set Breakfast probably called for.

Yes. Yes please.

He wished he had chosen a seat with his back to the wall. Not only did he have his back to the room, but he could not see out the window, and only had the plastic tomato sauce bottle in the shape of a tomato to look at.

But he thought it might look funny to change tables.

The woman pushed at the swinging door that led to the kitchen, and he could hear a fine day being forecast for the slopes and plains, plates being stacked with a great clattering, glasses clashing together, a tap drumming into a sink. A female voice said something that made a male voice laugh.

He supposed he could look rather ridiculous sitting in the solitary splendour of the DINING ROOM. He knew pretty much what to expect from the Set Breakfast. On a big oval plate with a blue rim, there would be the two flabby fried eggs, the watery fried tomato and the brittle bacon. White-bread toast, curled like a scroll, would crack in the toast-rack.

He sat staring at the sauce bottle. Now that the swinging door was closed again he could not hear anything from the kitchen. He wondered if they minded turning everything on, the big stove and the exhaust fan and everything, just to cook one Set Breakfast. He wondered if he should spare them the trouble and go down the road to the Acropolis. But then it might look as if he did not like the Caledonian's cooking.

Sometimes he felt the urge to apologise simply for existing, much less wanting breakfast.

Head Office had organised for him to meet the road gang's Leading Hand in the bar. The problem was, the publican was still cleaning out there from the day before. One eye was higher than the other and his nose was crooked. It gave him an unsteady wary look as he glanced up.

G'day, mate, he said, pausing in his mopping.

G'day, mate, Douglas said.

He hoped it didn't sound like satire. He wished he had got in first and called out *Morning, mate!* in a big hearty way. He perched uneasily on a bar stool. The publican pushed the mop backwards and forwards next to his feet.

You want a drink, mate, have to wait till I'm done here.

He unhooked his bottom from the stool.

Oh, sorry, he said. Mate. Should have said. Just waiting for a bloke.

He was standing in a puddle of water. The dirty strings of the mop were flicking around his boots.

Said I'd meet him here.

Suit yourself, mate, the publican said.

His lips were pressed together as if the mop took a lot of concentration.

Douglas got back on the stool, but tentatively, one foot

still on the floor. It was dark in the bar, glittering with wet tiles, and draughty, all the windows flung open. The great grey eye of the television hung over the bar and he kept glancing at it, and at the enigmatic handwritten sign on a piece of cardboard underneath it: TOUCH REGO BOWLO SAT. The publican hosed out the floor with a great blast of water, slapped over the metal counters with a lump of wet rag, stacked crates with a rattle and flourish.

The silence, under the blasts and crashes the publican was producing, had become strained.

Hot enough for you? Douglas finally said.

It came out croaky and he cleared his throat.

The publican looked up suspiciously from mopping around the cigarette machine.

Eh?

Douglas cleared his throat again.

Hot, he said clearly. Hot, isn't it?

The publican grunted and bent back to his mopping. The quality of the silence was now something you could snap in your hand. He had to get his feet out of the way quickly as the publican threw down a rubber mat beside the bar.

The doorway filled with the darkness of a bulky man with the daylight behind him. A big cheery voice boomed out into the bar.

G'day, Vince!

The publican straightened up from the mop.

Ah, Chook! G'day, mate!

He sounded like someone who had just been rescued. Hearing that, you could tell that Vince had not liked having someone perched on a stool watching while he cleaned the place out.

Douglas wished, as he often wished, that he had thought a bit quicker. He was a good enough thinker, but a slow one.

He stuck out his hand blindly towards the silhouette.

G'day, he said, I'm Douglas Cheeseman. From Head Office.

His hand was squashed in a strong meaty grip.

G'day, Doug, Henry Henderson's the name. Call me Chook, everyone does.

There was a short pause in which he could hear water dripping off the counter. It was getting into his boot.

Chook Henderson was only the Leading Hand, but he put himself in charge straight away.

We go in your ute, eh, he said.

It was not a question.

I'll drive. Show you the way.

He was no older than Douglas, but he looked a lot tougher. His face, crinkled up for years against glare, was seamed like a shoe, the tufty eyebrows coarse and vigorous. He had an old felt hat, and a big round belly that pushed his pants down so they hung off his hips.

He led the way out to the street and got in the driver's side while Douglas was still wondering how to say *no*.

He was a conscientious man. The ute had been issued to him. He was not supposed to let anyone else drive it. It was the insurance or something. Whenever you had a vehicle issued to you, you had to sign the Vehicle Requisition Form and the Blue Slip. You made a note of the mileage and how much petrol was in the tank. There was a place on the form for Pre-Existing Damage, too.

He had made the ute his own, driving down that morning from Sydney. They were his own browning apple cores in the ashtray, his own crumpled newspaper all over the floor, his own old brown jacket squashed up on the seat on top of his December issue of the *Engineering Digest.*

Chook Henderson was already reaching under the driver's seat to slide it backwards. His belly just fitted nicely in behind the wheel. He wound down the window and held out his hand for the keys and Douglas gave them to him.

Just like that. It was as if his hand did it all by itself.

He stood with his mouth ajar, wondering.

Chook already had the engine running, had the thing in reverse, the hand-brake off. He had not needed to be shown the trick about reverse, how you had to push the little button down on the gearstick before you slid it across. It had taken Douglas a moment to work it out when he picked up the ute at the car pool. It was the kind of puzzle he liked, and he would have been happy to show Chook.

This Chook did not need to be shown anything. The only thing holding him up was the bloke from Head Office, standing there looking as if he'd just remembered he'd left the stove on.

He came around to the passenger's side. Chook was pushing the newspapers to one side in a hospitable way. He saw the *Engineering Digest* and picked it up.

Temporal Variants in the Hydration of Portland Cement, he read, and tossed it on to the dashboard ledge.

Bit dry, eh, Doug?

He laughed a gusty laugh. Douglas wondered if he had made a joke. *Dry. Hydration.*

He laughed tentatively.

The *Digest* had seemed a good idea, back in Sydney. Catch up on a few back issues. Now he wished he had thought to put it in his bag. Over the years, he had found that it was hard to explain the attraction of the *Engineering Digest* to people. He had tried to tell them what was interesting about such things as the hydration of Portland Cement, but they had never seemed really convinced.

He stared out the side window. He did not know how you got to be a Chook Henderson. He had known them in the schoolyard. It seemed to come naturally to them. Perhaps it was something to do with your father, or whether you had brothers and sisters. Perhaps it was toilet training. He did not know how he had been toilet trained. It could be in the genes, or in the water. Iron in the pipes, something like that.

Whatever it was, it was too late for him now. He was good at working out the buttons on a gear stick and he knew a great deal about Portland Cement and other related subjects, but it seemed that he was no good with people. He had been told that more than once.

They left the shops behind, turned downhill and crossed the river. The bridge looked new, a simple job, pre-stressed concrete, three spans, he knew the type well. On the other side of the bridge there was a faded sign: *Karakarook North*. The road sloped around the hill along a ragged-looking street with no kerbing and guttering. The houses clung to the side of the hill, tilting on their foundations: blistered weatherboard places patched with stained fibro, the roofs rusting away, lattice unravelling from verandahs in long drooping strips, an old car up on bricks in every front yard.

Then without warning they were out of Karakarook, on

a dirt road running between rounded paddocks with clumps of trees and lopsided corrugated iron sheds that sent long crooked shadows out over the ground.

Even at this early hour of the morning the air that came in the window was so dry that Douglas could feel the membranes on the inside of his nose drying out. He imagined them cracking like old leather. A horse lifted its head from a pink bath that lay tilted on the ground beside a fence and stared at him with drops of water falling off its whiskery mouth.

Chook drove much faster on the dirt than Douglas would have cared to. As well as being careful about the Blue Slip and the Vehicle Requisition Form, he was a cautious driver. He had never had an accident, never even had a parking ticket. Risks were not in his nature.

Chook was driving with his right hand and rolling a cigarette with his left. While he did it he was not driving any slower. It was not an arrangement that made Douglas feel relaxed. The springs under the seat bounced and rolled and he wondered how much traffic there was, out here in the bush.

He felt the need to swallow. He wondered if he should offer to roll the cigarette for Chook, although he had never rolled a cigarette. He had taken a few timid puffs of joints at parties long ago, but he had never quite seen how home-made cigarettes worked. In design terms, there did not seem to be anything stopping the tobacco falling out the end.

This thing's buggered, Chook said.

He licked along the edge of the cigarette paper and squashed it around the tobacco.

Know what I mean?

Douglas could see that the cigarette was certainly a strange lumpy shape. He wondered if he should agree about it being buggered. He could suggest more stuffing. That would give it greater longitudinal strength. While he was thinking, Chook spoke again. There was an edge of impatience in his voice.

Your shocks, mate, he said. Your shocks are stuffed.

He glanced sideways at him and cocked a whiskery eyebrow.

Eh?

He stuck the cigarette in the corner of his mouth.

I'd a thought they'd look after their vehicles, up in Head Office.

Douglas had no wish to defend Head Office and any decisions it might have made about stuffed shocks. He glanced quickly sideways out of the window as if something had caught his attention, but there was nothing out the window to catch anyone's attention, only a drooping wire fence and a sheep with a big daggy backside.

Oh well, he said.

Chook glanced at him, waiting for more, but he did not say anything else, just got out a big blue hanky and sneezed into it.

Dust, he said, and laughed as if it was funny.

The road was winding uphill but Chook was not going to let a hill stand in his way. Douglas watched his big coarse hands throwing the ute round on the corners. The *Engineering Digest* was flung to the floor and he picked it up. He did not know where to put it so he sat holding it between his knees.

Chook smacked the gear stick down through the gears, forcing the ute along. The engine roared and snarled.

Douglas had not known that his mild-mannered white ute was capable of making such a sound. He glanced over at the tachometer. The needle was nearly in the red. He stared anxiously ahead, wishing for the crest of the hill. He could hear something rattling angrily underneath and the whole vehicle trembled with the strain. Chook was solid in his seat, his profile impassive.

He could not think of how to draw the position of the needle of the tachometer to Chook's attention in a tactful way.

They were over the hill now, rocking around the corners down the other side, and Chook was lighting the cigarette. Douglas watched him press the dashboard lighter against it so that it bent like a banana. Finally it began to smoke, and Chook blew out a few big blue puffs. He took it out of his mouth, pulled a shred of tobacco off his tongue, stuck the cigarette back on his lip, settled himself comfortably behind the wheel. He was ready now.

Douglas braced himself for a conversation.

Yes, Chook said.

He resettled the cigarette on his lip and blew out a lot of smoke on the word.

Glad to see the back of it, tell the truth, he said. Danger to life and limb.

He had to shout over the noise of the engine.

Douglas was feeling queasy from the bouncing and the smell of Chook's roll-your-own at close quarters. He seemed to have missed something. Chook seemed to be waiting for an answer. He thought there must have been a question. He tried to focus.

Greenies! Chook shouted.

He was shouting, but somehow Douglas could not hear him properly.

Chook swung the wheel hard to avoid something dark and dead in the middle of the road.

Douglas looked away and saw another lot of sheep out of the side window. Having to ask Chook to stop so he could be sick would be getting off to a pretty poor start. He made a vague answering noise that he thought Chook would not hear over the engine.

But Chook was not worried about what he was saying. He was enjoying his next thought.

Be saving the bloody dunnies next!

He laughed a big laugh with a rattly cough on the end of it. He took the cigarette off his lip, wound down his window, and spat.

Matter of safety, isn't it? he said. Responsibility to the public.

The phrase made him serious. He was watching Douglas, waiting for an answer. Douglas watched a corner approaching with a big pothole on the left-hand side and a tricky narrowing of the road.

You'd agree with that, wouldn't you?

It was clear that Chook was not going to stop watching him until he answered. He spoke up loud and quick.

Oh yes, certainly. Absolutely.

The feeling of wanting to be sick was making him break out in a sweat.

In the nick of time Chook looked at the road, skirted the pothole, got the ute around the corner. He seemed satisfied, although Douglas would have liked to know what it was that he had so earnestly agreed to.

He felt foolish, clutching his *Engineering Digest*. He opened the glove box, but the *Engineering Digest* was too big for it, so he had to go back to holding it.

No shortage of timber, those days, Chook said. For the bridges and that.

Douglas wished Chook would stop watching him.

Yes, he said. That's true enough.

He could feel Chook waiting for something more. He supposed it was a bit bland, but it was hard to think of words when you were about to be sick.

He could not see the speedo, but he could feel how the ute was sliding its back wheels out on the corners, and hear the rattle as stones were flung up against the paintwork. Pre-Existing Damage: Nil, he had written on the form.

He was pretty sure that even if he was not about to be sick he would still not know what Chook was talking about.

You'd think they'd be happy, Chook said. Saving the trees. But no, not on your nelly.

He laughed richly. Talking seemed to make him drive faster.

No, Douglas said vaguely.

He stared out the window at where two cows watched the progress of the ute and its cloud of pale dust. One had its mouth in a long funnel, mooing, but he could only hear the roar of the engine.

Talking made Chook go faster, but at least he looked at the road. When he was waiting for Douglas to say something he watched him. He was watching now, waiting for something better than that pale little *No*. There was another sharp-looking corner coming up.

How do you mean? Douglas asked.

This was not the way he wanted to die, tangled up in a

paddock with Chook Henderson and the ute from Head Office, with the *Engineering Digest* clenched in his white hand.

Happy? Who d'you mean, exactly?

All the bloody timber! Chook shouted. What they're on about, the greenies! Bloody possums and that. Endangered this that and the other thing!

He made a big gesture with one hand that made the ute swerve on to the wrong side of the road.

They want the old bloody bridge, see. The bloody Heritage. But they want the bloody trees too. See what I mean?

Douglas nodded, watching the *Engineering Digest* between his knees. He could not bear to see the corner coming towards them.

Well, he said.

He had to force himself to speak. It came out in a tiny squeak.

The timber is certainly a factor.

He could feel Chook still watching him.

A big factor.

Chook snorted, finally looked at the road, jerked the wheel around casually. Douglas could feel the back of the ute slide on the gravel, the whine as the wheels failed to grip. Then they were round.

You bet your bloody life it is, Doug! Chook shouted. A factor.

The word hung satirically in the air between them.

He looked out the window again. There was no sign of the river now, or the tributary with the *old bloody bridge* across it. He wondered how much further it would be, and whether he would be sick before they got there or after.

They don't want the bloody concrete, Chook bellowed suddenly, giving him a fright.

They're against the bloody concrete. Know what I mean?

Douglas looked around at last.

Against the concrete! he repeated.

Chook glanced at him and smiled a brown-toothed smile. He took a fresh grip on the wheel, settled back against his seat. Douglas could see how pleased he was to have finally got his attention.

How's that, then? he asked.

It seemed to him that Chook was driving less fast now. Concrete seemed to have something of a steadying effect on him.

Being against the concrete?

Not organic, Chook said.

He thought for a moment, and elaborated.

Not bloody organic enough.

He gathered the phlegm in the back of his mouth with a ripping sound and spat out the window.

It's the compost and earth-toilet lot. The bloody vitamins and let-the-bloody-chooks-free lot.

He gestured with both hands to demonstrate the letting-free-of-the-bloody-chooks and the ute sailed towards the bushes beside the road.

But concrete! Douglas said quickly.

Concrete!

His mouth faltered, trying to find the words to do justice to concrete.

Chook was not a man to wait around for the right word. He laughed a short unamused laugh.

Course it's organic!

One hand was holding the wheel casually, the other was out the window, elbow on the sill, hand gripping the edge of the roof so his shirt sleeve flapped in the slipstream.

Organic as bloody anything!

Douglas turned slightly towards him and put the *Engineering Digest* on the floor. He thought he was probably close enough to grab the wheel himself, if worst came to worst. The thing was to turn towards Chook in an interested way, but to keep his eyes on the road.

You've got no rot, no bloody maintenance at all!

Yes, Douglas said. I mean, no.

Neat and tidy! See you right for years!

Yes, he said again. Absolutely.

Chook grew quieter, put both hands back on the steering-wheel.

Nearly there, he said.

He coughed.

You'll find there's a bit of it in town, he said casually.

Douglas wondered what there was *a bit of* in town. As Chook turned to him and nodded, he noticed one eyebrow was tufted up, giving him a lopsided look.

Oh? he said, feeling helpless.

Nothing to worry about, Chook said.

Douglas was immediately anxious.

The bloody *Heritage Committee*.

Chook loaded the words with irony. He swung the ute around a corner, down a hill, and suddenly there it was, the tributary, and the bridge that was *a danger to the public*.

It was a cock-eyed little thing with a bend in it as if someone had given it a push in the middle. Chook switched the engine off and a hot humming silence established itself.

Knew a bloke once with a dick that shape, he said.

Douglas laughed. Then he wished he had not.

With his thumb Chook killed a fly trapped against the windscreen, and wiped his hand on his pants.

No worries, he said.

He glanced at Douglas, who nodded, but in fact he was full of worries, especially about the drive back. He would have to try to be sure to drive, except that he was not certain of the way. If he could not be the one driving, the next best thing would be to lead the conversation on to subjects less inflammatory than the bridge. Something nice and boring.

There was a lot to be said for being boring, and it was something he was good at.

He stood beside the stream, balancing on a big bean-shaped stone. Beside him a fallen tree had been silvered by years of floods and sun, the grain streaming like hair around the knots and holes in the wood. A small bold bird in a suit of green perched on it, cocked its head at him, and flew off. On the map, the stream was called Cascade Rivulet, but it was neither a cascade nor a rivulet, just a modest flow of water that travelled sinuously over rocks and logs in a series of shining bulges. It was a comfort, the way it kept coming, calmly obeying gravity, threading its way diligently down-hill, whether anyone was there to see it or not. It did not have to be authoritative or impress anyone. It just took the line of least resistance.

The bridge had not started life bent, but during some long-distant flood the middle of it had been pushed down-stream by a raft of drifting timber. Generally that was the end of it with bridges: they broke up then and washed away. But this one seemed to have chosen to bend rather than break. The centre piers had allowed themselves to be shifted bodily downstream through the sand of the riverbed and then, as the flood receded, they had planted themselves back in. On the top, the timbers of the roadway had slewed around on their bolts into a stiff curve that was higher one side than the other, like a shrugging shoulder.

Now the bridge looked weak, but it was not. It had been damaged, but the damage was the very thing that made it strong.

However, it was condemned. The file had come to Douglas Cheeseman, in at Head Office: *Replacement of the Bent Bridge*. It was a straightforward job. You demolished the old one, straightened up the approaches, and put in a prefabricated concrete beam. He had done it before, many times. The old timber bridges had all been built around the same time, so they were all wearing out together too.

Knocking down the old timber bridges was not his favourite job. He liked them, the innocent clumsy structure of them, the way the wood developed personality in its old age, although as a professional he could see how inefficient and over-engineered their structure was.

He was a good engineer. He had always been good at the sums. He sat at his desk with the surveyor's figures, doing the site plans and working out the specifications. The plans for the Bent Bridge were rolled up in his hand now.

Out on site, you were never parted from your plans. They were your Bible. They got dog-eared, yellowed, smeared with mud, peppered with little holes from where you had unrolled them on the ground.

But although so sacred, the plans were only the start. Once you got out there on the site everything was different. No matter how carefully done, the plans could not foresee the *variables*. It was always interesting, this moment when you saw for the first time the actual site rather than the idealised drawings of it.

He knew men who hated the *variables*. They had their plans and by golly they were going to stick to them. If the site did not match the drawings it was like a personal insult.

He himself liked the variables best. He liked the way that the solution to one problem created another problem further down the line, so that you had to think up something else, and that in turn created another problem to solve. It was an exchange, backwards and forwards. Some men thought of it as a war, but to him it was more like a conversation.

The variables had been the unexpected reward for getting through the exams and out on the sites. The other thing had turned out to be the bridges. They had a special fascination for him. He had been told there was even a word for people like him: he was apparently a *pontist*.

In the beginning, he had tried to get Marjorie interested in the bridges, but she had glazed over more and more as time went on. She had always made him promise not to *start on about your everlasting bridges*, when they'd gone out with other couples. *Just give it a rest, Douglas, people aren't that interested.*

He had bored her to death. It had been unreasonable to expect her to be interested. *Oh Douglas*, she had cried in exasperation one windy day on the Glebe Island Bridge. *Doug-las!* She had had a way of spinning out his name that had always filled him with apprehension. He blamed himself, now, for not catching on sooner.

In the end the pleasure of a good bridge had become one more private thing that you did not try to share.

He walked out on to the middle of the bridge, being careful to stay in the centre of the roadway. There was no guard-rail and, with the vertigo, he had learned to steer well clear of edges. He watched his boots, moving along the old timbers to the middle of the bridge. You were generally all right if you kept something in the foreground. When he was safely in the middle of the bridge he stopped, turned around, and carefully looked up. There was the ute, already dusty, and Chook leaning on the bonnet rolling another cigarette. Beside it was a tussocky paddock full of cows, and further back there was a rise with a ruined chimney and some poplar trees.

He suppressed the impulse to wave idiotically at Chook, and turned cautiously around, until he was looking at the other bank. A steep slope of bush, still in shadow at this hour, slanted down towards the bridge, with the road skewing around sharply through it, washed away into deep corrugations. It had been poorly planned in the first place, he could see that, with no thought for drainage. He knew without looking that the plans called for a new alignment that would cut in around the slope less steeply. The surveyor had marked it all out with fluorescent orange tapes that fluttered around the trunks of the trees that would have to be cut down.

He wondered if the Heritage Committee knew about the trees having to go, as well as the bridge.

He looked down at his boots and watched as they carried

him steadily, calmly, along the middle of the bridge. At the far end there was a loose fence-post that he pushed sideways, and he slid down the bank. It was steeper than he thought, and he arrived at the bottom in a shower of pebbles and dirt. In the silence he could hear them continuing to pour down the slope behind him.

Under the bridge it was cool and dank, full of rich organic smells. He stood with his boots sinking in the soft sand. The piers spanned a small glassy pool, each one disappearing into its own reflection. He looked at them with sympathy. His own teeth were somewhat similar, ringbarked at gum-line from years of unscientific brushing.

Pale sand fanned out underwater where the current slowed and shelved away into deeper, darker brown water against the far bank. Over there a dragonfly danced above a pucker of current. Upstream and downstream of the pool, the water bubbled mildly down through slopes of rounded stones.

There was a quiet secretive feel under here, crouching on the strip of damp sand. It was like hide-and-seek. He had always preferred to be the one doing the hiding. The water bubbling through the stones was like someone talking to you, keeping you company. Pale bands and twists of light reflected upwards from the water, stippling and shimmering over the dark timbers, making a secret upside-down world.

As he watched, a leaf twirled down out of the trees. It floated under the bridge where the water went black, and he waited for it to come out into the light on the other side.

He looked at the uprights, each one a whole tree trunk. Even after a hundred years shreds of bark still clung to them in places, and you could still see the knobs where branches had been roughly lopped off. It was not so much a bridge made of timber as a bridge made of trees.

There was no great engineering in these old bridges but he had noticed how often there was exceptional workmanship. Here, for instance, a neat bit of squaring had been done on the timbers of a joint so each one slotted in snugly against the other. The long-dead men who had built this bridge had even gone to the trouble of countersinking the bolt-heads, pecking out a tidy hole to get it all as tight as a piece of cabinetwork. It was tricky, working hardwood like that, but they had thought it worth doing.

True was the word carpenters used. It was as if they thought there was something moral about it.

In his books about bridges he had seen photos of the old-style timber-cutters with their axes, posing beside the stumps of huge trees. They stood in their waistcoats, the foreman with his jacket on, holding their axes. Under the heavy moustaches their faces were serious.

Now the Inspector had declared it *Past Repair*, stamped the words in red on the file, and Douglas Cheeseman had come along to knock it down.

It seemed like a mark of respect to confirm that the bridge was dead. He got out his Swiss Army Knife and was thorough, spiking his way along the underside of the bridge as far as he could go. In some places he came across rows of little holes where the Inspector had been there before him. When he had finished poking, he tapped with his knuckle and listened, like a man at a strange front door.

The corbels had had the worst of it, lying horizontally between the roadway and the tops of the piers. At first glance they looked sound, massive pieces of squared timber in which you could still see the marks of the adze. But the spike sank in up to the hilt, and when you looked closely you could see how the wood was mottled with rot, and the way the fibres were shrivelling away, contracting secretively into tiny cubes. When he knocked, the wood did not answer, only swallowed the sound like a sponge. He reached up and broke off a handful that went to powder in his hand.

He could see why the Inspector had got out the big red stamp. Replacing the corbels would be expensive. There was a high price on hardwood now that it was scarce, and on the skilled labour to work it, too. Not many people did anything with axes these days.

Even if you put new corbels in, you still had the problem of the water coming through the roadway and starting the rot all over again. The Shire Council had known what it was doing, demanding a concrete beam. Rain could pour down on it as long as it liked, and a flood might make it go a funny colour, but it would never rot and never bulge in the middle. No one would ever have to do any maintenance, or even notice it again.

Certainly, no one would ever think of making rude jokes about it.

He wished again that he had not laughed.

He laid his palm against one of the timbers, gently, as if it was an animal to be reassured.

Course, they had the timber for it back then, Chook said suddenly from behind him.

For a big man, Chook could move quietly. Douglas snatched his hand off the wood. He wondered how long Chook had been there, watching.

He moved away and felt his boots tear up out of the

mud. A fly started to pester him around the eyes and he flapped at it. No matter how early you got up, the flies were always there before you.

Plus, no chain saws, Chook went on.

He laughed, not unkindly.

Poor buggers, he said. They'd have been all day, buggerising around with the axes and that.

The fly was now several flies, and one was trying to get up his nose. It was funny, the way they left you alone until you needed to have your wits about you. They seemed to know when things were already tricky, and made sure they made them worse.

Hey, Chook said.

His face had taken on stern folds under his hat. He got out his pouch and teased out a shred of tobacco. Douglas waited. Chook was in no hurry. He slid the packet of papers out and wedged it under his armpit, sticking a square of paper to his bottom lip.

Know what the definition of a wilderness is, Doug?

The paper waggled on his lip like semaphore.

Can't say, Douglas said in a discouraging way.

He never liked jokes. He had been known to laugh long before the punch-line, out of sheer anxiety.

He watched Chook roll the tobacco into the paper and crease it carefully around, licking the paper with relish. He waited again. Chook lit up slowly, spinning it out.

What's between a greenie's ears!

Chook waited for him to laugh, and he did, but reluctantly. It was a forced and unamused laugh, cut short when a fly flew into his mouth and out again. He shut his mouth quickly and looked down. Where he had been standing thinking about the bridge he had left two perfect casts of his boots pressed into the mud, like the scene of a crime.

Chook tapped at ash that had not had a chance to form.

My wife's in with them, he said.

It was the most casual thing in the world.

The Heritage mob. Think we can get the bloody tourists here looking at the bloody bridge.

He put the cigarette back in his mouth and glanced at Douglas.

You know women, he said. What they're like.

Douglas nodded, although he would not have said he knew anything at all about women, what they were *like*. He and Marjorie had always been like an amateur job of carpentry, all gaps and putty that fell out after a while.

Tea-towels, Chook said suddenly. Pictures of the bloody bridge on bloody tea-towels. Mugs, drink coasters, the lot. She's gone right into it.

They stood in silence, looking across at the water.

Chook had the cigarette pinched between his lips, letting out big puffs of smoke every now and then like a boiler.

Playing-cards. On the back.

Douglas had the feeling that there was something else Chook wanted to say, possibly on the subject of women, and what they were like, but he did not want to hear it, and he himself had nothing useful to contribute.

In the silence the sound of the water bubbling down over the stones reasserted itself. Over against the bank where the water lay brown and still, a small fleet bird skimmed the surface, kissed its own reflection and spun away. A bubble broke the surface, then another.

They climbed back up the bank. Watching Chook's broad

back, on which a collection of small black flies was travelling, Douglas was planning his move. He would slip quickly into the driver's seat before Chook could get there. *I'll drive*, he'd say. It would be the most natural thing in the world.

But as he drew level with Chook, putting on a spurt so as to beat him to the driver's side of the ute, a small truck came bouncing along the potholes towards them and pulled up. Somehow he and Chook ended up with the truck between them, and Chook was having a conversation with the driver that Douglas could not hear. He saw them gesturing, saw the driver point toward him, saw Chook shake his head.

Hey, mate, Chook called. Stan needs a hand with some cattle that got out last night. Reckon you'll be right to get back to town on your own?

Yes, mate. Go ahead.

He had to try to keep the gladness out of his voice.

Go right ahead!

He liked the idea of poking around on his own, having a look at the ruined house, exploring. He watched the truck grind along through its gears over the bridge and up around the washed-out corner of road. For a long time after it had disappeared into the trees he could hear the gear changes, up the hill and off into the distance.

With the truck gone, he felt wonderfully alone. The sun glinted among the trees on the hillside, the bright new top leaves tossing themselves around on their stems as if waving. In the thick, shadowy undergrowth he could see the fluorescent tapes fluttering bright, like someone beckoning.

*

CHAPTER 5

HARLEY WOKE UP when a finger of white sunlight slanted in the window on to her eye and she was confused, feeling the stiff bedcover against her chin, seeing the light spread in an unfamiliar way on the ceiling. Outside, birds carolled and whooped in long melodious undulations of liquid notes. Somewhere further off, two kookaburras took it in turns to cackle and peal.

She got up and looked out at the backyard. It was still quite early, the sky a pale blue, sun slanting in low shafts along the dry grass, making haloes around the bushes. A big black bird swooped low out of a tree and posed for a moment on the top of the wire archway, then with a laborious flapping took off back up into the tree.

The dog was standing there, watching the window. She had not seen it at first because of the way it was not moving. It was as if it had been standing there, watching the window, all night. Its shadow stretched away, neat and crisp, from each of its paws. When it saw her at the window, it started to wave its tail backwards and forwards.

She had had to feed it the night before, of course. *But just this once,* she had told herself as she stood out in the dark backyard, giving it a tin of Pal she had found in the cupboard. *Definitely just this once.*

But from the way it was looking at her through the window with its head cocked on one side and its tail going backwards and forwards, it looked as if it might not understand about *just this once.*

She turned away from the window without acknowledging the dog. As far as she was concerned, the dog was as irrelevant to her as the tilting white plastic Garden Setting. Quickly she pulled on some clothes. Instead of leaving by the back door, she went through the house, finding herself tiptoeing past the Master Bedroom, and opened the somewhat majestic panelled front door. From the way it creaked and squeaked it was obvious that no one had used it for a long time.

She pulled it closed behind her as quietly as she could, but as she went down the front steps, the dog appeared around the side of the house. There was no fuss. It was as if they had been meeting like this at the foot of the steps for years.

She turned out of the gate. It was nothing to do with her if the dog was trotting along behind. It was none of her business, and she was not going to give it a glance.

She began to stride out, shoulders back, chest pushing forward through the air, her eyes on the silvery paddocks up beyond the last roofs of the town, where long stripes of pale early sunlight and soft mauve shadow folded themselves around the slopes.

A few doors further up the street, a very large woman was sweeping her front path with a tufty little dog beside her. Harley was carefully not looking at her, but she heard the sweeping stop. Out of the corner of her eye she could see the fat woman leaning on the broom, watching. She was not even pretending not to watch, and the tufty dog was watching too.

She put a pleasant sort of expression on her mouth, and readied herself for a quick bluff *Morning!* as she hurried past. But before she had time for that carefully-judged *Morning!* – not so cool as to be rude, but not so warm as to have to stop – the woman leaned the broom up against the fence and spoke.

Having a bit of a look-round? Your first morning?

It was impossible not to look, impossible not to slow down. Harley smiled in a way that felt sickly.

Hmm, she said. Yes.

The young woman was tremendously large and so fair she had no eyebrows, her big pale bland face like something beautifully washed. She had pressed herself up against her wire gate, to talk to Harley, and cushions of cloth-covered flesh bulged between the strands. Behind her on the lawn were various-sized balls, a wading pool, a tricycle with a wheel missing, a red plastic cape, a small pink gum-boot.

She was smiling and waiting. It seemed that she had really meant it as a question and was waiting for an answer. She did not seem to be playing by the city rules: *How are you good thanks and you* and then you went on. This woman actually seemed to be expecting a *conversation*.

The dog had stopped too, and was sniffing the nose of the tufty little dog.

Can't get up there, you know, the woman said. If it was a walk you were after.

Harley felt her face lengthening, her upper lip growing haughty. She reminded herself that this was the bush and they did things differently here, but she did not like being given answers to questions she had not asked.

Hmmm, she said again.

The young woman was still smiling calmly. She was not in any kind of hurry. She was just waiting for the next part of the *conversation*.

You want a walk, the woman said, you'd be better off going along Jupiter Street.

She smiled warmly and nodded several times. As far as she was concerned, it was self-evident where Jupiter Street was.

Jupiter Street, she said again. That's your best bet.

Still she did not point.

Lorraine's got her place done out nicely, she went on after a short wait. You'd be comfortable enough there.

Harley felt herself shrivelling up, curling away from this thing – this *relationship* – with this stranger. In the city there was a kind of politeness in pretending you were equally unknown to each other.

She felt her face stiffening.

Yes, she said, in a quelling end-of-conversation way.

But this rosy beaming woman might never have heard of *end-of-conversation*, or the tone of voice that told a person they had gone on long enough.

Yes, she went on serenely. Beverley's just had the twins, of course. Plus they've got the toddler, that's Kylie, and there's Brad, he's seven.

She smiled and nodded encouragingly at Harley.

You need your mother, times like that, don't you?

Her big solid body was like something inanimate, only the head nodding and smiling away on top of the solid pile of neck.

Harley heard herself producing words.

Yes, well thanks so very much.

It did not sound as if she was actually grateful for anything.

The face of the fat woman registered something. It was not a frown and it was not offence. It was like the look on the face of an actor registering that his partner had forgotten his lines.

There was a short pungent silence.

Round down along past there, the woman said, and finally pointed. Jupiter Street.

The bulk of her began to get itself turned around, like a liner, to point up the path towards her house.

Can't miss it, she said over her shoulder.

Harley felt her lips draw back across her teeth. It could not really be called a smile, but she was trying.

Thanks, she called after her. Thanks very much indeed.

Jupiter Street ran out of houses fairly soon, and on the edge of town it lost its confidence, the asphalt trailing away. Then it was just a dirt road, hardly more than a two-rutted track, traversing the side of the valley. You could see it slanting gradually down towards a ribbon of trees that showed where the river was.

She strode out, taking deep deliberate breaths. *Forty-five minutes to an hour*, the doctor had said. *Every day if possible.* At home in the city it was a matter of round and round the park, or through the congested streets trying not to step in the dog poo. An hour could seem a long time. Here, she could see that *forty-five minutes to an hour* was a much more elastic kind of thing.

It was obviously going to be another hot day. The flies had not found her so far, but where the sun slanted in across the ground the paddocks were already humming and ticking with insects. Lizards rustled under the dusty bushes beside the road and small solid-looking birds like fat china ornaments hopped in and out of the yellow flowers.

Ahead of her, long stripes of sunlight split by trees lay along the paddocks. A single long-dead pale gumtree stood in its necklace of ringbarking, casting a long intricate shadow out in front of it. Along the crests of the ridges there was a lacy effect where the pale sky showed through the canopies of the gumtrees. The bush on the ridges was not green so much as a dark and dusty khaki that went to black where the hills folded secretively into little creases. A bald shaved stripe where powerlines ran was the only straight line in a landscape that was all soft swellings and bulgings.

A group of cows was gathered around licking a rough brown block of salt. One looked up with a long straw of grass hanging from its mouth, staring at her like a yokel.

The dog trotted alongside her as if she belonged to it, as if it was being taken for a walk. It slowed when she slowed, broke into a run when she strode out quickly, looked where she looked. It was like a mirror trotting along beside her. But it was not because of the dog that she was walking. It was for herself, for her *dicky ticker*.

She took deep breaths, swinging her arms, striding out along the road. She could feel her heart pumping away in her chest. It sounded strong.

But it had sounded strong before, and then it had suddenly stopped. You could not really trust a heart.

Dicky ticker. She had lain on the narrow hospital bed

watching the doctor's young full-lipped mouth saying it: *dicky ticker*. He said it a lot, as if he enjoyed it, as if he was quoting, with amusement, some earlier, quaint, generation of doctors. She was confused from having nearly died, but she had wished he would stop saying it.

The nurses had talked about *infarction*.

None of them ever said *heart attack*. It had taken her a while to realise that was what had happened to her.

The gigantic pain had spread from her chest into her shoulder and down her arm and up into her jaw. The tremendous gripe of it had squeezed her almost to death.

She had barely been able to breathe, feeling the knots pulled tight around her heart. If she moved or thought the wrong kind of thought they would tighten further, and strangle her. She lay, not even blinking, watching the light and shadow on the white ceiling of the emergency room.

The doctor had all his long words about *arterio*-this, that and the other, and she listened and nodded. He had been kind, with his joky way of talking. But there on the white bed, under the cotton hospital blanket that kept you from being cold without exactly being warm, she had seen that all the *arterio* business was only an excuse. The truth was that her heart had finally decided to punish her. It had taken all these years, had let her go on with her *dangerous streak*, had watched to see if she could mend her ways, if Philip's death would make a difference. But she had not mended her ways: instead she had shrivelled inside, and clenched tight, growing wizened and stunted from so much unhappy history.

It seemed only right that her heart was finally turning on her.

Nurses came and went, tiny and far away beside the bed.

Doctors held her wrist, leaned in at her. Friends came and made mouth-shapes at her, pressed her limp hand. They had all talked about her second chance. She could turn over a new leaf. It was not too late.

They had all agreed how important it was to *unwind*. They made it sound easy, a simple choice you could make, *wind* or *unwind*. They made it sound no more difficult than choosing to *sit down* or *stand up*.

I want you to clench your right hand. Tight, tight, tighter, the soothing voice on the tape coaxed. *Now relax.* She had lain on the bed, clenching her fist, *tight, tight, tighter.* Then *relaxed.*

She was prepared to go through the motions, but she did not really believe in *second chances*. It was too late.

Somehow, it had always been too late. Even as a child she had known about being *wound*, like the swings she had played on with her sister. She would twist them up on their chains, forcing the seat around and around so it was coiled tight and ugly against itself. That was *wound*. It made you scream with the danger of it, the power screwed up in the chain, waiting to strike.

And in the end it got you.

The sun was lighting up every grass-head along the roadside with its own little glowing halo. A tall black horse galloped over to the fence and stood staring at her, a big spherical eyeball on each side of its head like a cubist painting. A muscle in its shoulder twitched under the hair. She hesitated, feeling an urge to go over, stroke its glossy neck, feel the big breathing warmth of it next to her. But when the dog sat down to watch her hesitate, she changed her mind. She did not want to be watched or waited for. The dog was quick, but not quite quick enough, and before it had time to get up again she stepped on the end of its tail.

It was not that she did it on purpose. It was more that she did not try very hard to avoid it.

It gave a sharp involuntary yelp, then quickly turned and licked her hand as if to forgive her. She snatched her hand away from the warm wet tongue and strode on, ignoring it.

A thick gumtree screwed its way up out of the ground, silvers and pinks roped like sinews along the length of the trunk. You could see that when the seed had sent up its shoot, something had blocked it, a stone perhaps, and made it come out twisted like a piece of string. Once twisted, it stayed that way, no matter how long it lived. The sapling would have been born twisted, and here was the mature tree, thick with years, still twisted. When it fell over, dead, the fibres of the dead wood would still show where, all its long life, it had been *wound*.

The dog was running on ahead of her, nosing at bushes and rocks, glancing back at her, panting, but when she caught its eye she looked away.

She tugged off her jumper and tied its sleeves around her waist. *Moderate to vigorous exercise*, the rosy-lipped doctor had said. *More than a stroll.*

She strode out hard, feeling the cuffs of the jumper wagging at her waist at each step. There was a certain cruel pleasure in forcing herself hard towards the crest of the hill. There was something of righteous punishment in it. The sun was in her eyes and she kept her head down. The muscles in the backs of her legs were starting to ache. She lengthened her stride to feel them stretch at each step with a small shooting pain. Take *that*, she thought. And *that*. And *that*.

They had told her that your heart had to be made to work.

The breath was coming hard now, her lungs burning, each breath like an angry little grunt. *That*. And *that*. And *that*.

If you made it work so hard it broke, that would serve you right.

The road corkscrewed around the corner and her arms skewed away strongly to get her up the last steep pinch. At the top she stood panting, feeling the heart thudding strenuously in her chest.

She stood listening to her chest pull the air in and expel it again. *In, out. In, out.* If she was having another heart attack, it would be hours, far too long, before anyone found her on this back road. It would be a long way to Livingstone Base Hospital, too, lying along the back seat of someone's car.

Too long, too far, too late.

If you were privileged with a second chance, you were obliged to be pleased, and be properly grateful, doing the walks and the unwinding. But after that no one could hold you responsible. You were not to blame if you did not get a third chance.

The dog did not seem to realise she could be having another heart attack. It came up and stood in front of her, panting up cheerfully as if nothing was the matter. Then it jerked its head around to snap at a fly and collapsed suddenly on its haunches, scratching convulsively behind its ear. Hair and dust flew out, each speck lit up radiantly by the sun.

Fleas, she thought. Nothing to do with me.

It looked as though she was not having another heart attack, after all.

She looked away up into the sky: the palest kind of blue, a big quiet light. High up, two birds were flying together, drawing a straight line through the air like aircraft in formation.

Just over the brow of the hill was a fork in the road and a flaking wooden sign. One fork pointed downhill towards CASCADE RIVULET, the other uphill, to HANGING ROCK. Someone had tied a stone on the end of a bit of string and hung it from the sign. She laughed aloud, suddenly, a noise like a bark.

The dog twisted its head to look up at her in surprise and she stopped laughing. She glanced around, as if someone might have heard her, laughing on an empty road, and looked at the rock again. It was not really all that funny.

Below her, she could see Cascade Rivulet glinting metallically between the trees. The road ahead of her turned a sudden sharp corner down the slope, so steep it had washed away into long corrugations, and then all at once there was the river, and the bridge.

She recognised it straight away from its picture in the paper, a humble little thing, the bend giving it an apologetic look. It was hard to see why the town was *split* on it.

She walked down to it, feeling stones rolling away from under her shoes down the slope. A white ute was parked at the far end of the bridge but there was no sign of anyone, only a flat paddock in which some cows stood all lined up the same way like ornaments along a mantelpiece.

She stopped in the middle of the bridge and looked down at the river. Sun shone through the transparent amber water and lit up rounded rocks just under the surface, and fans of white sand. Where a band of sun cast a slice of black shadow, the water was dark and secretive.

She wanted to go down there, under the bridge, and saw that the fence at one end had collapsed, the wooden posts leaning crookedly where the bank had been scoured out by flood. She would not have actually forced her way through anyone's fence. She knew how farmers felt about them, and about city folk who had no respect for them. But someone had been there before her. She could see where the post had been eased further sideways in the soft ground, and a rip down the dirt of the bank, where someone's heels had slid.

Underneath, the bridge was a quaint, clumsy thing, a clutter of primitive timbers wedged against each other into crude simple joints. Where each horizontal met a vertical, each had had a piece removed so they were locked tightly together.

It was like two people holding hands.

From a distance the old wood looked nothing more interesting than grey, but close up, each timber had its own colour and its own personality. One was pink-grey with fine streaks of red like dried blood in the grain. Another was green-grey with circular blooms of brown-grey lichen, the next was the bleached blue-grey with a kinked grain like an old-fashioned marcel wave.

She stood with her shoes sinking slowly in the damp sand, looking up into the underbelly of the bridge, feeling the muscles twitching in her thighs after the fast walk. It was all coarse and clumsy, but as well as the subtle textures of the grain, the shapes fitted together in a satisfying way, and there was what they called at the Museum an *interplay* between the light and the shadow that drew the eye back to look again and again.

She got a notebook and pencil out of her pocket and stood drawing squares and long rectangles that interlinked and interlocked, glancing between her page and the pencil.

When she had filled a page she turned over and started again. She spent a long time getting the angles right where one rectangle came in and locked into another. It looked so simple as to be not worth a second glance, but drawing it showed how complicated it really was.

When she had covered the third page she felt she had the shapes right, and started to shade the squares and rectangles with her pencil. *Light, dark, light, dark.* It was in no way a realistic drawing of the way the bridge looked, but it was what it might look like if you reduced it to its essence: simple squares and rectangles, simple lights and darks, arranged in a way that was not as simple as it seemed.

Suddenly the dog was down there with her, nudging her knee with its nose, and a piece of shading jerked past its border.

Bugger off, she said without looking, and kept going with the shading.

It licked its nose with a long rubbery tongue and panted up at her, but she went on steadfastly taking no notice. At last it pushed with its nose at her knee again.

Bugger off! she said

This time it was loud and angry, and she looked down frowning.

Then she saw that her feet were sinking into the damp

sand. Water was seeping up around them and was about to come in over the top of her shoe. She stepped back to where the sand was drier, her shoes making wet sucking noises as they pulled out of the sand.

The dog watched with interest. It cocked its ears at the sucking noise and went on watching the shoe-shaped holes she had left, as if they might make some other kind of interesting noise.

She glanced down at the dog at the same moment that the dog looked up. It closed its mouth and stopped panting, as if it thought she was going to say something. *Thank you, dog*, for example.

But she did not believe in talking to animals, much less thanking them. She turned away, put the notebook back in her pocket, and climbed up to the roadway.

From up on top, you would never guess how interesting it was underneath. The long squared timbers had been laid side by side in a plain way, and were simply held in place with big brown bolts. When the flood had come, and the bridge had decided to bend rather than break, each timber had swivelled slightly on its bolt. Some parts had been squeezed together, and in others long wedge-shaped cracks had opened up. But each individual beam had not moved very far. Beam by beam they hardly bent at all. To see that, you had to look along the whole bridge.

On the far side of the bridge she could see that another, more substantial road ran along beside the river on the other bank, joined by the bridge to the one she had used, making a big H-shape. She decided to take the other road back to Karakarook. There could be something wearisome about repeating yourself.

She could feel the sun on her back now, starting to get hot and harsh in her eyes. It was hard to leave the bridge, the water, the sense of stillness. The slice of shadow underneath was already smaller, shrinking in beneath, and blacker. In the middle of that crisp line of shade, the shape of her own head provided a knob, like a handle, of extra shadow.

From up here she could see the two shoe-shaped dents she had left in the sand, slowly filling with water but keeping their shape. Beside them were four smaller holes where the dog had stood. She could drop down dead, right now this minute, with another *infarction*, and long after she herself had been reduced to a smudge of smoke from a big busy chimney, the shape of her shoes would still be here. The shape of her shoes would go on proving she had been there, day and night, in light and in darkness, until the river rose and washed them away as if she had never been.

No one would know, though, except the dog.

Where the shadow met the light on the sand further along, she saw that there were two other holes in the shape of shoes, also filled with water. They were just like hers, but they were not hers.

As she watched, two big bumbling insects dipped quickly into the water in one of the other footprints, as if tasting it, and up again. Twining around each other they dropped into one of her own prints, hovered, and danced together out of sight under the bridge.

She moved her head and watched the shadow on the sand move too. A fly spun into her ear as if with an urgent message, then it was gone, leaving silence behind.

The sky was thickening into a hard blue. A cicada started

up, stopped, started again, was joined by another on a different pitch.

She decided to take it slowly on the way back. There was something to be said for having respect for a *dicky ticker*.

CHAPTER 6

Douglas waited until the dust of the truck's passage up the hill had settled, then walked a little way along the riverbank. When he came to a fence, he thought for a moment he would have to go back, but he found a sagging strand of wire and forced it down with his foot so he could get through.

He felt light-hearted, adventurous. He was a cautious man. It did not take much to make him feel he was having an *adventure*. There'd been no bush in his suburb, just street after street of tidy houses with red-tiled roofs and a front path with a curve that it did not need. But he'd been a conscientious Scout as a boy. He'd got his *Fire-Lighting* Badge and his *Tent-Erecting* Badge and had got a *Special Mention* for *Knots*.

The grass in the paddock was long, perfect for snakes. He thumped along, stamping his feet the way they had shown them at Scouts. He imagined the snakes, all over the paddock, waking up in the long grass, feeling the vibrations along the ground, sliding away.

Fire-Lighting, and *Tent-Erecting*, and *Knots*. He felt pretty confident about any of those, and he was all right on *Snakes*, too.

He was heading for the chimney of the ruined house, but the river drew him. He sat on a log, listening to the water chinkering over the stones, enjoying the way the casuarinas swept back and forth overhead with a soft whistling sound.

Over the river in the bush covering the steep hillside, a bird was making a lot of noise. The books always talked about birds *singing*, but you would not call this *singing*. This was little strong pulses of sound, like a small dense steel object being struck with a small dense brass hammer.

He tried it. *Bong. Ping.* That was hopeless. He did a kind of sucking-and-clucking sound with his mouth. That did not sound right either, and he was glad there was no one nearby to hear it.

He thought perhaps he would get a book about birds. It would be something to do while he was here, get a book and look up the different bird noises.

Around him the landscape ticked and hummed secretively, getting on with its own mysterious life. A line of tiny black ants ran along a stick, up and down two sides of a stone, and ringed a morsel of something. Two white butterflies twisted and flirted above a bush.

The breeze on his face, the murmur of the river, the big sky overhead: *Nature* was all around him, expansive, generous, like a hospitable host. He was glad Chook had gone, and glad he had stayed out here rather than going straight back to Room 8 and pretending the *Engineering Digest* had his full attention.

Suddenly he was aware that he was not alone. Not far away a group of cows was staring at him. A *herd*. He supposed you called it a *herd*.

They seemed to have horns. He wondered if that made

them bulls. He did not like the way they were watching him. If they had been humans it would have been extremely bad-mannered.

All at once he was sick of sitting on the log watching the ants, but he did not want to move. Moving could be an inflammatory thing to do.

A *herd* of bulls did not sound right. Perhaps cows as well as bulls could have horns. Some of these had horns and some did not. He would have liked to know what that meant. Underneath, they all had a twist of hair. He did not know what that meant either.

He had seen cows before on other country jobs. He had seen them in paddocks, chewing. He had seen them staring over fences as he drove past. He had even seen them close up, at the Sydney Show, standing in their stalls draped in prize ribbons, too fat to move, and a man waiting with a shovel held out under their rear end.

But he had never seen cows at such close quarters, and he had certainly never encountered cows who were so embarrassingly interested in him.

He sat looking hard at the ants. He was going to be as boring as possible, so that the cows would lose interest. It would be easy. He could go on being boring for as long as it took.

He sat very still and made his face go blank. A fly landed on his chin but he did not move. It crawled up on to the corner of his mouth like a slow torture, but he was determined not to brush it off. That might be interesting.

He thought of Chook Henderson. A man like that would not even notice a few cows looking at him. He would think it was ridiculous to give them a second thought.

Perhaps the hat was the problem. It had looked harmless enough in the shop, the most neutral sort of country-person's flat-topped felt hat, but it seemed to be causing tremendous interest here. He wondered if he should take it off, but taking it off might be even more interesting.

He stared at the ants, but he was not concentrating. A big foot struck the ground behind him and he glanced around. One cow had come up in front of the others. As he watched, it took another step towards him. It was a very solid foot with a lot of weight behind it, and it came down hard. The animal it belonged to was close enough now that he could see the long curly eyelashes, and a smudge of mud on its nose.

Curious, he told himself calmly. It was something he'd heard people say. *They're simply curious.* He stared back at the thing, noticing how its eyes were set wide apart on each side of its head. *Poor binocular vision.* He was probably just a blur, a kind of tall mushroom, a stalk with a hat on. That outraged and astonished look did not mean anything, it was just what it did when it was trying to focus. He'd had a teacher at school who did that, stood giving you the out-raged and astonished look until the whole class fell silent, and you suddenly realised it was you he was being outraged and astonished at.

The thing opened its mouth and mooed, a long deep sound with a little shrill hysterical thing on the end, and without thinking he mooed back. It was an uncharacteristic thing to do and he wished straight away he had not. The cow stared at him as if its feelings were hurt and took another step towards him. When it stopped again it was really very close. He could see a bit of grass stuck in one of its cavernous nostrils, and a little greenish froth on what he supposed you'd have to call its lips.

After what seemed a tremendously long time, it dropped its big brown head and started tearing at the grass. He could hear the muffled crushing noise as it ground away.

Being boring seemed to have finally paid off.

Smoothly, unprovocatively, boringly, he got up from the log and walked away sideways, keeping an eye on the cow. When he was able to get a tree between them, he turned and walked quickly up the paddock. Glancing back he could see that they were doing the I-am-outraged-and-astonished thing again.

It would be easy to get sick of cows.

The adventurous feeling had gone. He was feeling watched now. In the city no one looked. You were just another object taking up space on the footpath. Here you were huge and conspicuous, moving over the rounded bulge of a paddock. You could never be sure you were alone. There were cows, and perhaps people as well, watching you, screened by the hum of insects.

All this, grassy paddock, cows, trees – he had thought it was *Nature*. But now he could see that that was ignorance, or lack of imagination. It was not *Nature*. It was actually *property*.

That fence, for example, over beyond the chimney, was not just a picturesque feature of the landscape, put there to make the most of the perspective. It actually belonged to someone. Someone had paid money for it. So many days of labour at so much an hour, and so much for the posts and the wire. It was not decoration, it was a sum: cost of fence subtracted from number of cows contained by it, divided by the number of years it stayed up.

What he was doing was not *exploring*. It was *trespassing*.

He looked around from side to side as he walked up the paddock, swinging his arms vigorously. He was a person *out for a walk*, telegraphing his innocent intentions by a great attention to clouds, trees, birds. Country people were not big on *going for a walk*, but he thought they knew that *going for a walk* was something city people did.

His footsteps were unsteady on the rough grass. Grasshoppers sprang out of the tussocks with every step he took, like flights of little arrows. When two tiny fat birds swooped low in front of him he flinched. He was hot, could feel sweat running down his forehead from under his hat. *Slow down*, he told himself. *No need to panic.*

When he glanced back he saw that the cows were still staring at him. Some of them had just twisted their heads over their shoulders to stare but one or two had actually turned their entire bodies around.

Somehow at Scouts they seemed to have missed out on *Cows*.

Up close, the poplars and the chimney were disappointing. He'd been looking forward to ancient treasures in the grass, but there seemed to be no old bottles or bits of brass bedstead. At least here he was hidden.

Just beyond the poplars, two fences met at right-angles, and beyond that was the road, picturesquely curving up and away around the corner of the rise, like a road in a storybook. Seeing how close he was to the road, with his ute parked a little way further along, it felt silly to have got himself hot and bothered, panting here in the sun, just because a few cows had looked at him.

A willy-wagtail swivelled on top of a fence-post. One of the fences was higher than usual and one strand had a tin label with a picture of a lightning-bolt. He supposed that meant it was electrified. The other was a double fence with two separate barriers of barbed wire an arm's length apart.

He stood there in the quiet, wondering why you would want to make a double fence like that. His brain started to work on the little puzzle, going systematically through all the possible reasons. It could be to make doubly sure that nothing strayed on to the road. Perhaps it had turned out to be cheaper to put another line of fence in than repair the old. Perhaps they'd drawn the boundaries wrong the first time. Or perhaps it was to stop cattle being *rustled*. Did cattle really get *rustled*, though, outside cowboy movies?

There were situations where, even if you had got a *Special Mention* for *Knots*, it was still best simply to admit that you were out of your depth.

He was just embarking on the idea that a double fence would be doubly strong if you had something that was doubly powerful to be kept within it, when he heard a yell.

Oy!

He looked around but could not see anyone. When he took off his hat to see better, he heard it again, more urgently.

Oy! Oy!

Then he saw two things in quick succession: a person far away up at the curve in the road, gesturing and shouting *Oy!* and all the cows coming up the paddock towards him at a lumbering trot.

The person was still far away, a little figure in the distance, but the animals were close. They were closer every second. He had never seen cows behaving like this before:

running heavily in a pack, kicking up their back legs, butting each other with their shoulders, tossing their heads around, pricking each other's big round ribcages with their horns. As they ran, their bony hipbones were purposeful and their dewlaps swung vigorously from side to side.

There were more of them than he had thought, and he could see now that quite a few had horns. They were sharp, straight horns that were not particularly decorative. His wish to know whether they were cows or bulls had become an urgent anxiety within his chest.

The ground rumbled under them, and part of his brain busied itself with being interested in the way the sound was too low to hear. It was fascinating, really: he was actually hearing the cows with the soles of his feet, through the ground, the way a snake did.

He wondered whether he would hear them better if he lay down. Then his whole body would be like one long ear.

Perhaps they would think he was dead. That might be a good idea. You could hardly be more boring than dead.

He glanced at the double barbed-wire fence and imagined himself getting through it. The image that came to his mind was of his anxious bony bottom, pointing at the cows like a bull's-eye. It was not an encouraging picture. The other fence was too high, and there was the electric strand and the little picture of lightning. He did not know how many volts a fence like this might carry.

He imagined the way he would jerk and twitch like a puppet.

The cows were still coming on, but they had slowed down, shifting in a little crowd, pushing and shoving at each other with their hoops of ribs.

They were bold now, but he was confident that when they got closer they would lose their nerve. They would stop and go back to the staring business. He had already handled the staring. He was okay on that now. Cows stared and cows mooed, but if you were good enough at being boring they left you alone.

The voice of Chook Henderson in his head was rich and authoritative.

Show them who's bloody boss, mate! he was saying, and Douglas straightened up, getting ready to take a firm line.

But what if they were bulls? People were killed by bulls.

He found that he had picked up a piece of branch lying on the ground. Now he was a two-legged thing with a stick. He had the branch in his hand but he was trying not to think of it as a person *defending himself.*

But having the stick in his hand, he knew how frightened he was.

They were very close now. He could hear them breathing. There was one at the front that seemed to think it was some kind of leader. Its horns were very straight and very pointed.

He did not let himself think the word *sharp*.

When it lowered its head and looked up through its eyelashes at him he thought of pictures of bullfights he'd seen. The bulls lowered their heads like that when they were about to charge. He could see the mechanics of it. The head was perfectly shaped and the eyes were perfectly placed for being able to see while the head was lowered. Moreover, lowering the head brought the horns into exactly the right alignment to maximise damage to a two-legged thing that carried its soft part around its middle.

It was a lovely bit of mechanics.

But he was no bullfighter in little shiny slippers and tight sequinned pants. There was no cheering crowd. There could be no running around behind the wooden palisade, no shouting men on horses making the bull go away.

He was just a man in a paddock, sweating and holding a foolish piece of branch.

I am a human, he thought, and this is just a cow. I have to make it frightened of me. He waved the stick, jabbed it forward threateningly, yelled *Yah! Yah! Garah!* The cow – but perhaps it would be more realistic if he thought of it as a bull – scraped at the ground with a foot, took a step closer, tilted its head around so that the point of the left-hand horn was perfectly lined up with Douglas's stomach.

Actually, he thought, what bullfighters did was just like this. They flipped the cape and jabbed at the bull with their stick. They taunted it and goaded it, and finally it did the *lovely bit of mechanics.*

Maybe the stick was not such a good idea.

Now, he told the cow in a loud unsteady voice. Now, boy. Take it easy. There, boy.

He heard his voice and saw that the cow heard it too. It waggled its ears and shook its head as if a fly was bothering it. But it did not seem especially soothed. It went on scraping at a piece of ground with its front hoof and pointing its horn. He thought its eyes actually looked quite intelligent.

Whether it was a cow or a bull, it was not losing interest. Oy! Oy!

He glanced around at the person on the road. It was a woman, a big woman, making a wide looping gesture with both arms.

He saw this in a quick glance but he felt he had to go on watching the horn and turned back to the cow. When he risked another quick glance at the person, she was scrambling down the bank towards the double fence. He checked the cow again, took a few steps closer to the fence. The cow followed him. When he stopped it stopped too.

It was closer to him than it had been before.

He glanced behind him. The woman was at the fence now. She was close to him and that was a comfort. Another of his own species. But she was on the right side of the fence and he was definitely on the wrong side.

Oy!

He was not going to look again. There was no point in looking, and while he was looking the cow would get its chance. Someone on the wrong side of the fence calling *Oy!* was no use to him and it was important not to be distracted from the job of keeping the cow at a distance with the power of his watching.

Quick! Over the fence!

He glanced in spite of himself. A gate, perhaps, that he hadn't seen. A ladder. A pair of wirecutters.

But there was no gate, no ladder, no wirecutters. She was just standing waving her arms and wasting his time. The cow had moved closer while he had been thinking about wirecutters. No! he called.

His voice sounded high and thin. He wobbled his branch at the cow again and called over his shoulder.

How over?

That sounded ridiculous. He tried again.

How?

He did not want to get into a long discussion about it.

He needed to concentrate. If you kept your eye on the horn and kept moving, there was no reason why you would ever be jabbed. It was like tennis. *Eye on the ball.* He crouched towards the bull as if it was going to serve, holding the branch across both hands like a racquet. It seemed to help.

Suddenly the woman was beside him. He glanced at her in confusion before he remembered *eye on the ball.* It was nice of her to try to help, but she did not seem to realise the danger. He bounced from foot to foot and concentrated on the cow. There was something that did not add up about the fact that she was beside him, but he could not stop to think about it now. Stopping to think could be fatal. He felt powerful, bouncing like this on the balls of his feet. He could keep bouncing all day if he had to.

Quick! she said. Over here!

She pulled at his sleeve so he nearly dropped the branch. The cow was pawing the ground with both hoofs now but in doing so it was moving backwards. Getting a run-up, he thought. Here we go. Eye on the ball.

Quick! she shouted. Come on!

She was over at the electric fence, holding the strands apart. As he watched, she folded herself in through the fence and stood on the other side. It was like a magic trick.

Quick! she shouted, and held the strands apart invitingly.

She sounded exasperated. He watched himself run over to the fence and poke himself at it. He braced himself for the electric shock but none came. He braced himself for the thunder as the cows chased him, for the pain as the first horn got him in the bottom. Then he was through.

Up on the road, they did not look at each other. The woman looked away down at the cows.

He could hear himself panting.

Thanks, he said.

He laughed, although nothing was particularly funny.

He felt a hollowness like hunger around his middle, just where the horn would have gone in.

His knees were shaking so much he could feel the fabric of his pants flapping against the backs of his legs. He hoped she was not looking at them.

The woman was not looking at him. She was looking away down the road as if waiting for a bus. She seemed embarrassed.

Buggers, aren't they! she said.

She looked at him quickly, smiled suddenly, a big frank smile that lit up her face, then looked away again, at the cows.

He wanted to explain about the horns and how he thought the fence would kill him. He still did not understand what had happened, what she had done to make it safe. Was there a switch?

The cattle were away down there in the paddock, still staring up at them, but the ones at the back were starting to lose interest, turn away, rip at grass.

He was still holding his bit of branch, and suddenly laughed again, seeing himself waving the branch around. He could not be bothered feeling foolish or trying to explain. He was too happy feeling not impaled.

Thank you, he said.

It sounded insincere.

Really, thanks.

That sounded worse.

He flung his branch away down the bank. The cows

stared at it in an astonished way. He stood staring too, and had to remind himself to close his mouth.

Thought they were going to win that round.

He glanced down at them now spread out peacefully across the paddock tearing at grass.

The cows. Cattle, that is.

He looked at her.

What are they, bulls? Or what?

He laughed before she could say anything.

I don't have a grasp, really, of the cattle scene.

He smiled his uncertain smile, although not at her, and smoothed his palms against the front of his shirt as if drying them. He told himself to stop and pushed them into his pockets. Then he felt hunched and falsely over-casual.

There was a silence. With one toe he scraped a line in the dirt of the road. It was pretty much what the cow had done, he thought, and stopped. They both seemed to be looking down at the blunt line in the dust.

That yours, the ute back there?

Yes! he said quickly, over-enthusiastically, too loudly. He tried again more quietly.

Yes.

She said nothing. Now she was doing it too, drawing in the dust with the toe of her worn runner. She did a sort of half-circle. Next to each other, the line and the half-circle looked like some kind of message.

Together they looked back at the ute, small at this distance and sharp-edged in the landscape of woolly trees. It looked like a country ute, brown with dust around the bottom, and a long streak of something along the side panel. If you didn't know, you could almost think it belonged to a farmer.

As if in scorn at this idea, one of the cows, or bulls, lifted its nose and from deep in its belly let out a long melancholy trumpeting on several pitches, a kind of indignant yodel. They looked at each other and laughed. Her laugh was high and harsh, his a rumble and wheeze.

Look! he cried. They're laughing at me!

He thought it would make her laugh again, but her smile faded, and he saw that it might have sounded as if he was saying *You're laughing at me*. He said quickly, Not that I'd blame them!

He was almost shouting, trying to get it right.

She looked away, down at the cows. A frown like disapproval was clouding her face.

He could see she was a real country sort of woman, in her battered old shoes and the baggy tracksuit. Her face was brown from the sun, her cheeks coarsened by years of weather, but the blood flowed vigorously under the skin. Under the old track-pants, he thought she would have powerful legs, getting her along the miles of country back roads and over the paddocks.

He caught himself wishing she would invite him home. He could just sit in a corner of her kitchen while she got on with her life: people dropping in, the tea-pot never running cold, grandchildren being fed biscuits, dogs underfoot, the Country Hour going on the radio.

He would not be in anyone's way, just watching.

A brindle sort of dog with a big feathery tail was nosing around them. While she frowned at the dust, and he thought about how much he would like it in her kitchen, it came over and sniffed at him, its nose cold on the back of his hand, then stood panting up at him, took time out from panting to lick his wrist as if to taste him, then panted some more.

Look! she said.

Bunched together against the fence where the two of them had climbed through, the cows were now staring over. The grass in the next paddock looked just the same as the grass in the one they were in, but as he watched, one of the group lumbered up to the fence and stuck a foot through. The foot fumbled, its body lurched upwards against the fence, all four feet scrabbled at the wires as if the fence was a staircase. The fence swayed and sagged as the cow fought with it, dewlaps swinging, hindquarters jerking. A watching human could see that it would get stuck if it went forward. *Go back*, he thought. *Quick! Back!* His heart sank at the idea of having to try to free it and look foolish in a whole new way in front of this woman.

Finally the cow burst backwards out of the fence and turned away, then twisted its big head round to stare at the fence with a look of deep reproach.

When the humans laughed, it turned its head towards them and funnelled out a long sad *moo*. They both went *moo* back at the same moment and turned to each other, laughing. Between them the dog looked eagerly from face to face as if waiting to have the joke explained.

It was only when he was back in Room 8, standing in the middle of the room listening to a swell of lunchtime noise from the bar, that he realised he should have offered her a lift.

Idiot, idiot, idiot, he whispered.

He turned and turned in the room as if looking for a way

out. It was just as Marjorie had often said. He was good with figures and could tell you more than you'd ever want to know about bridges. But he *had no commonsense*.

At the window he gripped the frame with both hands and leaned out a little way. A car with a furry thing swinging from the top of its aerial came down Parnassus Road and when it had passed, an old man with hunched shoulders stepped cautiously out from under the awning of the Mini-Mart and headed across towards the Caledonian.

There was no woman with worn track-pants, no brindle dog. No way to be back on the road with her, thinking in time to offer her a lift.

Looking, regretting, not thinking, he glanced down into the alley between the Caledonian and the blue wall. Straight away the giddiness started to come at him from behind his eyes. There was an impression of a brick wall falling away from under him, of awful tapering height. The backs of his knees tingled and his feet were cold with the sucked-away emptied-out feeling. The frame of the window cut into his palms where he was gripping it. *Do not look down*, he told himself, and by force of will he made his head come up so that he faced the window in the wall opposite. Today the curtains were pushed back, and, from his high angle, he could see a piece of wooden floor, with a big white square like a sheet spread out, and what looked like a shirt stretched out in the middle of it. All around were stalky things that looked like the bottom of music-stands.

To help the giddy sickness retreat, he concentrated on the things that looked like music-stands. The Karakarook and District Musical Society? The Salvation Army, Karakarook Branch?

Sometimes being in the country felt like one long intelligence test he was failing.

Out on Parnassus Road, the brown dog that was always stretched on the mat outside the Mini-Mart sat up, snapped at a fly, and lay back down again. He watched, but nothing more interesting than that was going to happen on Parnassus Road for the time being.

Tomorrow, work on the bridge would start. He had all afternoon to wish he had not got into that situation with the cows, and to regret not being quick enough to offer the woman a lift. She could well have saved his life. Some kind of gratitude would have been in order.

He sat down on the side of the bed and picked up the *Engineering Digest*. It was turning into a long hot afternoon, and it would not end for hours.

CHAPTER 7

DARLING, HUGH SAID in a neutral way. He was tightening his mouth in the way he did, that was not frowning but not smiling either.

Darling, I think we've got too much citrus here.

He stood peering into the worm farm, holding one hand in a fist behind his back. Felicity thought he looked ridiculous, like someone dancing with himself, but he was the kind of man who never seemed to realise when he looked ridiculous.

Wouldn't you say?

He did not look at her, but went on inspecting the old orange peels.

The ratio has to be pretty much exact, he said.

He was looking at her now. He had always been good on *eye contact*. They had had workshops about it, during his Land & Pastoral training: *Eye Contact* and *Body Language*. It was for when you had to refuse someone a loan, mainly, but it had always come naturally to Hugh.

It meant he had nothing to hide, she supposed, but she had found the more he did the *eye contact* thing, the more shifty-eyed she herself became. Now, for example, she felt skewered to the landscape by the twin drills of his eyes.

In the first place, it's too acidic.

Her eyes were starting to go dry, keeping up the *eye contact*.

Then in the second place, it's too wet.

He had always liked having something to explain. He was a good explainer, and they had seemed a good match, because she was a good listener.

That's the second thing.

He paused. His eyes glanced away for a moment. It was as if he was checking the script, she thought.

The third thing is, there aren't enough worms yet. It might take a year, the instructions said. To build up to full . . . effectiveness.

He looked at her again. She felt blinded by the words. Time did not seem to be moving, but it must surely be time for him to go to work. Or was he going to stay home today, and tell her about citrus?

He meant well. She knew he meant well. And was good to her. He was a good husband. She could not complain.

Sometimes she caught herself wishing he was not such a good husband. Then she would be able to complain.

Compost was the closest thing he had to a hobby. He spent a lot of time setting up complicated new compost containers of various kinds, or forking the compost out to *aerate* it and then putting it all back in again, or simply standing, admiring his worms. She would go out in the twilight and let him show her what he had done, and she admired and praised. But for herself, she hated the secretive vigour of the worms, and the feel of dirt on her hands.

Their Nature Strip was the best in Karakarook. Even by the generous standards of Karakarook South, theirs was a nice wide one. It had been one of the things she had liked in the beginning, the Nature Strip. But they had not been there long before they had realised that because it was wide it was the place where the children in the street liked to play cricket.

William had wanted to join in with them, but they had not been a nice type of child for him to associate with. The peer group was so important, especially for that age group. Ten was a very impressionable age, and William was such a sensitive boy.

She had had to ask Hugh to speak to them once or twice, just in a friendly way. The problem was the noise, which was upsetting, and it made it so hard for William to concentrate on his homework. And when they went home, they often left behind the dented old rubbish-bin that they used for a wicket.

She had told him to suggest that they play on someone else's Nature Strip. Their own, for instance. But of course their own Nature Strips were bumpy and overgrown and lit-tered with dog excrement, and with the old lemonade bottles full of water that were supposed to stop the dog excrement.

Finally she had got him to plant a row of tea-trees down the middle of the strip. They had grown quickly, although they looked untidy, the way natives always seemed to, and they had certainly done the trick with the cricket. She had got Hugh to prune them last week, back to neat bush-shapes. She'd imagined how the spindly growth would thicken up into a row of nice dense bushes. She had even toyed with the idea of getting him to try some topiary. But this morning she had noticed that the wretched things had up and died on her.

We'd better go easy on the orange peels, Hugh said. Don't you think, darling?

She could see the back of his neck, where he could not. A crease was starting to develop there. As he bent to look at the offending orange peels, the crease disappeared. But when he tilted his head back up, she could see the skin fold itself back into the little crease.

The thing was, it must be happening to her, too.

Every time she nodded or looked up, the cracks on the back of her own neck cut in deeper. A person needed to nod, of course, to show they were paying attention. Now and then a person had to turn their head up, to unpeg the washing from the line, for example. But the less of that kind of thing there was, the better.

There was no real need to have your washing up above you. The thing would be to wind the Hill's Hoist right down, and stand on a box. Then the washing would be at face level. No crack-forming tilting of the head would be necessary. There was a box under the house that would do perfectly well, and when Hugh left she would get it out, taking care, of course, not to bend her neck any more than absolutely necessary as she did so.

Hugh looked at her again and smiled. She made herself nod. It was a small nod, just enough to make him look away. The smaller the nod was, the less the neck would crease.

In spite of her having nodded, Hugh was still watching her. Actually, she thought he was not so much watching her as keeping his eyes busy while he thought about something else. About citrus perhaps. He was trying to think of something to go on to. *In the fourth place.*

She had heard him get up to nine, one night, ticking the points off on his fingers. It had been something about the old bridge and how *Heritage* was well and good in its place, but that place was not a public carriageway. She had got quite interested, wondering what he would do when he ran out of fingers, and had almost been disappointed when he stopped.

He was looking at his watch.

I'll be off, darling, he said.

His face came over next to hers and his mouth did a little moist thing against her cheek. You called that *a kiss*. It was what husbands did. Wives could do them too, if they liked, but kisses were probably wrinkle-forming.

Felicity had heard that a cockroach could live for a month on a single grain of sugar. That was how careful you had to be.

At any time of the day or night, anyone could eat off her floor. She sometimes imagined them, down on the floor, the knife and fork in their hands, looking up at her. *Delicious, Felicity!*

When she had swept and mopped, she washed the broom and mop with boiling water and disinfectant. Then she liked to put them out in the sun to dry. She had read somewhere that sunlight had a *purifying effect*.

But there was a problem. If you took the things out into the sun for the *purifying effect*, you exposed your skin to the *damaging ultra-violet*. It had been scientifically proven that ultra-violet was one of the quickest ways to get wrinkles.

She had timed herself, and even hanging up the mop and broom as fast as she could, she had worked out that it added up to nearly six hours of exposure to the ultra-violet in the course of a year.

Perhaps she should wait till sunset for that, too, but then where would she keep the wet mop and broom until then?

It was a bit of a dilemma.

The best she could do was to go into the bathroom straight away afterwards, and put on the special Creme Jeunesse from Honeycutt's. There was a right way to do it, as there was a right way to do everything. You *smoothed* it in with a *gentle upwards motion*. You had to be careful not to *rub* or *stretch* the skin.

The thing was, if you were not careful, and did it the wrong way, the positive effect of the cream would be offset by the negative effect of the way you were *rubbing* and *stretching*.

When you thought about it, nothing was really simple.

And actually, that was wrinkle-forming, too, thinking about the way nothing was simple.

It was not that she had any *lines*, much less *wrinkles*. For a woman of her age she had the most youthful face of anyone she knew. Other women of her age definitely had *lines*. Some of them had what could only be called *wrinkles*, although they called them *laugh-lines* to make it sound better.

She was not going to get *lines*, or *laugh-lines*, let alone *wrinkles*. It was simply a matter of thinking ahead, and being vigilant. The bending of the neck, for example. Until she had seen the damage it was doing to Hugh, she had not thought of that, but now she was aware of it, it was just a matter of adding it to the things you had to remember.

She had always been nice-looking. It was only sensible to acknowledge that. It was not boasting. Really, she did not care one way or the other. If it had been up to her, she would just as soon have been born plain.

Growing up, though, she had discovered that her smile had

solved most problems. It had got her out of the frowsty little cluttered house, away from the smell of unwashed milk bottles and the worn-out, the second-hand, the patched-up, the home-made. She had climbed up and out – the Palmolive ad was going to be just the start of something really big in modelling – smiling her lovely smile, tossing her lovely hair, and had put her beginnings behind her as if they had never been.

Now she looked in the mirror and smiled that same smile, but it was not quite as it had been. It was hard to say just exactly what it was. Something around the eyes – or was it the curve of the cheek, or the set of the mouth? – was not quite the way it had been.

There were days when she was pleased she had always been a little vague about her age, even with Hugh. He never forgot her birthday, always had something pretty for her. But she was the only one who knew exactly what year the original birthday had been, and even in the privacy of her own mind, she was finding the precise name of the year softening and blurring.

Sometimes she thought she would rather be dead than old.

The Creme Jeunesse was shiny on her face in the mirror. She imagined the cells swelling rosily. There was some kind of special enzyme or protein in this one, that *replenished* the cells. She liked the idea of *replenishment*. It could make up for the damage life did to your skin.

Smiling, for example. Smiling did immense damage. People did not realise, smiling away recklessly. The corners of the eyes screwed up, the cheeks creased, the upper lip stretched. She had tried it in the mirror. The bigger the smile, the more lines it etched into your skin. The more often you smiled, the worse the lines got.

She was not going even to think the word *wrinkle*.

Of course, a person had to smile from time to time. But you could be careful, and only smile when necessary.

There was always a time, just after her lunch – just a few lettuce leaves and a piece of tomato, it was perfectly easy not to have anything more, and you had to be careful not to clog your system – and before it was time to pick up William from school, when time seemed to slow down and stop.

The silence in the house could be suffocating then. She felt as if she was swelling like a balloon under so much emptiness. The afternoon, and her life, stretched away in front of her, every boring bead-like minute of every boring bead-like day lining itself up to be got through.

She walked from room to room, hearing her high heels on the polished boards. The clock ticked discreetly from the mantelpiece in the living-room and she heard the scrabbling sound of a bird's claws over the iron roof of the laundry outside the kitchen window. A crow further up the hill mourned through the warm still air.

There were times when the afternoons threatened to last for ever.

After the little *awkwardnesses*, Hugh had thought that she had needed an *interest*, and she had tried many *interesting* things. Pottery had seemed promising, but the clay ruined your hands. Her hands had been like crocodile skin while she had been doing the pottery.

She had liked the idea of being able to speak French, and

improving the French she had done at school had been a nice *interest* for a while, when they had been in Lismore. *Accent aigu! Lips back everyone!* Miss Marshall at the Evening Class had cried, and spat enthusiastically, getting her own lips right. Miss Marshall was a big-bosomed vulgar woman with no inhibitions, and the class had all laughed and tried it, watching each other.

But in her own quiet house after the classes, all by herself, the blinds drawn against the afternoon outside, she had never felt like getting her lips around French.

Quilting had been good for quite a while. She had done the quilting when Hugh had been in the Bathurst branch. It was complicated and fiddly, which was a good thing for an *interest* to be. And if you followed the instructions to the letter, you could get it absolutely perfect. She liked that about it. She had read that *the art of quilting is the art of fudging*, and had closed the book. She preferred the books that made it sound hard.

She still had them all. My *research*, was the way she thought of it. To start with, she had arranged them in alphabetical order by the author's name. But that had looked untidy because they were all different sizes, so she had put them in descending order of height instead. That looked much neater, although it was a little bit hard to find anything.

She'd had all the proper equipment: the rotary cutter and the self-healing cutting-board and the plastic templates and the special needles and special thread for the quilting. She had liked to think of them as her *tools of the trade*.

She sometimes regretted all the fabrics. She'd had them in clear plastic boxes on the shelves that Hugh had got the man to build in the sewing room of the Bathurst house. The *plains* had been graded in colour from ROY to BIV, and each box was labelled according to whether it held *yardage*, or *fat quarters* or *skinny eighths*, or *scraps*. There was a section for *Checks* and one for *Spots*, and another big one for *Florals*.

There had been a bit of a problem, with fabrics that had both *spots* and *checks*, or *florals* that were also *stripes*. Would you call a checkerboard a *Check* or a *Black-and-White*? It had worried her until she had hit on another category: *Overlaps*.

She used to go in there sometimes, just to look. Sometimes she had wondered whether that was really the thing she liked best about quilting, filing the fabrics properly. *You should be running the Land & Pastoral, darling*, Hugh had said. *You're so efficient*.

They had a good laugh about that, the idea of her running the Land & Pastoral.

He was always tremendously encouraging about her *interests*.

Only God can make something perfect, was the idea, according to the books, so a quilt was supposed to have a little mistake in it. Putting the mistake in had always given her a lot of satisfaction. You put a blue triangle in where it should have been green, that kind of thing, or a stripe instead of a check.

It was just another part of the perfection, really, not being perfect. But it only counted if you were not being perfect on purpose.

She had stopped quilting when she realised how it aged you. The problem was the tendency of your mouth to purse as you sewed. It was the concentrating, and the getting it right, and it was important to get it right, but getting it right made fine lines appear around the lips. The other thing was that you could get into the habit of hunching over the hand-sewing. She had watched other women, sewing and pursing and hunching.

Having a baby had been a wonderful *interest* for her, and in the beginning it had all gone wonderfully well. In the ante-natal classes the teacher had praised her belly-dancing exercise and even asked her to demonstrate it to the class. She had memorised all the special words: *dilation* and *perineum* and *vulva*. They were like *tools of the trade*, if you were having a baby.

The only problem had been that Hugh would not pinch her hard enough for the pain-practice. Sometimes he could be almost too kind-hearted. *Go on*, she had to hiss. *Harder.*

All over the room men were grimacing as they pinched the soft skin on the upper arms of their wives, as if it was they who were being hurt. The wives had their eyes closed, breathing through their noses. *Breathing through the pain*, it was called, while the men screwed the skin round.

When the teacher told them to stop, everyone smiled bravely, and glanced around at all the other couples smiling bravely. The women looked uneasy, thinking *but that was only my arm*.

One couple was not smiling bravely. It was the couple who had been half-hearted about the belly-dancing. The woman was the one who had gone *Urgh* during the video. Now she was sitting white in the face, rigid, tears rolling down her cheeks, and her husband, a big beefy man with a belly cut in two by his belt, folded his hands over and over each other as if he was washing them.

There was a silence in the room while the tears ran out of the woman's eyes. The man looked down at his lap. Outside a siren wailed past the window and skirled away on a diminishing note down the avenue.

Her labour was going to be perfectly straightforward. She knew that when the time came she would know that the pain was only the muscles of her uterus squeezing the baby out like toothpaste. It would not be *pain*, it would just be *contractions*. It was very simple.

The labour room shone, the floor waxed and gleaming, the bedclothes stiff with cleanness, and she was *coping* well. The doctor came and told her how well she was *coping*. She was breathing, *one two three release*, *pant-pant-pant pause*, and she was doing the belly-dancing, hanging on to the back of a chair, feeling the hospital gown, open down the back, swing against her calves.

Night came on. There was a sense of buses full of people grinding along home outside, everyone hurrying, anxious. She kept looking at the big white-faced clock on the wall, as if she was running late for something important. When Hugh, that anonymous person she knew to be her husband, put the lamp on, there was no escaping the fact that a whole day had gone by.

They made her lie down on the bed while they looked up inside her, and when they told her she was still *only two centimetres dilated*, she was confused. How was it possible, when she had been doing everything perfectly?

Lying on the bed while they examined her, she saw a great brown smear of old blood on the metal shade of the big ceiling lamp. She wished she had not seen it. Some other woman had lain here with baby and blood pouring out of her, something going wrong, urgent voices calling *Bring that lamp down!* and a bloodied gloved hand reaching out for it, pulling it down, leaving behind this nasty brown secret.

With nightfall, the wolves came into the room and tore at her by lamplight. They snarled and barked, long rough sounds, or was it she who was snarling with the ripping and gripping of it? There was the start of outrage, and behind that was panic.

Each pain, or *contraction*, came on her again and again, starting as something faint, like a most distant rumble of a train far away in a tunnel, but it came on and on. She heard a high silly little-girl's voice call out, oh, it's *coming* again, it's *coming*, and it roared, gnashing, flailing its way over her, staying for longer each time, and even as it receded it was coming again. All she needed was one moment, just a moment to take control of things again, but it would not give her that moment.

There was nothing to put between herself and the pain now. The belly-dancing was pathetic, and she had lost track of the panting. All those things were absurd, ridiculous, a child's games. She was not person plus belly now, making the belly go in and out, left and right. She was nothing but belly now, that great bully of a belly taking her over completely. She was flattened, betrayed, a husk on all fours on the floor like an animal, her face contorted, and the belly mocked her.

The baby they gave her to hold at last was that belly, the face in the wrappings staring blindly with dark-lashed eyes.

There was no *love* or *joy* in that stare. It did not care who you were, or how good you were at belly-dancing and remembering words like *perineum*.

She held it, the way you were supposed to, but there was no warm gush of love for it, only the feeling that she would rather put it away in its little perspex hospital box, because a parcel in a perspex box was something she could look after perfectly. She had done her homework, and read the books, and knew, for example, that cabbage leaves would relieve the tight swollen feeling in the breasts before the milk *came in*. It was good to know a thing like that. She laughed with the other mothers in the ward, pushing the clammy leaves down under their dainty nighties. One refused, asked the nurse for pain-killers instead, but that was not the right thing to do. At this stage you had complete control over everything that went into the baby. It was irresponsible to take pain-killers when a cabbage leaf, properly applied, would do the job.

She got the feeding right, too, and even when she went home with the baby she stuck precisely to the system they showed her at the hospital. She had written it all down to make sure she got it right. Nine minutes on the left side, then burp for thirty seconds. Nine minutes on the right side, then burp for one minute. She even got a little timer so she could be sure.

She did not like to say anything, but she watched other mothers drag out their weary-looking breasts from bras that you could see were not quite *fresh*, stuff the nipple into the baby's mouth and go on talking, go on even drinking a cup of tea, not paying attention, not timing the feed, going on talking or drinking tea until the baby simply fell asleep with the nipple sliding out of its mouth in a little puddle of drool.

She got the nappies perfect, too. She found a way of

doing the nappies that was as neat as an envelope around a letter. What a pleasure to flick out a clean nappy, fold it left over right, right over left, up through the middle and pin – with your hand underneath, naturally, so as not to stab the baby – and there it was, a trim white parcel of bandaged bottom, all your own work.

William was a rather blank kind of boy now. Sometimes she noticed a furtive anxious expression on his face that made him look like one of his own guinea-pigs. But she could not complain. He was a good boy and did his homework and kept his room tidy and brushed his hair without being asked, and never gave any trouble.

She could not understand mothers with children who were naughty. She heard them, answering back cheekily, refusing to eat their carrots, leaving the house with their shoe-laces undone. She saw the mothers shrugging, giving in. She did not tolerate any of that. You made it clear to children what was expected, and then you made sure that they did it. It was as simple as that.

William was too old now to be an *interest*, but recently she had discovered the best *interest* she had ever had: herself. She had the Creme Jeunesse, and the Defoliant Masque. She had the row of dear little ice-coloured bottles: the Oxidizing Humectant, and the Rose-Hip Astringent, and the Guava Enzyme Scrub, and the Day Creme and the Night Creme and the special Eye Cream that cost so much, but you only needed a little bit. She had the Bruised Oatmeal Face-Pack Programme in the cupboard, and always had plenty of cucumbers in the fridge. It was part of getting it all absolutely right, knowing about the old-fashioned things as well as the scientific ones.

She knew that other people put the radio on, or watched television, while they lay with the Oatmeal Pack on their face and the cucumber slices on their eyes, but she did not need television or the radio. It was enough to think about the way each cell of her cheeks, her chin, her neck, was being *replenished*.

The trouble was that you could forget about everything else. You went on picturing the little cells, one by one, swelling juicily, and one thought would lead to another, and time could get away on you.

One awful day she had simply forgotten to pick William up from school. Fiona had come home with him in the end, and had stood knocking at the back door. She had been so deeply absorbed in thinking about the *replenishment*, it had taken her a while to realise what the noise was. When she came to the door with the Oatmeal Pack still thick on her face and a cucumber slice stuck to her nose, Fiona had given her a bit of a funny look, and William had rushed straight into his room and slammed the door.

After that she had got herself a dear little alarm clock with an unusual striped face. There was a solution to every problem, if you had the will to solve it.

You still had to be vigilant. Even lying down, thinking about *replenishment*, you had to be careful not to let your eyebrows draw together, concentrating. Under the Oatmeal Pack the concentrating would show on your face in the form of a *line* which might at some later time harden into a *wrinkle*.

She tried hard not to think about anything at all now when she lay down. The trouble was, trying not to think about anything was in itself something you had to concentrate on. Even concentrating on not concentrating could be enough to make your eyebrows draw in towards each other. So, as well as remembering not to concentrate on *replenishment*, you also had to remember not to concentrate on *not concentrating*.

There was a lot to remember.

It was a full time job, really, remembering everything.

CHAPTER 8

LORRAINE SMART'S BASKET was too dainty for big Harley Savage. She felt it dangling from the end of her arm like a silly little decoration as she set off down Delphi Street towards the shops. She felt as if she was pretending to be someone else with this little dainty basket, someone not dangerous. *Lah le lah*, the basket seemed to say. *Happy days. Nice smiles. Happily ever after.*

Above such a basket, she felt that her face was more forbidding than ever. *Look out*, her face said. *I bite.*

The dog was not too dainty for her. Like her, it was a big coarse thing. It could probably turn dangerous, too.

After the walk in the morning she had given it a dish of water. *Just this once*, she reminded it, although not aloud, and shoved quite hard at its shoulder with the side of her foot when it got too close.

She would get rid of it this morning. Somewhere between the Mini-Mart where she would pick up a few groceries, and Alfred Chang Superior Meats where she would get something lean for dinner, and the Cobwebbe Crafte Shoppe, where Coralie was expecting her, the dog would disappear. It would just go, the same way it had just come.

In the meantime it trotted along beside her, keeping pace when she stopped, out of a city person's habit, at Jupiter Street, to *look to the right and look to the left and look to the right again* before she crossed. The only traffic was two magpies pecking at something squashed on the bitumen.

When she stopped, the dog stopped too. It looked where she was looking, then up into her face. It was right beside her when she got to the shops.

They seemed to crouch under their wide awnings, the windows heavily shadowed. She imagined shopkeepers peering out at her. The *woman down from Sydney*. The *Museum woman*.

The awnings had her confused for a moment. There was ALFRED CHANG, SUPERIOR MEATS, on one in elaborate italics, and there was ALFRED CHANEY, VALUER AND AUCTIONEER, on the next one. The windows were different. Alfred Chaney's was gold lettering arching across the glass, some kind of coat-of-arms thing and letters after his name like a brain surgeon. But behind the gold lettering the shop was dark, nothing there except an empty cardboard box and an old milk carton.

Next door there were no layers of gilt lettering, but the lights were on, illuminating a sloping display counter of shiny metal with cardboard containers of dripping in a tidy triangle like ninepins, and a neat stack of tins of tongue. There was no meat on display, only a glossy, deeply coloured picture of a carcase drawn over with dotted lines showing where it could be cut into joints.

As she watched, a large hand reached into the window and arranged two sprays of bright green plastic fern beside the containers of dripping. The dog's tail was beating against her leg. It was looking eagerly in the direction of the fly-door.

She turned her back on Superior Meats.

Across the road was the schoolyard, with a picket fence painted Department of Education cream and several well-worn pepper-trees. The flag drooped from its flagpole in the sun and a little glaze of heat lay over the bitumen playground.

Next to the school there was a shop with DRY & PIECE GOODS in raised plaster on the facade, but the flaking paint along the awning said BAKERY, and in any case it was closed. Someone had taped newspaper up over the windows, but so long ago the sticky-tape had dried out and the newspaper was curling down off the glass.

Two men turned into the bar of the Caledonian and above them on the verandah that reached out over the footpath a woman shook out a rug. Harley could see little flecks of dust floating down on to the cars nosed up to the gutter underneath.

The window of the Mini-Mart displayed an arrangement of plastic fly-swats that had been there so long that they were furred with red dust, a tin of Solagard, a tea-pot in the shape of a thatched cottage, three faded boxes of Uncle Toby's Oats, a blister pack of screwdrivers and a packet of sewing-needles. Right at the top there were buckets in six colours.

Thick plastic strips hung in the doorway to keep the flies out, one bandaged at hand-height with masking tape. When she pushed the fly-door behind the plastic strips, the hinge squealed and the bell jangled above her head. Out of the corner of her eye she saw that the dog was making itself comfortable on a piece of footpath, as if the two of them had been coming to the Mini-Mart for years.

Inside, the shop was dimly lit with fluorescents that were missing a few tubes, so it seemed very dark after the brilliance outside. There was something about it more like an institution than a shop: the pale green paint, the expanses of shiny lino floor. She felt too large between the shelves, nearly knocking over a pyramid of tinned peaches, brushing against a bouquet of tea-towels.

She stood in the dim shop holding the basket in front of her. Through the doorway she could see the flaring brightness of Parnassus Road baking under the sun. And just there, paws crossed in front of it, patiently watching the door, was the dog.

She was sure it would just go, but it had not just gone yet.

At the *Pet Food* section, she walked quickly past. It was nothing to do with her. At the next aisle she reconsidered, turned back. She had used Lorraine Smart's tin of Pal, so she would have to replace it. As her hand went out to take the tin off the shelf, she reminded herself that she was not in any sense buying it *for the dog*. She was buying it *for Lorraine Smart*. She dropped it in the basket without looking, moving on quickly.

Harley had gone into the laundry at Lorraine Smart's once or twice, but the message on the brown-paper bag over the taps was always the same: DO NOT USE. Under the bag, the taps looked normal, but it seemed better to be on the safe side and just do her washing in the kitchen, in a bucket. However, although Lorraine Smart's house contained many useful items, there were no buckets.

But apart from the ones in the window, she could not see any in the shop, either.

Beyond the long bare wooden counter, a still shape that had seemed part of the shelves moved sideways.

May I help you? it said, spreading its hands on the counter, revealing itself to be a shrivelled old man with crooked glasses and a big hairy mole on his ear.

I'm after a bucket, she said, trying to be friendly, *unwound*. A plain old bucket. For some washing.

The man took his hands off the counter and began to pick at the skin of his palm.

A bucket, he repeated. A plain old bucket.

Yes, she said.

He looked at her through his crooked glasses. They made his face look peculiar, and she saw that one of the lenses was cracked clean across and glued together with yellow glue, beaded along the mend.

Sorry, he said, and smiled. Just sold the last yesterday.

He sounded pleased. The glasses were slipping and he screwed up his face to push them back.

But, she said, and turned side-on to the counter, so that the buckets in the window were directly in his line of vision, the white glare of the street beyond them.

She did not want to be rude.

I *thought* I saw some in the window, she said doubtfully, as if the six plastic fly-swats might have caught the sun in a funny way and looked like six buckets.

Oh! he cried, and released his face so that the glasses slid down his nose again. Oh, those. They're the display.

He stood smiling at her, very much at ease. The silence extended. She imagined plucking the mole-hair on his ear-lobe and seeing him wince. She was surprised to find that she had said, Well, can't I buy one?

The frown returned to his face.

Buy one?

She nodded and he sighed a big heavy sigh.

That's the display, he said again, patiently.

This is the bush, they do things differently here, she reminded herself. But she heard her voice louder, sharper.

Why can't I buy one?

He shot back with the answer like a snake striking.

That's the display, he said. It shows what stock we carry.

She was getting hot. She could feel herself filling with rude things to say to him. She made an effort to speak very calmly.

Okay, but can't I buy just the one? Any colour will do.

No, see, he said, patiently, but with an edge of determination in his voice. It may not matter to *you* what colour it is, but there might be someone needs a particular colour, yellow for example, he might need (*he or she,* she corrected in her mind), or red, or whatever, blue. Now if he (*or she*) looks in the window and sees no yellow, or red, or whatever, blue, he'll think (*she'll think*) we don't carry it, when we do.

But you don't, she said, too loudly.

Oh yes we do, the man said, smooth and quick. She saw that he'd had conversations like this before. We just don't happen to have one at the minute.

They faced each other across the counter, the light reflecting off his glasses. A car revved up juicily across the square and drove away. A distant dog barked twice.

She could feel the rage rising in her chest, hot like brandy fumes, up into her face. The muscles in her arm were getting ready with a little extra load of blood, to slap her hand on the counter. Her voice had the words ready. *Come*

ON, *for God's sake,* it would shout. *Just sell me one of your bloody buckets!*

She waited, breathing, thinking of nothing but breathing, reminding herself that this was the moment when bureaucrats behind desks reached into their drawers, pulled out a different kind of form and said, *Now I might be able to do it if you were a P-85.* You were in business then, the bureaucrat's power established, and you could be oozily grateful to be a P-85.

But this was the bush and they did things differently here. Instead of the bureaucrat getting out the P-85, and everyone going home happy, the man with the mended glasses and the strangely red-faced woman continued to stand with the counter between them.

She left the shop, blind with irritation, and almost tripped over the dog as it came forward with its tail beating the air, sniffing at the string bag. She did not look down, but she knew it was there, following a pace behind, as she walked stiffly away from the Mini-Mart.

There was a fellow watching her over outside the Caledonian, a long lanky fellow curved against the wall. She stared back rudely, and he looked away.

It was true that a leaf had two sides, but when you *turned over a new leaf,* the *new leaf* was very like the *old leaf.*

Jay-walking recklessly across the empty space of Parnassus Road towards the Cobwebbe Crafte Shoppe, she tried to breathe steadily. She clenched the hand not holding the basket. *Tight, tight, tighter.* Doing it out in public she realised it was the same as making a fist.

And relax.

She was determined to start off on the right foot with Coralie this time. She would not mention *family*, and then clam up about it. She would not say how hot it was, either. That was stupid in a place that had been hot for three months and would go on being hot for another three.

Coralie was behind the cash register again going through dockets. She looked up and smiled when she saw who it was.

Hello, Harley said.

That sounded all right, but before she could stop herself, she went on.

Hot, isn't it?

But Coralie did not seem to mind.

Bushfire weather, she said, and went on counting dockets. When she had counted the last one she looked up and smiled over the tops of her glasses.

Not to worry, she said. We got the blue ribbon for Hose-Rolling last year.

Harley did not understand, and thought Coralie must be making some kind of suggestive joke. She laughed politely, feeling her face stiff with the false smile.

The bright red glasses must have seemed cheering, original, when Coralie had bought them. She would have smiled at herself in the optician's mirror. Harley could imagine her thinking the word *zany*. Now they were a joke that had gone on too long.

Under the glasses, crow's feet were etched in hard around her eyes from a lifetime of squinting at the Karakarook sunlight, and the skin there had gone crepey. But her breasts poked out jauntily under her tee-shirt and her hips were round in the tight jeans. Harley thought Coralie could be as old as she herself was. But Coralie had made a different decision about how to present herself to the world. Harley would never have tried *zany* red glasses or tight jeans. For years she had always chosen clothes that made no promises.

Coralie was smiling now, a complicated sort of smile that did not want to embarrass Harley but did not want to seem to laugh at her either.

No, look, she said, and pointed up behind her on the wall, above a dinner-set in the shape of black and orange pumpkins, at a row of pennants.

See? Karakarook Volunteer Bush Fire Brigade. Hose-Rolling. First Prize.

Oh!

It was foolish and patronising to have laughed.

But you're right, Coralie said quickly, and smiled a simpler sort of smile, and winked. There's a bit of off-duty hose-work goes on, too.

They could have a good laugh together about that.

Someone in Karakarook seemed to like padded coat-hangers. There were a lot of crocheted ones in orange wool and a lot more in pink, with white ribbon threaded along them. There were some more done in ruched pink satin trimmed along the bottom with lace. The expensive ones were done in hexagon patchwork. There was an abundant supply of glasses-cases, too. You could get them in crocheted wool, crocheted cotton, hexagon patchwork, satin embroidered with flannel flowers, or petit point.

When she picked up one of the coat-hangers and

squeezed the foam padding, it was nasty: flabby, like something left too long in the sun, and she felt her face draw down in disgust. Remembering Coralie was watching her, she made the corners of her mouth turn up, but then she thought she might look as if she was laughing.

She coughed, and tried to start again with the shape of her mouth.

Picking up a full-skirted doll she recoiled as her hand disappeared under its hollow skirt.

That's for your spare toilet roll, Coralie said. Don't go in for them myself, do you?

No, Harley said.

The way I see it is, we all go to the toilet, Coralie said.

Harley picked up a big striped bedsock that stretched in her hand into a huge thing like a Christmas stocking.

Mrs Stott, Coralie said. Well, she knits a bit on the loose side.

She opened the till with a ping and started sorting the money.

So you've got family out this way, did you say? she asked.

But as if to soften the intrusive sound of this, she took off the *zany* glasses and polished them on the hem of her tee-shirt. Without them, she looked like someone who could have worries of her own.

It made Harley feel she should make an effort.

I had my Gran and Grandpa, she said. Out Boolaroo way.

This was true, although not what she had been thinking of, that first day, mentioning *family*. But it struck the right tone, that *out Boolaroo way*, and it was nowhere near Badham. Her connection with Badham was no one's business but her own.

But they're long gone.

Coralie glanced at her.

Dead and gone, like, do you mean? she asked.

Then she bit her lip as if regretting the phrase. To reassure her, Harley spoke quickly.

That's right. Dead and gone.

It was a funny phrase, when you thought about it, but of course it was right. *Dead* was not always *gone*. You could think about the *dead* every day of your life, so that it seemed they would never, ever, be truly *gone*. Philip, for example. She went on quickly, to forestall any thoughts about him.

They got very old, she said.

Philip had not been old, of course. He had not been as old, when he *took his own life*, as she was now. And of course it had been a mystery to everyone. *Out of the blue* was another phrase she had taken refuge behind. No one had ever been able to make any sense of it, although she was weary now at the thought of how everyone had endlessly tried.

He had left a note. The police had found it on the bench: the writing pad that he used for personal letters, and one of the special disposable fountain-pens he liked. They had been disappointed because they did not think it went very far towards explaining anything

Dear Harley, it said, and a comma. That was all. *Dear Harley, comma.* He had shaped the comma, with the special black pen that he bought by the dozen, in his orderly way, putting the receipt away carefully, and in the time it took to write *Dear Harley* and the comma, he must have thought about her, because that was what you did when you started a letter. *Dear Harley, comma.* As he wrote, he must have seen her in his mind's eye as she was to him.

Whatever he had seen, it had made him put down the pen and get on with the thing he had so carefully planned.

The comma had never stopped haunting her. It did not explain anything for the police, and she let people go on saying it happened *out of the blue*. But she knew it had not happened *out of the blue*, but because of her. *Dear Harley, comma*. She was that dangerous, that a man could go and do to himself the thing that Philip had done rather than go on thinking about her.

Coralie had her head in the till again. There was a silence in which she flicked at banknotes to get them all the same way up, slid them into the till, flipped down the clip to hold them in place.

Harley felt the story of the grandparents ought to be finished off. At least it would fill the silence for a moment.

And then they died, she said. Just, you know, of natural causes.

It came out sounding a bit funny. Thinking about Philip, and trying not to think about it, had somehow made the words come out not quite right. If there was someone else here with Coralie now, they would be making rueful frog-faces at each other behind her back, faces that said, *Bit of a funny one, isn't she.*

And she – she would tighten herself up against being worked out. There were too many things she did not want to have to remember, too great a sense of needing to be wary. Her mouth would never look right.

It was a kind of fear, but they would think she was being haughty.

*

She was tired, thinking about it, and moved away to the shelves. Buying something was at least a way of not having to go on talking. It would show *her heart was in the right place*, even if it was not.

There were several shelves of unattractive khaki-coloured pickles and some kind of intensely black jam, but under that there were some jars of marmalade of a jewel-like amber hung with fine curls of peel.

These are good, aren't they, she said, holding one up to the light. Real Show quality.

Coralie laughed, a big hard surprised laugh like a sneeze.

Oh, that was me did those, she said. I did them.

She sounded almost angry.

I couldn't get anywhere with the sponges, not fluffy enough, and Marj Pump always wins the Preserved Fruit, so I thought I'd have a go at the marmalade.

She held a jar up to the light and frowned at it critically.

It's darker than you'd really want it, she said. The blessed sugar got too hot.

Harley guessed she would have said *the bloody sugar*, if she had not been on her best behaviour with the expert from Sydney.

What sort of fruit is it? she asked.

She was not really interested, but it was a way of trying to get back on the right foot.

Coralie had got a little rag and had wrapped it round her finger. Now she was pushing it between the buttons of the cash register, cleaning out the dust.

Yes, well, that particular one was the Sevilles. The rest of them aren't worth a bumper, your Navels and your Valencias.

She wet a fresh fingerful of rag with spit and wiped along

between the buttons. After a moment something occurred to her and she added quickly,

Course, there's plenty swear by Navels and the rest of them. I'm not saying they're no good. Only I personally like to go for the Sevilles.

Her lips pressed together as she squeezed her finger along between the buttons of the cash register.

Harley could see that it was Coralie's turn to feel that she had made a mistake. She seemed to spread it like a disease, being *wound.*

Oh no, she said, I agree about the Sevilles.

Coralie looked up, pleased, from the cash register.

Then you know about Sevilles! she exclaimed. Most people think they're blessed mandarins.

She leaned forward eagerly over the table. Harley tried not to draw back. She had not meant exactly that she *knew* about Sevilles.

Now, do you use the muslin bag, Coralie said, or how do you do it?

Harley put the jars down on the counter and made a big thing of getting out a hanky to wipe her fingers.

Well, she said.

It seemed too late to explain that she was just being polite.

She had watched marmalade being made one afternoon a long time ago, in a house she and her first husband had shared with others. Her memory of that afternoon did not involve any kind of bag, or muslin in any form.

Coralie drew back over the counter and ran her rag along the top of the register.

Course, she said casually, there are those who just cut it all up and bung it in, she said. Nothing wrong in that.

Harley was looking down, concentrating on wiping a little speck of nothing off the lid of one of the jars. There was a pause.

What I do, Coralie said, is I get a muslin bag, about so big. I put all the rubbish in there, the fruit and the pith and that. For the boiling-up.

Harley nodded in a neutral sort of way. She remembered the boiling-up part, the orange-smelling steam filling the kitchen. She remembered getting a bit tight with George while the boiling-up part was going on. They had had fun, laughing at the fussy little man in charge of the marmalade.

Actually, they had been rather nasty to him. In the beginning, George had liked the *dangerous streak* in her because it made him laugh. It was only later that he stopped liking it.

A man with big ears under his hat came into the shop. He nodded at her and when he took his hat off, she recognised him as the man who did not know how to get through a fence. She smiled, but it was too late: he had already turned away and was staring at the coat-hangers as if they were interesting.

Now it would look as if she had snubbed him. Not in town two days, and already she was getting it wrong.

Coralie seemed to have lost interest in the marmalade, just in time for Harley, who was starting to feel tight in the chest from having to pretend to *know about the Sevilles*.

We're on our last legs, here in Karakarook, Coralie announced. Freeway cut us right off, so Livingstone got the McDonald's. And Badham got the Prison Farm.

It seemed to Harley that Coralie was being careful not to glance at her.

She had made that problem, all by herself. She had not needed to mention *family* at Badham, but some devil in her mouth had made sure it popped out, and now it was a little knot in the thread of things with Coralie.

Coralie was going on. She was speaking quite loudly, as if she wanted the man to hear.

We don't get the passing trade like we used to.

The man was somewhere behind the rocking-chair, looking at the beanies. Harley tried to keep an agreeable expression on her face, for when she could catch his eye.

Coralie watched him for a moment, her lips pursed, then leaned over the counter.

Help you with anything at all?

Harley thought the tone she was taking was not quite the right tone to take with a customer.

He ducked his head, smiled vaguely without looking at the women, mumbled something, moved around to the bedsocks. When he picked one up it stretched like a concertina as it had for Harley, and he put it down hastily.

We've got to get the tourists, Coralie declared. As a matter of urgency.

She was starting to sound like someone at a public meeting.

Instead of pulling things down that will bring them in.

When she was not speaking, the shop was silent, in a deafening way. The man dislodged a painted door-stop and it fell on the floorboards with several different kinds of clatter.

Sorry, he said, and laughed.

They already got rid of the bridge here in town, Coralie said. Could have been a real drawcard. Old, you know, and a bit tatty, the way the tourists like. That was the Shire. Stacked the meeting.

She was quite shrill now, and sounded angry.

And now the old Bent Bridge, she said.

She made the words *old Bent Bridge* very clear. They carried, easily, to every corner of the shop. The man would probably even have heard them from outside.

The tourists would love it. That's why the Heritage thing, she said, and nodded at Harley.

It seemed best to nod back.

The Museum and that. You'll see, tonight at the meeting. We've got no shortage of ideas.

She straightened up and stared towards the man, although he had got himself behind a stand now.

There's more upstairs, she said loudly. Feel free to look round, won't you.

He came out from behind the stand. The way he did it, it looked as if he might have been trying to hide. He smiled again, and mumbled something, and suddenly went out of the shop. Harley still had the agreeable expression on her face, but it was turned towards an empty doorway.

Coralie was staring after him sternly, but suddenly laughed.

Did you see him drop the bedsock! she cried. Enough to frighten anybody off.

She put the jars of marmalade in a plastic bag.

Here, take these. On me, love.

Harley took the bag, and thanked her. It was simpler to just take it than to get into the business of the muslin bag again.

Anyway, she knew that Coralie knew. She had looked at her, and known that the expert from Sydney had never made marmalade in her life, with or without a muslin bag, and for some reason best known to herself was fibbing about it.

Outside on the street, the man with the hat had already vanished. That was a funny thing about little places like this. They had a way of swallowing people down into themselves and leaving everything empty.

The dog followed her back up the hill to Delphi Street, but Harley did not so much as glance at it. It thought it had another day's reprieve, and in a way that was true, because of the way she had kept on forgetting to ask anyone about it. But a reprieve was all it was.

She could hear its nails clicking on the footpath, the air panting in and out of its chest, but she did not look around.

CHAPTER 9

THE MECHANICS' INSTITUTE was a high gaunt room with a stage at one end and a pressed-tin ceiling with flowers picked out in blue and pink. Against the green walls, the effect was of molecules recoiling violently from each other. In the middle of the room was a big table with a group of people drawn up to it like a dinner-party.

All the faces turned towards Harley as she came in, and straight away she started sneezing. It was the ceiling fans whirring away so hard, wobbling in their sockets far above, stirring up dust that smelled of feet and furniture polish and disinfectant. Between her sneezes, the hot room thrummed as if about to take off.

She groped in her bag for a tissue, sneezing all the time, and when she had the tissue to her face she went on sneezing some more.

The faces around the big table watched as if mesmerised. It was starting to be like something out of the *Guinness Book of Records*. Finally Coralie pushed her chair back and went over to a switch on the wall. The fans slowed down.

Bless you! she called. Bless you, love!

Finally the sneezing stopped, although her nose still tickled. Thanks very much.

She could hear how her voice was thick, as if she had been crying.

The faces all turned towards her seemed green in the fluorescent light, Coralie's hair so black it was almost purple. She supposed her own nose was red and her eyes shrunken after so much sneezing. Without the sneezing, and the tissue up in front of her face, she felt exposed to the glare of so many strange faces.

She had made an effort that evening, getting ready for the meeting of the Karakarook Heritage Museum Committee: put on lipstick and her African dress, and fluffed up her hopeless hair in one of Lorraine Smart's many mirrors, to try to hide some of the uncompromising shape of her skull. Under the fluffed-up hair her face was as intractable as ever, but she had practised a warm smile in the mirror, one that did not show her fang-like eye-teeth, or look patronising.

She had not practised the sneezing.

They had all written their names on a piece of paper that Coralie passed down to her. *Coralie Henderson, Leith Cousens, Merle Armitage, Helen Banks.* In old-fashioned careful copperplate gone a bit wobbly, *Beryl Trimm.* Someone called *Felicity Porcelline* had done circles instead of dots over her *i*'s. *Bert Cutcliffe* was a large firm cursive, underlined. *Alfred Chang* was tiny secretive letters like the Rosetta Stone. More names ran on down the side of the page.

Good evening, she said, and an alarm immediately started up somewhere close. Two notes went on insisting, piercing, seeming to say it over and over: *you're weak, you're weak, you're weak.* She stood helplessly under the noise, pinned to the spot, accused. *You're weak, you're weak.*

Suddenly it stopped in mid-note. The silence that

followed seemed to throb: big, solid, an object in its own right.

That'll be the alarm, someone said.

It was an Asian man, smiling easily around at everyone as they laughed, settled themselves on their chairs, glanced around at each other.

Good evening, she tried again.

Coralie nodded away, smiling encouragingly, the picture of someone being *all ears*. Harley wondered if she looked nervous, the way Coralie was being so reassuring.

My name is Harley Savage.

As if cued by the name, an old woman, her face a cob-web of lines, unfolded a plastic bag in front of her and started to feel around inside. Everyone looked at her, but she went on obliviously, pawing clumsily at it and filling the room with the loud ugly noise. A middle-aged man in a shirt and tie frowned across at her, tapping his biro on the table.

Assuming the Asian man was *Alfred Chang*, the man with the biro must be *Bert Cutcliffe*.

Finally the old woman found what she was after, another plastic bag in which there was some small soft object. She put it on the table in front of her, where the plastic creaked and popped as it slowly uncreased.

With an effort, Harley made herself stop watching the bag unfold. She smiled around brightly. What with one thing and another, she seemed to have lost the thread. She was the expert from Sydney, and everyone was waiting. They had come out after dinner, when they could have been watching telly, or taking advantage of the off-peak STD, to talk about setting up a Heritage Museum in a small and undistinguished country town that had run out of steam.

She glanced down at her notes. *INTRO*, it said, unhelpfully.

People usually thought museums wanted the heirlooms, the cameo brooch, the engraved silver tea-pot, the lace christening robes that had come out from England with the great-great-great-grandparents.

It was a safe bet that Karakarook was full of lace christening robes and silver tea-pots. They always survived because they were never used, just brought out now and then to be admired.

The trouble was, the same things that had survived in Karakarook had survived everywhere else as well. No one was going to turn off the freeway to look at somebody else's great-grandmother's silver teapot.

What would put Karakarook on the map were the things that were so ordinary that no one had thought of keeping any of them. Ordinary dresses and baby's jumpers and men's work-shirts, and all the improvised things made for their houses by people who never had enough money to buy one from the shops.

Those things did not survive, because no one thought they were worth keeping. They were just used until they fell to pieces, or were thrown away as soon as you could afford something better. There was a kind of shame at keeping an old pair of children's overalls made from cut-down man's pants, or an apron made out of a sugar-bag. It was like admitting you picked your nose or farted. *That old thing!* they always exclaimed when Harley asked for them. *That rubbish!*

Things only survived by accident. Harley had found the *Ploughshares Quilt*, now in a humidity-controlled environment at the Museum, in a fruit box full of *terrible old things from Grandma* that had been about to go to the tip, in the back of a garage in Tenterfield. The now-famous *Beamer Collection* of work-clothes had been wedged into a hole in the side of a shed to keep the rats out.

Those were the things that would bring the city tourists. They would exclaim at the improvisation, the ingenuity, the thrift, and would go back to Sydney feeling they had been in touch with the real *spirit of the bush*.

Everyone had something on the table in front of them, but Harley did not think anyone would have brought their *old rubbish*. The old woman – probably *Beryl Trimm* of the shaky copperplate – had her hand on whatever was in her plastic bag, as if someone might run in and snatch it away from her. The Asian man had a shoebox in front of him, bulging with something that needed two heavy-duty elastic bands to hold it closed. Across the table from him, an over-dressed blonde woman kept looping her hair behind an ear and rearranging the handles of a cloth bag.

Harley had learnt from experience that the idea of the *old rubbish* was best led up to gradually.

Let's see what you've brought, she suggested, and like a good hostess Coralie glanced around, then volunteered.

My mother made this, she said. For her glory box.

She unfolded a large and elaborate white tablecloth with a lot of drawn-thread embroidery along the sides and some very ornate Mountmellick Work in the central medallion.

There were the napkins too, but they got lost.

Mmm, Harley said. Lovely workmanship.

It could break your heart if you thought about it too much, the amount of Coralie's mother's life that had gone into this tablecloth. She picked up the complicated scalloped edge, where the corner turned like a military operation.

Beautiful, she said, and meant it, even though it was no good to any museum.

Gives me a headache just looking at it, to be honest, Coralie said. But my word Mum was proud of it.

She folded it up, holding the middle under her chin like a bedsheet.

Go on, Merle, you're next, she said to the woman next to her.

Merle was wearing a blue tee-shirt with a knotted scarf printed around the neck in red, and the woman next to her was wearing the same thing, only with the colours the other way around. Next to each other the way they were, they were like a practical joke. They looked as though they had gone to the same hairdresser, too, and had their hair tidied away into the same perms.

Each one wanted the other to go first. *Go on, Merle. You first, Helen.*

They looked to Harley like best friends, the way they were laughing at each other, and it was only natural that best friends would have the same taste in clothes. *I like your top, Helen*, Harley could imagine Merle saying. *And my word that's a nice one you've got there, Merle*, Helen would answer.

The one with the red top and the blue scarf-pattern had a pair of white lace gloves her great-aunt had made. *Not for wearing*, she explained. *You just carried them in your hand. To church and that.* A woman across the table whose eyebrows were the same sandy red as her cheeks was interested in how you did it with the tatting shuttle, but she found it hard to visualise and the explanation became complicated, and everyone threw themselves at length into the business of whether you went *front to back* with the shuttle, or *back to front*.

Harley sat at the head of the table. She kept a smile on her face and breathed very steadily. *In. Out. In. Out.* She was not in the least bit *wound*.

Helen, or was it Merle, with the blue top and the red scarf-pattern, had brought along the lace christening robe that had been handed down in her family for five generations. Someone wanted to know whether she had ever had to wash it, and there was a long story about a baby who had brought up his breakfast on it. *Not stewed plums, luckily,* she said, and they all laughed, but then they were interested when she told them that the best thing was horse-shampoo because it was exactly the right pH. Someone else got out her address book to write down the name of the horse-shampoo, which had a complicated spelling.

While they were still sorting out whether it was two *k*s or two *m*s, the woman with the hair that had to be looped back all the time opened up her red corduroy bag. It had cloth handles, and a strip of velcro to keep it closed at the top, and a label in one corner, like a stamp, with her name and address on it.

Harley could guess what was inside.

The sound of the velcro unripping made everyone stop listening to the way you spelt the name of the horse-shampoo. When the woman lifted out a quilt folded in tissue and spread it out, they all went *Ooooh!*

It was an antique crazy quilt, made out of hundreds of

little pieces of velvet and satin, each one a different shape and outlined in thick yellow embroidery. There was a scalloped black satin border and a black satin backing.

Every museum in the world had dozens just like it.

The woman leaned over the table towards Harley, who could see the way she had outlined her lips with a fine line of bright lipstick. She had painted the exact shape she wanted, even if it was not quite the shape of her lips.

The lips cut out the syllables one by one and put them together.

My husband's great-grandmother made it.

The lips were very careful to articulate the *t* on *great* and the *d* on *grand*.

According to family stories it's well over a hundred years old.

A woman with a lot of dark-brown moles on her face shook her head and made a clicking noise with her tongue. Coralie said *My word!* in a bright way.

It's always been properly looked after, the woman with the blonde hair went on.

I keep it in naphthalene.

There was a short silence around the table.

In what, did you say? Coralie asked.

Harley had always admired people who did not mind being the one to ask the silly question. She had always minded, and never asked.

Mothballs, the woman said, and pushed her hair behind her ear again.

In moth-balls.

You could hear how it was really two separate words.

People were leaning forward over the table now and hands were beginning to reach out towards the quilt.

A tiny crease of anxiety began to take shape between the woman's nicely drawn eyebrows. She pulled the quilt gently away from them.

Oh, I think we'd better not touch it, don't you?

The hands kept following the quilt as she drew it back, and her pretty little face tightened.

Not too much.

Getting the *t* on the end of *not* separate from the *t* on the beginning of *too* seemed to be making the crease deeper, but she had got the quilt folded up again now, and back in its bag.

A very large woman brought a piece of patchwork the size of a handkerchief out of a brown paper bag. With a little shock of surprise Harley realised it was the woman who had told her to go *up along Jupiter Street* that morning. It was not really surprising, of course, Karakarook was only small, but a city person had to remind herself how small a world this was, how everything overlapped with everything else.

My Nanna did the miniatures, the woman said.

The patchwork was like an opal, brilliant colours shining densely together.

She liked the little tiny ones.

She spoke very calmly and sweetly, not hurrying, looked down and smoothed the dress over her front.

Because she was big, probably. Like me.

There was a silence in which the fans revolved gently against the ceiling.

The woman whose face was peppered with moles broke the silence.

Big is beautiful, pet! she called.

While everyone was laughing, she seized her chance.

When I was a girl out West, she started, Well, when the governesses came, the first thing they'd do would be they'd knit a jumper for the jackeroo.

Everyone smiled, got themselves comfortable in their chairs. There was a sense of people settling in for a *yarn*.

Well, she said, looking around, pleased, I've knitted that many bloody jumpers!

Harley moved her sheets of paper over each other with slightly more of a snap and rustle than was necessary. She looked at the names on the list. *Glad Fowler*, this one might be, or *Marjorie Pump*.

The woman glanced over at the rustle of the papers.

Well, she said quickly, I'm sick of the old chenille, and I've decided I'm going to die in my own bed at home, so I said to Don, I'd better make a bloody fabulous quilt so's I'll make a nice corpse.

The laughter went on a long time. Harley laughed too, politely, with the surface of her face. But it was too easy to see the woman with the moles as a corpse, stretched out waxy in her coffin, folds of maroon satin around her face, the moles standing out dark on her dead skin.

She wondered if everyone else could too, and whether that was why they were laughing so long.

But the woman with the moles was pleased with herself. She looked around the table, folded her arms over her bosom, smiled. You could see that as far as she was concerned it was only a figure of speech. She did not really believe she would ever be a corpse.

But the mention of quilts had started them all off reciting the names of their favourite patterns.

The woman who had written down the name of the horse-shampoo had brightened.

Drunkard's Path! she called out, and blushed.

Bear's Paw! Coralie shouted. *Bow Ties!*

Oh, *Blazing Star*, the fat woman said. You should see Lorraine's *Blazing Star*!

The woman with the crazy quilt waited for a pause and pushed her hair back again.

I've always found that *Flying Geese* makes a very effective border, she said.

Harley had heard it called *refained*, the way she spoke.

But I've found that puckering tends to be a problem.

Everyone was silent for a moment, but then the woman with the moles brayed out,

Oh, I still go for the old *Log Cabin*. With the red in the middle for the fire in the hearth.

The woman with the vowels did not try to compete with any more information about her puckering borders.

Or remember *Courthouse Steps?* one of the printed-scarf women said. Just like *Log Cabin* except the darks and lights are opposite.

All over the room, people were nodding and smiling to show they knew about *Courthouse Steps* too.

But what about the really old things? Harley interrupted.

She had not meant it to be so abrupt.

The old shabby things?

It might have come out louder than she had meant.

Patched and mended, you know, she said more softly.

All around the room, glad smiles were fading.

The old bush quilts, for instance, she tried. Put together out of old clothes, things like that.

There was no response from the faces in front of her.

She glanced down at her notes. *Australian vernacular*, it said. She tried it.

The Australian vernacular!

It had sounded good, back in the Museum in Sydney, discussing it with the *Curator* in brackets *Textiles*. Here under the fluorescent lights of the Karakarook Mechanics' Institute hall, *Australian vernacular* did not sound nearly as good.

She heard her voice go stringy, trying to explain.

You know, made out of flour-bags sometimes? Just to keep warm? Some people call them waggas.

No one seemed to have heard of waggas.

The silence was like a substance that you had to push back with your bare hands. She went on desperately flinging words at it.

Rough as anything. Rags inside, for warmth.

From their blank faces you would think they had never heard of rags, either.

All the old horrors! she cried.

Her voice was over-bright, trying to be jokey.

The old horrors we hide out the back!

She heard her voice, too sprightly, and felt her face stretch, smiling too hard. The solemn moon faces were all turned towards her blankly. Even Coralie's encouraging smile had gone stiff.

Harley wondered if she was the only person in the world with *horrors out the back*.

The patchwork of her own that she had brought to show them was fingered doubtfully. It was the one she called

Shearing Shed #5, with little triangles that did not quite match up together, and big odd trapezoid shapes in many shades of grey.

It was a feature of Harley Savage's fibre art, the way she made her seam-lines not quite line up. It was one of the things that *held the surfaces in dynamic equilibrium* and *wittily subverted the form*. This one, *Shearing Shed #5*, was one of a series she was quite pleased with, that took the big simple shapes of country sheds as a basis for *lights* and *darks* to fit against each other in interesting ways.

When you had been sewing as long as she had, it was actually quite hard, getting the seams not to line up exactly. But she already knew that many people, the ones who knew a lot about *Log Cabin* and *Bear's Paw*, only saw her patchworks as a series of mistakes. They could not see past the fact that the seams did not quite line up, and the way the stripes of the fabrics ran in different directions, and that the quilting was just done on the machine, and not even in proper straight lines.

Oh, contemporary, Coralie said. Never done contemporary, have you, Merle?

She was like a hostess with a difficult dinner-party. But Merle had not *done contemporary* either.

There was a pause, then Coralie found a word that was both polite and truthful.

It's very different, she said. She raised her voice. Very different, isn't it, Mrs Trimm?

The old lady did not seem to have an opinion as to whether it was *different*. She was fingering a part where raw seam edges created a fringed effect. It had always been one of Harley's favourite parts of this particular piece.

Is this on purpose, dear? she asked. Did you do this on purpose?

Harley looked at her watch. It said half past seven.

Yes, she agreed with Mrs Trimm. She seemed to have been here, smiling hard, for hours.

It was on purpose.

She wondered if her watch might have stopped.

CHAPTER 10

AT HIS AGE William did not need to be taken to school. In fact he was always nagging her to let him walk there on his own. But she knew that *on his own* meant *with the others,* the rough uncouth boys who had skateboards and said *I gunna* when they meant *I'm going to.* Not appropriate companions for William, who was quite bright, but had to be encouraged to take his homework seriously.

She had walked down to the school with him today, and waved as he went in, although he never turned around to wave back, and then she had come back and cleaned up the breakfast things, and mopped the floor. Hurrying to get the mop out in the sun, she realised she was frowning.

It was one more thing to remember, not to frown while you ran outside with the mop.

Then she stripped the beds, turned the mattresses, and got the freshly-ironed sheets out of the cupboard she thought of as *the linen press.*

She loved the feel of the crisply ironed fresh sheets snapping out over the bed on a cushion of air, and the glassiness of the starched pillowcases. It was only logical that the slippery texture of a thoroughly starched and ironed pillowcase would minimise the dragging effect on the skin of the face.

As she made the bed it brought a picture from her childhood. It was not a picture she wanted to see, but just for a moment, before she could blank it out, she did: her mother, flat on her back, asleep in the musty double bed, stretched out under the bedclothes fully dressed from when she had come in late from the Mail Exchange the night before. Her face pointed straight up to the ceiling, the shoes still on her feet made peaks in the bedclothes, and the handbag had kept her company all night, at the ready on her arm.

She put the picture away from her. There was no point in dwelling on things like that. You *put them behind you*, and did not look back.

She tucked the sheets hard under the corners of the mattress. *Hospital Corners*. Her mother had had no idea how to make a bed properly, had never heard of *Hospital Corners*. Felicity had learned about *Hospital Corners*, and starching, and the importance of turning mattresses on a daily basis, from Hugh's mother, who had taken her under her wing. *I've always wanted a daughter*, she had said. Felicity had had to stop herself saying, *And I've always wanted a mother*. It might have sounded a little bit funny, seeing her mother was still alive.

She had sent away to Sydney for a new book that had diagrams of chin-tightening exercises. You started by pulling the mouth out sideways into a kind of leer. Then you tensed the muscles around your neck and jaw. She tried it in front of the bathroom mirror. It was rather grotesque.

However, she could see how it exercised all the muscles that held up your chin. They stood out in a frill of tendons around your jaw.

It was probably very good for you, even though it did make you look as if you were being electrocuted.

She did it six times, and then the muscles began to ache. *No pain, no gain.* That was what the books said. So she did seven more.

Hugh said he did not care, and he probably meant it. *Darling, I'd love you even with wrinkles,* he had told her, many times. She thought it was probably true. He was not one of those men who would trade in their wife once she got old, and replace her with something that had no *laugh-lines.* Hugh was a man who liked life to stay the same. She thought he had made a sort of agreement with life, that he would not demand too much of it, if it left him alone.

He liked the Land & Pastoral that way. There was not much margin for surprise there.

It was nothing to do with Hugh, the staving-off of the laugh-lines and so on.

It was something more private than that, and more important.

She did another chin-clench in the mirror. The trouble was that although making yourself look electrocuted tightened up the muscles around your chin, it also creased the whole of the lower part of your face up into *lines.*

The question was, whether the *chin-firming* effect was enough to make up for the *line-forming* effect. It was yet another little dilemma.

And now here she was, frowning about the dilemma itself. It seemed that thinking about almost anything led to a dilemma, and where you had a dilemma you had this little pucker between the eyebrows.

She smoothed it out with a bit more Creme Jeunesse.

That was better. But as soon as she forgot, she knew something under the skin would swell back into the smoothed-out place and make that little buckle in the skin again.

You had to fight the feeling, sometimes, that your body had a mind of its own. But a person could not be on guard for ever against themselves.

The woman from the Museum was apparently a well-known person. That common-looking Coralie from the craft shop had told her that the PM himself owned one of her patchworks.

But Felicity had noticed straight away that the woman had been neglecting her moisturiser. Every time she smiled, cracks in her skin radiated out from her eyes. *Laugh-lines*, indeed.

And she should do something about her hair. With that big face she needed to make a bit more of her hair. A good perm, perhaps. The lipstick was on crooked, too, and it was the wrong colour. With that sort of skin she should never wear that sort of pink. She could have told her that the dress was a bad mistake. That big ethnic sort of pattern, brown on cream, looked more like a tablecloth than a dress. Being so big herself, she would do better to avoid big patterns like that.

Moreover, she had happened to notice that the button on one of the square pockets over the breasts did not quite match the ones that did up the dress down the front. The woman had probably lost a button from the front and replaced it with this one from the pocket, and put the one that did not quite match on the pocket, where it would not show so much. She had made the mistake of thinking the not-quite-matching button would be a little secret between herself and the dress.

You lost buttons, naturally. Buttons were often sewn on very poorly. These days, as soon as she brought any garment home, she went over the buttons and reinforced the stitching with proper button thread.

However, you still lost a button now and then, and they were surprisingly hard to match. She had lost a pretty little button off her pink silk once, and had sent away to Honeycutt's for a match. The first one they sent was not satisfactory and had had to be returned. The second had not been completely satisfactory either. There had been some attempt at unpleasantness, but she had a good carrying voice on the phone, and the vowels she had learned to copy from Hugh's mother stood her in good stead with people in shops.

It was true that you could disguise the fact that buttons did not quite match by taking one from somewhere less conspicuous, as this woman had done.

But it meant it was not perfect. You always had something to hide.

The meeting had started well enough. The woman from the Museum in Sydney told them her name, and welcomed them, and congratulated them on the idea of the Karakarook Heritage Museum. She had not giggled or said *um* and her posture was good.

But then she let people waste time, talking about the obviously unsuitable things they had brought along. It was polite, she supposed, but you could let politeness go too far.

She had not gone along to hear Merle Armitage, with her glasses still crooked – it would be so simple just to pop in to Livingstone and get the man to straighten them – explain how you made the gusset for the thumb of a lace glove. It was not even real lace. Then Mrs Fowler had gone on and on about knitting jumpers, when anyone who knew anything about knitting knew that her casting-off was always much too tight.

Something could be done about disfiguring moles like hers. She could mention it to her discreetly some time. There was a man in Sydney who did wonders with moles.

Mr Cutcliffe was there, wearing the same polyester tie he always wore. He had brought along a terrible old shirt, the antique collarless kind, with a big brown stain on the front. Personally, she would not have given it house room.

One had to be cordial and courteous to Mr Cutcliffe, because he was William's teacher, but he was not really up to much. She was not completely happy with the school. These little country schools, how could they get the quality staff? More than once she had heard Mr Cutcliffe say *anythink* in an unguarded moment.

Once upon a time, long ago, she herself had said *anythink*. Everyone in her family had always said *anythink*. But once she was meeting different kinds of people at Honeycutt's, she had quickly learned better. By the time she was going out with Hugh she hardly had to think before she said the word. *Anything*. There was a pleasure in getting it right, and knowing you had got it right, and making sure other people knew you got it right. *Anything*.

Ben Hall's shirt, Mr Cutcliffe had said, and Felicity had thought he must be some local football hero, until he had added, *The one they shot him in, there's the blood*, and she remembered the bushrangers.

The worst thing about the meeting for the Museum Committee was that Alfred Chang had been there. He had brought along a whole lot of funny old black-and-white photographs. They showed Karakarook as it had been in the beginning, a raw naked town surrounded by hills littered with cut-down tree trunks as thick on the ground as spilled toothpicks. The big plane trees along the driveway of *Heatherbrae* had not even been planted, and the Post Office and Town Hall were bald and new, and beside them the Mechanics' Institute had grand iron railings out the front that were not there any more, and a sort of colonnade that had been filled in with fibro.

They had been in his uncle's things, he said, when he died, and had come to him because the family knew he was interested in photography.

The way he spoke, he seemed to think it was all quite normal, as if his uncle was just like other people's uncles, whereas of course his uncle must have been Chinese. It was almost as if he did not realise that being Chinese was unusual.

Photography's a bit of a hobby with me, he said. I've fixed up a darkroom and a bit of a studio. Up above the shop.

He was telling the woman from the Museum, of course, but it had seemed to Felicity that he had been speaking directly to her.

While everyone was looking at the photos and exclaiming at how *different* it all was, and how it was all *just the same*, he held one out to her across the table.

Here, Mrs Porcelline, he said.

There was that same silky thing in the way he said her name. The way he said it, it actually sounded slightly rude.

This one might interest you. The bank, when it was first built.

He made her lean right over the table to take the photo. He would have been able to look right down her front. It was the only problem with the little pink top. The other thing was, as he gave her the photo, his fingers brushed hers. It could have been an accident. Anyone looking would have assumed it was an accident. You had to know about him being in love with her, to know it was on purpose.

She felt sorry for him in a way. Going to so much trouble, coming to the meeting, all the business with the old photos, just so he could sit across the table from her and touch her fingers.

She looked at the photograph of the Land & Pastoral, although it did not interest her. The shadows of the stone pediment were very sharp and black on the paper, and there were two men in a buggy in front of it, and a blur that was probably a dog running past.

When she passed it back to him she was careful to slide it across the table. That way, their fingers would not touch again.

But he would not take it back.

Keep it, he hissed in a stage-whisper, so everyone looked.

Keep it, Mrs Porcelline.

He would have gone on hissing at her across the table all night, so she smiled and mouthed *thank you* across at him, and put the photo away in her bag to show how grateful she was.

After that she kept her face turned away, looking along towards the woman from the Museum. She could not see, but she could feel him, watching her, for the rest of the night. She did not look, but she made sure she kept her chin nice and high, and the corners of her mouth turned up.

Although supposed to be such an important person, the woman from the Museum had not seemed to be all that interested in Great-Grandmother Ferguson's magnificent old heirloom quilt, that had come down to Hugh. It looked as though she did not fully realise just how valuable it was. Felicity had been prepared to point out the piece that was said to be out of her wedding dress, and the embroidered spider's webs and butterflies, but did not feel she had been given the opportunity.

Not that she had any intention of leaving Great-Grandmother Ferguson's quilt in the Karakarook Heritage Museum. She would make it clear that it was simply on loan – she had seen that, in art galleries, *on loan from so-and-so* – and when they left Karakarook at the end of the year, she would take it with her.

Rather than showing the proper interest, the woman from the Museum had gone on about *old horrors*. She had talked about *old horrors* as if they were something you might want to have, and bring along for other people to see. Personally, Felicity thought the appropriate place for any kind of *old horror* was in the incinerator.

There had been a little moment's *awkwardness* at the end of the meeting. She did not want to remember it, in fact she had already put it behind her. No one would guess that it was what she was thinking about now as she stood in front of the mirror, smoothing the special cream around her eyes.

It had been nothing more than an instant's *awkwardness*, and no one who had witnessed it knew about the other, larger, *awkwardnesses*. Hugh knew about the larger *awkwardnesses* but did not know about this small *awkwardness*. Only she herself knew about both, and her secret was safe with her.

Frankly, in a little place like Karakarook, you would not think that there could be too much scope for *awkwardness*.

The woman from the Museum had been saying that other museums sometimes took photos of all the things in their collection before they stored them away, like a kind of catalogue. Alfred Chang had volunteered to do it.

I've got the studio set-up, he said.

Felicity had felt him glance over at her.

It wouldn't be like a professional, but I'm free. If you'll trust me.

It seemed to Felicity, although she was not looking, that he was speaking straight at her. She was not looking, but she could feel him, across the table, watching her.

All at once it had seemed a kind of moral dilemma. It would be terrible if the bank manager's wife did not appear to trust the butcher. And how much worse considering he was Chinese. And in love with her.

Oh, yes! she found herself crying out. I'd love you!

That was wrong.

To do mine, I mean!

She had almost been shouting.

Why had she done that? Jumped in so fast, and called out so loud?

In the mirror her face smiled calmly back at her, a smooth, slightly smiling, unlined face with special cream on its eyelids and nothing to reproach itself for.

That was the first *awkwardness*, she thought. There had been enough *awkwardnesses* to start ticking them off on your fingers, because there had been a second little *awkwardness* not long after the first one.

At the end of the night, when everyone was scraping back their chairs and gathering up their things, she could not find her handbag. She looked around among the clutter on the table and heard herself saying in a high voice, a voice just about to tip over into being the kind of voice that would make everyone stop and look around: *My bag! I've lost my handbag!*

There was a little silence, and then Mrs Fowler announced it in her carrying voice.

She's lost her handbag. Mrs Porcelline can't find her handbag.

Felicity could not help noticing how she made it sound like *hambag*.

Everyone scuffled around, looking for it, and then in the end, it turned out it had somehow got all the way over the other side of the table, where Alfred Chang was sitting. He picked up Helen Banks' antique baby's shawl, and there it was, her own little tan bag, swinging out from its concealment in the folds of the shawl.

Watching her face in the mirror, she wondered now whether it had really been an accident.

Not to worry, Mrs Porcelline, he had said.

She tried to remember just the kind of smile he had given her.

Here it is.

Then he was coming around the end of the table towards her, holding it out.

Oh! she heard herself exclaim.

It was too loud again.

Oh! Goodness! However did that happen!

She laughed and then she stumbled over the leg of her chair, and somehow there she was, falling against Alfred Chang's chest. She put out her arms, just a reflex, and for a moment – well, for a moment it was almost as if she was hugging him.

She got herself upright in a blink. Really, in terms of time, it had hardly happened.

The trouble was, then she laughed. It was just to show how it did not matter at all. Just a little laugh to throw it off.

She remembered the laugh. It had not been quite right, the laugh. Mrs Fowler had looked at her, and so had Coralie Henderson, and all at once there was a whiff, like a fart, of something extremely *awkward*.

She had watched the photo of the bank in the incinerator, this morning: it had fallen in face-upwards, and had begun by writhing in the heat like a thing in pain, curling itself almost in two and then suddenly folding out flat again. She had watched as the flames poured all over the brown surface and swallowed up the columns, the men by the buggy, the blur that was probably a dog.

A lot of very smelly black smoke had poured out of the top of the incinerator. Even when she clanged the lid down, it kept gushing out from the chimney. Perhaps the paper was really some form of plastic. Plus, there were chemicals on the surface of the paper, the actual electrons or atoms or whatever it was that had made up the picture. Toxic, probably.

She could see the smoke drifting out over the backyards of Karakarook South. Other people would smell it, but they would not know it was coming from her incinerator, and even if they did, they would not know what she was burning, and once the smoke had gone, there would be nothing left whatsoever.

That was the nice thing about burning. Once things were burned, it was just as if they had never been.

Chapter 11

CORALIE HAD GIVEN Harley elaborate instructions about getting out to her sister's place on the Yuribee road. She had been watching out for the landmarks, and had passed the little creek, and the big red hay shed, but she was starting to think she must have missed the burnt-out car.

In the city it was gauche to be on time, but she had a feeling it might be different in Karakarook.

Just a bit of a barbie, Coralie had said. *Out at my sister's place. Just a few people.*

The Yuribee road was a homely little thing. Yellow flowers bobbed along the broken edges of the road and the thick stems of thistles burst up through the bitumen. There were no cuttings and no culverts. It was a matter of up around the hills and down the other side. The Datsun laboured up, whined down, swinging out on a sharp corner so the back wheels snatched at gravel.

The landscape was laid on in layers, the distant mountains the airiest of blues, overlaid with the curves of hills, each a darker blue, until the closer ones were almost black with thick bush softening every contour of the land like mould. In the foreground each individual hill had only a remnant cap of bush, and where the slope grew gentle it had been cleared altogether into a band of bleached bare paddock.

At the end of a line of pine trees there was a sagging post-and-rail fence, where a group of cows nosed at the straw-dry grass. One seemed to have given up and was standing pensively staring into the distance, its shadow a small black shape underneath its belly. A cockeyed shed near them seemed to be kneeling sideways into the grass. In the next paddock, all by itself, was a small brick dunny with a pointy roof, like a miniature church.

There it was finally, the burnt-out car, upside down, with a small tree growing through the driver's window. She had to *go past that*. Then there would be a sharp bend, and she had to *go past that*, and she had to go past the shed and yards, but not far, because when she got to the gate and grid, she had to turn in there.

She felt a little clutch of fright, getting out of the car to undo the gate. It had been like this for a long time now. There was that sense of all the faces turning towards her. *Oh, it's Harley.* In that moment, when she could feel them all visualising what had happened with Philip, she had to gather her personality around her like a cloak. It was for protection, but she knew it could look like bad temper.

The first gate was held closed with a chain-and-pin arrangement, but the pin had twisted in the wood of the post and it took her a moment to work out how to twist it back around so you could lift the chain over it. Some sheep nearby raised their heads and watched her suspiciously. She found she was over-acting innocence. *Just here for a barbie*, she was explaining in her imagination. *They're expecting me.* As she drove through the gate and got out again to close it behind her, the sheep tossed their heads in fright and scattered away with their bandy back legs looking silly. From behind an egg-like boulder that had been cracked in half by a tree erupting out of it, she could hear them going *Baa! Baaaaah! Ba-ah!* in an indignant way.

Each of Coralie's sister's gates was kept closed by a different arrangement of chain and loops, some from the shop and some home-made out of fencing-wire. Coralie had told her there were three of them, not counting the first one, but she had lost count when she came over a rise and saw the house in front of her.

From a distance, as she drove up the last stretch of potholed track past the last gate, feeling all her loose flesh jiggle and jolt, Coralie's sister's *place* reminded her of Gran and Grandfather's *place*. There was the same bald paddock in front of the house, the same bush-covered hill behind it, the same kind of big black pine tree at the side. There was even an old bulbous-nosed truck, its red paint turned to pink powder, standing up to its doors in weeds, that was just like Grandfather's old Dodge.

She got out of the car, hearing how loud the door-slam was in the midday silence, and took a deep breath of the sweet straw-scented air.

Oh, here's Harley!

She wished she had some other Harley she could offer them.

But now Coralie was coming out smiling from the verandah, where she must have been waiting for her. From the back of the house she could hear voices, splashing, children shrieking.

Good on you, pet, Coralie said. Glad you could come.

From the sound of it, she had thought Harley might not come, and that was clever of her, because for a while it had been true. *An attack of gastric,* she had planned. *What a shame.* At the last minute, though, she thought of all the complications *an attack of gastric* would cause. Coralie would come to the house, and want to look after her. She would have to pretend to be sick, then pretend to recover, but not too quickly.

In the end, it was probably easier to face *just a few people*.

She followed Coralie around the side path past the water tank and along beside the chook-yard. The chooks' water bowl was a cracked pink bathroom hand-basin with the plug in, tilting on the ground. Stretched out on the wire with plastic clothes pegs, a fox-skin had shrivelled and cracked in the sun.

She felt her mouth jerk into a spasm of premature smile, as if practising, and made it stop. It might look funny to come around the corner with a big smile already stuck on.

She need not have worried, because just as they came into the backyard, someone threw a cupful of something at the barbecue and orange flame erupted with a *whump*. Everyone jumped back. *Steady on, Don,* someone shrilled. *Call the Brigade, quick!* someone else called, and a man's voice shouted, *Not to worry, love, we're all here,* so they were all laughing and only half paying attention when she and Coralie joined them.

There was the barbecue with the men around it poking at the cooking meat, and a big table in the shade under a tree, the food all covered with little domes of fly-wire, and a square of bright blue swimming-pool where children were jumping in, splashing up water that was like chips of glass in the sun.

Coralie's sister Donna was just like Coralie, only without the glasses, and her hair was dyed red instead of black. She fussed around Harley, getting her a drink, getting her a little biscuit with cheese on it. Then she and Coralie stood side by side, smiling at her, as if at handiwork they were proud of.

A big man who had been methodically splitting wood for the barbecue put his axe down and wiped his hands on his blue singlet so he could shake hands.

My husband Henry, Coralie said, rather formally, but then she laughed.

Mind you, nobody calls him that.

Call me Chook, he said. Everyone does.

In fact, Harley thought, he did look a bit like an old boiler, stringy in the singlet. It was the kind of dangerous, or at least nasty, thought she had hoped she might be able to avoid, *unwinding* in Karakarook, the kind of thought that belonged to the *old* side of her *leaf.*

To make up for it, she tried to be especially friendly.

You're in the Heritage Committee too, then? she asked, but she could see straight away that was wrong. Coralie and Chook exchanged a glance.

Not exactly, Coralie said.

Not on your life, he said at the same moment.

It's a bit of a sore point, Donna explained unnecessarily. As a matter of fact.

In the little silence, the man who had brought the old bushranger shirt to the meeting came up.

Mr Cutcliffe, you remember? Coralie said.

Mr Cutcliffe sat Harley down on a stool he had brought for the purpose, and sat on another himself, and started to tell her a lot of things about the bushrangers. *Wonderful*, she kept saying. *Goodness.*

Chook went back to splitting kindling with small deft strokes of his axe, and Coralie and Donna went over to the food table to do things with plates. *Really?* Harley said. *Fancy that.*

Then the fat woman, the one whose Nanna made the miniatures, was standing beside Mr Cutcliffe with a plate of meat.

Here you go, Mr Cutcliffe, she said. Salad's over on the table, you know your way around.

She took his place on the stool.

He's the teacher, she said, watching him go over to the table. Mr Cutcliffe. Taught me, too. And look, I'm Leith. I know how it is with names.

Leith smiled peacefully over towards the swimming-pool.

He's real good with the kids, Mr Cutcliffe. But you don't want to get him started on the bushrangers. His mother was a Hall, see, and he's that proud of it.

She shifted on the little canvas stool and it creaked dangerously.

Now listen, Harley, she said, and Harley tightened herself up against whatever was coming. She was going to be told she had done something wrong. Perhaps she had left one of the gates open on the way in.

Sorry you missed out on the bucket the other day, she said in her slow smiling way. Grandad's a bit funny about the display.

Harley nodded, and tried to make her smile as peaceful as Leith's.

Perfectly all right, she said. No problem at all.

But it made her giddy. She had come very close to losing her temper with *Grandad*, had nearly shouted at him, slapped the counter, stormed out of the shop. If she had, everyone in Karakarook would have known within half an hour. Here in Karakarook there would be no hiding a *dangerous streak*.

The Asian man came over with a plate full of food for her, and another for himself, and with another strained creak from the stool, Leith got up.

Alfred, isn't it? Harley said, remembering the tiny secretive writing on her list.

Then she wondered if that might be wrong, too. Perhaps he liked to be called *Mr Chang*, the way Bert Cutcliffe obviously like to be *Mr Cutcliffe*. Or *Alfred Chang* might have been someone else, and now he would think, *she thinks we all look the same*.

Yes, he said, only I'm Freddy to my friends. Like the frog. Call me Freddy.

He smiled at her, a frank cheerful boyish smile, although she could see, close up like this, that he was no boy.

Try this rump, he said. Butchered it myself.

They chewed the steak together in silence for a moment. It was very tough. Harley tried not to let him see how her jaw was straining at it.

Tough as old boot leather, he said cheerfully.

Harley was getting ready to protest that no, it was *lovely*, such a *good flavour*, and *not really tough at all*, but he got in first.

Leave that, he said. I'll get you some snags. No need to be polite.

*

173

After the snags he took her plate away.

Got something to show you, he said.

He did not quite take her by the hand, but the gesture implied it, and it seemed impolite not to follow him. Coralie glanced up and did something with her face that was some kind of message, but at that distance it was impossible to know what it meant. In the far corner of the garden, bushes screened them from the party and the light turned green, filtering down through a big tree of some thick shady kind.

The butchering tree, Freddy said. Grandpa was cook out here in the old days.

He pointed up into the leaves, where a thick branch hung directly over their heads.

See? The hook. Hang the beast up on that, slice it down, all the guts fall straight out.

If he was trying for shock effect, he had picked the wrong audience.

Oh yes, Harley said, but she was already moving to go back to the party. As she was turning, Freddy was suddenly in front of her with a hand gripping her elbow.

Know what Karakarook means? he said.

She could feel his thumb, stroking the skin just above her elbow.

In Aboriginal?

Taking her elbow had brought him very close to her. He was shorter than she was, chunky and muscular, and was watching her in a certain kind of intent way.

It means elbow.

She knew that intent look. She had received it a lot in her younger days, in spite of her lack of *looks*. She knew what it came from, and she knew exactly what it led to. It was flattering, in a way, to be getting it at her time of life, and from a man certainly not lacking in charm.

Number two husband had been like this Freddy: that nice lopsided smile, that nuggety quality. Like Freddy, he had given off a kind of steam of sexuality, an innocent animal vigour. He had flirted with anyone. It did not mean anything. It was just a reflex, the way you saw the kids in Newtown going along trying the handles of all the parked cars, just on the off-chance. Occasionally, often enough to keep them trying, one of the doors would open.

Freddy was to be congratulated for being willing to give such unpromising material a try. In Karakarook there'd be a terrible shortage of new doors, not much room for *just on the off-chance*. You'd know everyone, and they'd know you, and there'd be no room for secrets. A new person, and especially a new person who was just passing through, would be an opportunity you would just have to take when it was offered.

Poor Freddy was not to know how entirely her history had made such intent looks irrelevant. Not so much unwelcome as simply obsolete.

She resisted the impulse to laugh.

To demonstrate what he meant, he crooked his own arm, the one that was not holding hers.

Because of the bend in the river.

Crooking his elbow and holding it up to show the way the river bent had brought him even closer.

Well, she said, and moved herself away just slightly. That's an interesting piece of information, Freddy.

He caught the tone straight away and dropped his hand from her elbow.

They looked at each other. He was not surprised, not disappointed, just weighing up whether it would be worth trying again.

Any time you need information, he suggested, watching her.

Thanks, she said.

She heard the dryness in her tone and for an instant she was sorry. You would have a few laughs with this Freddy.

Elbows, knees, he said. Body parts in general.

I know where to come, she agreed, and allowed herself a smile.

From over at the barbecue, someone called out *Bring us the lemonade while you're there, love! Bottom shelf of the fridge!*

Back with the others, heat pressed down on everything. People had found places to sprawl under the big leafy trees. They had gone quiet, conversation progressing in fits and starts with long pauses in between. Even the children had stopped hurling themselves at the water, and had disappeared somewhere.

Coralie came over and sat beside her on the grass.

I see you've met our Freddy, she said.

Harley could hear how she was feeling her way.

You could start a scandal in Karakarook that way. Go behind the bushes with the butcher for two minutes. One person noticing would be all it took.

Not telling you about Karakarook, Coralie asked. What it means in Aboriginal?

Well, as a matter of fact, yes.

Coralie gave a sudden admiring laugh that made Donna's husband glance over from scraping the barbecue.

Doesn't waste any time, our Freddy.

They both watched Freddy getting beers out of an esky and handing them round.

Not a bad bloke, Coralie said. Got his mother and his auntie out on the farm, they're neither of them well. You've got to hand it to him, looking after them the way he does.

She glanced at Harley.

But it's, you know, limiting for him.

Harley watched Donna's husband, a calm, smiling man whose tee-shirt said JACK THE RIPPER with blood dripping off each letter. He was hoisting up a little girl who had run out of the house. She sat astride his hip, picking at the thick rubbery paint of the blood.

So have you got a husband at all, yourself?

Harley could tell Coralie meant it to sound casual, but it came out a bit blunt.

She rushed on, covering it up.

Don't take any notice of me, love. We're all stickybeaks out here in the bush.

Then she left a silence.

I did have, Harley said. But he's gone.

Her own laugh took her by surprise.

Not dead and gone. Just gone.

It was true, more or less. It was completely true of two of the three husbands. True of the majority.

Any little lie that was necessary to keep covered up the way in which the third husband was *gone* was a kindness. There were times when everyone was happier with a little lie.

Coralie turned her glass, looking at the way the light made the beer look like honey, put it down on the grass, made a reasonable assumption.

They do that, don't they, she said finally. They can be bloody idiots.

Donna came over to them. She had a plastic bag full of something she wanted to show Harley, but could not bring herself to. It was interesting, watching someone else being shy.

Go on, pet, show her, Coralie said, but Donna was half-angry.

Oh, it's nothing, it's just a lot of rubbish.

Exactly! Coralie cried, and turned to Harley. Just what you said, wasn't it, pet, about the rubbish?

It was not hard to see who wore the pants in that relationship.

But Harley was not going to get involved in this one.

Oh, well, she murmured diplomatically. Well, you know.

Coralie grabbed the bag and pulled out a handful of what was in it: tailor's samples of dark wool, dozens of them. A couple of the squares dropped out of her hand and Donna quickly bent to pick them up. Now that Coralie had got the ball rolling, Donna was braver.

Mr Sinclair's grand-daughter gave them to the fete, she said. But nobody wanted them.

She held up a lustrous navy-blue with a faint grey stripe.

I could have told her that, but you can't, when it's a fete, can you?

I'd have bought them, Harley said. Like a shot.

They were quality wool, dense sombre colours, mint condition. She actually felt her mouth watering at the idea of piecing them together.

Want them? Donna said. You're more than welcome.

She held the bag out. Harley had to stop herself snatching it and pawing greedily through the squares.

Just what I needed, she said. I'm doing a sort of pretend wagga. Based on the old bridge, you know?

This threatened to create the sort of silence that had greeted *Australian vernacular*, but Mr Cutcliffe rescued the moment. Ah, show and tell, eh? he said, coming over. Ten and a half out of ten, girls.

Coralie and Donna laughed, even though Harley did not think it was much of a joke, but after a moment she felt she should join in too. Mr Cutcliffe looked round at them all going *heh heh heh*. You could see how pleased he was to have made them laugh, even if they were only being polite. It was worth the little effort, to see the pleasure it gave him.

It was a new idea for Harley. In the city you could avoid people like Mr Cutcliffe, who did not know when enough was enough on some subject dear to their heart. You could pretend to be terribly busy. The word *deadline* could be used or you could be *just on your way out of the house*.

But out here, she could see people went by different rules. You did not just pick out the best bits of life. You took the whole lot, the good and the bad. You forgave people for being who they were, and you hoped they would be able to forgive you. Now and again you were rewarded with the small pleasure of being able to laugh, not uproariously but genuinely, at a small witticism offered by someone who was usually a bore.

More than the heat and the flies, that was what made the bush feel like another country, where anything was possible.

*

She had not had anything to drink, but getting into the hot car at the end of the afternoon – now she realised why everyone else had parked further over, where the shade had come around – she felt a little light-headed.

In Sydney she was used to people one at a time, and only the ones she already knew. She seemed to have stopped meeting fresh people. All the ones she saw knew the story about Philip. *Oh, it's Harley*, she saw them think. *And there was Philip.* The story lay like a stain across everything they said and everything she said. Certain words created a certain kind of silence. Conversations inched forwards carefully across a chasm.

Everyone knowing had its good side. No one expected a great deal. If things came out sounding peculiar, allowances were made. But it had its bad side too. It was like being attached, permanently and irrevocably, to a big lump of something dead and ugly.

A long afternoon in the company of so many new people, none of whom knew anything about her – how dangerous she was, for example – had left her feeling that her head was not quite attached to her body, or perhaps it was that her face was not attached to her head. That face had created small speeches of a blameless kind, smiled at things other people had said, had managed to be nothing worse than perfectly normal.

She was still smiling as she drove back through all the gates, still holding herself ready to be agreeable, still arranging innocuous sentences in her mind. Apprehension had become a habit that created its own difficulties, but nothing had been asked of her this afternoon that she could not manage. In a small way it was something to be proud of.

At the last gate, as she was looping the piece of fencing-wire over the rusted bolt, she suddenly wondered whether she had closed the very first gate, back near the house, the one with the piece of chain and the little fencing-wire hook. She had been smiling, and teasing herself with the idea that life might be different if you lived in the country, and she had not been paying attention to the gates. She stood with her hand on the warm metal of this last one, trying to remember.

A sheep came towards her and went *baa* in a tremulous way at her. It made it hard to concentrate. She frowned at it and it became indignant. *Baa-aaah! Baa!*

She could remember undoing the chain on that first gate, working out the way the hook went, and even remembered pushing the gate open. It hung too low and you had to heave it up, but the corner still dragged along through a groove in the dirt. She remembered that, and she remembered driving through it. Then her memory went blank.

She stood for a long time, staring down at the dirt.

Finally she undid the last gate again, got into the car, and went all the way back through the three gates, being careful to close each one. When she got to the third one, hoping Donna was not watching the smoke-signals of her dust, she found that she had closed it after all, the hook fast on the chain.

By the time she got back to the road, she felt she had been opening and closing gates all afternoon. But at least she had not done anything unforgivable.

CHAPTER 12

OUT AT THE Bent Bridge, the men were having their smoko. They had got the fire going, twigs crackling under the billy, the flames invisible in the brilliant morning light. Smoke drifted away blue under the trees and turned the slanting sunlight into great organ-pipes of powdery light.

The red-headed one they all called Blue opened his sandwich up, showing the flap of grainy grey devon inside. He had caught the sun across his bare freckled back and his eyes were bloodshot.

Er, yuk, he said, and peeled it off the bread.

It was stuck like wallpaper.

Keep telling Mum I hate devon.

He flung it into the fire where it lay across a stick, curling, darkening, starting to sizzle. He stuck the two slices of bread back against each other.

The sauce is all right but, he said, and bit.

With the bulldozer shut down, it was very quiet. When one of the men leaned forward and lifted the lid off the billy with a stick to toss in a handful of tea-leaves, the metallic clink was like a single clear note of music.

Douglas unwrapped the sandwiches the woman had made for him at the Acropolis Cafe. Curried egg and lettuce.

They slipped down, insubstantial. The bread was slimy in his mouth, smooth and white. Nothing to chew on. He was generally a bit fussy about his bread but there was nothing but Tip Top at the Acropolis Cafe, although you did have the choice of white or brown.

There had been a snow-dome on a shelf in the window, with a tiny plastic Parthenon in it, and a pair of dolls dressed in the little white tennis-skirts of Greek guards. He had slowed down on his way in, to glance at them, and had seen the poster, up behind the Parthenon. SAVE THE BENT BRIDGE.

He had jerked in mid-step and stopped to read it. HERITAGE, it said, and there was a grainy black-and-white photo. Along the bottom, in red, it said TOURISM POTENTIAL OUR LIFEBLOOD.

He had glanced around as if caught out. A tall thin man, all chin and ears, was leaning against the boot of a car, scratching his chest through his shirt and staring. Douglas met his eye and looked away quickly up the street. In that direction two men with bellies that hung comfortably over their belts were standing beside a ute where a black and white dog panted in the tray. They stopped talking and seemed to be watching him, too, their faces unreadable under their hats.

Chook had said *a lot of old women*, but he might have been speaking figuratively.

The woman who made his sandwiches had brown hair like the icing on one of her own cakes, with lush little waves and crests, and a gold inlay that showed when she smiled. He felt the poster blazing behind him in the window as he stood there watching her slicing and filling.

He hoped that she might think he was from the Pastures

Board, or the phone company. But after she had given him his change she had said *Nice day for it, out at the river,* and he had known that she knew.

In a place this size, you had to assume everyone knew.

Still, she'd been nice enough. She had made his sandwiches carefully, with the filling all the way to the crusts, and had picked out the least chipped lamington for him.

Today Chook was wearing a tee-shirt that said I'D RATHER BE FISHING. He had introduced the men, but had gone too quickly. Now it seemed to Douglas that they had all been called Stan or Len, except for Blue and a tiny little sharp-faced man they called Lofty.

They all sat around the fire with the sandwiches. He was glad of the fire. It gave you something to look at other than the faces of all these strangers.

He seemed part of the circle of men, but he was not, not really. He sat on his share of the log they had rolled over near the fire, and smiled uneasily when he was not dealing with the curried egg and lettuce. They talked among themselves, jerking out the words too quickly for him to catch, getting rid of them as if they were hot. They had no problems understanding each other, but to Douglas it was like a foreign language of which he could only catch the odd phrase. *That is piss-poor,* he heard. *My word.*

He kept his eyes on the fire, trying not to bolt down his curried egg and lettuce.

Wests have got a ton of guts, eh? the man next to him on the log said, and Douglas had to ask *Pardon?* again.

This man was wearing a tee-shirt that said TOO MUCH

SEX MAKES YOUR EYES GO FUZZY in fuzzy letters. The second time, he said it more clearly, so Douglas could understand the words. Now the problem was, what did they mean?

It was always like this out on site with the men. He made a point of reading the sports page for just these moments, and tried to memorise a few things so he could say *Vaughan's peaked*, or *They'd be better off sacking Stannard*. But when it came to it, the conversation always seemed to go in some other direction and needed information he had not memorised, or when it came to the moment, he could not remember if it was Vaughan or Stannard who had *peaked*.

Ah, he said. Ah, could be, you know.

He crushed up the paper from the sandwiches and threw it into the fire.

Could certainly be. Yep.

It was not what you would call *scintillating*.

A different kind of man, a man who was *good with people*, would know all about *Wests* and their *guts*, and would have a few jokes ready for a situation like this. He'd take the initiative. The Stans and Lens would be turned towards such a man, listening, laughing, giving each other glances that said, *Good bloke, eh*.

However, he was not that man, never had been, never would be, no matter how many sports pages he read up on. It was one of the reasons he was not back in Sydney striding around in a hard hat on a big job, with a hundred men waiting for him to point his ruler. It was one reason he'd been given this tinpot little bridge to do.

That, and the vertigo, of course.

*

He'd never liked heights, and had been prepared to confess to it. But his mother had told him he would grow out of it, and the professor had told him he would get used to it. He had told Marjorie, not long after they were married, but she had just laughed. *An engineer, scared of heights?* He had laughed, too. She was right. It was funny.

He had tried to pretend it was a weakness he did not have, and pretending had worked, until the job came up on the Port Gordon Bridge.

The South Tower was a smooth concrete thing, with a temporary lift that crawled up and down, just a tin box with wire mesh on the sides. When he and the Site Engineer stepped in he felt it sink and tremble under their weight. On the green fibreglass of the Site Engineer's helmet there was a red cross and *First Aid* stencilled in authoritative white letters.

You could see it as reassuring. Or not.

Licensed to carry total 750 kgs, a chipped enamel sign said, and he had started a complicated sum in his head incorporating the estimated weight of himself and the Site Engineer, plus the big drum full of chain in the corner. As a rule, numbers lined up neatly in his mind's eye, but now the numbers were evaporating from one end of the sum as soon as he got the other end right.

Then, with the sum still not finished, the Site Engineer was winding a lever with a black knob around through half a circle and, after a sickening jerk, the lift began to move slowly upwards.

He had prepared for this moment, the night before. He had explained it to himself. The lift would not be moving relative to the people inside it, so the trick was not to look out. If the people inside the lift kept their eyes fixed on their own shoes, they would not have to know that they were tee-tering up through the air.

Do not look down, he told himself. *Do not look down*, the order went out to the eyes. But they looked down just the same.

Things on the ground had already become shockingly tiny. Big drums were shrinking to cotton-reel size as he watched. Men's helmets were like pimples bobbing around on the ground. A concrete truck was no bigger than a matchbox toy.

A tingle like an electric shock ran up from the soles of his feet, into the backs of his knees, a horrible creeping feeling, as he watched the tiny helmets shrinking away beneath him.

When the lift jerked and stopped dead at the top of the tower, he held his breath.

Here we go, mate, he heard the Site Engineer say. I said, here we go.

He remembered in time how to nod and smile, and erased from his mind the fact that he was about to step from the lift to the tower, across 120 metres of empty air. He would fall at the rate of 10 metres per second per second, more or less. It would probably seem like a long time.

The platform at the top of the tower ran around the four sides of a hole in which men were working on a tangle of reinforcing rods. As soon as he got out of the lift he grasped the scaffolding-pipe railing. It felt solid. But he knew the whole platform, and the railing he was hanging on to, was only a flimsy temporary thing. It could easily break away from the tower and shred apart. Everyone on it would be little dolls tumbling headfirst, legs and arms spreadeagled, bouncing down the sides of the tower at 10 metres per second per second, more or less, until they hit the ground and broke.

There was always someone passing with a camera. As a child he had pored over the books in the library, drawn to them with a sick fascination: people caught by the camera falling from windows, off ladders, out of the arms of firemen.

He had his hand gripping the railing. He hoped it looked casual.

Don't look down, he instructed himself, but he caught a flash of light from below, and looked straight down at the waters of Port Gordon, bright and wrinkled with sunlight. Miles down he could see a little splinter of darkness gliding along the brightness, giving out flashes of light that dipped and flared together, the oars of a boat so tiny it was invisible except for the sparks it was giving off.

With a lurch like a vomit he remembered where he was. There was a lost pulsing ache in the soles of his feet, and a hot weakness around his ankles and knees. There was a dangerous lightness in his head now, as if it was floating away, weightless. The tower appeared to be swaying.

The thing was, he could not be sure if it was the tower swaying, or himself.

Now he was sweaty and dizzy, and hot and cold at once. He must not move. Whatever happened, he must not move. He must go on hanging on to this piece of gritty pipe. He must keep his feet just exactly where they were. If he kept them locked on to this plank, he would not spin away into space.

He heard someone moan. It could have been himself.

*

Later he had read up on the vertigo business. There was a purely physiological basis for it. It was not a moral failure.

He had tried to explain it to Marjorie. *A kind of spirit level in our heads*, he had tried, but she did not seem interested in the idea of a spirit level in the head. *The eyes have to get a vectoring fix on something*, he said, but she had glazed over by then.

It was a pleasure, understanding it, and up to a point it helped. He knew now to keep something in sight in the foreground, and to hang on to something. There was no shame in hanging on, if it helped.

But the word had gone round about the day he had had to be sedated and carried down on a stretcher from the South Tower of the Port Gordon Bridge.

He was a good engineer, but it had gone against him, professionally. That was why he was a small-job man. He was a small-job man, and his new boots were pinching like buggery.

Stan, or Len, or someone, was coming round now with the billy, filling everyone's mug. His big cracked hand grasped the wire handle and poured, the tea split by the wire.

You right like that mate? he asked. You right?

Douglas did not know what was being asked.

Yes, mate, that's fine, he said.

No, you right like that? Stan or Len asked again.

They both stared at the tea, locked into some problem of communication. The tea was so dark it was almost purple.

Chook was sitting on another log opposite him. He was solid, his whiskery ears had authority. His feet were big, solid on the ground in their steel-toed boots. All those Lens and Stans were solid too, with their jerked-out remarks, drinking the mouth-curdling tea.

He felt like the only flimsy one.

We got sugar, Chook translated, and pointed to a grubby paper packet of sugar near the fire, puckered around the top from being grasped in big dirty hands.

No milk, but.

That's fine, Douglas said again.

To prove how *fine* it was he took a sip, but flinched back from a burnt lip. The tea was so strong it made his mouth shrivel. He wondered if it was too late to ask for the sugar, being passed around now from hand to hand with a tin spoon.

He felt Chook watching him, summing him up. It was tricky, being the engineer. You had the authority. You had to take responsibility. If anything went wrong, you were the one all the faces turned towards.

His first job, years ago, there'd been a bloke like this Chook Henderson. Douglas had been young and green, and had been only too happy to let someone else take charge. Before he knew what was happening, there'd been some kind of Union thing happening about tea-breaks, some other complicated thing about a bloke with a bad back.

In the end he'd had to trail into the town and phone Morton Street. *Sorry sir, the men have downed tools. What do I do now?* Young, and green, all right: but not too bright, either. He'd heard that loud and clear in the voice that came back down the wire.

He took another sip. He felt his upper lip was a strange tensed shape, but he had got some of it down, and Chook was looking away at last.

If he were German or Venezuelan, it would be all right to be sitting here stiff and foreign. But if you were Australian, you were supposed to feel at home in the country. The *bush*, rather. They seemed to call it that, even when it was just plain old paddocks.

The message had come through loud and clear at school. *An Australian* was a man on the back of a horse, rounding up sheep or cracking a whip at a lot of cows. So the kids at Kogarah Public School, who had never seen a sheep or a cow except at the Show, had had to learn how to be *Australian* off the blackboard.

Australia Rides on the Sheep's Back. He could remember the way Mrs Linney had written it up on the blackboard in her curly writing. He had copied it down neatly in his exercise book while Mrs Linney explained about it being a *figure of speech*. Then she had written up *eleven and a half sheep for every man, woman and child.*

An earnest and conscientious child, he had felt a particular wordless anxiety about it. He had taken that *child* personally, and worried about the eleven and a half sheep that must be his, toiling over some parched hillside.

They had sung *Click Go the Shears*, and written down the words *ringer* and *blue-bellied joe* in their books, and next to them what they meant. He had forgotten now, but he had once known. They had recited *I Love a Sunburnt Country* and tried to believe they did. Douglas Cheeseman's pale freckled skin did not love a sunburnt country, and for a long time he had thought a *sweeping plain* was something to do with woodwork, but he had sung as sincerely as the rest.

He had thought you could simply apply yourself to it,

and learn to be the sort of *Australian* you were supposed to be. He could see now that it would never be that simple.

When he put the tea down and got to his feet, everyone looked up at him. It was as if they thought he might be going to make a speech. *Welcome, men, to the Bent Bridge Project.*

He had not planned any speech. As he spoke to Chook, he felt his face going red, the way it did when too many people looked at him.

Just having a quick check of that alignment, he said.

He was not asking permission, but when Chook turned the hand holding his salad roll so that he could see his watch, it looked a bit that way. A piece of beetroot fell out and landed on the dusty toe of Chook's boot.

Fair enough mate.

In Chook's voice was only the politest minimum of surprise that someone would not take their full tea-break.

The men were still looking at him, standing waiting while Chook checked his watch. The young one was watching with a hand up under his singlet, artlessly scratching a soft round stomach and showing a big innocent belly-button like a baby's.

He wished he had just gone on sitting. At least he was inconspicuous, just sitting minding his own business, getting on with his lamington. Although he was *not quite right* doing that, he was not definitely *wrong*. Wanting to go back to work before you had to was definitely *wrong*.

He walked over on to the bridge and stood safely back from the edge, looking upstream, where the little river threaded its way between slopes of rounded rocks and stretches of sand.

From over at the fire behind him he heard the chink of an enamel mug against the billy and someone laughed. His back was stiff, his shoulders tense. He felt hunched like the bridge.

It was easy to feel small under the big harsh sky. The sun fell on to his hat, his shoulders. He could feel it burning through the shirt. You could underestimate these country suns. They could seem kindly, but there was something metallic and unforgiving about them.

He had his slide rule with him, the old Pocket Log Duplex Decitrig in its tan leather case that he had bought as a student, still cocked to multiply 1.285 by something in the middle of the scale. It was many years since he had used it, and it showed his age, even owning one. The young blokes exclaimed over it as if it was a papyrus scroll. But it was a comfort. At moments like this, he liked to have it in his hand. He got it out now, although he had no need to calculate anything. *The Engineer at Work.*

If it had been up to him he would not knock down this little bridge. He could see clearly what could be done. You would take up the timbers of the roadway, labelling them so you could put them back together the same way. Then you would replace the rotten corbels. Then, before you laid the roadway back, you would cap the whole thing with concrete, the same way Dr Liu had put the gold inlay on his back molars. Then the roadway could be bolted down on top of that. It would be good for another hundred years, but it would still look more or less the way it did now.

He spread out the plans on the planks of the roadway and

squatted over them. His own shadow fell black over the lines and figures. He was glad to be able to get a pen out of his shirt pocket and make a note. *Bearers and piers essentially sound*, he wrote. *Corbels failed.* He took his time, making sure every letter was nicely shaped, bent studiously over the plans.

But as he wrote, he went on thinking, and he saw that it would not be enough simply to make formwork on top of the bridge and pour the layer of concrete. If you did it like that, the bridge and the concrete would never be married together properly, and with all the movement in the old bridge, the concrete would crack, no matter how much steel you incorporated. It would let the water in, and you would be back where you started. Worse off, in fact, because you would not be able to lift off the concrete slab for future repairs. It was the kind of thing that made the job interesting: the way an answer created another question. It was why, in spite of never knowing things like why Wests had *a ton of guts*, he would prefer to be out here, in the thick of the problem, rather than back at Morton Street behind a desk.

Cap with concrete, he wrote, and then a big question mark. As he was shaping the question mark, with one part of his mind thinking that the shape of the question mark was the same shape as the bridge, another part of his mind showed him, like a snapshot, what the answer was.

Instead of pouring the concrete in situ, you would make formwork on the ground and precast the cap in sections. You'd cast the girders right into the concrete, which would shrink tight around them as it set. You'd cast it upside-down, of course, which would mean that the part that would be uppermost when in use – that is, the bottom when it was cast – would be stronger, because of the tendency of the blue metal to sink through the mix. The sections could be pinned together, and the roadway put back on top of them.

It was a beautiful solution, elegant and simple, and economical too.

Modules, he wrote. *Precast with girders incorporated. Pinned to slab.*

It was a lovely solution to the problem, but he would not mention it to anyone. Mr Denning had been a good solid engineer in his day, but he was not a man to grasp a new idea quickly, let alone welcome it. Head Office liked things nice and simple. He could imagine the shape Mr Denning's face would go if he tried to explain about the module idea. He could hear the way he would stumble and fall over his words, and how silly Mr Denning's silence would make them sound. Another, braver, man might be prepared to do it, but he was not that man.

As he was carefully capping the pen and clipping it back on to his pocket, he got a whiff of Chook's cigarette. Without really looking, he could see him out of the corner of his eye, standing by the fire with his hands on his hips, smoke billowing from his face, watching *the engineer at work.*

A fly landed on Douglas's chin and crawled up towards his lip. He was afraid that if he waved it away Chook would think he was waving at him. He tried to snort it off without moving, but it was one of the sticky little fearless bush flies and it stayed put, until, with the smallest movement possible, he brushed it off. He heard someone cough loudly but resisted the impulse to turn and look. Several flies were now crowding on his hand, where he had brushed the first one away. It seemed to be true, what they said: *Kill a fly, ten more come to its funeral.*

Up on the road the bulldozer started with a grind and a roar. A small cloud of black smoke floated down from it and melted away over the water. The engine coughed and died and he heard a scornful shout from Chook.

He rolled the plans up tightly and wedged them under his arm. No one but himself need ever see the note he had made on them. It was all too easy to imagine Chook's face. *You some kind of a greenie, mate?*

He could see the cows, still in the paddock where they had chased him. From here, the fence looked insignificant, the cows innocent, merely a picturesque addition to the landscape, calmly moving from tuft to tuft of grass, eating away like cows on a calendar.

He realised he was rehearsing a conversation. *Express my thanks. Lunch, or perhaps afternoon tea?*

He could not seem to stop himself, hearing more pompous words shape themselves in his mind. *Give me great pleasure. Gesture of appreciation.*

It was ridiculous, the idea of talking to her like that. The backs of his knees tingled when he thought of it, as if Harley Savage was a great height.

He coughed and turned around, watching where the bulldozer had already made a long raw rip in the paddock. Chook was standing on a mound, pointing like Napoleon.

It was quite simple. Next time he saw her, he would just say *Hello!* and smile. He might make a remark about cows if it seemed appropriate, but he would not do anything foolish.

*

CHAPTER 13

HER FATHER HAD been a big handsome man with a fine head of hair, a paintbrush in his hand, skeins of paint threading along the canvas making a bird look like an angel. He was the famous James Appleby Harley Savage, son of Harley Talbot Appleby Savage, brother of Norman Backhouse Savage. It was an illustrious family.

From when she was old enough to hold a pencil, the little girl Pixie Appleby Harley Savage had been taught about vanishing points, and was made to work out at the start where the horizon was going to be, and how to make things at the front bigger than things at the back. No matter how young, she had never been allowed to scribble. Nor had she been allowed to do stick people, or square houses with symmetrical looped-up curtains at every window and a carefully curving path to the front door with a round tree on one side. It was *uncreative* and it was *unimaginative* to do drawings like that, and even at a young age she picked up that there was something else not nice about it which had a name later on, a favourite word of Mother's: it was *vulgar*.

Her father's hands skimmed across the paper and out of the end of his pencil came a bird, a twig for it to perch on, behind it a branch. *See? Like that.*

It was an illustrious and gifted family, but it seemed that *the gift* had passed Pixie by. Even after so many patient lessons, from the end of her pencil came only hard ugly lines, and a bird that looked like a surprised tadpole.

She was ashamed of her big muscly legs and her round face. But the shame of this grotesque bird was unendurable.

I don't want to be artistic, she cried, and heard the silence, saw the ring of shocked faces.

Oh, but you are very artistic and terribly creative, her mother said quickly, with something like fear in her voice.

There was a silence in which no one agreed.

In your own way, of course.

Someone cleared their throat.

And these things blossom later on sometimes.

At school they had known she was an Appleby Savage, and hoped for wonders. They were even willing to see them where there were none. It had taken a long time, but finally they came to expect no more wonders.

Use your imaginations, girls, Miss McGovern would say, but what Pixie drew was never what Miss McGovern meant by *imagination.* Pixie was interested in the veins on the leaf, and in the *xylem* and the *phloem,* in *transpiration* and *photosynthesis.*

You make a plant look like a machine, Miss McGovern accused.

But you must be good at art, her best friend Gillian had said. *Because you're no good at maths.*

Her sister, of the fascinating wide mobile mouth, the far-set cat-like eyes, had always been a proper Appleby Savage. She had had the Appleby Savage *gift,* as well as long brown legs that looked good in shorts. Celeste had known about things at the back being smaller than things at the front without ever having to be told. She had a way of being dreamy, dishevelled, lovely even in her old pink flannelette pyjamas, thinking interesting thoughts behind her lovely green eyes. Celeste's birds made Father laugh with surprise and pleasure in a way Pixie's never did.

Celeste had other knacks, too. She was good at catching Pixie in moments when she would rather have been alone. Celeste's reflection would join Pixie's frowning into the mirror. *God, Pix,* she would say in her sophisticated way. *That lipstick! Makes you look like a shopgirl.*

She was not the older sister, but acted as though she was.

Why did you call me Pixie? she asked her mother once, when puberty was making her look into mirrors. *You were such a beautiful baby,* her mother said, and smiled into the air at the memory of that beautiful baby, not at the face of her plain daughter.

Later, she learned the expression *jolie laide,* and hoped it might rescue her. *Oh, I'm a jolie laide,* she had tried telling a hairdresser, airily. But the hairdresser had not known what it meant, and when she had tried to translate, it sounded silly.

She had to recognise, in any case, that she was not interestingly ugly. Not enough to be a *jolie laide.* She was simply ordinary: ordinary brown eyes, ordinary brown hair. An ordinary small nose, an ordinary mouth. No one would ever find her fascinating across a crowded room. *So like your grandmother,* her mother had sighed.

Mother had always made her go on trying. *You never know who you might meet,* she had said, and done that little winsome thing with the corner of her mouth that she did so well.

As a child, she could not do much, but she could refuse to answer to the name of the beautiful baby who had turned into herself. *Harley*, she insisted. *My name is Harley*.

James Appleby Harley Savage the celebrated painter had frequently said that *All Nature is Art*. But the *Nature* he had in mind was some flowers arranged nicely in a vase, or a landscape with a tree two-thirds of the way along the left-hand foreground.

His in-laws' shabby farm, everything grey and blistered in the dry and the heat, dirty-looking sheep everywhere and too many flies, was not the *Nature* he was thinking of. And Mother, for whom that cracked lino, those warped weatherboards, that curling roofing-iron, had been home, wanted nothing better than to put it behind her, a sentimental memory among all her *nice things*.

However, it was at Gran and Grandfather's farm that plain awkward Harley had been happiest. Celeste was usually not there. She hated the farm, and in any case popular Celeste was usually invited to someone's beach house or snow lodge for the holidays.

When Harley thought of Gran now, it was of her bending down to the door in the fuel stove with the curly black-on-yellow enamelled letters on the door, AGA. Gran called the stove *Agatha*, affectionately, as if it was one of the family, although Grandfather called it *the range*. It was black and mysterious with many doors of different sizes, and made a peaceful enclosed roaring when the fire was going. On the top were metal rings fitting one inside the other that Gran moved around with a stubby metal tool. Underneath the rings was the fire. It had taken Harley a long time to see that the more metal rings you took off, the more fire licked at the bottom of the pot. The rings were what turned the stove up or down.

Gran would move around the kitchen in what she called her *pinny*, which was what Mother would have called an *apron*. But none of Mother's aprons had been made from an old dress with the sleeves taken out and split up the back from top to bottom, and Mother's aprons never actually got dirty, the way Gran's *pinnies* did.

If Grandfather was away in the paddocks, and she needed more wood, Gran would go outside the kitchen door and stand blocks of wood up on the chopping block to split them neatly with the axe. Harley was proud, helping her carry them inside, and Gran never seemed to notice, or care, that her jumper got covered in bits of bark.

Gran did not care much about being neat, although she was clean. Days had gone by sometimes before she would remember to brush Harley's hair. The days were busy but peaceful, and went along entirely without the benefit of clocks.

Grandfather did the sheds and the paddocks in the old felt hat he always wore, that had cracked open along the creases. When he came in at the end of the day he'd stand in the kitchen and take the hat off, revealing a forehead as white as a scar. *What's for tea, Mother?* he would say, and whatever Gran said, he nodded in a satisfied way, hung his hat on the wooden peg, and went to wash his hands.

At the farm she slept in the closed-in back verandah. *The sleepout*, Gran called it, and Harley was anxious the first time, thinking *the sleepout* might mean she had to sleep outside, in the country darkness full of strange noises and things rustling secretively that might want to bite you.

But she came to love the sleepout. You were not completely *in*, but you were not exactly *out*, either.

She loved waking up there, under the heavy home-made bedcover Gran had put together out of pieces of the kind of material men's suits were made of. The pieces had been cut into triangles and sewn together in a simple pattern: *light, dark, light, dark*. It was filled with something that made it bulge in strange ways.

Lying pinned under the weight of the bedcover in the morning, listening to the chooks waking up and Gran clanging Agatha's door, she could lose herself in the pattern. *Light, dark. Light, dark.* Somehow it was a comfort. Close up, the pattern was harder to see because some of the dark *lights* were almost the same as some of the light *darks*. But even if you were too close to see that the pieces went *light, dark, light, dark*, you knew that that was what they did. You knew you could count on it being there, whether you could see it or not. *Light, dark, light, dark.*

Gran had sewn everything: sheets sides-to-middle, pinnies from worn-out dresses, curtains when something was on special at Woods' in town. The machine ran magically backwards and forwards to patch the seat of the grandfather's overalls. Once she had made a loose-cover for the couch, a huge flowered creature writhing under the needle as she hoisted its mass around, little Gran enveloped in a tangle of pockets and corners and dead-end tubes, emerging out of it at last and fitting it triumphantly around the bulges of the old couch.

As a little girl, she stood beside Gran watching the thread

winding through the little hooks and loops on the top of the machine, and the unfathomable workings of the thread coming up out of the hole in the silver plate under the needle. No matter how hard you looked, there was a moment when it did something too fast for the eye, and came back up holding the bottom thread.

She sat on the floor behind the machine, watching Gran's feet in their serious black shoes with the bunion-bulges, treadling up and down like semaphore. She watched the dark simple workings, furred with oily dust, the big solemn flywheel turning, the sinister endless loop of the belt running into the hole in the wooden casing.

Never touch, Gran had said, cross with the gravity of it. *Never ever.*

But when Gran left the room, she turned the wheel at the side, the shiny silver metal cold against her palm. She was frightened then, the way the needle leapt down into the hole, and tried to turn the wheel the other way to make it come back up. But the needle was stuck fast, seized tight by whatever lived in the little hole.

Gran saw, straight away. *Didn't I tell you*, she said, *never to touch the machine?*

She frowned and her voice was as stern as Harley had ever heard it. But even when it was stern it did not have the bitter edge of dislike that came into Mother's voice, and Father's.

Harley felt very small and wicked, standing next to Gran in the silent room.

Somehow she was always in trouble at home, for breaking things with her clumsiness, being rude without having meant it, or not being very good at anything. *Why can't you be more like your sister?* her father had shouted once in exasperation. So it had become a habit, lying. It always seemed simpler.

It wasn't me, she had said to Gran, and made her eyes go round with honesty.

But it did not seem to be a game that her grandmother knew how to play. She did not accuse, the way Mother and Father did, and pincer her in logic, wear her down with it until she gave in. Gran's face just came over puzzled. *It's all right, lovey*, she said. *You were only being inquisitive.*

But Harley had to go on, adding layers to her lie. The cat had jumped up through the window and pushed the wheel with its paw. She had seen it. It was trying to catch a beetle that was hiding under the machine. No, actually it was a mouse. A black and white mouse.

She felt her face swelling, shiny with the desperate lies, and hated Gran then, with her puzzled loving smile.

When Gran died, Harley and Celeste were not told for a long time. They were not taken to the funeral, or to the funeral of their grandfather, who *went* soon afterwards.

Grandfather left a display case of war medals, up on the wall near the bookcases, and three leather-bound school prize books in the glass-fronted bookcase. But of Gran there was very little left. There was an ugly Chinese vase that turned out to be worth a lot of money, and there was a rather good *piece*, as Mother called it – a cedar knife box that she used for the second-best set.

The memory of their grandmother faded quickly.

She asked Mother once what had became of the rest of

Gran's things when the farm was sold. She made her voice casual. Mother was vague. *Oh*, she said. *Those things? They went to a good home, darling.*

There was one *thing* in particular that she was thinking of: the old bedcover. She would never have admitted to it. It could not be compared with the valuable, though ugly, Chinese vase or the cedar *piece*. Mother would think it was rather odd to care about a smelly old thing made of rags.

But the loss of the bedcover was a grief to her. *Light, dark, light, dark.*

There was a tightness in Harley's chest when she thought of her grandmother. It was that she had not said goodbye. She wished she had just five minutes of time back – just two, or even one would do – to kiss her goodbye.

And tell her she loved her. That was the main thing. She had never told her she loved her. Instead, she had lied to her, and been silent when she should have spoken, and curled away when Gran had stroked her hair, or given her a kiss smelling of flowery old lady.

Yet Gran was the one who had always loved her. She was the only one who had never judged or scorned.

It was like a hole at her heart, when she remembered her.

As a child, cloth had always been a comfort. At night she had soothed herself to sleep by imagining that she was in a warehouse full of rolls of fabric, row after row into the misty distance, and no one watching her. Gloriously alone, she felt each kind of material as she wandered, or unrolled great lengths of it and watched it furl around her feet: crisp cotton, crackling with starch, silk that floated away like water as she went to grasp it, springy muscular wool with the warm thick smell of winter. Something about yards and yards of it, that was the thing: something about unreeling it off the bolt, hearing the thump as the bulk of it hit the wood of the counter, polished by thousands of bolts of fabric sliding over it.

Lying private in bed she could take her time, and no one was there to think she was a fool. After even the worst of days, thinking about rolls of fabric brought sleep.

She had asked her friend Gillian once what she thought about when she was going to sleep, and Gillian had said *Oh, what I did in the day, what I'll do tomorrow.* She had suspected that Gillian had some secret comfort too and was not telling, so when Gillian said *What about you,* she said, *Me too, what I did in the day, what I'll do when I get up.*

They were best friends, but they did not share anything that mattered.

At home there were no pieces of men's suiting, but there was a rag-bag of expensive scraps left by scrupulous Mrs Longfellow who made Mother's frocks.

She waited until Celeste was out and the house was quiet. Then she tiptoed into the Sewing Room to find the rag-bag, and took it back to her own room. She closed the door, and listened again to make sure no one was near before she got them out and spread them over the floor. She had not really planned to, but found herself cutting them into triangles, and arranging them next to each other on the floor. *Light, dark. Light, dark.*

It was interesting, the way a piece that looked lovely on

its own could stop looking lovely when you put it alongside another piece.

But also, a dull piece could become a jewel next to certain other pieces.

And it was a kind of magic, the way no piece was either a *light* or *dark* by itself. Any of them could be a *light* or a *dark*, depending on what it was next to.

She had to remind herself to go on breathing, the pleasure of it was so private.

When there was a tap on the door she jerked around in fright, knocking against the lamp so it toppled off the table, and there was Celeste, standing in the doorway, staring.

God, Harley, she said. What are you doing here crouching in the dark?

She came in and looked down at the pieces of cloth arranged on the flowered carpet.

What's this, a still life or something?

She was amused, prepared to patronise.

Harley felt the heat coming up into her cheeks. The room was suddenly hot. Celeste was staring, waiting, smiling a little.

She looked at her lined-up scraps through Celeste's clever eyes. As a *still life* they were very dull.

All at once the wish to talk about it was impossible to resist. Once she explained, how could Celeste fail to see the loveliness of it, the lights and the darks, the pattern, the way the light *darks* and the dark *lights* sorted themselves out if they were part of a pattern?

No, she said. This is my patchwork. There are lights and darks. See?

She had not finished arranging them, and there were gaps in the pattern where flowered Axminster showed through.

You have to stand back, she said. To see.

It was clear that Celeste could not see, although she stepped back and put her head on one side so her hair swung against her cheek.

Lights and darks! she exclaimed in a falsely interested way. How do you mean?

It was not very clear, with the carpet showing through, and the way the dark *lights* were similar to the light *darks*.

Well, Harley said.

She could see it was a mistake to try to explain.

This one – see? – goes with this one.

Separated from the rest, the bit of material was just a fraying scrap.

Celeste put it down and picked up another.

And this?

In Celeste's long-fingered pale hand it was just a limp dingy thing.

That's a light, she mumbled. If it's with a dark.

Celeste tossed it back on the carpet and looked at Harley, hunkered down beside her scraps, twisting up awkwardly at her.

But patchwork! Celeste said. Harls, that's just craft!

Celeste was famous now, fascinating, she had *openings*, was long-legged in tights from Berlin and a haircut like a sculpture. She was in the paper now and then and always looked good in the photo.

Harley had learned to call cloth *fabric*. What she did now was called *Textile Art*, and there were books about it. Some people called it *craft*, and some people called it *art*, but

Harley had stopped caring about what you called it.

She had made a career out of it, the *lights* and the *darks*. She had made a name for herself out of suiting fabrics. *Harley Savage's monochromes*. They were not real scraps, of course, or even real tailor's samples. These days they were just pretending. She bought the fabrics, had them sent from Milan and Hong Kong.

You would not have gone to bed under any of her patchworks, but the PM had bought one, and the Museum had several stored away in the basements.

In the back of her mind there was always Gran's bedcover. Every patchwork she made was an attempt to reconstruct the way Gran had put the lights and darks together, the way they had not been absolutely regular, the way the pieces had not quite lined up so the whole thing seemed to vibrate. It seemed so simple. It seemed there was nothing to it.

But Harley had found that there was no end to the ways you could put *light* and *dark* together.

Chapter 14

He was good at the window now. He could go over to it confidently and hold on to the frame, and once or twice he had actually put his head all the way out, although he had been careful not to look down. The books all agreed that you never got over vertigo, but you could learn to accommodate it.

He grasped the frame now and put his head cautiously out into the night. The slice of Parnassus Road he could see from his window was stone-coloured in the light of the moon. The shadow under the shop awnings was like a solid substance. A streetlight outside the Mini-Mart stuttered and sputtered. *Defective tube*, he thought. *Shire being stingy with the maintenance.*

A hot little breeze gusted down out of the grey hills beyond the town, bringing dry medicinal smells in from the paddocks, catching up a sheet of newspaper and spinning it along until it flapped around an awning-post. Somewhere above his head something creaked and scratched against something else. He would have liked to look up, but looking up could be even worse than looking down, especially if you were twisting out of a window.

Instead he looked down at an angle into the window

across the alley. Tonight the curtains were pushed back and the room was full of brilliant white light. He could see quite a big piece of lit-up floor. The white sheet was still there, with the shirt spread out on it. As he watched, a man's legs came over and stood beside it, and a hand reached down with something he recognised after a moment as a light meter. He went on watching, even when the legs and the light meter had gone, but the shirt stared blandly up into the lights and nothing further happened.

He turned back into his room. He tried lying on the bed reading, but the light was so grey the print started to dance in front of his eyes and the way the bed sagged made his back ache. He wished he had brought some light reading. He had finished the piece on *Hydration in Portland Cement*, but although there was something on *Flash Set* that looked interesting, he did not feel like it at the moment.

The *Engineering Digest* was a good read, but you had to be in the mood.

He sat up and pulled his boots on, then crept down the stairs and past the bar, where he could hear a companionable burr of men's voices and the cricket results being read out from the TV.

A normal man would go in there now, and not be worried by the way all the faces would turn to look at him. A really normal man would not even notice that they were looking.

As he passed the alley, he glanced up and saw that the thing that had creaked and scratched above his head was the D of CALEDONIAN, swinging from its screw.

By night, there was something sinister about Parnassus Road. As soon as you left the circle of light cast by the

Caledonian, you were in a world of glimmerings and strange shadowed movements. The butcher's shop was lit only by a small globe that dimly illuminated the containers of dripping in the window. You would never guess that upstairs, light was blazing. As he turned to cross the road he caught the flicker of his own movement reflected in the stainless steel of the display.

He went along under the awnings, staring into the window of the Mini-Mart where a dim blue bulb lit up screwdrivers, tins of paint, some fly-swats, a row of buckets. Behind them cold white light glowed from the fridges along the back wall, filling the shop with sombre shapes and shadows.

He supposed that, prowling along the footpath, his hair stiffly disarranged by the wind, he could seem as shadowy and sinister as the street.

Where Parnassus Road met Virgil Street the strip of shops ended with the Acropolis Cafe on the corner. Across from the Acropolis was a park with a big elaborate cairn in polished granite, and in front of it a garden bed where, by the grey light of the moon, he could make out the word ANZAC done in marigolds.

A rusting wire circle from a florist's wreath leaned against the base of the cairn, dried stems still sticking out like barbed wire. Cut into the stone and done with gold leaf that gleamed in the moonlight were the words: *To Our Glorious Dead*, and under that an alphabetical strip of names: *Allnut, P.J., Anderson T.F., Edwards, M.A.* At the bottom, like a bureaucrat's curt stamp: REMEMBERED, with the gilt fallen off the B.

He had never liked the gold-leaf lists, but you could not admit that to anyone.

His own father had been a famous war hero. Was in all the books. His was a name everybody knew. *Douglas Cheeseman, VC.* The *other* Douglas Cheeseman. Even now, when people heard his name, they'd look thoughtfully at him. *Douglas Cheeseman,* they'd say. His mouth would stiffen up, ready for it. *Any relation of* THE *Douglas Cheeseman?*

He had never felt his name was his own. It was always as if he had borrowed the name of the famous hero, or stolen it.

He himself – the *second* Douglas Cheeseman, Douglas Cheeseman *the lesser* – had been born a month after his father was killed. He knew it by heart: *ensuring the safety of his men at the cost of his own life.* He knew every detail. On its way home after a successful mission, the Lancaster had caught fire high over France and no one had been able to get the extinguisher to work. There was a business of a jammed pin. The crew got out by parachute while Douglas Cheeseman *the first* had stayed at the controls, and by the time they were all out, it was too late for him.

Douglas Cheeseman *the second* admired courage as much as the next man, of course. It was a quality he knew himself conspicuously to lack. He had hung his head, hearing the story of his famous father yet again, guilty in the knowledge that he would not have had that kind of courage.

There was another, more private and unsharable guilt. It was a thought that had to be suppressed every time it tried to surface: that the men in the Lancaster had not needed courage so much as someone with a bit of mechanical expertise. Someone who understood jammed pins.

An engineer, for example.

As a boy he'd had to go to Legacy afternoon teas with the

old war comrades. *Oh, Douglas Cheeseman*, they'd cry, peering at his name tag. *You must be the son.* They were hearty, glad.

But Douglas Cheeseman the son was not the man his father had been, and had a certain shifty-eyed reluctance to agree about what a legend his father was. After a while their big meaty faces would grow disappointed, and they would turn away.

Alive, his father would have been just another irritable man putting off mowing the lawn, making the bathroom smell of farts, taking wrong turnings on the way to Katoomba.

Dead, he could do no wrong.

Douglas Cheeseman the second knew he was a clumsy jug-eared boy, and had had to accept that he was not only no good at sport, but nothing special at lessons, either. He had always hated the way his face tended to fall into a rather stupid look. He was not stupid, he knew that, but his face sometimes was. He had spent his life avoiding his reflection in shop windows.

He had loved his mother, but she had never been cosy. Nothing gave when you hugged her. Flesh did not yield to flesh. Hers was the engineered perfection of expensive foundation garments. The boys at the school where she taught – not his own school, thank God – had called her, *Her Ladyship* behind her back, for the erectness of her spine, the arch of her pencilled eyebrows, the perfection of her smart little suits and her sharp narrow shoes.

His mother had always been a mystery to him. She had shed a few tears – appropriate, controlled tears, nothing embarrassing – every Anzac Day at the Cenotaph, and

Douglas had stood beside her looking up at the bronze soldiers in puttees staring off above his head, and the same kind of alphabetical list as here. *In Memory of Those Who Fell.*

When he was little, it had been necessary to explain to him that this was not *falling* in the sense with which he was all too familiar. As an awkward child, accused in the school report of *Poor Gross Motor Skills* for his inability to kick or catch balls, he had been prepared to extend his full sympathy to *those who fell.*

How had his mother really felt, as she went forward to lay the wreath? When she saw the name up there in gilt: *Cheeseman, D.J.,* did she think of how she had laughed with a man made of flesh, at the way their chests had stuck together, in bed on hot afternoons, making rude rubbery noises? How did she feel, running her eye down that alphabetical list, *Adams* to *Yonge,* seeing that sticky chest, that laughing mouth, as *Cheeseman, D.J.?*

He wondered, but he found it hard to imagine his mother's chest without its foundations, making rude noises.

All his life he had wondered why she had given him the dead hero's name. She should have known it would be asking a lot of any son. Even if he had been handsome and clever, captain of the cricket team and life of the party, he could still not have lived up to his father, smiling confidently out of his silver frame on the mantelpiece. How much less could he do so, being that hangdog boy, carrying his hidden cargo of guilt?

He turned away and headed up towards where the hills were whale-shapes against the navy-blue sky. Away from the stony light of Parnassus Road and the grim little sinister shops, under the big empty sky, there was a feeling that anything might be possible. Somewhere frogs creaked and croaked and other things made secretive clicking noises, getting on with their invisible lives, driven by urgencies and delights known only to themselves.

His senses felt clarified by the dark. It was not a barrier but a fluid medium, bringing him sounds and smells that lapped him around. Swimming through them, Douglas was no longer hunched under the weight of his shortcomings. He felt his shoulders pull back, his spine straighten, his senses come to the alert. He stood on a corner enjoying the way the moon lay on its back and slid in a dignified way behind the curve of a hill.

Since the divorce he had found himself often walking at night. It was not that he was any kind of Peeping Tom. He had no interest in ladies in their underwear. It was more the chance you might learn something. The thing he would have liked to learn was not something you could ask anyone, although it was so simple. *How do people get on?* He had the feeling that others, somehow, had been born knowing things about how to manage with other people that he himself had been born without. The lives of others, men and women rubbing along together, held a fascination for him. He peered into windows, soaking up other people's lives as he had once soaked up the logic of the distributed stress-load.

Walking quietly down a narrow dunny-lane beside houses, he could see straight into a brightly-lit room, a bulb pouring down yellow light on a table, like a still life: wood grain, white doily, fruit bowl, oranges incandescent under the light. It was vivid but uninformative. The trappings of domesticity could not help him, the doilies and the polished wood and the bulb where visible molecules of light seemed to stream outwards. The room waited, and he waited, but no-one came to show him how you did it.

He paused under another window, hearing meat sizzling, smelling cooked lamb. He liked walking at dinner-time. He liked that sense of happy families around the table, tucking in. There was a rattle of cutlery, a low-frequency rumble of voices, swelling music from something on television. A woman called out *No two ways about that, love*, and laughed.

Further along a window threw a square of yellow light on to the road and lit up a hand-painted sign on a gate that had been altered to read BEWARE OF THE FROGS. Behind the window someone was washing up. There was the deadened clatter of dishes in water, the muffled knocking around of the brush in the suds, then a smash and a cry. First the smash, then the cry. Then immediately a man's voice, querulous from some far room, on a questioning inflection. Right over his head a woman's sharp voice, exasperated, shrill, called out, *Yes, I dropped a bloody plate!*

He wondered. Did that – that querulousness, that sharpness – mean people at the end of their tether with each other? People worn down by years of annoyance, years of the words never connecting, years of the obvious always being spoken, the important things never mentioned: did it mean that? Or was it a man and a woman who knew that crankiness could be a kind of intimacy?

He moved on. It was bad enough to have bored his wife into leaving, but it would be worse to be discovered lurking in the dunny-lane. *I was seeing how other people do it*, he might say, but a copper would take a dim view.

On a street of big old houses, like boats moored in their gardens, he paused on the nature strip, beside a bush, glanced in to a lit-up living-room and there she was, the woman of the cows. She was standing leaning over a table looking down at something. As he watched, the dog gave him a fright, coming out like a welcoming host and suddenly licking his hand loudly, not barking, seeming to remember him from the last time they had met.

Her tee-shirt was coming undone along the shoulder. He could see the lips of the seam spreading open along her shoulder so that skin showed.

Marjorie would never have dreamed of wearing a tee-shirt coming undone along the shoulder. But then, Marjorie would never have dreamed of wearing a tee-shirt of any kind. She would have said that it *didn't do anything for her*. It had been important to Marjorie that things *did something for her*.

It was obvious that this woman did not care if things *did something for her* or not.

He stood there for a long time, watching. When you stood still, you could hear the way the frog noises mounted to a crescendo *cr crrr crrrrrrr* and then stopped so that you could hear a *tick, tick, tick, tickticktick, ticktick, ticktick-tick*, and some kind of very high *eep eep eeep*. Then the frogs started up again. If you were inside a house, you did not hear any of that. But standing outside, holding your breath behind a bush, you heard it all very clearly.

Now she was arranging something on the table in front of her and, as she flicked and lifted, he saw it was pieces of fabric that she was laying out across the table. Then she picked something up and ran it across the surface with a grand gesture like a dancer's. He watched as she picked up fabric, laid it down, ran the tool across it again. Each time she picked them up, the pieces of fabric were smaller.

Her big plain face was serious, brooding, as she cut and flipped the fabric. She stepped back, cocked her head on one side, rearranged the fabric again.

He wished he could see what it was she was so interested in, laid out on the table.

He quelled the phrases as they rose into his mind again. *Very pleased if you would be my guest.* She would be embarrassed. You show some bloke how to get through a fence, and suddenly you're stuck with him: some bloke with big ears and a hungry kind of look in his eyes, being an embarrassment.

She would refuse, but in a tactful way, and that would be embarrassing too.

He had given it a lot of thought, and he had definitely decided not to suggest anything.

CHAPTER 15

THE THING ABOUT the school was, it was almost opposite the shops: there was the Cobwebbe Crafte Shoppe and the Caledonian, and next to that was Alfred Chang Superior Meats. Very handy, for picking up a few chops for dinner on the way home. But it meant that as Felicity waited for the children to be let out in the afternoon, she knew she was in full view of the butcher. He could be standing there, behind the triangle of dripping-containers, watching you from across the road. You would never know whether he was or not.

Not that it mattered, of course. She did not even know why she thought of it.

But she did, every afternoon, and looked forward to going down to the school.

When they had first come to Karakarook, the other mothers at the school had all looked alike to her. She had recognised them only by signs: the tall one, the one who was always smoking, the fat one.

They were nice enough women, and good-hearted, of course. They had invited her to join the Red Cross and the

Country Women's Association, and play tennis with them on Tuesdays, and now there was this business with the Museum Committee. She did not want to be stand-offish, and Hugh had encouraged her to join in, so she went along to the Red Cross now and then, when they had an interesting speaker, and she had made some lovely lamingtons for the school Lamington Drive, and the Museum Committee had seemed promising.

So she knew them all now, to say hello to, but there was no one she wanted to see very much of. They just did not share any interests, really, and most of them were *letting themselves go* shockingly.

The other thing was that when you were the bank manager's wife, it could be a little bit tricky. You did not want to look stand-offish, but you did not want to get too close, either. It could be awkward if there turned out to be a problem later about an overdraft.

The one who was always smoking, Angela, was leaning against the fence today, talking to Lois, the one whose bra and petticoat straps were always drooping down over her upper arms. She was forever plunging a hand in for one or other of them. She did not seem to realise how awful it looked. Angela had a cigarette in her mouth that was flipping up and down as she talked. The lighter was at the ready in her hand, thumb poised to spin the wheel, but she could not bring herself to stop talking for long enough to light it.

Felicity did not approve of mothers who smoked. There was a great deal of literature on the subject. Apart from the effect on children, there was the effect on your own complexion. It was well-documented that smoking could add a decade to your age by the time you were fifty.

She smiled at the woman with the earrings in the shape of parrots. Fiona. She knew Fiona quite well. William sometimes played with her son and although Fiona allowed the boys to play with toy guns, of which Felicity did not approve, on the whole it was a friendship to encourage, since the boy seemed quite bright.

Felicity would not herself have worn earrings like that, and if Fiona did a little reading in the magazines she would know better than to use that kind of eyeshadow. She looked red in the face today and her hair needed a comb. A bra strap was showing.

Felicity smiled, but cautiously. Fiona sometimes let things get on top of her.

She herself was wearing her nice navy pants, very good quality from Honeycutt's, and the blue top with the *little touch of white at the throat*. She could have told Fiona, if she was interested, about the way the *little touch of white at the throat* bounced light up under your chin, so that any little pouchings and darkenings of skin would disappear.

She smiled, and made sure she was standing up nice and straight. Posture was so important. She glanced over towards the shops, but their windows looked back blankly.

If he were ever to suggest some photos of her, of course she would laugh and refuse. She was a wife and mother, after all.

Refuse, but nicely.

Fiona was pushing the stroller over to Felicity. The baby was in it, looking cranky, and there was a lot of shopping hanging off the back, and little Darren was holding on to the side.

These children are eating me alive, she cried as she came up to Felicity.

She laughed as if taken by surprise by the words that had come out of her mouth. But she could not seem to stop.

Sucking the marrow out of my bones! she cried.

She was almost shouting.

Out of the corner of her eye, Felicity saw something moving behind the window of Alfred Chang Superior Meats.

Fiona laughed, high and insistent, like the call of a bird. Felicity smiled, but in a small way. She would not want anyone to think she was really close friends with Fiona.

Yesterday I *counted*, Fiona began, and stopped to laugh again.

The laughing was making the parrot-earrings tremble and twitch. Her lips were stretched tight over her laugh, showing teeth and gums. She was laughing, of course, but if you took a photograph at that moment, you would have said she was in pain.

I *counted*, she repeated, the words broken up with the laughing. I counted how many times he said *Mum I want a biscuit*.

She broke off and looked away to check where Darren was, and saw him over by the fence with a stick.

Darren, put that stick down please.

She turned back to Felicity.

Thirty-seven! she cried. No, put it *down!* Before I gave in.

Darren stared at her with his lip stuck out and banged the stick along the railing of the fence.

Darren, I said put it down please. No, Darren, *no!*

Now Darren was holding the stick like a rifle and another child was approaching, unsteady on its feet, a big wad of nappy between its knees. It was Janet's little boy, but Janet was not watching, over by the gate showing something in a magazine to Pat. Darren was shooting this child, who stood wavering, then put out a fat arm, a fat hand, to touch the end of the stick. Darren was crouching down with one eye closed, shooting him again and again while he smiled and reached and wavered.

Fiona, calling out *Darren! No!* let go of the stroller and ran towards him. She was not laughing now.

As she let go of the stroller, the weight of the shopping hanging behind pulled it over backwards, and the baby in the stroller went over too, still strapped in, on top of the shopping. It began to scream *Maaaaah maaaaaah.* Fiona, halfway to Darren, glanced back, but Janet's little boy had wavered closer to Darren and Darren was jabbing the stick and making shooting noises. Janet's little boy was about to lose an eye.

Felicity did not ever like to interfere with other people's children. But Angela and Lois and all the others were looking now, and it seemed sensible to pick up the stroller. With the shopping hanging off the back, and the roaring baby, it was very heavy, but she got it upright. She felt herself grimacing with the effort, and looking awkward, straining to lift the stroller.

Over at the fence, Fiona was almost within reach of Darren, but Darren shot her a grinning look, not a nice look at all, and jumped around, putting Janet's little boy between himself and his mother. The end of the stick brushed against Janet's little boy's face. He recoiled, staggered back with his hand to his face, lost balance, fell heavily on his bottom. The mouth squared, wet and red. He started to scream.

Darren was pointing the stick at his mother now and she grabbed the end of it and pulled. He leaned back against the pull, she gave a tug and then he had fallen over backwards and hit his head against the fence. Lying sprawled on his back, he roared out of a big gaping mouth.

Janet had rushed over now and snatched up her child, still screaming. She was fingering his face, peering. *Where does it hurt, sweetie?* There was hair everywhere, and tears.

The bag of oranges on the back of the stroller had burst in the fall. The baby in the stroller was still screaming in high broken jabs of noise, twisting against the straps, kicking, arching its back as if in agony. People were picking up oranges and giving them to Felicity, but there was nothing to put them in so oranges were spilling out of her arms.

Then Leith, with her little girl beside her and the baby on her hip, gave her a plastic bag out of her hold-all, and Lois came over to help. Felicity had to keep holding the stroller with her hip so the weight of the rest of the shopping would not pull it over again, and try to get the oranges out of her arms into the bag Leith was holding. She knew she must be looking very awkward but she tried to keep her face smooth and not let her bottom stick out as she bent over the stroller.

Now classes were out. Big children were everywhere, pushing. It was the first thing they learned when they got to school, how to stick their elbows out and barge. Their backpacks bumped around, knocking little ones over.

There was William, over on the steps, looking round, not seeing her in the crush. He humped his backpack on and pushed towards the gate. He was with, but not quite *with*, some of the boys who said *gunna*. She worked her way around a group of little girls to try to intercept him. *William!* she called, *Oh William!* She was quite close, but he did not hear. He was actually out the gate, setting off along the footpath with the others, when she caught up with him.

Darling, she cried, and put her arm around his shoulders. He shrugged it off. But just for that moment, it would have made a lovely photo, if anyone had happened to be nearby with a camera. She glanced over at Alfred Chang Superior Meats and there he was, Alfred Chang himself, standing in his doorway, definitely looking towards her. He probably waited all day for the chance of this glimpse of her. *Darling,* she said again, but William had already moved away, and she was only saying it into the air.

CHAPTER 16

DOUGLAS HAD BEEN in Karakarook a week now, but he was always the only one at breakfast. The woman did not even have to ask any more, but just nodded when he came in to the Dining Room and went away to order his Set Breakfast.

The hinges of the swing door creaked and thumped now and she came out balancing the toast-rack on the edge of the plate, the cup and saucer in the other hand.

There you go, love, she said, and whipped out the local paper from under her arm and spread it open next to the plate.

Seen this?

BENT BRIDGE TO GO, the headline blared, and there was a full-colour picture of the bridge, and next to it the sketch they had done at Head Office, to show what the new bridge would look like. Here in the paper it was called an *artist's impression*, but it had only been Bob Partridge up on the third floor. Under the photo of the old bridge was a sub-heading: *Danger to Public, Says Engineer.*

He heard himself blurt *No!* It was like a shout in the quiet room. He wanted to turn the paper face down but the woman was looking over his shoulder.

Should have gone years ago, she said. See, the Main Roads pays for the bridge, but the Shire cops the maintenance.

He nodded. He knew that, about the Shire being responsible for the maintenance, but it seemed polite to make a little *hm?* and nod.

At least there was no photo of him.

They've been a terrible nuisance, the greenies, she said. Troublemakers, the lot of them.

He got to work on the Set Breakfast, bolting down the eggs, slicing hard across the bacon, slurping at the tea. The toast was embarrassing, the way it exploded into crumbs when you tried to butter it, and the watery grilled half-tomato kept sliding off his fork.

Yes, he said, for something to say, but was sorry then, because it sounded as though he agreed with her.

He did agree, they were troublemakers. But it was not as simple as all that. Sometimes, trouble needed to be made.

He had often found there was a grey area between agreeing and disagreeing, as in this case.

The swinging doors thumped again and the publican came out with a tray of glasses that he put down on a table with a clash, and came over to stand beside the woman.

Greenies not giving you any bother?

Um, he said, and swallowed a mouthful of bacon.

About the bridge, the publican said loudly, as if Douglas was deaf. They giving you any bother at all?

Glad to see the back of it, the woman said.

Danger to life and limb, the publican said.

The school bus and that, the kiddies, the woman said.

Standing in the way of progress, the publican said, and like a snake striking, Eh?

Now they were both watching Douglas. His mouth tried

out various words. There was *yes*. That was not quite right. There was *no*. That was not quite right, either.

There were times when life seemed to be one big grey area.

The woman finally took pity on him.

You'd agree with that, she said kindly. Being a professional.

She turned to the publican.

He'd agree with that.

Douglas got the last mouthful of toast and egg down and slid the knife and fork together. The woman reached in straight away and took the plate.

That's right, she said, as if he had spoken. We're right behind you, love. One hundred per cent.

It seemed to take a long time to get himself out of the Dining Room and away from the two faces watching him. He felt them looking at the enormous size of his ears, their blazing heat, their flapping and blushing stupidity. The back of his neck felt exposed, blushing like his ears as he progressed in a zigzag way through the thicket of tables and chairs.

Something about being watched was making his bottom move in a strange way, and thinking about it was making it worse.

Out on the street the air was ruthlessly clear and he seemed to be the centre of Karakarook's attention. Two women glanced at him as he crossed the road. A man in overalls stopped opening his car door to have a good look. A truck passed and someone stared at him out the window.

He did not think he was imagining it. Undistinguished invisible Douglas Cheeseman was suddenly conspicuous in the hard glare of Parnassus Road. *Danger to Public, Says Engineer.*

It was fame, of a kind. But like that other kind of fame he was reluctantly familiar with, it was unwanted.

CHAPTER 17

HARLEY COULD ALREADY see how you would stop finding the Cobwebbe Crafte Shoppe funny. This morning PEACE ON EAR seemed quite normal.

The dog walked beside her, glancing up from time to time, its tail brushing against her leg, a stick in its mouth. It seemed to enjoy carrying a stick around. When a dusty truck drove by with a brown dog in the tray, running from side to side and barking, the dog beside her looked, stopped, pricked up its ears. She could see it was trying to decide whether to drop the stick so it could bark too.

It was quite funny, really, but she had no intention of laughing.

The dog had not packed its little suitcase and gone home. Nor did it seem about to. It drank the water she gave it *just this once* every day, and ate the *just this last time* can of Pal.

Today was the day she was going to be decisive about it. Somewhere in Karakarook was someone who would claim it, and this morning she would find that someone, and walk away without a dog.

Parnassus Road had a flattened look under the huge pale country sky. Nothing interrupted the blank white light that poured down everywhere. The sun was already hot, and even at this hour the shadows were very black and crisp, as if cut out of black paper and laid on the ground. The parapet of the butcher's shop cast a shadow that looked like a badly cut slice of bread, wider at one end than the other, and the Cobwebbe Crafte Shoppe laid a big blocky shadow across the footpath.

A dusty car drove past on the road and slowed. Someone invisible behind the windscreen stuck a hand out and waved, and she waved back.

She was getting used to the way people did that, out here in the bush, and had finally learned how to wave back before it was too late. She liked the way she was getting to know who they were from their cars, and the way they knew who she was from hers. That was how you did it here: you did not wait to recognise people, you assumed you knew them, and you assumed that they knew all about you, because they all did.

She liked the way she knew the people she met down on Parnassus Road when she did her shopping. The trip became a series of conversations under the awnings. They were like ants, stopping to exchange a bit of information between their feelers before they went on.

Bert Cutcliffe had invited her down to the school and in a hot hall filled with the sharp metallic smell of many children – their feet, the bananas in their bags – she showed them Mrs Trimm's teacosy in the shape of an echidna, and the ancient rotary egg-beater, and the doily that said KEEP THE HOME FIRES BURNING. She did not know the children, but they knew her now, and sang out *Hi Miss Savage!* when they saw her.

It was a new feeling, like being without the layer of your shell that was called *privacy*. She would have said it would be claustrophobic, to have everyone know you, but it did not seem to be like that.

The way no one knew you in the city, the way everyone *respected your privacy*, had always seemed safe. Now it was looking a little bleak.

Children were streaming towards the school in a last-minute flurry. Boys ran towards her with their packs bumping around on their backs, skirting around her and the dog.

Sucked in! one yelled at the other.

Get stuffed!

They were like her boys had been at that age, big and rough. It was just more proof of her *dangerous streak*, not having let them get a dog. She could see that now.

The youngest had made the biggest fuss. He had seemed hardly to notice when his father was not there any more. *Too young to take it in*, people said. But the thing about the dog had become an obsession. He had done endless drawings of dogs and left them around the house for her to find, had got books about dogs out of the library, had thought up dozens of dog names. Then he had started the tantrums. He had got into a kind of habit of hurling himself on the floor when things went wrong, and screaming and screaming until he more or less blacked out and could be put to bed.

He had dogs now, but they did not seem to make him happy. There were some things that you had to have when you needed them, or it was too late for ever after.

She had not really been paying attention at the time, of course. She had been in no frame of mind to think about a dog, with Philip so suddenly dead.

Upset: that was the word they had used. *Poor thing, she's upset*. But she had not felt *upset*. She had not really let herself feel anything. The feelings that were waiting for her, on the other side of a cool coping, could not be survived. So she had *dealt with it well*, had used the phrase *a death in the family* on the phone to people, as if it was just that, a simple *death*.

There were sometimes worse things than mere death, but they were too bad to think about.

A smartly dressed woman was coming towards her, hurrying a neat boy along. She recognised the woman from the museum meeting and was pleased with herself for remembering.

Hello! she said, and got a nice smile ready on her face.

But the woman did not notice her.

What about your library book? she was asking. And your homework? The project? The disasters?

Her voice was drilling away at the boy.

And did you get the excursion money I left for you? And the note?

The boy's face was blank. He did not say anything. It was as if his mother was simply not there.

When the school bell buzzed, a few stragglers made a run for it, and suddenly Parnassus Road was empty except for a man crossing the road with a long fluorescent light tube under his arm, like a Frenchman with a loaf of bread.

In the Mini-Mart, she was glad to see it was Leith behind the counter rather than *Grandad* with the mended glasses.

Hello again, Harley, she said as she started to punch in the items.

This was the moment. *Followed me home*, she had planned to say, with a nice easy laugh. *Followed me home, you know how they are.*

But while she was still rehearsing the nice easy laugh, Leith was speaking.

Don't know if this is any good, she said, and brought something out from under the counter wrapped in a plastic bag.

Grandad's been using it for putting the super on the citrus.

It was a ladle, that you might use for soup or stew. The handle was an old metal file, ground down to a tapering point, and joined with three brass rivets to a piece of tin hammered into a bowl shape.

Harley felt it warm in her hands, could feel the texture where the tin had been painstakingly rounded.

Grandad thinks it might have been his dad made it, Leith said. But who'd know, after all this time.

Many hours of fiddly work had gone into it. Someone had tapped away at the bowl and ground away at the handle, and filed the brass rivets until they were like inlaid gold.

If all you wanted to do was get stew out of a pot, there were easier ways to do it. She had seen dippers made with a tin can and a piece of fencing-wire that would have done the job just as well. But just getting the stew out of the pot had not been the point with this one.

She imagined them sitting together, the man and the woman, by the flickering firelight, a big iron pot on the hob with the ladle in it, the baby asleep in a cradle made out of butter-boxes, and outside the bush heaving and whispering, and the dew falling cold out of the air, nothing for miles and miles but the trees scraping their chilly leaves together in the night wind, the little bead of warmth and light of their hearth puny, but powerful too, in all that darkness.

A labour of love.

There were times when the corny old phrases suddenly made sense.

She felt almost shy of the ladle, as if it were something too private to stare at.

It's good, she said, but her voice stuck in her throat somehow and she had to cough, and let Leith come around the counter to pat her on the back.

It was not till she was back out on the footpath, squinting into the hard white light beyond the awning, the ladle wrapped in its plastic again in the basket, that she remembered the dog. There it was, glancing up at her as if to say *Where to next, Harley?*

The youngest had brought a dog home one day. *It followed me home, Mum,* he had said, and squinted up at her from the bottom of the back steps. *Just followed me, honest.*

Until this moment, meeting the gaze of this dog, she had forgotten about that.

She had not believed him, naturally. They had had an argument about it. *Dogs don't just follow people home,* she had said. She remembered, reluctantly, how nasty she had been. She had ended up shouting, as she had too often. *What do you take me for, an idiot?*

It was starting to look as though she might be.

As she wheeled away from these thoughts, she found herself suddenly face to face with the man she had had to rescue from the cows. This time she spoke up quickly, to make up for seeming to snub him that day in the Cobwebbe Crafte Shoppe.

Oh, hello, she said. Didn't recognise you.

She could not imagine why she had said that, since she had recognised him straight away this time.

His face broke into a big eager smile that transformed it.

I wanted to thank you, he said, so fast the words tripped over each other. For the other day. You know, with the cows.

He did not seem like a tall man, with his diffident shoulders, the humble tilt of his head, but his face was up on a level with hers.

I thought I'd, you know, had it, he said. Stupid of me not trying the fence.

He smiled so his crooked teeth showed. He did not seem to remember he had said all this before. She nodded as if he had not, and smiled.

Oh well, she said.

She realised she was trying to think of a way to save his pride.

You weren't to know the fence wasn't turned on.

He shook his head emphatically.

I'm just a duffer, he said. I'd be no use to you on a desert island, anything like that.

It sounded rather personal: *no use to you*, as if he had been thinking of the two of them, alone together on a desert island, and himself looking to be *of use*.

He seemed to be thinking that too, biting his lip as if to punish it for what it had said.

His ears seemed bigger than ever when he blushed, and they blushed too, warm and rosy. He looked away at the dog and when he patted his leg it came over straight away, pushing its nose into the palm of his hand. Then it rolled over on to its back and he hunkered down to scratch around the hard knobs of its nipples. The dog's eyes narrowed to slits of ecstasy and its hind leg scratched in sympathy, although its ears were still cocked alertly towards Harley.

He looked up at her.

I should have given you a lift, he said. I only thought of it too late.

She was about to explain about the *forty-five minutes to an hour*, but suddenly he looked straight up at her and in an odd high-pitched way said,

Would you let me take you to lunch, or afternoon tea? As a way of thanking you?

Before she had taken this in, a man in a blue singlet came out of the alleyway, poking a ladder between them. They stepped back from each other quickly, as if they had been too close.

Scuse me, mate, he said. Coming through.

It seemed to take the ladder a long time to pass between them.

When he had gone they were left staring at each other.

Yes, she said.

It was just the word that came out of her mouth. It was as if it was just the first word that her mind came upon, while it was busy remembering the way he had looked down in the paddock, waving his branch at the cows, and the way, together up on the road, the toes of their shoes had pulled grooves in the dust as they spoke.

Her mouth opened again.

Of course.

Why *of course?* There was no *of course* about it.

But although the words had popped out by accident, they set things in motion that had a momentum of their own.

The Panorama Cafe, he said quickly. Out on the Jurgo road?

Now he seemed in a hurry to be gone.

Tomorrow, around the three mark?

Even as he was speaking he was backing away, making a little waving gesture with one hand.

Yes, she heard herself call. It's a date!

She had meant it to sound light, airy, inconsequential, something of a joke. A *date*. With such a woman as herself, the idea of a *date* could only be ironic. The way it came out it sounded simply strange: coy, but huge and loud. The dog glanced up at her as if startled.

He was nodding and still backing away, as if from Royalty, and nearly bumped into Coralie, who was suddenly there behind him with a carton of milk in her hand.

Whoops-a-daisy! she cried, and looked from him to Harley.

With one last jerky wave, he was turning and more or less fleeing into the doorway of the Caledonian.

Coralie watched him go. Then she turned her attention to Harley.

Know that bloke, do you?

No, Harley said. That is, not really.

She did not, only knew how the sun had lit up his ears from behind, so they were like translucent pink flowers, and she did not know why she remembered that so well.

Coralie went on standing with the carton of milk in her hand, waiting for more.

Know him I mean, Harley added. She did not know where to start about the cows, and the fence, and the way he had clutched the stick. She had only been joking, calling it a *date*, but somehow, as a joke, it was hard to explain.

*

CHAPTER 18

FELICITY FOUND THE entrance without difficulty, in the lane behind Alfred Chang Superior Meats, and went in boldly, through a back yard with a choko vine wandering over the broken fence, and into the doorway. There was a dim staircase with green lino on the treads. She looked up to where the top of the stairs went away into shadows and gripped the handles of Great-Grandmother Ferguson's quilt bag more tightly.

She was, very kindly, arranging for Alfred Chang to photograph Great-Grandmother Ferguson's quilt for the Karakarook Heritage Museum. Actually, the woman from Sydney had talked them into calling it the *Karakarook Pioneer Heritage Museum*, because she said that would give more the *flavour of the collection*. Felicity thought it made it sound a bit amateurish, but the others seemed to like the idea of pioneers. Several of them had even mentioned their convict ancestors, almost as if they were something to be proud of.

Anyway, that was all there was to it: arranging for the photographing of the quilt. It was true that Alfred Chang was in love with her, poor man, but there was nothing she could do about that. Men were always doing it, falling in love with her. Could she help it if they found her attractive?

There was nothing underhand about it and certainly nothing in the least bit *awkward*. She did not mind who saw her go into this doorway, and she did not know why she was a little breathless, even before she had gone up the stairs.

At the top there was a big hot open space with screens partitioning off smaller spaces. The nearest screen was covered with photos: of dead gumtrees silhouetted against the sky, of rounded boulders nestled against each other like eggs, of various orange sunsets. There were a lot of photos of a fat Chinese baby sitting naked on a sheepskin laughing, and several family groups with the same baby being held up by various people dressed in their best.

She called out in a tentative way.

Hello? Hello?

There was no answer. The windows were all covered with black curtains, but over in the far corner behind some screens there was a pool of brilliant white light, and she went over towards it.

All around her, shadows went off into deeper shadows. A lamp on a tall stand swayed like a dandelion as she passed too close to it and she flinched back, then tripped over a coil of flex, and on the rebound from the flex barked her shin on a metal box. What with the heat, and the clutter, and wondering if Alfred Chang was watching her, she felt a little disoriented.

Behind the screens was an open space with lights pointing down at a white backdrop spread out on the floor. Lying on the backdrop, very small and shabby, was the old shirt Mr Cutcliffe had brought for the Museum. It lay in a clean blaze of brilliance, a sad little wrinkled thing. Above it a camera stared down from a crude gantry.

She stepped into the lit-up area, on to the white paper. You could almost take hold of the light in handfuls. It bounced up from the white floor and ricocheted off the walls of darkness all around, making a cocoon of radiance, a magic circle with herself at the centre. The blackness was like a living thing around the whiteness: solid, organic, shifting its boundaries, receding and advancing as the pupils of her eyes dilated and contracted. She could feel them doing it, operated by some mechanism beyond her control.

She peered out, shading her eyes with her hand.

Hello?

The blank whiteness of the light swallowed up the word.

Hello?

Being under the lights made you see yourself in a different way. She had learned that, doing the shoot for the Palmolive ad. You looked at yourself from the outside, as if you were someone else. You watched the various parts of yourself moving: *Head up, dearie! Just put that leg forward, yes, lovely,* but the person tilting her head up or putting her leg forward was not quite the same as you yourself.

Mr Chang?

That sounded ridiculously formal, and for some reason her voice had a tiny quaver in it.

Alfred?

That sounded much too familiar.

Is anyone there?

Alfred Chang stepped forward into the light, short and chunky, a roll of flex over his shoulder like a mountaineer. Light engulfed him, made him crisp and unreal, his face flat, without shadows. She could see a few black whiskers on the side of his cheek where he had missed a patch, shaving. His stiff black hair swallowed the light.

She felt a little pulse of something when she saw him. Like apprehension, or stage-fright, but it was not those.

It was knowing he was in love with her. There was always something rather exciting about having a man, especially someone as strange as a Chinese man, in love with you.

She could not help noticing that there was a button missing on his shirt so that it yawed open. She could actually see a crease of honey-coloured stomach and his neat little navel.

She looked away quickly.

She wished she had not called him by his first name. She had never done it before and she did not know why she had done so now. It would only encourage him.

He unhooked the flex from his shoulder and laid it on the floor.

Call me Freddy, he said. I'm only Alfred on the awning.

He came nearer and watched her face closely as if measuring the light falling on it.

She had been told more than once that she was one of those people the camera *fell in love with*. The man who had taken the photos for Palmolive had told her he had never seen anyone the camera *fell in love with* quite so much. *Irresistible* was the word he had used.

Thank you, she would say, if he suggested photos. *It's terribly kind of you to offer, but I don't think it would be appropriate, do you?*

Appropriate was such a useful word.

His hair was very dry and brittle-looking. She had never been this close to him before, to notice. She knew just the conditioner he should use. Also, he needed a haircut. Being a little short of stature he would be better off with a nice neat head of hair. She could almost feel the scissors in her hand, and had the thickness of his hair sitting neatly over his ears.

As well as having the missing button, the faded paisley shirt was too tight, and you could see big peg-marks on the shoulders. She realised she had never seen him before without his striped apron, not this close anyway, except of course the night of the Museum meeting, and he had been sitting down then, so you would not have noticed a thing like a missing button. Or a navel.

I've always been Freddy, he said. Like the frog.

He kept pulling up his jeans, as if they needed a belt. When he did that, hoisted them up, you could see a bulge just there. They were frayed just there, too, around the zip.

She looked away, naturally, but could not help noticing. It was really very badly frayed.

She heard herself giggle.

Alfred was my father's name, he went on.

She thought he was probably trying to spin things out, poor thing, to make this little meeting with her last as long as possible.

So one of us had to be Freddy.

Felicity went *Oh?* in an interested way. That did not seem quite enough, and he was still watching her, so she added *really?*

That sounded just a bit too much. She smiled, and tried to think of something to say that was neither too much nor too little. He might think she was over-conscious of his being Chinese if she made a comment about his name, which was obviously not Chinese, not the Alfred part of it anyway, and that might be tactless. She thought that if you were Chinese you would want to be as normal as possible in every other way.

She knew he lived with his mother, out of town some-where, and his sister or auntie, someone like that. He was definitely not married. But you would think the mother or the sister would sew the button back on his shirt, and per-haps try to do something about the fraying zip, too.

In her mind's eye she had the shirt off and was matching the button with the ones in her box. It was a standard pearly men's-shirt button, not hard to match. Now she was thread-ing her Number 7 Crewel with her Dylko Reinforced Thread, colour white – being careful not to purse or hunch – and was stitching away.

Now she was knotting the thread on the button and snipping it off, and he was pulling the shirt back on.

He was still watching her. She felt the light falling full on her face from the source beyond the screen. She made her-self smile slightly, the way she knew smoothed out the skin of her face in a nice way. She tilted her chin up, just frac-tionally. It was only in certain lights that her chin was inclined to let her down. She did not know what sort of light this was but she thought it was possible that it was the kind in which her chin let her down.

Is that your family, the photos out there?

That was polite but neutral, and broke the silence that was developing.

She wondered if he knew that she knew that he was in love with her.

He nodded.

My sister, he said. Her family.

He did not seem very interested. His hair blazed backlit in one of the lamps. He seemed to be waiting for her to say something.

They're lovely photos, she heard herself gushing. So . . . intimate.

That was not really the word she had meant. *Intimate*. It did not sound quite right. She hurried on, before the word could become large in the silence.

About the quilt, she said. When should I come back for it, do you think?

She had thought of the word now. *Informal*. That was what she had meant. *Informal*. It would look funny, though, to go back and explain that she had meant *informal* rather than *intimate*.

How would Friday be, Mrs Porcelline?

She thought perhaps he did know that she knew. She had a sense that he was trying to catch her eye.

Excellent! she said.

In trying not to catch his eye, she felt she was looking rather shifty. She gave him one of her *lovely smiles*, to make up for looking shifty.

That seemed to be all, but he did not go back to coiling the flex.

Bit of a mess, he said cheerfully, looking around.

Her eyes were used to the lights now and she followed his glance. Just out of range of the lights there was a jumble of tawdry grubby things: a chair with ragged tapestry upholstery and carved wooden claws, a red velvet chaise-longue, a spindly palm in a pot. She recognised the fluffy sheepskin from the baby photo, and the barley-twist table the smiling family was grouped around. There were black metal lamps heaped up in an angular pile, a bag full of squares of yellow cardboard, a heap of striped fabric, a litter of polystyrene wig heads, and clots of grey flex everywhere.

Hugh's mother had often said, looking out the window of the car on Sunday drives, *No one is so poor they can't sweep up their yard.* But clearly, Freddy Chang had never bothered to get himself organised. Perhaps he thought it made him artistic, a romantic figure.

It was funny, really, and rather sad, a Chinese trying to cut a romantic figure.

The white backdrop that the shirt lay on was just a length of thick paper pulled down like a kitchen towel from a long tube hanging above. The edge was ragged and dirty, stuck down to the floor with bits of masking tape, and she could see dirty fingerprints and footprints on the white.

None of that would show in the photo, though. The shirt lay on the middle of the paper, where it was clean. The photo would show nothing but clean brilliant light. You would never guess the dirt that was beyond the image. It was a kind of magic.

Her own feet were the centre of radiating wedges of shadows that overlapped and interlinked and re-formed themselves around her feet, half-shadows and quarter-shadows. When she moved, they moved too, but they stayed attached to her feet so that she was always at the centre of a web of light and dark.

She wondered whether you could get rid of all the shadows, if you used enough lights, and arranged them scientifically. They would have to be forced under your feet. They would still be there, under the soles of your shoes. But no one would see them.

She imagined how it would be, to look around yourself, front, back, sides, and not see a single shadow anywhere. She would like to ask him if it was possible, but he might think it was peculiar.

Oh well, she said.

That was good as far as it went, but the silence seemed to call for something further.

What sort of thing do you normally photograph?

That was a good question: interested, but not too interested.

Portraits mainly, he said. I do a fair number of portraits.

He was watching her closely.

Life studies. You know.

Did *life studies* mean *nude*? She had a feeling it might.

You'd be a natural, you know, he said. I can tell.

She already knew that, but it seemed modest to pretend.

Oh? Really? Do you think so?

From when she was young, people had always said *You take a nice photo*, looking through the album. Later on she had been able to show them the Palmolive ad, and they always said the same thing: *Oh, you've got good bones*, which was really missing the point, as the Palmolive ad had not been interested in her bones.

No one ever saw the ones where she had not *taken a nice photo*, because she had always popped those straight in the incinerator. Anyone could be caught at an unflattering angle.

Under Freddy Chang's gaze, she tried to keep her chin up in the way she knew gave her a rather nice yearning sort of look. *Look as if you're thinking about white lilies*, the Palmolive man had said from behind the camera. *Smooth white lilies*. When she had lifted her chin and obediently thought about lilies, he had called out *Lovely! Perfect, dearie! Now just push the dress off the shoulder, sweetheart, that's the way. Just a bit more, there's a girl.*

Lovely, Alfred, or Freddy, said. You'd come up beautifully.

He put his hands up to make a frame and looked at her through it. Somehow it was not like simply being stared at, if someone was pretending you were a photograph.

Lovely, he said again.

After a moment he dropped his hands and came over to stand next to her. He pointed at the sad old shirt lying under the light.

That's the shirt they shot him in, he said, and moved closer, as if to see it from her angle.

Ben Hall.

She did not like to move, because he might be offended, but she felt he was a little close.

Hard to get the blood-stain to come out sharp.

The dense black shadow of his body lay over hers.

Not squeamish about blood, I hope, he said solicitously, putting a hand on her arm for a moment.

It was probably the moment he would especially treasure later on, when he thought privately about the time she had come to see him: the moment he had touched her.

Oh no! she exclaimed, too brightly.

Didn't think so, he said, and watched her.

There was a silence. She could not think of anything to say about blood, or not being squeamish about it.

Didn't think you'd be inhibited. About that sort of thing.

Oh no! she said again, and laughed, and under cover of the laugh she moved away a little. No point in tantalising the poor man.

When he left her to go over to one of the black-draped windows and rattled the heavy curtains back along their rod, the daylight that fell into the room seemed cold, gritty, almost dirty beside the hot thick light from the lamps.

She hoped he was not offended that she had moved away, and it seemed only polite to move over next to him and look out the window too. Out there she could see the flaking brown-painted brick of the side of the Caledonian, so close it looked as if you could touch it.

Not much of a view, Freddy said, but he kept looking out.

She glanced down into the narrow brick-cobbled alley that ran between the shop and the Caledonian, where a broken rubbish-bin lay on its side, but then she remembered that looking down could give you a double chin, or the appearance of one, even if you did not really have one, so she tilted her head up. She was confident that she had smoothed the foundation into her neck this morning, as the magazines told you to, so there was no line between the *flesh colour* out of the bottle and the *flesh colour* that was the colour of your actual flesh.

There was even less to see looking back up at the wall of the Caledonian: a rusting fire escape, a small window, the woodwork painted the same flaking brown as the wall, and above the window, the sign that said CALEDONIAN, with the D hanging upside-down above the window.

Nice and private, Freddy suggested.

She had just been thinking the very opposite, that it was not really private at all with the hotel window so close, so she agreed too vehemently.

Yes! Oh yes! Lucky, isn't it!

Then there's always the curtain, Freddy said, and suddenly dragged it across the window again.

If you're, you know, up to something you shouldn't be.

She glanced at him because with the curtain closed there was nothing else to look at, and then she laughed.

She could hear herself doing it again: a long peal of laughter. It was not really all that funny. In fact, if you thought about it, it was not funny at all. She did not know why she was laughing. In fact, it hardly sounded like her at all, but some other woman, much more reckless and easily amused than she herself was, behaving *inappropriately* with the butcher.

She would have to do something about the laughing. It was just a matter of will-power. *No more of that laughing,* you told yourself. It was that simple. *Control yourself, Felicity.* That was all there was to it.

CHAPTER 19

AT THE BARBECUE, Harley had met the young man at the garage, the one with the rose tattoo on his arm. She had met too many people that day, and now she could not remember his name, but she knew he was someone's son, or nephew. Everyone in Karakarook was related to someone else. At the barbecue she had admired his tattoos, and he had rolled up the sleeve of his tee-shirt to show her how the dragon went all the way up to his shoulder.

He had promised her a chest of drawers made of kerosene tins for the museum, and offered to pick up the old range that Mrs Trimm was donating. *I've got a lot of time for history*, he had told her. *Like to see the old things kept*.

He leaned in intimately at the window, in a toxic aura of petrol fumes.

There was a sign, he said. But it's buggered. Best bet is, watch out for the kero cans. There's four of them.

Kero cans, she said doubtfully.

Bloody good letterbox, he said. On their sides.

He slapped at a fly on his forearm.

Only thing is, got to watch out for snakes.

Snakes! she exclaimed.

My word, he said. Put me hand in for the mail once,

come out with a bloody great diamond python wrapped around me bloody arm.

She wondered privately how a diamond python would be able to climb up the pole and into the kero can, and also why it would want to. But she did not ask.

When he had shot the nozzle back into its housing, he turned towards her again and frowned, wanting her to be sure.

Four of them, he said, as he screwed the cap back on the petrol tank. Can't miss it.

In the end, enjoying the little song the wind made in the window-frame and the way the roof-racks thrummed, she passed the kero cans and only caught sight of them at the last moment, hidden in tall yellow grass. When she stopped and wound down the window, a dry papery smell came in on the warm air. She could see the post now, standing upright in the long grass, and the *buggered* sign propped up against it: *Mount Olympus Panorama Cafe*.

On the narrow side-road, the engine seemed very loud in the stillness of the afternoon. The road began to climb. As she passed a gate with FAIR VIEW on it, a flock of birds burst up in fright, then settled back along the roof of a shed that was collapsed at one end as if it had been sat on.

The car began corkscrewing up the mountain, and trees crowded in over the road. Straggly bushes hung by a thread from the edges of the cuttings, the gnarled knuckles of roots gripping the stones. The Datsun swung out on a sharp corner and for a moment the back wheels snatched at gravel.

She felt a kick of anticipation as she remembered where she was going. A *date*. But she did not know why she kept thinking of it as a *date*, when *dates* were so obviously something buried under the weight of her unhappy history.

When he blushed, as he had blushed getting his invitation out, you could see the sandy eyebrows that were otherwise camouflaged by the sandiness of his skin. She thought of him now, winding the wheel around on the corners. He had a way of looking at you sideways, as if you might bite.

She wondered what he was doing at the Caledonian in Karakarook. He did not seem to have the personality to be a manufacturer's rep. She could not imagine him opening a case of samples of fly-swats or tea-towels and enthusing. He was more likely a public servant, someone from the *Egg Board* or the *Wool Board*. Probably not from the *Cattle Board*, though.

He might get dull on the subject of eggs, or wool. She was starting to wish her mouth had not taken it upon itself to say *yes, of course*.

The last few corners were so steep the Datsun had to be jerked into first gear. The car ground away up the dirt road as if boring against an obstacle.

She took the last bend too fast, hearing the gravel spurting up around the wheels, and burst into the parking area at speed. The white ute was already there, neatly backed in beside a tree waiting for her. She jerked to a stop in front of it and for a moment they stared at each other through their windscreens. She switched her engine off and in the silence a bird went *cachinka cachinka cachinka tweep!* and a twist of bark fell, spinning over itself, between them on to the ground.

He came around to Harley's door and leaned, tentatively, in at the window, fingers curled over the sill. He bent himself in at her humbly but said nothing. She went on gripping the wheel in the approved ten-to-two fashion. Now that it was upon her, she was not sure how to go about this *date*. She breathed steadily.

You found it okay, he said at last.

Oh yes, she said, more eagerly than she meant to, and opened the door without thinking. He had to unlock his hands and get his head out of the way quickly.

Sorry, she said.

No, my fault, he said.

Another bird told a long story: *Pee, perepp, pereep! Anch anch, anch coop cooop coop coop trill!* In the transparent heat each droplet of sound was clear and echoing, as if snipped out and pasted on the air.

The tea-room was oily, the wood panelling sticky with streaked orange varnish. Someone had stuck up posters of other places. Gaudy flowers: SWITZERLAND. A glassy canal: HOLLAND. Grenadier Guards: BRITAIN. Flies circled at face-level. The tables were laid with white lace plastic tablecloths ingrained with dirt and in the middle of each was a clutter of clouded shakers and bottles.

Along one wall was a greasy glass case full of souvenirs. Tea-towels with waratahs. A fluffy platypus with a green plastic beak.

Hand-made signs were taped everywhere. *Do NOT touch display PLEASE. Kindly ASK for assistance. Do NOT lean on glass. NO change given for PHONE.*

One side of the room was all glass, beyond which was the view: a great sheet of blank landscape, its colours bleached by distance, its contours flattened by the height. Cloud-shadows lay like dark mats across the patchwork paddocks.

They were the only customers.

From behind a flowered curtain, dirty along the edge at hand-height, came the sound of thick crockery being crashed into a sink.

It's not very, um, I'm afraid, he said.

He gestured at the view.

But the view is. Well.

He stared out at the bland landscape beneath.

You can see a long way. Um, obviously.

He pulled out one of the wooden chairs and swatted at a fly that was trying to land on his chin.

You can see the river, he said hopefully, and pointed.

She craned to see.

But not very well.

She looked at his face and saw the way his mouth was, under his moustache: how he was biting his bottom lip in his teeth, hard. She knew, without knowing, that he had grown the moustache to hide behind. It was just what she would have done if she had been born a man.

He glanced up as if feeling her watching and met her eyes before looking away again. She had the impulse to say something reassuring but could not think of anything.

It was starting to look as though he might be as bad at *dates* as she was.

At least they had that in common.

She had not planned to, but she found herself having uttered a sudden laugh. The crockery behind the curtain had fallen silent so it was a loud sound in the tea-room, startling the Grenadier Guard and the beady-eyed green-beaked platypus.

He stood gripping the back of a chair hard, holding it out for her. His shoulders were hunched as if under a heavy overcoat. In the silence after her laugh, the gnashing of the crockery started again, louder.

In that humble hunch of shoulder, that desperate grip on the chair, she suddenly saw how it all looked to him: the circling flies, the dirty plastic tablecloths, the boring view, herself laughing. She heard how her laugh could have sounded like a laugh of scorn. It was, or could sound like, a playground laugh. *Made you look you dirty chook.* That kind of laugh: unkind.

Sorry, he said in a generalised kind of way.

A laugh once laughed cannot be unlaughed, and she could not think of anything to say, to soften the scorn of it.

She took the chair from him, feeling where it was warm from his hand on the top rail. As she sat down, her knee hit some part of the table underneath the hanging plastic lace. The table tilted and the sauce bottle fell over and began to roll. They both reached for it at once and then both drew back to let the other do it. The bottle fell with a crash on the wooden floor and began to roll slowly underneath the table. When they both bent down for it at once, they nearly cracked their heads together.

Sorry, they both said at the same time.

She let him get the bottle and sat up straight, feeling the blood a hard red in her cheeks. He did not look at her, but put it back on the table and carefully lined everything up in descending order of height: the greasy salt and pepper shakers, the sugar dispenser full of lumps.

She watched his hands doing it, his big blond knuckles.

They needed to get on with the *date* part of the date, the part where they had a conversation that was more than a lot of apologies.

*

She saw that he had his back to the view.

Sit round here, she said. Where you can see.

But before he could answer, a hand reached out to push back the curtain and the woman came over to them. She picked up the bottles and held them against her while with a damp grey dishcloth she wiped at the plastic lace table-cloth. They sat watching the movement of the dishcloth between them. When she had finished, she went back behind the curtain.

They call that crumbing down, Harley said. What she did.

Crumbing down? he repeated. Crumbing down. Ah. Well.

There was a silence. The woman came back with her pad.

Two teas, he said, with scones.

He looked at Harley. Unless you'd like coffee. Or something.

She shook her head.

Two teas, then, he said. In a pot, please.

A pot? The pots are just pots for one, the woman said warningly.

Yes, he said. That will be fine. But not too strong, please.

Not too strong? she repeated. It's just the bags. Just the one bag then was it?

He was keeping his eyes on the underneath of the order pad. One hand was gripping the thumb of the other, hard.

Yes, he said. One bag will be fine for me.

When she had gone he let go of his thumb and hid his hands away under the table. He looked at Harley. A fly circled lazily and landed on the salt shaker between them.

I'm a bit fussy about my tea, he said. But there's something to be said for being realistic.

He flapped his fingers at the fly, which flew up briefly

and landed on his shoulder. The woman had put the bottles back in the wrong order, and he lined them up again, from right to left this time.

Harley was not looking for rings. She was certainly not looking for rings. But there was a ring, just the same: a plain band on his little finger in some kind of dull metal.

It was too dull to be a wedding ring and besides, it was on the wrong finger. Unable to think of anything to say, she went on thinking about it.

He was a lean man now, but perhaps he had been even leaner once. Perhaps he had married as that young, even leaner, man, and had thickened up.

She looked out at the sky, where distant clouds formed and melted away like thoughts. He'd have had to explain to his wife. *Darling*, he'd have said, and explained about the ring not fitting. *But I still love you, darling*.

She found it hard to imagine his mouth saying such words. Somehow, he did not have that kind of mouth.

But other people, their lives, their love affairs, were always a mystery, the way they seemed to be able to reveal themselves without fear.

We're sitting on a rarity, he said suddenly.

Harley twisted around to have a look at her chair.

No, he said. No, the mountain was what I meant. A basalt remnant.

He glanced around at the deadened landscape below as if it had called out to him, then went back to studying the arrangement of the bottles.

Are you a geologist? Harley asked. Knowing about basalt remnants?

That was good. *Making conversation*, it was called.

Oh no, he said and laughed. I'm an engineer.

He looked at her sheepishly.

Dead boring.

She started to say something, but he cut across her.

Great conversation-stopper at a party, he said. Telling people you're an engineer. Clears the room.

She did not have a chance to find the words to tell him she was not such a *people*, because the woman was between them again to set out the tea things. Some of the tea slopped out of the silly little elaborate china tea-pots on to the table-cloth and some of it went on a scone. They were very small scones on a rather large plate with a scalloped edge and embossed roses. There were two tiny china pots in a tortured tulip-shape full of jam and cream.

He poured his tea quickly, even before the woman had finished setting everything out, but it was already so strong the roses inside the cup were almost invisible. When he tried to lift the cup to his mouth she saw that he could not get his finger inside the handle and had to grasp it in an awkward sideways way.

When she lifted her own cup she had the same problem, and the cup burnt her knuckle, as it must have burned his.

The table was now crowded with objects but there was not actually very much to eat. They each took one of the tiny scones and spread the cream and jam. The tulip-shape disguised the fact that the pots did not actually contain very much of anything at all. With the scones gone, the plate looked very large and empty.

Harley had decided not to comment on any of this, to save his feelings. But her mouth seemed to have made a different decision.

I wasn't hungry, actually, she found it had said.

Horrified, she listened to the words continue to come out of her mouth.

I had a heart attack, it went on. Not that long ago.

He was listening hard. He had eaten his entire scone in one go.

She was suddenly feeling overheated. The African thing she was wearing was actually rather thick, although you thought of Africa as a hot place and therefore a place of cool clothes.

So I have to watch, you know, what I eat.

He nodded again and dabbed at his mouth, which was quite clean, with the paper serviette.

Plus, I'm supposed to walk a lot, so I walk a lot. Here. In Karakarook, I mean.

He was watching her as she talked. She could not seem to stop. She was afraid she might go on telling him things about her heart attack until the Panorama Cafe closed.

She made a wild grab at a subject that was not herself or her heart attack.

I've been noticing your ring, she said. It's unusual. Isn't it?

It was like a call for help.

She watched her own big hand suddenly shoot out across the table and take his, turning it over to look at the ring.

It's my engineer's ring, he said.

He stared at it as if he had never seen it before.

We all have them.

Now he was the one who could not seem to stop.

Engineers, that is. They give them to us when we graduate. They're made of iron. Originally, anyway. From the Montague Bridge, you may have heard of it? Famous collapse back in the 1890s. Great loss of life.

He twisted the ring round and round.

It reminds us, you know. Of what can happen.

It was as if he was looking for something on the ring, the way he was turning it and turning it.

If you don't do your sums right.

How fascinating, she said brightly.

She wished she had not, because she had found it to be, in fact, fascinating. The trouble was, *How fascinating* did not sound as if you were fascinated.

Sometimes, the harder you tried to be sincere, the falser it came out.

No, really, she added.

That made it worse.

Outside, the afternoon went on and on, sun pouring down blankly from the sky on to the few scattered clouds and the flattened landscape below. A big black bird circled slowly on extended wings on the same level as the windows, curving around and around, carving a spiral through the air.

Douglas was trying not to look at the view, although it was what he had brought her all this way for. They were far enough back from the edge, and there was enough framing around the window, to make the hot weak frightened feeling controllable, but it was better, on the whole, not to look out.

He thought he had probably come to the end of the subject of the ring, and he sat trying to think of something else. There was more he could tell her about it. How Kipling had written the *Oath of Engineers*, for example. But a person was not supposed to *go on and on*, in conversation. You were supposed to take turns.

When she had taken his hand, he had seen how large and strong hers were, the nails square and short. Her watch had a big frank stare like a man's.

And what are you doing in Karakarook? she said finally.

Oh, he said, pleased to have a new subject. I'm here to put up a new bridge.

Then he thought that might sound boastful.

Just a very small one. Whack in a concrete beam.

She nodded, and looked as if she wanted to hear more.

It's something of an interest with me, concrete, he said. As it were.

He wondered why he had added that.

Concrete! she exclaimed.

People have the wrong idea about concrete, he started. They've got this idea it's not natural, but it's just calcium carbonate, dig it up out of the ground.

She nodded and he was encouraged. All his life he had wanted to convince people to give concrete a chance. It was the most unjustly despised material. When you said *concrete*, all people thought of was cheap high-rise towers with stains running down the sides, ugly schools with obscene graffiti, underpasses smelling of piss.

It was not good at bending, that was true. If you wanted it to bend, you had to combine it with steel, which bent rather than broke. The strength of the concrete, the flexibility of the steel: it was the perfect marriage. The thing no one seemed to really appreciate about concrete was the way it was a kind of negative. It just took up whatever space was left vacant for it. You could say it revealed the shape of the imagination.

And yet people snorted when he tried to share his enthusiasm. *Concrete!* they would go, and their eyes would start to flicker past his shoulder, looking for someone better to talk to. Even in at the Department they thought he took it a bit too seriously. At the Christmas party one year they had made him a Christmas stocking out of concrete, for a joke. *Just what I always wanted*, he had said, being a good sport, and everyone laughed, but then turned away to their own conversations.

Did you know, he began, that it's not really a solid at all. It's really a very thick liquid.

She looked startled, and he rushed on.

It actually keeps on flowing even after it's set. It's called creep.

Creep? she repeated.

They don't understand it, he said. What it does when the water hits the mix. They know what happens but they don't know why. On a molecular level, I mean.

He was afraid he was losing her, and rushed on.

People want to pretend it's something else, he cried, trying not to shout in the quiet room. He felt a fleck of saliva jump out of his mouth.

They make it into blocks, pretend it's stone. Cover it with pebbles, that sort of caper.

He could not believe he had said *caper*. She was watching him closely, but he did not know what her look meant.

Like vegetarians giving you lentils in the shape of a chop.

Too late he thought *but what if she's a vegetarian*. He could only press on.

It's an insult to the chop, plus it's an insult to the lentils.

She laughed suddenly, showing sharp eye-teeth, but he was not sure whether she was laughing at the idea of insulting a lentil, or at him.

Ever looked at how a freeway curves? Or a pedestrian over-pass? Or what about those wheelchair ramps? Pure poetry!

She had stopped laughing now.

If it was expensive, it would be a cult.

He stopped himself. There was more to say, but he thought the look on her face might be the one he had become familiar with over the years. *Glazed over*, they called it. It meant you were bored.

Sorry, he said. I'm being a bore. My wife always said I was a bridge bore.

He wished he had not mentioned *my wife*. It was too complicated to go into, the divorce and so on.

There was a little silence.

And you? he asked. What brings you to Karakarook, Harley?

He hated the way that sounded, like his mother doing her *gracious* thing with the boys.

I'm helping them get their museum going.

Pardon?

A Heritage thing. For the tourists.

Oh!

I work for the Applied Arts Museum in Sydney. Textiles, mostly.

Oh, he said again.

He wished he could think of something else to say.

They're turning up some fine old things. Bush quilts and so on.

He nodded, wondering if he should ask what a bush quilt was. The way she talked, she assumed everyone knew what they were. Maybe they did.

They both looked out the window, but there was

nothing to say about all the different kinds of brown lying flattened under the sun. The conversation seemed to have run into a cul-de-sac again.

The dirty curtain was pushed aside and the woman came over with the bill, putting it face down in front of him.

They both looked at it.

Like a prompt card! Harley suddenly blurted on a laugh.

Her big finger pointed to the words printed on the back of the bill: THANK YOU.

He laughed in a high-pitched way that sounded frantic. Then there was a silence in which they looked at each other's chins, at each other's shoulders. They did not quite look at each other's eyes.

Good view, she said. Shame you can't see it.

It's okay, he said, and gave a kind of guffaw. I'm not good with heights, actually, he went on quickly, to cover up the guffaw. They had to sedate me once, to get me down off the top of the Port Gordon Bridge.

She might as well know how hopeless he was.

The South Tower. On a stretcher. Quite funny, in retrospect.

He laughed, demonstrating how funny it was in retrospect, but she did not join in.

The curtain parted again and a metal bucket with a mop in it was propelled out. With a great rattle and clank, the woman drew the mop out of the water and squeezed it between the rollers of the bucket, then started flopping it around on the floor. A strong carbolic smell filled the room.

He glanced at Harley. She glanced at her watch.

Better be going, he said, quickly, before she did.

She unhooked her handbag from the back of the chair and stood up.

Thank you for the tea, she said, but a fly landed on her face as she spoke, and she frowned and brushed at it, so the words had an ironic sound.

He suppressed the impulse to start apologising again. As he got his wallet out and glanced uncertainly towards the woman with the mop, he had one last look at the big bland sheets of distant scenery laid out below. Standing up, the height started to give him the starey sick feeling. He looked away quickly.

Her back seemed very large and powerful, walking away. He wondered how he had ever found the courage to ask her out, and whether he would ever dare to do it again.

She drove home filled with lightness like a balloon inside. As she bowled along the road, seeing the white ute up ahead now and again, and seeing its dust in the air above the road, she sang out loud. *Dah DEE, dah DEE, dah dee DAH, the WILD colonial boy.*

He was not such a duffer as he seemed. The thing about the concrete was interesting, and he was right about freeways, although it sounded a bit silly until you thought about it. She had once nearly had an accident on the approach to the Harbour Bridge, getting so involved in the way one curve of the roadway moved around and across another one as the road curved upwards.

It was funny how you could live your whole life surrounded by something as ordinary as concrete, and never think of it as special, until you met someone who did.

It occurred to her that *being a duffer* might be something he did to protect himself, the way *having a dangerous streak* was what she did.

The way the shadows laid themselves out along the ground from the base of trees, the way the rounded paddocks curved away like cheeks: it all filled her with silly pleasure. Some sad-looking sheep in a paddock stared up as she passed, and she shouted out the window at them, *Buck up, sheep!* and they looked apprehensive and began to move tentatively along in a line.

When they had nearly hit their heads together, reaching for the sauce bottle, it must have looked quite funny. She wished now that she had laughed. That would have been the right moment to laugh, not the other moment. He would have been able to join in. They could have laughed at themselves, together.

But they had not, just pretended nothing was happening. She supposed it was like that, on a *date*. Especially a *first date*. She caught herself thinking, *next time*.

As she turned on to the main road, a truck passed with *John & Kevin Ridgely, Water Bores* painted along the side in curly writing. He had said his wife called him a *bridge bore*. She knew without having to ask that he was divorced. Something about the way he said it. *My wife*. She could tell him about *John and Kevin Ridgely, Water Bores*. He seemed like the kind of man you could make that sort of joke with.

Late afternoon was easing its way into evening, out here where the sky took up so much space. The shadows were starting to lengthen and above her a flock of cockatoos was creaking along through the sky. Where the sun was lowering itself towards the horizon, small elegant clouds had lined themselves up and were preparing to turn pink.

There's the view, he had said, as if she might have overlooked it, and had made a grand undulating gesture of his palm like an opera singer.

Remembering, she laughed aloud.

CHAPTER 20

FELICITY LIKED THE Defoliant Masque. You put it on and then you lay on the couch with the blinds drawn and behind it you could be somewhere else for a little while. She dabbed it on thickly, being careful not to pull at the skin of her face. The Masque smelled of avocadoes, but looked like plaster. The whiteness of it made her eyes look rather dreadful: yellow round the whites, and unfriendly. They stared at her coldly.

She knew it was her own face, of course. Who else could it belong to?

Alfred Chang, or Freddy, had been very cordial. He had not been *inscrutable* at all. He had a nice smile. You had to hand it to the Chinese, they always had good teeth.

Through the gap in the shirt she had not only seen his neat little navel, but also a feathery line of black hair coming up from inside the frayed jeans. Further down, behind the ragged fly, the hair would be thick, of course, like a little nest for what lay in it.

Above the basin the mask watched, staring back blankly from the mirror. She met its eyes boldly. No one would ever need to know what it was thinking. Not even herself.

He had kept on pulling up the zip on his jeans, where it

was ragged, right in front of her. He had not seemed to know he was doing it. He did not even turn away. He pulled up the zip, and every time he pulled it up she could see the big bold bulge.

She had no idea why she kept on thinking about the zip on Freddy Chang's jeans.

Her plaster reflection did not know, either.

Suddenly, for no reason at all, she remembered what Linda McLennan had told her at school about Chinese people. Actually Linda had not called them *Chinese*, but something else, but it would be racist to remember what it was. She had told her that Chinese *did it* through a hole in the sheet. Linda had made a circle with her thumb and finger, to demonstrate. *Just big enough, you know, for the man's thing.*

She cleared her throat and felt the Defoliant Masque crack.

You could put a patch over the ragged part, but it would be tricky, with the thickness of fabric in that particular area. It could be a mistake. A patch could have the opposite of the intended effect. It might actually draw attention to the zip, rather than the reverse. It might draw attention to the whole groin – or *loin* – area. A sort of codpiece effect.

Thinking about it, she felt something in her own *loin* area, a sort of heat or weakness, a little melting-away sort of sensation. The Defoliant Masque stared back. It did not know what she was talking about.

You would need to take off the jeans first, of course, if you wanted to patch them.

Even with the Defoliant Masque she did not like to meet the eyes in the mirror when she thought about the taking-off of the jeans.

She went to the fridge and got out two slices of cucumber and lay on the couch with them on her eyelids. They were cool and heavy and made you feel as if you did not want to move, as if your body was a large clumsy appendage attached to you.

Behind the eyelids, her blood ebbed and flowed, ripples and currents of greater darkness through the darkness. She had already set the little alarm clock. Now she could simply give herself up to the blind world behind the cucumbers. There was a ragged fly there that bulged, and when you touched it, it fell open, simply fell open, and there it was, the thing that had been making it bulge. She went through it again, just to be sure. There was the ragged fly, and it fell open, and there it was. She could feel it on her own body, pressing against her warmly, insistently, hard but soft as well. It moved against her and made her melt from the centre out, melt right away into the darkness.

Later, the cucumber slices were flabby on her face and the Defoliant Masque felt gritty. She filled the basin with warm water and splashed it up over her face, feeling the Masque running off, taking the dead cells and the *toxins* with it. *Exfoliation* was the technical term. She was *exfoliating* herself. She let the water out and without opening her eyes refilled the basin with cooler water, splashing again and again until she had washed away every last remnant of the old face.

With her eyes still closed, she patted her face dry with the special super-soft towel. Then she opened them. There she was in the mirror.

There was always a little moment of disappointment. It

was never quite the transformation you hoped for, when the Defoliant Masque came off. It was simply her own face, still, and the eyes that stared back at her out of it knew all about her, all her little secrets.

He had told her to come back on Friday for the quilt. She would take William to school, and then go straight across, first thing. It would not look as if she was impatient. It was only sensible, rather than make two trips.

When she had given him the quilt bag, he had put one hand on her wrist and the other on his chest, where his heart might have been. *I'll guard it with my life*, he had said, and she had laughed again as if it was terribly witty, to cover the funny feeling of his fingers holding her wrist.

She smoothed the moisturiser gently into her cheeks and around her mouth, stroking upwards on her neck. She was not going to think about him any more. In particular, she was not going to think about the frayed zip of his jeans.

CHAPTER 21

THE SCONE, AND more especially the cream on the scone, had tasted funny in spite of being so small, and by the morning after the *date*, Harley had a fierce headache that had her left eyeball in a burning grip, and she had already been sick twice. It appeared that it was the *attack of gastric* that she had conjured into being the day of the barbecue.

She rang the Mini-Mart, and Leith promised to send a boy up with some tablets, and she crawled back into bed, a sick animal hiding itself away in its burrow. Outside, the cicadas whirred away indifferently, as if from another world altogether.

All she could remember of her *date* now, apart from the scone that was just about killing her, was how full of pathetic elation she had been, how she had behaved like a lovely young girl on a *date*, not an old trout too dangerous to be let out. She hated herself for that singing on the way home. Who did she think she was, some peach-cheeked girl?

She squirmed in the bed, feeling the sheets creased and tangled underneath her, punishing herself with thoughts of how she had taken his hand in hers and turned it over, looking at the ring. He had probably thought she was keen on him, and looking for an excuse to touch. He had been polite about it, and not snatched his hand away, but he must have wondered. Her face felt hot and swollen, thinking about it.

She could not get the picture of Douglas Cheeseman out of her mind. She tossed angrily in the bed, trying to erase his face. He had a little tuft of hair that stuck up at the back, where he could not see it. She couldn't stop thinking about it now. You could see that he brushed the front part very carefully, but the tuft stuck up obstinately, like a little flag with a message he was unaware of. Throughout their conversation her hand had wanted to smooth it down.

There was no getting away from the fact that she had been *interested*. That was the banal truth of the matter, as smug and insipid as a Hallmark card. It was foolish and grotesque, and it was dangerous, too.

It was like starting to slide down a slippery-dip: there was a point where you could still stop yourself. She was at that point. It was not too late to pull back, before gravity took over and everything went wrong.

The details of what went wrong were different every time, but one of the things she recognised was the feeling that *this time will be different*.

She had been *interested* in all of them at the start. With the first there had been a proper wedding, and a trip to the shops with her mother-in-law, a kindly woman puzzled by her son's choice in wives, to pick out the dinner service. She had never looked at plates before, felt too big to be safe in the china department, had felt the need to pretend that she knew how you made a pot roast. On the day of the wedding, looking at her big plain face in the mirror, not *jolie*, not even *jolie laide*, the whole thing had felt like a play she had found herself in by mistake.

In retrospect, you could have seen it coming.

The second, the one Freddy Chang reminded her of, had had a smile that fascinated her, that started at one corner of his mouth and moved slowly across. She had thought she would never tire of it, but it had become a tyrant in the end. It went with the *looking deep into her eyes*, and she began to feel choked by so much adoration of a person she knew was not herself, so lacking as she was in adorable qualities. He had tried to encourage her with her patchworks, but she had refused to be encouraged. *It's just craft*, she had said when he admired anything. *And anyway, it's no good.*

There was a certain logic in it when he put his hands around her neck and squeezed, one night, in sheer frustration. It was not a serious attempt at murder, but it gave them both a way out of a situation that had arrived at an impasse.

She had gone out and bought a big old car she had fallen in love with, glamorous but unreliable. It was in that car that she had met the third husband. Philip was inclined to be masterful. The car had stalled, yet again, on the middle of the Harbour Bridge, and would not re-start. She had got out in rage and smacked the bonnet with the flat of her hand, and kept on smacking it until Philip had stopped his car and got out and taken hold of her wrist. *I'm a doctor*, he had said in his fruity, confident voice. *Stop that at once.*

She had married him for that fruity, confident voice, and for that calmness. He never got upset, never showed anger, never shouted. Even when she clumsily broke the special chair with the tricky turned legs he had half-made in the shed, or chipped his best chisel, he was never angry. It was almost unnatural, the way he never lost his temper. He considered it a sign of weakness. *Losing control,* he called it when other people did it. *Losing control* was something he never did, not even right up to the very last second. The way he kept such a tight grip, even on planning his own intricate death, had always been one of the worst things about it. In a way he was still in control, even now, having presented her with a fact she could do nothing about, the indigestible fact of his suicide.

Taking his own life was the phrase people used. *He took his own life.* It made it sound almost reasonable. But they had not been there.

When the doorbell rang she sat up in bed and swung her feet out, dragging her way into her dressing-gown. The sleeve got stuck against itself and the more she dragged at the neck the more trapped her hand was against a blind dead-end of fabric. Her jaw clenched tight and her lips flattened. She growled in her throat as she jerked at the wrapper, hearing herself snarl, a primitive enraged sound like a thwarted animal.

Finally the sleeve gave and her hand slid through. She lurched up from the bed, grabbed the edge of the sunroom door, hurried to the front door and opened it.

She had just enough time to see that it was not the boy from the Mini-Mart who stood there, but Douglas. She had a moment to notice how his hair was kinked in at the sides from where he must have been wearing his hat. Then the colour leached out of everything. He stood there with the kink in his hair and a funny look on his face, but he was in black and white.

There was a sideways slewing in her head, like lying down

drunk, a deep dangerous interior shifting and welling. It was like being a potful of jam after you poured in the sugar.

She felt her hand go up to her mouth, although the feeling was not quite localised in her mouth, or even her stomach.

If I close my eyes, she thought, it will be better. But closing her eyes brought the bright seething blackness closer and now her throat was somehow swelling, thickening. Beyond the man at the door she could see Lorraine Smart's parched front garden, flaring out as if overexposed, and now everything was so brilliantly white it was black.

She pushed roughly past him and was violently sick on Lorraine Smart's front path. She had wanted to get as far as the bush by the fence, but her body had had its own ideas.

He made her go back into the house, pushing her along with an arm around her.

I was sick too, he was saying. I just came. To see if you were all right.

She wanted to crawl in between her sheets and block him out, take her sickness and put it to bed in privacy. But he did not let her lie on the bed or put her head on the pillow. He had his arm around her and, somehow pushing with his hip, he was making her go over to the chair in the corner. He grabbed the back of it with his free hand and shook it like a dog so everything went on the floor: grey old bra, jeans, socks still in a concertina from where she'd ripped them off, a shoe that jumped and clattered.

You've got it worse than I did, he said. I'm terribly sorry.

She did not want to hear him being sorry.

Sit down there, he said. Go on.

She did as she was told, staring at the dust-balls eddying on the floorboards as he made the bed.

I thought it tasted funny, he said. I should have said something.

The bedclothes flew out smooth, cushioned on air, the way his wrists flicked at them.

It's my fault, he said. I'm sorry.

No, she said. Thank you.

She meant *Go away*.

There, he said. Get in there now.

He stood as she gathered the dressing-gown around herself and shuffled across to the bed.

I'll be all right, she said.

Just go away.

He was about to say something when the doorbell shrilled again. She shut her eyes. She heard him leave the room, heard a rumble of voices at the door.

In a minute he came back with a box of tablets and a clean glass of water.

Don't look after me, she said.

She had tried to think of a more gracious phrase. She thought she had thought of one. This was not what her mind had thought it had prepared, although it was exactly what she meant. But he did not take any notice. He put the glass down and went on pressing out pills.

No, he said.

He held out his hand and she took the pills from his palm and swallowed them.

I mean, she said, just leave me alone.

It seemed he had not heard her. Perhaps she had not spoken. He was gathering up the smudged glasses from the bedside table and going out of the room.

Now she could hear him out in the kitchen. She knew

just what it was like out there: the greasy water in the sink from yesterday where she had suddenly given up, the grey scum, the wet toast wallowing, the canted piles of crusted dishes and the lines of black ants threading in and out of a crack in the window-frame and over to the sugar scattered on the bread-board.

She made herself small in the bed, hating the thought of him seeing all that. There was a silence from the kitchen. She imagined him looking, wondering where to start. *Go,* she thought. *Just go.* It seemed unbearably intimate to have him looking at her squalor, fishing the wet toast out of her sink and smelling the rankness of her rubbish-bin. No amount of sex could ever be so intimate.

She heard him gently – so as not to disturb her, but she was tense, listening to the tiny noises – close the kitchen door. She could hear the little scratch as he unhooked the apron from the back of the door and the squeak of the cupboard door as he got out the detergent. The dirty water in the sink made a dreadful sucking sound as it ran through the plughole.

She listened as he washed the dishes. Then she heard him opening and shutting drawers, looking for a clean tea-towel. Then the clatter as he put everything away. Then there was another long silence.

She heard the scratch on the door again as he hung the apron back up, the squeak of the back door and the clatter of the rubbish-bin lid as he took the kitchen tidy outside to the bin and emptied it.

When she heard his steps come towards the sunroom door, she heaved over in the bed, pulling the sheet up around her ears. She was asleep, she was deaf, she was dead.

He tiptoed over to the bed and leaned over looking down at her. She could feel his gaze like a physical thing, urging its attention on her, but she squeezed her eyes shut tightly. *Go away,* she mouthed silently under the sheets.

At last she heard him tiptoe down the hall, open the front door with the long melodramatic creak it produced if you did it slowly, and shut it behind him.

When she woke up she knew she was better. On the kitchen bench was a note.

Back later on, it said, *to see how you are. My apologies again.*

D, it was signed, as if he was the only *D* she knew. It was like the note a husband might leave a wife. She stood looking at it. *How dare he,* she found herself thinking. *How dare he.*

She screwed it up angrily. The kitchen was reproachfully clean. Everywhere she looked she saw he had been there, wiping, arranging, cleaning. She was dizzy with the closeness of him, giddy with the intimacy of it. She was better, but she had to cling to the table with her fingers, overwhelmed by the feeling of him all around her, like a vacuum sucking her into itself.

If he comes back, she decided, *I won't open the door.*

But that would not work. He was the kind of man who would break the door down if he thought she might have fallen over unconscious in the bedroom. There would be no escaping him.

She felt hot, congested with the claustrophobia of it.

She would open the door, then, but only to say thank you. She would be cordial enough, but there would be no encouragement in the way she said it. If he tried to make conversation, she would go limp. *Yes*, she would say, and *No*, and *I'm not really sure*. She was not going to be rude. But she would not give him even the smallest sliver of herself.

He would get the hint eventually.

CHAPTER 22

WHEN HE CAME back later, birds were gathering for the night in a big incongruous date-palm in someone's back-yard. He knocked and waited, looking up into the tree. The bird book had not seemed like such a good idea in the end. He found it quite easy to imagine the jokes Chook would make about *birds*.

When she opened the door he saw straight away that she was better. She was civil enough, but did not ask him in. Actually, she did not even open the door very far, just talked to him around the edge of it.

Yes, she said, and *No*, and *not really*, and she said *thank you* a lot, in various ways. *Thank you so very much*, she said. *Thanks very much indeed*. Gripping the edge of the door between them, she said it over and over: *thank you, thanks, thank you very much*. He had brought her a bunch of grapes – cling-wrapped and squashy, but the best he could do in the Mini-Mart – but she waved them away. *I don't think so, thanks*, she said through the chink in the door.

Walking back down her path, he looked up into the date-palm again as if he was interested in the birds. He was, in a way, but not as interested as all that.

He had to take the grapes back to Room 8 and eat

them himself, sitting on the side of the bed, thinking about her.

She had seemed to like him at first. She had listened when he told her about concrete, not *glazed over* straight away. She had seemed genuinely interested.

But he had gone on too long about it, as usual, and she had picked him for a bore. The Panorama had not been a good choice, either, the sticky silence that had surrounded them, and the woman with the mop. A man with more imagination would have come up with something better.

He wished he had not told her about the Port Gordon Bridge. When he'd got to the bit about the stretcher, she laughed, although she tried to pretend she was just coughing.

She would go back to Sydney, and the man who had taken her out to tea in a cafe full of flies and got excited about concrete would just become a funny story for dinner-parties.

It was the thing about a little place like Karakarook: you kept seeing the same people over and over, and being reminded of how you had got it all wrong.

He did not really mean *the same people*. What he really meant was, *the same person*.

Standing beside a verandah-post outside the Caledonian – not exactly hiding, more just standing still – he saw her, the day after he had washed her dishes, coming out of the shop with the tins of paint in the window. He prepared a smile and even got his hand up for a sort of wave. But she got into her car without even glancing in his direction. He waved away a fly that was not there and stood squinting across the road. As she turned her head to reverse out he saw the strong tendon in the side of her neck and her stern profile. He watched the brown Datsun all the way down Parnassus Road, until it took the corner at St Brendan's fast enough to make the pigeons flutter up in fright from the ridgepole.

A day or two later he'd seen her coming out of the Acropolis with the paper under her arm, frowning, the dog at her heels, and later the same day outside the Mechanics' Institute, looking huge beside a tiny woman in tight jeans, waving away the flies and nodding at what the woman was telling her.

Today, here she was standing with the butcher outside his shop. He watched as she made some kind of big humorous gesture that made the butcher laugh, his black hair gleaming like onyx in the sun.

He could see that she had not wasted any time in making herself at home in Karakarook. He felt a sort of helpless admiration for the way she was able to have a conversation with the butcher that was obviously not about meat. It looked as if it was more fun than a conversation about creep.

He watched her hand draw the joke on the air and remembered the way those fingers had felt, taking his hand, turning it over, looking at his ring. He must have bored her silly about the ring. As if she would be interested. At least he had not gone on about Kipling.

He saw her, and on several other occasions he thought he did. He waved at a woman coming out of the bank one day, a man-shaped sort of woman, big torso, broad shoulders, skinny legs. He waved, and actually broke into a sort of eager trot, but as she turned to open the door of her car, he saw it was not her. He dropped his hand and stood watching as she reversed out and drove away, reading her bumper sticker: OUR BALLS ARE BIGGER, with a picture of a soccer ball.

It was not really anything like her, and he felt a fool, running.

He did not think she had noticed him, on any of the occasions he had watched her. He knew he was not a very noticeable kind of man, being more the kind who faded into the background.

Marjorie had always bought him neutrals. *So handy*, she had said. *Go with anything*. Now he was here on Parnassus Road, Karakarook, *going with* the peeling paint of the Caledonian. He had never minded, before, being such a neutral sort of man. But watching Harley Savage stride purposefully, gesture decisively, laugh in that big confident way, he wished he could find it in himself to be a different and less invisible kind of man.

Chapter 23

On Friday, Freddy was waiting for Felicity at the top of the stairs. It was funny seeing him again, after thinking about him the way she had been.

She turned her thoughts away quickly from the precise way in which she had been thinking about him.

He was smaller than she remembered, as if her mind's eye had made him swell. She had started to think of him as quite a tall man, but here he was, smiling in that way he had, and not much taller than she was herself.

She had been right about how muscular he was, though, the way his shoulders were padded with little packets of muscle. And, although she was not even going to glance at them, she could see that he was wearing the same frayed jeans.

She was not quite herself with him today. She smiled her nice smile and said, *Oh, hello!* in the way she said *Oh, hello!* to anyone, but somehow there was a *Freddy Chang* who had taken up residence in her mind now, the personal, private *Freddy Chang* who made her melt away behind her cucumbers. But that *Freddy Chang* was not the same as this *Freddy Chang*. This *Freddy Chang* did not know anything about the things that other *Freddy Chang* got up to in the privacy of her own mind, and it was important not to mix the two of them up.

She would keep it cheerful, friendly, wholesome. He would never know, and she did not have to know either, really, about her own, private *Freddy Chang*.

Mrs Porcelline, he said.

It was a kind of smiling sigh. He did not seem to mind being in love with someone he could not have. *Unattainable.* A lot of men went for a woman who was *unattainable.*

Come along through, Mrs Porcelline, he said. Just stay close to me, it's a bit on the dark side.

He went off fast ahead of her, chunky but nimble, like someone doing ballroom dancing: *step to the left, step to the right.* He did not look back to see if she was following. She tried to match him step for step, so close she could smell the chalky cotton of his shirt, and something warm and fleshy underneath it. He was so close she could have touched his back with her hand. When she followed him around a partition, the last dim light was cut off and in the total blackness she ran straight into his back.

Oh! Sorry!

My fault, Mrs Porcelline, he said, or whispered. Should have warned you what was coming.

Then there was nothing, just rustlings and small metallic noises and something that might have been a grunt. The darkness enclosed her like water, fitting itself snugly around every fold of her body. In the dead blackness it was harder to remember that the *Freddy* she had at home in her mind was not the same as the *Freddy* who was here with her now, somewhere, doing something. You could imagine – *one* could imagine, not exactly she herself – that he was taking his

clothes off. There was the tiny dragging noise of the belt
being undone. And now the rustle of the button at the top
of the ragged zip.

Behind the zip was, well, the thing that lived behind his
zip, that made it bulge, that wore it out from bulging, so
that it needed patching. The idea of Freddy Chang's zip had
a very familiar feel in her mind, as if the thought had been
used over and over again, in every possible way, up and
down, quickly and slowly, in the dark, in sunlight, with talking, without talking.

She caught herself thinking about it now, but it was all
right, because no one could see what she was thinking.

Suddenly light burst down from a high lamp. She cried
out from the shock of it, flinched away covering her eyes.

Oh! she heard herself gasp. Oh, help!

But his clothes were still all done up tight, and he
was not even looking at her, and turned away, reaching
up to tilt the lamp so the hard white light burned down
sideways.

They were in a space she had not seen before, an office
in an alcove of screens. There was a desk and a filing cabi-
net, and a typist's chair with a rip down the middle of the
seat, and a couch covered in beige vinyl. He took a big
manilla envelope from the desk and gave it to her. When he
had finished giving it to her, and she had finished taking it,
he went on standing very close to her, as if the envelope was
made of glass and he was waiting to catch it if it fell.

Tell me what you think.

He was close enough that he really only had to whisper.

She tried not to fumble, getting the envelope open, feeling him watching her hands.

The photos of Great-Grandmother Ferguson's quilt were very professional-looking. The quilt looked rich and sump-tuous, and did not show a single pucker or shadow. He had laid out the scalloped edge so the slight irregularity did not show at all. Only someone who knew, such as Great-Grandmother Ferguson, but she was dead, and herself, but she was not telling, and now Freddy Chang, who had made sure no one would know, would ever guess that the quilt was not absolutely, perfectly square.

Lovely! she exclaimed. Perfect!

He had come around next to her, looking over her shoul-der at the prints.

He was so close, he was almost cheek-to-cheek.

He did not seem to be aware of how close he was. He was innocently engrossed in the photos, a purely professional interest. She should not be thinking of the fact that if he turned his face towards her, he would be able to stick his tongue right into her ear.

In fact, she was definitely not thinking that.

Perfect, she said again.

She shuffled through the pictures, trying to think of what to say to fill the silence.

Not a single wrinkle, she said.

She had not really meant to use the word *wrinkle*. There was another word, but she could not think of it.

She heard herself laugh, that laugh she did with Freddy Chang.

Not wrinkle, she said. More, well . . .

But having got so far, she could not think of any word but *wrinkle*. Somehow, the word *wrinkle* was stuck in her mind, and for some reason, along with the word *wrinkle*, was a picture of Freddy Chang's, well, *organ*, a neat little folded thing soft in its nest of hair, its *wrinkles* slowly smoothing out as it swelled and filled.

She peered more closely at the quilt and pushed her hair back behind her ear. It fell forward again and she was glad to feel it like a screen hiding her cheek. She smiled in the way she knew looked girlish, glad, innocent. From trying it in the mirror she knew it was the kind of smile that gave her a sweet little dimple.

A person with a dimple like that would only have the most wholesome thoughts.

Crease, of course. That was the word she should have used. Not *wrinkle*.

Crease, she said.

It sounded rather loud.

Crease, I mean.

There was a long silence. She could feel her fingers slimy on the gloss of the photos as she stared at the quilt and its lack of *creases*.

Yes, he said casually, as if continuing an earlier conversation. I get a bit of use out of the couch, as a matter of fact.

They both looked at it.

The couch was a terrible old thing. The vinyl was the kind that stuck to the backs of your legs if you sat on it with a short skirt. At one end there was a small dingy cushion. It was quite safe to look at it, because no one would think *casting couch* of this cheap old thing. No one would think, *You would have to get on top of each other.*

She could not seem to think about anything but two bodies on the couch. It would hardly be wide enough for two. The more she tried to think about something else, the more she thought about it.

But it was all right. No one would know as long as you kept on smiling nicely.

More relaxing than you might think, he said.

It was not that Freddy Chang was being suggestive. He was just talking about how you could have a nap there in the middle of the day when business was slow downstairs. Any other possible meanings were purely in her own mind. That mind of hers seemed to be getting away from her.

Suddenly he took hold of her elbow. She could feel his whole warm palm, cupping her elbow.

Know what *Karakarook* means? he asked.

His thumb was pressing a dent into the flesh of her upper arm.

Oh! No! she cried. How do you mean?

She was confused by the closeness of him, the way he was gripping her arm, almost hard enough to hurt, the heat coming up out of his palm, into her elbow. And what was he talking about?

Elbow, he said, and took hold of her other arm, cupping the elbow there as well. It brought him around in front of her, very close. It was as if they were about to start dancing, except there was no music to make it all right.

In the Aboriginal language. Karakarook – means elbow.

She could actually feel the heat coming off him, he was so close.

Oh! she exclaimed again.

She was blushing under the lights. Her whole body felt as if it was one big hot blush. But it was all right. He probably could not see, or if he did he would just think it was just blusher. He could probably not tell the difference between blusher and a blush.

She felt his fingers slide up her arm, under the sleeve of the pink blouse. His fingers pressed into the flesh there as if he was playing the piano, but his face did not show anything in particular, although he was not being particularly *inscrutable* either.

It was as if his fingers were secretively spelling out one kind of thing, while his face was doing something else.

She had replaced the buttons on this particular blouse with some that she had thought were more attractive and they had turned out to be just a little tight in the button-holes. It meant that it had become a bit hard to undo the buttons.

She could not imagine why she was thinking about that just at this moment.

Because of the way the river bends, he said.

One of his knees was pressing against her leg, edging itself between her thighs. He seemed unaware of it, telling her the little detail of local geography. It would seem as if she had a dirty mind, if she told him to stop. *Stop what, Mrs Porcelline?* His face registered no knowledge of what his sly knee was doing, and what her sly mind was noticing.

Like an elbow, he said.

He was so close she could feel the puffs of air on her cheek as he spoke.

Know what I mean?

She was losing the thread of this conversation. What did he mean, *Know what I mean?*

In spite of herself, her legs were slowly parting under the gentle insistence of his knee. It was as if her legs were no

longer under her control. Part of her was busy trying con-
scientiously to work out what he meant by *Know what I
mean*, but another part of her was doing this other thing.

My word it's bright in here, she blurted out suddenly,
loudly.

He let go of one of her elbows, leaned sideways and
reached up roughly to switch off a lamp so it reeled on its
stalk.

Better, Mrs Porcelline?

CHAPTER 24

HARLEY WAS DRIVING the old Singer like a car with a dubious gearbox, riding it hard. The table shook, the floor rumbled from the hammering of the machine. Her knee shoved at the worn metal lever, her hands flew between the wheel at the side and the fabric, pushing it through, dragging the thread down against the blade at the back, snapping it off.

The patchwork was like a dark pelt spilling into her lap as she turned and flipped and folded. All the small squares and rectangles of fabric drank the light. Even the extra, yellow light beaming down over the needle did not make the fabric bright.

She had covered several of the mirrors with towels, but the room was still full of reflections like pools of glimmering water. Every time she moved she glimpsed an answering shadowy movement, a flickering from all around the room.

Something made a noise outside the window and she glanced around quickly, over her shoulder. Her reflections in the mirrors all glanced around quickly too, a crowd in the room with her, furtive, stopping when she looked at them. She sat rigid, listening. The reflections were still, but she knew they were there, watching.

She sighed and held up the patchwork. To her it was

obviously inspired by the shapes of an old wooden bridge. But to anyone else it would probably just look like something gone wrong. Stitched up next to each other, the pieces all looked the same: the *lights* and the *darks* all looked dirty and drab under the yellow light. The whole thing was shapeless, puckered, a wounded creature with a sad brown look. It bulged along the edges, thick and lumpy. The seams did not quite line up. It was *on purpose*, of course, but no one in Karakarook was likely to know that.

Outside in the big rough country night, the dog was standing, waiting for her to feed it. It did not bark or whine, but she knew it was there, waiting to be fed, still patient, still optimistic, even though the square of the kitchen window was black now, all the noises and smells of dinner gone.

She had thought it was enough to be neutral with the dog. She had thought that was possible: to be neutral. She had never hit it, but she did not pat it either. It was true that she bought it dogfood, but only ever one tin at a time. She had let it rest its chin on the seat-back beside her as she drove, but she had never given it a name.

However, she could see now that there was no such thing as being neutral with a dog. A dog had an all-or-nothing approach, and to this dog, *just this once* was the same as *for ever and ever*.

She could see she should have been firm with it from the start. That very first day, she should not have let it get into the car. She should have handed the problem to Coralie then and there. *It's not my dog*, she should have said. *I don't want it.*

She supposed she had been flattered by the dog's attention,

the way it had chosen her, the way it seemed to like her. She told herself, grimly, forcing the fabric along under the needle, that it was naive to think it liked her. *Sucked in*, as the tough boys down at the school would say. It was just that she was the one who opened the tin of dogfood. As far as the dog was concerned, she was just an elaborate extension of the tin opener.

She had let herself be flattered, and now she was stuck with a situation she should never have allowed to develop. The thing was, there was no way you could explain to a dog. You could not say, *I was wrong to encourage you*, politely but firmly. You could not say, *Thanks so much, but I have had enough of you now*.

The solution was to stop feeding it, and she was going to start tonight. For a while it would think that she had simply forgotten. It would wait patiently. She had learned how patient it could be. In the morning it would be hungry, and by tomorrow afternoon it would be extremely hungry. Some time tomorrow night, or at the worst the day after, it would finally get the hint.

There was a rustling close by outside, then a dull tap and a swish. Then nothing, only distant noises: the frogs again, some kind of plaintive honking, and far over in Karakarook North, a tiny distant squeal of tyres on a corner and a thin faraway car horn.

She felt herself straining to hear the small nearby sounds. When she turned her head deliberately to meet herself in the nearest mirror she saw how pale her face was against the room full of shadows behind her. Lit from below by the yellow light of the Singer, her face was stern with listening too hard: cruel, angular, her eyes shadowed, inhuman, unfeeling. She did not intend to look that way, but she did.

The roof gave a loud creak, then another. It was like slow footsteps.

She wished now that she had not mentioned the bridge patchwork to Coralie. Donna's pieces had got her excited, but everything looked good in the beginning. It was only later, putting the pieces together, that it turned into something less than you had hoped. It seemed she would never learn that was the way things always were.

It made it worse at the end, if you had been eager in the beginning. It was better never to be enthusiastic.

Coralie would be understanding. She could imagine her coming close, putting her hand on her arm, the way she did. *Not to worry, pet,* she would say. *No worries.*

But she did not want to be understood. She had to go on. There was no use hoping to make it different now, or better. It would simply have to go on being what it was.

She bowed her head to the Singer again, head down like an animal, feeling all her obstinacy driving her on. She worked quickly, fitting her corners together, lining up her seam allowances just slightly off, pressing the seams open. The shapes repeated themselves under the yellow light: *light, dark, light, dark.* She set her mouth hard round the pins and felt her cheeks shake as she jerked the threads down hard and snapped them off. She caught sight of herself again in one of the mirrors: her mouth was sardonic with the pins bristling between her lips, her face fierce, her shoulders angry.

She got up abruptly and went over to the black square of window to try to close the curtain that never worked properly. She felt exposed and ridiculous, standing in the window as if on a stage, pulling at it. She jerked hard, something gave with a bang, the way it always did, and the curtain slid reluctantly across.

Outside she heard the dog bark once, a deep confident bark. That was its way of reminding her. Just the one courteous little bark. Just to let her know it was still there, still hungry.

Instead of going back to the discouraging heap of fabric on the table, she sat down on the couch. She was upright, polite, like a visitor. Lorraine Smart had been reading a glossy magazine with ARE YOU HAPPY? on the cover. She flipped through the pages. Happy faces smiled back at her, holding casseroles and babies, telling her about Virgo's February, being pleased with their lipstick.

You could do a quiz to see if you were HAPPY, but Harley did not do that. When she came to that page, she turned quickly on.

No, she wanted to tell someone. No, I am not happy.

It was silly, and she would not, but she wanted to cry.

Later, trying to sleep, she lay on Lorraine Smart's lumpy daybed, watching the sky outside the window. It was like the sleepout at Gran's: *inside*, but *outside* too. The stars were big, close, busy twinkling away to each other. In the country, looking up at the sky at night, it was hard not to start thinking about eternity. Thinking about eternity was supposed to bring on calm and cosmic thoughts. It was supposed to be good for *unwinding* you.

It did not seem to be having that effect. She lay stiffly staring into the dark, trying to breathe evenly. With the light off, the night was suddenly full of many small surreptitious noises. There were rustlings and swishings that could be the sound of wind in the leaves. But they could also be the anxious and unhappy small noises made by a hungry dog ranging around the backyard, wondering what it had done wrong.

She hoped it had given up when it saw the last light go out, and was lying down now on its sack, preparing for sleep in spite of its empty stomach. She hoped it was not still standing out there, ears pricked forward, tail poised ready to wag, watching the back door for her to appear there with the chipped enamel plate and the tin of Pal.

She lay on her back, clenching her fists. *Tight, tight, tighter.* Something in the backyard made a sharp snap. *And relax.*

Her neck was rigid with the strain of holding herself still, listening. She felt she had become one big ear, swivelled out into the backyard.

Tight, tight, tighter.

She could feel her fingernails digging into the palm of her hand.

And relax.

Her hand was *relaxed*, but the rest of her was not. She was getting a cramp in one leg from trying so hard to *relax*.

It was a relief to fling back the covers and go out to the kitchen. The light sprang on so harshly she had to cover her eyes. The door of the cupboard banged angrily as she got out the tin of Pal, the giant size, big enough for a whole kennelful of dogs. The Mini-Mart had *just sold the last* of all the smaller tins.

She opened the door and her shadow, very black, zigzagged away from her feet down the back steps, the light behind her sending a frail yellow wash out into the blackness of the backyard.

The dog came up out of the shadows straight away, not

at all surprised, right up the steps to her feet. It waved its tail, panted, shifted from paw to paw, backing clumsily down in front of her, one step at a time, turning on each to make sure she was still there. She held the green enamel plate up in the air and pushed at the dog with the side of her foot. She did not exactly kick it, but it had to move quickly.

At the foot of the steps it turned and stood staring up at her so intently it forgot to go on wagging its tail. It smacked its mouth closed with a slurp of its tongue and cocked its head sideways at her. Its eyes went from her face to the plate and back again.

When she put the plate down on the square of pink concrete under the Hill's Hoist, the dog was on it before it touched the ground. It ate in ugly gulps, jerking the food down. Even after the food was gone, it went on licking the plate so hard it was pushed around and around the square of pink concrete with a desperate scraping noise. Finally the plate was clean, smeared only with dog spit, the pink concrete dabbed with darker patches where its tongue had gone looking for every crumb. Then it looked up at her with its ears pricked so hard it looked painful.

It was the look of *adoration* that filled her with a kind of panic.

No, she said.

It was the first time she had said anything to the dog. Its tail beat faster, backwards and forwards.

No! she said, louder.

The dog did not seem to realise that *no* was a rejection. It only knew the difference between words and not-words. As far as the dog was concerned, a *no* was just as good as a *yes:* it was a *conversation.*

She jabbed into the tin with a spoon, raking out another plateful. *All right then*, she thought angrily. *Take that, then.* When the dog had eaten that, she scraped out another, thumping the spoon furiously on the plate. *All right, go on.* Then a third. Still the dog gulped the food down, chased the plate around the concrete with its tongue, panted up at her for more. She stabbed angrily at the last of the red jelly in the tin, slopping it furiously out on to the plate. *Take it then, if you want it so much. Go on.* This time the dog only sniffed and mumbled at the food. Suddenly it bucked, jerked, and on a hoarse abrupt bark brought it all up.

The bird started up again with the only words it had. *Come here! Come here, Johnny! Johnny!*

She made a disgusted grunt and hurled the empty tin at the fence. The bird squawked once and was silent.

In the grass near the steps, a cricket went on blandly. *Tickticktick ticktick ticktickticktickticktick.*

Back in bed, she thought of the dog, hungry again, sniffing at its vomit out in the dark. She could imagine the puzzled look it would have. She imagined it coming up to the steps, looking up, meek, silent, prepared to wait.

She thought of herself, vengefully hacking the dog food out of the tin. It was always like that when things turned into *relationships*. Where there were relationships there was no avoiding *meanness, malice, fear, guilt*. Every kind of *danger*.

She lay awake for a long time. It was a hot night, but her feet seemed cold.

*

CHAPTER 25

IT HAD BEEN Coralie's idea to put up partitions in the Mechanics' Institute to make a series of little bays, each one like a real kitchen or bedroom or laundry. The partitions were up now, and so were the shelves and benches. There was a smell of fresh paint from where Harley and Coralie had done them. They had had to leave the blue and pink ceiling because it was too high to deal with, but at eye level it was all white now, ready for the exhibits.

Harley was doing the labels today, a boring job, but people took things more seriously if they had a proper professional-looking label. Coralie had brought an ancient typewriter to do them with that was almost a historical artefact in itself. Sometimes with the museum business it was hard to know where to stop.

Coralie had made a chocolate cake for them to eat before they started, but when she cut it, it was still runny in the middle.

Not to worry, she said. Eat it with spoons, that's all.

She had brought a bottle of Pimm's, too.

Thought we needed a bit of keeping up our strength, you know, while we work.

Outside a harsh dry wind rattled something on the roof

and a branch kept tapping against the high windows. The Pimm's made a cheerful party sound as she splashed it into the glasses.

Harley took a swallow and coughed.

Like it, do you? Coralie said. I'm partial to a Pimm's on a hot day.

Mrs Trimm's range had been fitted by Leith's husband into the HEARTH AND HOME room, with a wooden mantelpiece over it. The effect was very convincing. Mrs Trimm's range was called REX in black bas-relief, the way Gran's had been AGA. Harley imagined them: *Agatha* and *Rex*, having their Golden Wedding Anniversary.

AND SO TO BED had the narrow sapling stretcher, and the butter-box cradle and the fruit-box dressing-table with the cretonne ruching. There was a strange yellow velvet object with a hard triangular base, that had come with a note in tremulous old-lady's handwriting explaining that it was the jawbone of a Tasmanian Tiger made into a pincushion. That sat on the chest of drawers made of kerosene tins, and up on the wall behind it was a picture of a rather podgy kangaroo made of little brown things glued on to a sheet of wood. Harley had thought at first they were pellets of sheep shit, but they turned out to be gumnuts.

More was on its way. A baby's high chair from butter-boxes had been promised, and a Coolgardie cool-safe. Someone called Pearlie had promised an original jute-bag wagga, and someone else out near Badham had sent word through Coralie that she had a pair of boots home-made by her great-grandfather, mended with nails, and did that count as Heritage?

There would be more than they could ever display, but Freddy Chang was doing well with the photos. He seemed to have really thrown himself into it. Sometimes, now, when she passed the shop, she saw the sign propped up in the window: *Closed. Back 3 p.m.*

Hope Freddy's business isn't suffering, Harley said. He's always in the darkroom, by the look of it.

But Coralie laughed, fanning herself with a big glossy photo of a boomerang-shaped doily.

I wouldn't worry, pet, she said. Some of us have got a fair idea what goes on at lunch time in Freddy's dark room.

She was careful to make it two words.

Know what I mean, pet?

A blowfly came at them out of nowhere, buzzed the cake, settled for an instant on Coralie's hair, zigzagged away and burred against a window. Outside, Harley could hear the wind going on and on.

Chook and I came courting here, Coralie said suddenly. He had a key and that, from being in the woodchop team.

She stood up and smoothed her skirt down over her hips, looking around the hall.

Used to come here and pash in the dark.

She sat down again and poured herself another Pimm's.

I thought he was that good-looking. He's thickened out now, type of thing. Plus he was a bit of a hero, being State Champ.

She sipped at her Pimm's as though it were hot.

Do anything with an axe, made a toothpick for a bet once. But he's not much of a conversationalist. Not at home. And I like a chat, type of thing.

She glanced at Harley.

Plus I'm a stickybeak, as you know.

She swallowed Pimm's and smothered a burp.

Pardon me. Now you're not a stickybeak, are you?

But, not waiting for Harley to find an answer, she got up and went across the hall to where the blowfly was hysterical against the glass, pulled the cord that worked the high window. Suddenly the fly was gone. It left a large silence behind.

Now, pet, she said, and Harley felt the familiar little pulse of apprehension.

Have a look here.

She had something tied up in a sugar-bag.

Made it for Chook to take rabbiting, she said. Donkey's years ago.

Her strong short fingers were being patient with the knot in the string at the neck of the bag.

Not that he rabbits much any more, she said. Anyway, we've gone over to the Dacron now.

She reached into the bag with both arms and pulled out a clot of fabric: a bush quilt, pieces of faded fabric over something lumpy inside.

There's Auntie Em's blue coat, and there's my pink dress I got from Farmer's.

She touched the square of pink flowered cotton.

My word I loved that dress.

The back was made up of squares of calico with a picture of a big red flower and the words *Wagga Lily Flour* stencilled on each piece. The stitches had come apart in the middle so you could see what was inside.

Woolly socks were good, Coralie said. Open them out flat, the tops, where they weren't worn.

There it was, a grey sock-top with a maroon stripe.

Everything had been flattened out and roughly tacked down on to the backing with big looping stitches.

The kids wanted me to chuck it out, Coralie said. Mum, they says, it's a dirty old thing, get rid of it.

Once on the sapling bed it looked less lumpy, and you could see how the big piece of *the dress from Farmer's* balanced the various pieces of *Auntie Em's coat*.

They stood admiring it. Coralie thought it should go the other way up, so they turned it round and stood back to admire it again. Then Coralie turned towards her with a flash of her glasses.

What did you think of the Panorama, anyhow? she said casually. My niece, that's my sister's Janelle, she works up there now. Just part-time.

She tweaked at a pucker, leaving a convenient silence.

Harley felt herself warming visibly with a blush that started in her chest and spread evenly outwards like a stain in water. She remembered the way she had cannoned into the table, the way he had fussed about the tea, the silences that had fallen between them. Janelle could have made it into a good story. *Oh, yes, definitely made for each other*, she could imagine Janelle saying, and everyone laughing. *Definitely love at first sight.*

Under new management, Coralie said at last. But Janelle says it's just the same as the old lot.

There was a silence in which Coralie waited. The wind was snapping something against the roof. *Tap, tap, taptaptap.*

I saw him, you know, Coralie said. Outside the pub.

Harley bent over the bedcover, smoothing down a lump that sprang back up as she flattened it.

Who do you mean? she said, although she was afraid she knew. He. Who, he?

Hearing herself, she wondered if the Pimm's might have been a bit of a mistake.

The bloke from the Roads Department, Coralie said. That you went up to the Panorama with.

Again she held open an inviting silence.

You didn't see him, she went on at last. But I did. I got a good look at the way he was watching you.

The tapping on the roof was irritating. Harley kept wanting to look around, even though she knew there was nothing there.

Oh, him! she said. That was nothing.

She went back to the table and sat down at the old typewriter.

It was nothing, she repeated, rolling one of the index cards in. Nothing at all.

It might have come out vehement, she was trying so hard to make it casual. The letters on the yellowed keys seemed supernaturally crisp as she concentrated on them. QWERTY. UIOP.

Coralie came over and put the Pimm's away in the basket.

I better stop, that Pimm's is knocking me right out.

She picked up their glasses, but did not go anywhere with them.

Seems a nice enough bloke in himself.

Behind her all the inquisitive citizens of Karakarook, all 1374 of them, were waiting to hear what she would say.

I helped him out, that was all, Harley tried.

The whole of Karakarook would know that he had come to the house, too, because of the boy from the Mini-Mart. She stopped herself explaining further: *but it was only to see if the scone had made me sick too.* That would make it sound as if it mattered.

He wanted to thank me. It was nothing important.

The hall seemed very quiet, the air expectant. The tapping was loud and urgent.

Coralie took off her glasses and polished them on the hem of her skirt.

Well, she said. In that case.

She put the glasses back on and looked at Harley.

In that case, you might want to come in with us on the petition. About the bridge.

She hesitated.

We're going to go out there. In a body, type of thing, to give it to him. Plus a blockade, if we have to.

It seemed she was not satisfied with the glasses. She took them off, breathed on the lenses, polished them once more. Harley could see the way they shone in the light when she put them back on.

We thought, you know, it might put you in a difficult position, type of thing, if you and him, you know.

No, Harley cried. Not in the least!

In the gaunt space of the hall it sounded very loud and angry.

Well, Coralie said. That's all right then.

Harley could feel another expectant little silence developing. She drew the list quickly towards her and started typing, keeping her head down.

SOUP LADLE, about 1890

A labour of love. Without meaning to, she gave a scornful little snort at the idea, and felt Coralie look at her enquiringly. She kept her head down.

STEEL FILE, BRASS RIVETS, TIN.

Then she saw that the label was upside down, the lined

side of the card showing. She ripped it out of the machine with a harsh ratcheting and tore it up.

Suddenly there was knocking, loud and peremptory, against the front door of the hall. Harley got up so quickly from the table that she hit her leg against the corner.

Whoops! Coralie said, and watched as she strode down towards the door.

She got her face ready for him. *No thank you, not today.* He had a nerve, chasing her all around town. Who did he think he was?

But when she opened the door, there was no one out there wanting to get in to talk to her, only the wind jerking at a loose piece of fibro. She stepped out and looked up and down the road. Parnassus Road gaped back at her. A drink-can rattled its way steadily along the gutter, driven by the wind.

She waited, but no one appeared in either direction. You could see for such a long way up Parnassus Road, you could be sure that no one was going to arrive at the Mechanics' Institute soon, or at any time in the near future.

Just the wind, she called down the hall to Coralie.

Her voice sounded angry in the space between them.

No one there.

CHAPTER 26

YOU HARDLY HAD to touch Freddy Chang's zip and it fell open.

The first time, Felicity had sounded surprised.

Oh!

She had sounded surprised, and in a way she was, because Felicity Porcelline would never dream of undoing the zip of the Karakarook butcher. It was simply that, well, here they were, and his zip was undone.

After that first time, she had not bothered to be surprised. It could not be she herself who was doing it, but it was best not to look too closely at the mechanism by which the zip of the Karakarook butcher fell open.

Once the zip was open, Freddy Chang became all of a piece. The bulge of flesh over his hip joined with the V-shaped sling of muscle that ran down into his groin and held his soft organs. The springy hair of his pubic area ran up into a narrow black line of hair to his navel and tapered away up towards his smooth brown chest.

Naked, he was not untidy any more. It was an interesting fact that a naked person did not look untidy. Naked, Freddy Chang was no longer Chinese, either. She never thought about him being Chinese when he had no clothes on, even though she had never done it with anyone Chinese before.

They always did the poses before they did what she liked to think of, vaguely, as *the other thing*. The poses got her in the mood, and by the time she had done the poses for a few minutes, the *Felicity Anne Porcelline* who was *the wife of the Manager of the Karakarook Branch of the Land & Pastoral Bank*, whose floor was clean enough to eat off and who never, ever forgot to moisturise before she went to bed, was not paying attention.

What sat under the lights, doing the poses, was just skin. It did not go by any rules because it did not need to think. It did not seem to care about anything. It did not even wear a wedding ring. That was in the handbag, on the floor near the door, getting dust on the suede. *Felicity Anne Porcelline* would never put her good bag down on the floor like that to get dusty, but the skin took no notice of the dust on the suede, only arranged itself in various poses, one after the other, peach-like and perfect under the lights.

Marvellous! Yes! Perfect!

His photos were always excellent. Every time she went back, he showed her the ones from the time before. *You could have been a professional*, he always said. *Honest.*

The face on the prints smiled back at her: winsome, thoughtful, surprised, serious. It could do all the expressions. And always young. In the photos, you would have thought she was no older than thirty. Younger even. Twenty-five.

It was nothing like *love*. It was not even that she *liked* Freddy Chang particularly. They certainly had absolutely nothing *in common.* He did not *make her laugh*, or impress her with his *sincerity* or his *good manners*. His body moving inside hers did not result in anything that could be given the status of *passion*. It was nothing to do with him, in a way. It was just two organisms, panting into each other's mouths and calling out.

Out of the lights, with her clothes back on, there was no way to think about what was happening. Out of the lights, his jokes were not funny, and he needed a haircut, and there was no escaping the fact that she was a *married woman* having an *affair with the butcher*. Out of the lights, viewed cold, it was simply an act of madness. In a little place like Karakarook it could only be a matter of time.

There was a kind of sick ecstasy, knowing it was only a matter of time.

She glanced at the clock beside the couch. She had brought it from home, the little one with the unusual black-and-white striped face that usually warned her to take the cucumbers off her face.

The first time, there had been a little crisis, because they had fallen asleep on the couch. That is, *after*. It was surprising how comfortable that ordinary old couch was, when you opened it up. She had woken up in a fright, hot and sweaty, and seen on her watch that it was nearly ten minutes after school finishing-time. She had raced down the stairs still scrambling into her blouse. Freddy had gone with her to the foot of the stairs, just in his underpants, and given her a big kiss, right there in the doorway, and just as she turned away from him, she had glimpsed, through the open gateway at the end of the yard, a group of boys going along the lane.

She had a feeling that William was one of them, although they were out of sight before she could be sure.

She had crammed the buttons into the buttonholes and raced up the hill to the house, and had managed to get there before him. That meant he must have dawdled with the other boys, and she had roused on him for that, and for walking home without her when she repeatedly told him not to. She had just been delayed very briefly, down at the shops, because Coralie needed to have a word with her. About the Museum, as a matter of fact. About Great-Grandmother Ferguson's old quilt, actually.

It was only after he had gone off to his room, sullen and silent, that she looked down and saw that all the buttons of the little blouse were in the wrong holes.

Now, before she did anything else, when she first got there, she set the clock.

It was twelve o'clock. The alarm would ring at a quarter to three. That gave her plenty of time. She left it vague just what it gave her *plenty of time* for.

What's the time? Freddy asked.

Twelve o'clock.

She preferred it when he said nothing, but she had found there was a way of having a conversation without really having one. Your mouth made words, and part of your brain even supplied them, but you did not allow any actual thinking to take place.

Nearly three hours, then, he said. Two and three-quarter hours.

Felicity Porcelline would be embarrassed to be with someone stating the obvious like that. Hugh's mother had taken her out to lunch before they were married and told her

Always start from the outside with cutlery, Don't let your husband see you in curlers, and *Never state the obvious.*

It had been good advice, and had stood *Felicity Porcelline* in good stead over the years. But Hugh's mother was not here to hear Freddy Chang stating the obvious, and *Felicity Porcelline* did not seem to be listening. The skin on the couch was the only one there, and it could not care less.

She swivelled on her hip to press herself against Freddy's warm stomach. He was like a powerful little machine, generating its own heat from within.

Plenty, she said. Enough and to spare.

How many more weeks of term? he asked.

Two, she said. Then it'll be the holidays.

Actually, the skin found it soothing to state the obvious.

We'll be right, he said. We'll work out something.

He laughed in a vibrating burr that she felt through her own flesh.

In bank hours, that is.

The couch creaked with his laughter.

No bank holidays coming up, I hope?

He pressed himself into her. He was ready again. So was she.

CHAPTER 27

LOOK, SAID PRINGLE, and nudged Douglas. A little cluster of cars and utes was gathered near the southern approach, and a clot of people was coming along the road, a small procession in the landscape.

Douglas had seen documentaries about Bolivia where processions like this straggled through the landscape. Religious festivals, harvest thanksgiving, that kind of thing. But this was not Bolivia. It seemed unlikely that this was a harvest thanksgiving procession.

The men were watching him. He could feel them behind him, not watching the procession but watching him. Someone coughed, a big airy cough. They knew what was happening. They were waiting to see what he would do.

The engineer. The one in charge. Whatever it was, he was the one who was going to have to deal with it.

The group of people stopped at the end of the bridge, but a small black-haired woman in red glasses kept on coming. She walked right up to him, flushed and stern-looking, and looked him challengingly in the eye.

We know you're nothing to do with it, type of thing, she said.

It sounded as if she had rehearsed that part.

But we've done out this petition.

She held out a sheaf of papers stapled together.

Go on, she said, and shook the papers at him. It's got to be seen by the high-ups, in at Head Office.

She bit her lower lip and he realised that in spite of her confident, rehearsed voice, she was nervous. Behind the red glasses he could see her eyes: hazel, flecked, not unfriendly.

In an automatic way he took the papers, feeling them warm from her hand. Then he wished he had not. Having the papers in his hand made him part of whatever it was that was happening. He tried to give them back, but she took a step away out of reach, shaking her head.

You show them that, she said. You tell them.

It was a petition, set out like a proper legal document. *Whereas Your Majesty,* he read at the top, and then a whole lot of dense writing in which he saw the words *known as The Bent Bridge.* The pages were dog-eared, the column of signatures amateurish-looking, with different kinds of pens, different kinds of writing.

The Shire went behind our backs, the woman said. Stacked the meeting, type of thing.

The light winked off the red glasses.

Took no account of the heritage value, she said.

That part was all rehearsed too.

She seemed to have run out of words now. She stared at him as if hoping he would say something she could answer.

He said nothing, just went on looking blindly at the pages of writing. He had no words. He certainly had no *Whereas Your Majesty* sort of words. He could not think of anything to say about Heritage value or the tourist aspect. There was a bad taste like fear in his mouth.

There seemed no reason why this frozen moment should not go on for the rest of the day, or even into next week. But finally the woman turned away and went back to join the others. He watched her go, wondering what would happen now. The group seemed to be mostly women, some with strollers, several with what seemed to be picnic baskets, a couple of elderly ones with home-made-looking floppy cloth hats. There was a little skinny man standing with one hip up, one down, his hands clasped in front of his privates, and a chunky Chinese man, his black hair gleaming in the sun, and an older fellow, standing to attention like one of the Legacy types, with a wide tie flapping sideways. At the front of the group was a gigantic young woman swaying a baby on her hip, a toddler beside her gripping the teat of a bottle in her teeth and staring solemnly at the man all by himself on the bridge.

He was a naughty boy. He was in big trouble.

The woman in the red glasses was speaking to them all. *Go home*, Douglas hoped she was telling them. *Everyone just go home.* He watched hopefully, but when she had finished, no one turned to *go home*. Instead the little crowd began to shrink and flatten, as everyone sat down on the road. The woman in the red glasses perched cross-legged in front of them, and the huge woman bent down awkwardly on one hand, lowering herself slowly sideways so her tent-like dress ballooned around her, and finally lay stretched full-length on the roadway, the dusty timbers disappearing under the flowers of her dress.

Behind them, the bulldozer was big and dangerous-looking, the edge of the blade glinting in the sun where rocks had scraped through to the bare steel. The sun rained down steadily on them all. It was surprisingly quiet, considering how many people were gathered on such a small bridge. A bird called, unworried, from its bush. *Cheep cheep cheep a whee!*

He was reminded of the outdoor classes he had had on site, as a student. It seemed a long time ago, those innocent times. The students were always invited to sit on the asphalt of some new road or the concrete of some new bridge, while the professor talked. Some of them never sat, no matter how long the professor talked. They would stand, shifting their weight from foot to foot as the lecture went on, as if there was something meek about sitting.

He himself had always sat down straight away, and he wished he could do it now, go over and sit with everyone waiting for someone else to work out what came next.

An untidy man with frizzy blond hair and two cameras slung around his neck seemed to be taking photographs of everyone. Beside him was a young man with a spiral notebook, counting the crowd with his pen jabbing the air. When the frizzy man turned the lens on Douglas, he realised too late that he had his mouth open. The sheaf of petition in his hand, his mouth agape. He could imagine the picture.

He turned away, ducking his head. There were the friendly old planks of the roadway. It might be nice to count them. *One, two, three, four.*

While he counted, he let himself imagine a happy ending to all this. He would finish counting, and when he looked up, the people on the bridge would be gone. He would go over to the ute, get in and drive back into town. He imagined Room 8, how quiet it would be, and what comfort the *Engineering Digest* could offer. If he wanted something more exciting, he could go downstairs and watch the butcher rearrange the tins of tongue in his window.

He got to the end of one row of planks. *Fifteen, sixteen, seventeen.* He could see out of the corner of his eye that the people on the bridge were still there. They had done what they were going to do. It was his turn now.

Another man, that *leader of men* who followed him like a scornful shadow everywhere he went, would know what to do. A *leader of men* would take his hat off, stand up nice and straight, and take charge.

Ladies and gentlemen, such a man would say. He would have a good carrying voice. It would not come out as a bleat, as his own tended to when he tried to make it loud. *Can I have your attention!*

But what came next?

You are wrong about concrete, he wanted to shout. *May I have your attention, ladies and gentlemen. Did you know that concrete is actually a very thick liquid?*

He felt a ball of sweat trickle down his spine.

Concrete is the form of imagination, ladies and gentlemen, having none of its own.

They were words, but even he knew they would not be the right ones.

Suddenly he saw Harley Savage in the crowd. She was wearing a big hat with a floppy brim that partly hid her face, but now that he saw her, he wondered how he had missed her before. It would take more than a hat for him not to recognise her.

He could not see the expression on her face under the brim, and as he watched, her hand went up and pulled it down further. He could only see her mouth and chin now, but he would know them anywhere.

She was saying something to the Chinese man next to her, the mouth shaping itself around a story. The Chinese man smiled a sudden white smile, threw his head back, laughed aloud. In the still air, he could hear it quite clearly: *Ha ha! Ha!*

She had probably just told him about the cows, and the way he had looked when he poked his stick at them.

Now the Chinese man was telling her something. Her mouth was smiling, interested. She nodded and glanced over at where Douglas stood with the petition still held out as if someone might come along and relieve him of it. He knew that she saw him. You could hardly miss him, standing there in the middle of the bridge. But from the way she glanced at him, no one would ever imagine that she had once taken his hand in hers, or shared a plate of the world's tiniest scones. She was leaning back on her hands now, staring at him. He had not thought she was that kind: to enjoy being part of a crowd, watching the one on the outside, to see what he would do.

She stared blandly, watching him suffer.

The sun was making him dizzy, or perhaps it was the unanchored sense of things slipping away from him. He did not know if it was heatstroke or just humiliation. I am under compression, he thought, subjected to a load beyond my capacity. My molecules are rearranging themselves into planes. I cannot stretch any further.

Catastrophic failure. It was what concrete did, if it was asked to do something it could not do.

*

Finally, the woman with the red glasses saved him. She stood up and came over, right in front of him, so he felt like a bully towering over her.

He could see the man with the cameras, crouching down low so the photo would make him look even taller, the woman even tinier. It would make a good front page. *David and Goliath*. Something like that.

What I'd suggest, she said kindly, is get on the blower to your boss. We're ready to do a blockade. You tell him that.

He stared down at her. From this angle he could see the roots of her hair, where the new growth was coming in grey underneath the black.

The blower, he repeated. A blockade.

Yes, she said patiently. We've got the sandwiches and the Thermoses and that.

She stared up into his face, waiting. He could hear the bird still going on and on in its bush. What a life. Nothing to do all day except hop around on a twig going *cheep cheep cheep a whee*.

Okay? the woman with the red glasses was saying.

He made himself nod and smile, although he was not quite sure what was *okay*.

We'll go now, she said.

She seemed to be waiting for something, so he nodded and smiled some more.

Long as you get straight on to your boss, and hold off on pulling it down.

She made him shake hands, like a man would, to seal the agreement, but he misunderstood at first and thought she wanted the petition back. He felt Harley watching as he fumbled with the petition, finally got the woman's hand in some kind of peculiar sideways grip.

Even after everyone had got up and gone back to their cars and driven away, he went on smiling automatically, frightened of what might happen if he stopped. He felt large and alone, and his eyes seemed to have gone stary and strange. It was possible that he was about to burst into tears.

He could hear the bird again: it seemed to have become two birds now. *Cheep* CHEEP *cheep a whee! Bic bic bic bic whip* WHIP*!* It was like a conversation, except of course that birds did not have conversations.

Harley Savage was the only one who had not gone. She was coming towards him, her head down so all he could see was her hat. She was not looking at him, but he could see that she was planning to say something.

Perhaps several things.

She was not wearing the torn tee-shirt today, but the knobby African thing she had worn to the Panorama Cafe. There was a slit on each side that he had not noticed before, that made it flap around her calves as she walked. It had a vigorous barbaric look, the pattern emphatic, energetic, bold as a danger sign.

She was close enough now for him to see some kind of primitive ornament on a strip of leather around her throat, carved out of bone perhaps, possibly a dagger. It was a decoration, but it was also a weapon.

He put his hat back on and took a step sideways, as if he might get out of her way. He could feel the smile still on his face, but he was pretty sure a smile would not be required for the sort of conversation they were about to have.

She stopped, within talking distance but not close, as if observing some invisible frontier, but the dog did not seem to recognise any frontier. It ran up gladly to him and circled several times sniffing at his trousers and once, quickly, politely, into his crotch. Then it did a figure of eight and flopped down in the dust between them.

When she cleared her throat, it was like the principal getting ready to *have a little chat* with you.

Tell me, she said, casually, still not quite looking at him. Who makes these decisions?

She was smiling a sweet but menacing smile.

About pulling things down?

He was taken by surprise. It was not the question he had expected. *Not me!* he wanted to blurt. *It wasn't me!*

Well, he started, and stopped.

In the silence the panting of the dog between them was very loud and eager, like another, more enthusiastic, language.

Look, he said.

It was always a mistake to start with *Look*.

I've got a lot of sympathy for the Heritage aspect, he said.
Oh? Yes?

Her face was sceptical, resistant, an eyebrow arched wryly.

But the Inspector from Head Office has done the Report.

He hated himself for the way he was reverentially capitalising everything.

Given it the thumbs down, I'm afraid.

He heard himself in astonishment. He did not think he had ever talked about giving something the *thumbs down* before.

The timber is rotting right away. The corbels.

That sounded a bit too technical, as if he was trying to silence her with his special knowledge.

The what?

Because, see, the roadway lets the water in, and then it can't get away.

That wasn't too technical, but it wasn't terribly clear, either. He was not trying hard enough, somehow, and he knew it was because his heart was not in it. All it took was a man who was brave enough to get on to Mr Denning and make him listen to the modules idea. A brave man would have done it as soon as he saw the first poster in town. A man such as his heroic father, for instance, would not have thought twice.

Instead, here he was, unhappily going through the motions of defending Head Office.

And so they rot.

Can't you just put new ones in?

The timber is scarce these days, you see. Plus, there's not the skilled labour to work it.

He found he was ticking things off on his fingers. He hated people who did that. He did not think he had ever done it before. He put his hands away in his armpits.

For the corbels alone, you're looking at a helluva lot of old-growth hardwood.

Some other dreadfully jovial man had taken over his mouth. He stopped in despair.

He could see a small pale scar on her chin that he had never noticed before.

It's an environmental concern, he said at last.

Now he sounded like a Forestry Commission pamphlet.

Look, he said. This bridge took fifty-odd mature old-growth eucalypts to build. Fifty-odd, minimum.

She was watching him now and the frown had gone. Her

face was blank with thought as she visibly pictured fifty-odd trees.

He followed up his advantage.

That's fifty families of possums, give or take a few.

He started the sum in his head, say conservatively four possums per family, fifty times four was. Next he could talk about the birds, and then he could move on to the snakes. People tended to forget reptiles, in the scheme of things.

She was looking away again, past his shoulder, away over to the bush. He could see how her bottom jaw stuck out in a way that gave her an obstinate look.

It's just a matter of facts, he said, loudly, convincing himself. You can't just wait till a bridge falls down. Can you?

It was a mistake, asking a question, even a rhetorical one. She did not respond, and his words winged away windily into the quiet afternoon.

In the long silence he could hear the men murmuring together behind him. Someone coughed that thin cough again.

He saw a frown start between her eyebrows, and he went on quickly.

Whereas, you whack a concrete beam in, see you right for a century.

He stopped, wishing he had not used the word *whack*.

Yes, she said. I know you're keen on concrete.

She allowed a pointed silence to fall.

What are those tapes? she said finally. Round the trees.

She pointed so the sleeve of the African thing fell back and showed her arm, the muscles under the tanned skin.

He turned to look, although he knew exactly what she meant.

That's where the road's going to go, he said.

He swept his arm up and down along the line.

Cutting in round the side of the hill.

There was a silence. He glanced at her. She was staring up at the hillside.

The trees? All those big trees are going?

He was like a man holding the gun to his own head and pulling the trigger.

Yes.

He gave the word an upward inflection, as if it was not just *yes*, it was *yes, but*. Something would come along so that he could somehow make a *yes* into a *no*, and stop her looking at him this way.

Nothing rescued him. She went on looking at him, waiting.

So they're going, she said flatly. All those trees.

In a kind of panic he started to count them to himself. *Four*, and three more in a bunch, that made *seven. Eight. Nine* and *ten*. And more further up.

He would be perfectly happy to go on counting all day. *Eleven, twelve*.

He could imagine the noise of the chainsaws. There would be no *buggerising around* with axes. He could imagine the drama of the trees crashing down one by one. Chook would love it. *Fourteen, fifteen*. They would lie there dead, and the dozer would push them in a pile to one side. They would stay there until the bracken and the blackberries finally hid them. *Seventeen, eighteen*.

She was staring coldly at him, waiting.

Yes, he said.

It came out in a whisper. Yes, he made himself repeat, louder. They're going.

His voice sounded very puny to his own ears, as if travelling a long way through empty air.

The dog suddenly jumped up as if someone had called it, and a moment later a small truck appeared along the road in clouds of yellow dust. They moved to opposite sides of the bridge to let it pass between them and it crossed the bridge in a long rumble and clatter that ripped the silence. He could feel the bridge tremble, could hear the bolts tinkling and straining at each other. He even thought he could see a sort of ripple in the roadway as the truck went over, and feel a buckling under his feet.

When it had ground away up the badly cambered corner, the man and the woman were left standing in hanging dust.

He could not think of anything to say that would not sound like *I told you so*. He scraped at the roadway with the toe of one of his boots. They were scuffing up quite nicely now.

Yes, she said, as if he had been lecturing her. Well, I'd best be getting along.

She did not meet his eyes, but turned and was off, away down the road to the brown Datsun. She opened the door and the dog sprang in. They looked as if they had been doing that particular bit of teamwork all their lives. He stood watching until the car disappeared around the corner.

He was the wrong man for this situation. He knew that. He wished there was someone he could go up to and tell. *Look*, he would like to say, *I'm the wrong man for this. Ask anyone.*

Anyone, in the form of Harley Savage, tall and powerful, would willingly agree. But there was no one to tell. There was only he himself, a flimsy man alone with his shadow, scuffing at the roadway with his boot.

Taking the long view, the whole business of the Bent

Bridge was unimportant. Taking a long enough view, the whole idea of bridges was meaningless. The sun would decay and explode at some point in the future, and no one would ever again have to worry about anything.

The long view was usually a comfort to Douglas, but it did not comfort him today.

When something fell with a clang over by the ute, he looked around. The men were all gathered there, staring at him. Chook met his eye but looked away quickly and busied himself with a big thorough cough that involved taking the cigarette out, clearing his throat, and spitting into a bush. A startled bird shot out.

Hey Chook, Douglas tried, going over to him. What was that all about, mate?

Chook was busy bending down now, doing something with a jemmy.

Don't know the first thing about it, mate.

Crouched down into himself, his voice was muffled.

Haven't got a clue, mate.

Chook had become the smallest and most compressed of men, kneeling over his jemmy. Suddenly, he took up almost no space at all.

Be saving the bloody dunnies next. That had been a good laugh. But where was he now, when things had stopped being funny?

Douglas stood looking down at a bald spot on Chook's head he had never known was there. *You're just all talk, Chook*, he realised. It was a kind of dizziness, the surprise of it. *You're all hot air*, he thought in something like wonder. It was what he had heard men say of each other, and had never understood until now. *Just a big bag of wind.*

*

CHAPTER 28

THERE WAS A particular place he was going tonight but he was not prepared to admit to himself where it was. If he ended up there again, it was not on purpose. It was just that this was a small town, there were not many streets, it was only natural.

Behind the bottlebrush the grass was flattened now from his feet standing there so often.

He was not really *hiding*. He was not really even *looking in*. He was just *out for a walk*, the way anyone might be. One foot was actually up in the air, in the very act of *walking*.

A few days after the petition, he had been in the paper again. The woman at the Caledonian had made him look at it, standing over him at breakfast that morning. He had stared at the little dots that made up his own face on the newsprint of the *Livingstone & Shire Weekly Clarion*, stooping threateningly over the small figure of the woman with his mouth hanging open. In the photo his ears were sticking out at a remarkable angle. *LAST BID TO SAVE BRIDGE*. They had got his name wrong: they had called him *Chessman*, but at least he had not made the front page this time.

Not that good a one of Coralie, the woman in the pub had said. *Not like her at all, really.* He had hoped that it was *not like him at all really,* either, but that was probably too much to hope.

He did not want to be any more famous in Karakarook than he was already. He did not want to make the headlines again: PEEPING TOM CAUGHT.

But there was no one out at night in the streets of Karakarook to be convinced about the *walking*, and after a while he came out from behind the bush and forgot to keep one foot ready in the walking position.

She was there again tonight, brilliantly lit in the yellow rectangle of the window. On the sideboard he could see the fruit bowl and a jumble of ornaments. On the wall a blue striped bathroom towel was draped over something square. Perhaps it was a picture she did not like, some gaudy print that had got on her nerves.

It was something he did himself in motels, where the pictures were screwed to the wall for the other kind of people, the ones who liked the pictures so much they wanted to take them home.

She sat, frowning down at an old-fashioned black sewing machine on the table in front of her, a strip of red flannel round its middle stuck with pins, painted with elaborate gilt scrollwork around the upper curves. The electric cord coming out of its back was thick, rubbery and twisted like an umbilical cord. The sewing machine sat very black in the rain of brilliant yellow light from the bulb above the table, shedding its own small extra pool of even yellower, even brighter light from its own small lamp, the circle of warmth falling on the needle winking bright.

He could see a curved metal lever coming out of its base. You must work the machine by pressing against the curve of the lever with your knee. A clever bit of design. Left your hands free.

He could not see what she was bending over at the machine, and took the few steps to the fence, but even craning over it he still could not see. After a moment he opened the gate, lifting it up so it would not scrape on the path, and tiptoed over the dry grass. Now he was right outside the window, looking straight in through the gap in the curtains.

There could be no story about being *out for a walk* now. He felt unsteady on his feet, taking shallow inefficient breaths, as if he had suddenly come to the edge of a great height. He made himself take a deep lungful. Absurd. A man his age.

He could see that the little pieces of fabric had been sewn together into larger units, and now she was stitching those units together, holding them up, putting them against each other, putting pins in and taking them out. The thing was growing quickly as she pinned and stitched, was already big enough to cover the top of a bed.

Marjorie had embroidered things. She had done a table-cloth once that she told everyone *nearly killed her*. She had a pretty puffy box, all frills and satin padding, for her embroidery things. You could not open the lid unless the handle was pushed fully back. Very poor design. But the poor design of it had not worried her, only the risk of his hands, dirty from a day on the site, coming near her table-cloth.

The way this woman was frowning down at the fabric made him think of how she looked when she smiled. He remembered panting on the dusty road, clutching his stick, the cows bellowing down behind the fence. There'd been a certain way she'd looked into his face. He went through it again in his mind. They had turned together to look at the cattle and then she had looked at him and smiled.

Brightly lit up like someone on a stage, she frowned into the pool of yellow light, squinting at the eye of the needle, threading it. Then he could see her give a long sigh and pick up two of the little pieces of fabric. She stared down as they moved smoothly through the machine, all her attention focused on the fabric, the needle, the circle of light.

He could see her profile, absorbed, stern, as she guided the fabric under the needle, then reached through to pull down the threads against the cutter at the back.

It was silly, torturing himself with watching her, but he could not seem to stop. He watched as if to memorise it all, as if his memory of her smile would have to last him a long time.

He could hear the thrumming of the motor, and see how large and strong her fingers were, pushing the fabric through the maw of the sewing-machine. She was like a mechanism herself, he thought, a well-designed and well-fuelled piece of machinery. Or a beam of reinforced concrete. *Oh Douglas,* he could hear Marjorie, exasperated, *everything's got to be your everlasting concrete!*

It was true, though, and Marjorie was not here to listen to him thinking it. He was flimsy, trussed around, bolted stiffly together into an ugly rigid muddle of members to disguise the basic weakness of the structure. But she had both the strength of the concrete and the flexibility of the rein-forcement. The greater the load, the stronger she would get, standing planted solidly in bedrock. She would be able to stretch under tension. She was not brittle. She was flesh and bone together, bending without breaking. It was what he loved about her.

The thought took him by surprise.

Love. He did not know if this was what was meant by *love.*

He had felt something for Marjorie which he had always thought must be *love.* There had been the feeling that she was something very special, and fragile. It was a privilege, being her husband, and the husband of such a woman had to show he deserved it.

He never had deserved it, and so it had seemed only fair when she left.

The feeling that he had had for Marjorie, which he had always thought of as *love,* was not the feeling that he had now, watching this woman through the window, her hands deft under the pool of light.

She was standing now, holding up the thing she had been working on, so he could see it was a patchwork, and he could make out the squares and rectangles of light and dark, and some kind of dark-on-light border around the edge. She flung it out over the back of the couch and stood back with her head on one side, looking at it severely, her mouth a grim line.

You could see she was the kind of person who would be inclined to see the faults in a thing. The patchwork looked all right to him, but he could see that she did not think so.

He imagined saying something to her about it.

What a great job.

That would sound patronising.

Very interesting.

That would sound as if he found it *boring*.

Extremely interesting.

That would sound as if he thought it was *extremely boring*.

Fantastic workmanship.

You could hardly go wrong with *fantastic workmanship*.

The only thing was, she might ask him exactly what it was he found so *fantastic*.

Also, she might think *fantastic workmanship* was sexist.

Fantastic workwomanship. *Fantastic workpersonship*.

Anyway, she would not be fooled. She would know he was only trying to curry favour.

He remembered the way she had laughed, enjoying the company of the man next to her on the bridge. How coldly she had watched him, standing there with the petition in his hand. Thinking about it made a kind of emptiness inside.

As he watched she turned and came over to the window. He stood frozen beside the bottlebrush, not breathing, looking straight into her face. They were separated only by a few metres of warm night air and a pane of glass. He was close enough to see the light winking on the pins between her lips.

She reached up above her head, pulling at the curtain. It did not move and he held his breath as she jerked at it. From this angle her neck was cabled with powerful tendons. The curtain suddenly gave and jerked across the window in front of his face.

The dog panted up at him. He could feel its tail beating against his leg like a code and bent down to scratch the hair behind its ears. He felt as if he had lost or forgotten something. There was the feeling of a gap, where something important belonged. Something was floating away from him. It was tapping him on the shoulder: going, gone.

He supposed it would be like this now, for the rest of his life. Outside, with the curtains shut in his face. Outside, looking in.

CHAPTER 29

IT SEEMED THAT Freddy was starting to enjoy all the secrecy. He made a big thing of play-acting when they met in the street. *Morning, Mrs Porcelline!* he always called in an exaggeratedly casual way, as if she was just the same to him as any of the others: *Morning, Mrs Trimm!* or *Morning, Mrs Fowler!*

Then he started embroidering it: *Morning, Mrs Porcelline, school holidays coming up are they?* or *Morning, Mrs Porcelline*, he'd call, *lovely light for a photo today*, and gesture around as if he meant Parnassus Road.

Now, perversely, it seemed she was never alone in the shop with him: now, when she did not want anyone there, Lois or Fiona dawdled for hours over their lamb's fries and sausages. She could see Freddy enjoyed it. *I do a good sausage*, he'd say seriously. *Though I do say it myself.* He would catch her eye through the gauze then, and wait until Fiona was glancing away. Then he would give her a wink. *I like a nice fat sausage, don't you, Mrs Porcelline?*

She was there with William one day, asking for *six short-loins*, not half an hour after he had been making jokes upstairs about how *long* his particular *short-loin* was, and he gave her a big rude wink through the fly-wire. William had not seen the wink, she was sure, and anyway he was much too young to put two and two together. But it was a risk.

It was bad enough that she had to go the back way to the studio, along the dunny-lane behind the shops, wearing her big hat pulled down low over her face. It was actually more dangerous doing that, in a way, because the windows at the back of the shops and the hotel overlooked the lane, and if anyone had seen her, it would have been hard to explain what she was doing there in the dunny-lane in the middle of the day.

It made her tired, just thinking about it.

But she could see that he loved all the scheming. Upstairs in the studio he had worked out a way of balancing a screen across the top of the stairs so it would make a lot of noise if anyone tried to come in, and had got interested in the idea of a trip-wire and a bell, even drawn a lot of diagrams. Then he had wanted her to get involved with a complicated system of signals in code, based on the arrangement of the things in his shop window. *If the tins of tongue are on the right of the dripping, it's okay for you to come up*, he explained, *even if it says Closed. If they're on the left, it means I really am.*

He had laughed at his own ingenuity, and she had seen the tongue in his mouth as he laughed: strong, red, muscular.

But codes and secrets were no part of her pleasure. They meant that you knew what you were doing, and that was exactly what she did not want to know.

The worst time was the day she had come out of the shop, after she had been alone in there with Freddy and he had wanted to fondle her through the flap in the gauze. She had come out a bit flustered, feeling red in the face, and the old woman, Mrs Trimm, was sitting in the gutter right outside.

She was a funny old thing, half gone in the head. Ninety-eight, someone had told her. She sat there with her sandshoes in the gutter – in the city you would think she was an old wino, but the Trimms were a good family in the district, apparently – and when Felicity came out she twisted around to look up at her from under her old straw hat.

Hello, dear, she said out of a face that was a web of deeply scored wrinkles. I'm just waiting for my lover to bring the car around.

She slapped her thigh, laughed.

I mean my mother!

She laughed again, stamped one of the sandshoes on the ground.

No, no, I mean my daughter! I'm waiting for my daughter!

And there she was, the daughter, a weather-beaten middle-aged woman driving up in a truck.

Mrs Trimm got up and smoothed down her shabby old skirt as if she was the belle of the ball.

I'm losing my marbles, she leaned close to tell Felicity confidentially. On and off, like a light-switch on the blink.

But just before she turned away to climb up into the cab of the truck she gave Felicity a wink, and when she was up in the seat, she looked out the window at her and did something with her finger against the side of her nose that might or might not have been waving away a fly. Felicity stood in the midday glare, watching the truck shrink away down Parnassus Road.

There were times when the light in the country seemed bright enough to burn the flesh right off your bones.

*

CHAPTER 30

CORALIE HAD TOLD Harley about a swimming hole down at the river. *Never been measured, it's that deep*, she had said. *There's a fault, type of thing. Some bloke come and said.*

When she set out it had seemed a pleasant enough day, but long before she got near the river she was hotter and crankier than she had ever been in her life. It was turning out to be a city person's silly idea. The day had become a *scorcher*, with an angry little dry wind that burst out of nowhere, funnelling along the valley, whipping her along so that she could feel the back of her skirt snapping against her calves. Every gust was like a blow. The ground along the road was littered with switches of leaves ripped off and flung down. Birds were frantic, darting and wheeling low in the sky, blasted by a gust, then dropping into a hole of stillness.

The sky had a strange bruised look to it, and things seemed to have gone a funny colour. Somewhere away in the National Park there was a bushfire, Coralie had said, and even so far away it was having an effect on the sky above Karakarook. Shadows were not right. Everything was very sharp and small, like things looked at through someone else's glasses.

She was angry with herself for the words she was finding

for the wind. Like *the breath of a furnace.* But she had never felt the breath of a furnace, so what did she mean? Like *opening an oven door.* But it was nothing like opening an oven door. This was not a wind that was going to be domesticated by words.

She hated the wind, the way it hurled itself at her in raw gusts of heat. She hated the grasshoppers, humming hoarsely out of the grass. She hated the cicadas, the pressure-waves of drilling that felt as if a blood vessel in your head was about to burst. She hated the dog, trotting now in front, now behind, panting noisily. She could not bear to look at its tongue, red and desperate, hanging out, drying.

Anyone with any sense was inside on a day like this, behind closed curtains, stretched out on the couch. Only she was the city fool, inching along a dusty road towards an inadequate river.

She could see now why Coralie had given her a funny look when she said she was going to walk out to the swimming hole. She should have climbed off her high horse, asked her advice. *Don't you think I should?* It would have been easy, and nicer than making her face go glassy when Coralie was obviously waiting to advise her.

Serves me right, she thought grimly.

The funny light seemed to have done something to the way she was moving. Her arm, swinging out in front of her as she strode along, seemed too big, or was it too small? She was conscious of her knees going up and down like piston-ends under her skirt. There was a sense of things having stopped, except for the sound of the blood in her own ears, and the way her knees were continuing to move up and down.

Somewhere in the distance, in between the blasts of the wind, she could hear a dog barking, on and on, and a rooster crowing reedily as if the strange light made it think it was dawn.

Behind her she heard a car approaching, and she moved over on to the stony verge to let it pass. But it did not pass. It slowed down and followed her at a walking pace until she looked around, annoyed. It was a white ute, but she could not see the driver behind the reflections of trees in the windscreen. She stared, and with a jerk it accelerated and stopped just ahead of her. Dust billowed around, fell on her face, her mouth, went up her nose. She was sneezing and coughing at the same time and wiping tears out of her eyes, feeling the grit on her face turn to mud, when the driver got out of the ute and she saw that it was Douglas Cheeseman.

He got out and came over to her, frowning.

Sorry! he cried.

He was flushed, whether with the heat or self-reproach she did not know.

Sorry about the dust! he cried.

He swiped at it with his hat, stirring up more.

Making it worse! Sorry!

Something was tightening in her. She looked away from him. She wished another car would come along and rescue her from the closeness of him, the way he was watching her now.

Just wondered if you'd care for a lift, he said finally.

The words had a stiff rehearsed sound. He met her eye for a moment, then looked away.

You know, in this heat.

He was apologetic, but there was something dogged

about the way he stood there in front of her. He was not a man who would give up easily.

She should have said *no*, right from the start.

Her throat felt full of dust, drying out the words. She shook her head and made some kind of gesture with her fingers, and finally swallowed enough spit to speak.

No, she started, but her voice seized up on the dust again.

She coughed, feeling him watching her.

No, she said. I'll walk.

It was partly the dust, but she could hear how her voice sounded very thin and cold.

He stood there patiently with the dust in his eyebrows, the sun beating down on the thin sandy hair on his crown. His shirt was wrinkled and stuck to his chest with sweat and his shorts were loose around his skinny legs.

She realised she feared him, as being a man too easy to do violence to. Or was it herself she feared?

She clamped the hat down tighter on her head against the wind so the brim hid her eyes. Now she could see only his boots, standing in the dust, and his hands dangling defencelessly.

It's too hot, he said. Let me take you.

But before he had finished, a cold stern voice, from which the dust had gone, spoke out of her mouth, out of her stunted and dangerous heart.

I'll walk, thanks.

He received this like a large ball thrown at his head: turned aside, blinked. A blast of wind gusted into his face, laden with the pale dust, and he closed his eyes against it.

He went on standing there while she walked around him

and on up the road past the ute. She kept the hat down. She could see the edge of the brim, and the road moving past her feet.

He drove past so slowly it seemed to take hours, and so far on the other side of the road she could hear the tyres snapping against stones on the verge. She did not look at him, but put her shoulders further back and got her chin up like someone enjoying their constitutional. A fly, excited by the expanse of sweaty cheek and nose, harassed her but she would not turn, would not acknowledge the white ute creeping along on the far side of the road. Even when it had passed, drawing its funnel of yellow dust behind it, she continued to stride along through the haze of fine dust as if she did not notice it.

Only when the ute was out of sight round the next bend did she put down her basket, take her hat off, flail it at the fly, wipe the sweat off her forehead. A crow whined sardonically and she turned to frown at it.

The river fell down a short rock-face and turned a dogleg corner, and there, hidden in the armpit of the hill, was a big dark body of still water that sucked the sunlight down into itself.

She had vaguely imagined a clear blue pool out of a picture-book. She had not expected it to be this dirty brown, with the wind roughening the surface so that it looked solid. Sparks of white sunlight glinted and winked harshly against the ripples.

The far bank rose up steeply, covered with dense bush that was tossing itself around frantically in the wind. So many leaves clashing together made a brittle sweeping sound.

She was standing on a kind of beach of pale rounded stones, where a few stunted she-oaks struggled up and cast thin patches of shade. In every blast of the hot wind, the trees whistled and hissed with a noise like fire.

When she picked up a rock and hurled it towards the pool, it disappeared into the water with hardly a splash. The wind gusted over the place, rubbing out the ripples.

Awkwardly she sat down on the stones, her legs sticking out stiffly in front of her. The stones were not made for sitting on. A fly hovered near her eye and she flapped at it irritably. It circled back and tried the other eye. She flapped it away again. It avoided her hand, but languidly, unconcerned. It could do it all day, circle and land, circle and land. It could go on for ever. She could not.

Even in the shade, the heat beat up from the bleached stones. The sun was a solid malevolent weight and the wind brought no coolness. Sweat had stuck her shirt to her back and made her toes slimy in her sandals. Everywhere she looked her eyes met glare.

She had planned to swim naked. She had imagined it: the clear blue pool, framed by graceful drooping branches, herself, her skin sliding through the water.

But she did not want to undress here, or go into the pool. It was the wind, and the roughness of the water, and the ugly darkness of it. It was the trees tossing themselves around angrily, and the way the sun fell so harshly out of the sky.

Trudging back the way she had come was an exhausting prospect. She imagined it. *How was your swim?* She was not quite sure who she heard asking the question. Coralie, it could have been. Or him. Douglas, the engineer. *How was your swim?* She would have to admit that she had walked all that way and then come back without going in the water.

She turned suddenly and stared across the pond as if she had heard someone calling, but the wind blew on indifferently, covering everything with its noise.

She had made a mistake. She was prepared to admit that. But she could not go on sitting there, with a fly circling and landing, circling and landing. She bent forward and took her sandals off, then stood up to undo her skirt, teetering awkwardly on the stones.

The dog, lying panting in another patch of thin shade, watched as she stretched her tee-shirt down. The stones were hot, and nasty to walk on, but she made her way over to where a flat brown rock jutted into the pool, and sat down with her feet dangling into the water.

On such a hot day, it should have been pleasant to have your feet in a river, but the water was too cold, the air too hot. Her body, happy only in such a narrow band of temperature, felt fragile. Too hot, too cold: either one was fatal.

The dog was splashing along between the rocks on the edge of the pool. Its wet paw-prints on the dry rocks vanished as soon as they were made.

It glanced over at her, panted, licked its nose, then as if setting an example it waded purposefully into the water and began to swim towards the other side. She could only see the top of its head, cutting through the water, leaving behind a vee of ripples. A dandelion head skimmed along the water, rolling along the surface, very white against the heavy brown.

Quickly, like downing medicine, she slid over the edge of the rock into the water, feeling with her feet for the bottom but not touching anything. Under the water her body was an unfamiliar amber shape that shadowed away into darkness, the tee-shirt ballooning up around her armpits. When she held up a hand it looked like someone else's, sallow in the metallic light reflected from the surface.

The cold slowly wrapped itself around her. The further down into the water you penetrated, the colder it got.

She stroked slowly across the pool, parting the water quietly in front of her. At every stroke she could feel it painting itself against her skin, washing another layer of warmth off her body. She swam shallowly, keeping herself up out of the colder depths. It was thin and slippery water that seemed to draw her down, rather than buoy her up, so that her movements felt laboured, as if she had forgotten how to swim.

She paused to rest, treading water. Down in the darkness beneath, her feet were gripped by the cold. Moving them was like pushing heavily through some thick dull substance.

In front of her, a duck spread its wings, thrust its webbed feet out ahead of it, and skidded into the water with a hiss. Its invisible feet pedalled quickly, propelling it along as secretively as if on ball-bearings. The reptilian head turned this way and that, and for a moment the tiny round eye stared coldly at her.

She seemed to be a long way from the bank. It was an effort to go on treading this thin water. She seemed to be pedalling away furiously, just to keep her chin above the surface, and her legs were tiring. The tee-shirt was a dead weight now, dragging at her shoulders.

She looked back to the bank, where the basket and the

towel were crisp-edged miniature things and trees cast confusing shadows on the rounded stones. The brown water seemed to have done something to her eyes that made the world look colourless.

Along the bank there were many shifting shadows, but none of them was the dog. The emptiness of the pond was suddenly frightening. It was as if she was the only living creature in the world. It was just herself and her shaky heart.

Alone had always seemed like freedom. Suddenly it seemed like a life sentence.

Hey, she called.

The sound rose up thin and silly from the surface of the water, a grasshopper voice under the big empty sky. It was swept away, rubbed out by a gust of wind that shivered across the pool and puckered the steely surface. Three ducks flew up suddenly with a great clatter of wings.

Now that she had stopped moving, the cold was penetrating her body, cell by cell replacing warmth and energy with a numb inertia. Weakness was spreading up her legs, along her arms, into her shoulders. Cold closed around her chest like a hand. Her legs were stuck in something too dense and resistant to kick, her arms had become ponderous.

Something seemed to be going wrong with her breathing, too, as if sandbags were pressing in on her from all sides. She felt her mouth straining open for the air she needed to keep the legs moving, the arms circling, the heart believing in its mission. She could hear her breathing, in and out of her mouth, like someone else's: ragged, rasping, on the edge of panic. *Unh, unh*, she heard herself. It was like a plea. *Unh. Unh.*

Hearing herself, she was frightened.

Help, she called, without conviction.

The noise of the wind and the water and the leaves scraping against each other flowed back smoothly over the word as if it had never been.

It was like being on two different planets: her head was up in blasts of hot air, her body was in the unmoving cold of the water. When a gust of wind hit her in the face like a blow she let her head slip below the surface.

Underwater was a serene and silent amber world, hung with languid fragments of leaf and twig that eddied away from her hand. After the torment of the wind, it was peaceful.

It seemed that the water was making an inviting space within itself. She did not feel cold any more, only weak. Legs and arms floated at a great remove from her. Messages from the brain did not seem strong enough to overcome the paralysis that had settled into her body. She imagined it, like a dye, a softness working its way into every cell.

It did not seem to be like having an *infarction*. There was no pain, spreading like lava along her limbs. There was no struggle. There was only a feeling of yielding to the inevitable.

Like this? she thought in amazement. *This? Now?*

No one would ever find the body in this unmeasured water. There would just be her sandals on the bank, and the picnic basket. The dog, too, perhaps, panting towards the place where her hand had come up for the last time.

Not my heart, after all, she thought, and wanted to laugh. It was a shame there was no one to share the joke with.

They might even think she had done it on purpose, *taken her own life*, drowned it like a bag of unwanted kittens. She had thought about it, in the past, when things got complicated: how much simpler it would be to just go out the back and shoot herself. It had seemed a simple solution, even rather romantic.

But that was before Philip had *taken his own life*. People did not understand that if a person had driven a man to *take his own life*, they no longer had that option for themselves. They had to go on living with themselves, doing their best not to remember certain things too clearly, until they died *of natural causes*.

Not remembering was harder than you would think. It took up a great deal of energy, and even then, memories sliced through the not-remembering, as sharp as ever. The saw, for example. It had stopped before it got all the way through his neck. It had jammed in his spinal column. The high whine of the straining motor was what had taken her to the shed in the end, and when she pushed the door open the first thing she noticed was the melted-plastic smell of an electric motor seizing up.

At first glance she had thought it was an accident, and her scream had been an angry one, that the machine had done this to him. When she saw the string he had rigged up, and the ingenious arrangement of pulleys and counter-weights to pull him down on to the blade, it was not possible to let it in. Her insides had erupted out of her mouth, had gone on and on in spasms, rejecting it.

She pushed the memory away, as she had been doing for all those years, but as she pushed, she saw something new in it. If she drowned now, it would turn out that Douglas would be the last person to see her alive. He would probably be called on for evidence. *She was walking along the road,* he would tell them. *That was the last I saw of her.* She could imagine it, the bewildered look on his face. *I wanted to give her a lift*, he would keep telling them. *But she said she'd rather walk.*

They would turn out to be her last words, what she had said to him. *I'll walk, thanks.* She had looked into his face – the last face she would ever see – and spoken those words, and had seen him recoil as if from an unexpected missile.

Those words could sound like proof. *Wanted to be on her own*, they would explain to each other. *To take her own life.*

It brought her back to it again: he would be the last person to have seen her alive. She knew what that meant, to be the one left looking at a space where someone had recently been. Philip had just gone out to the shed, after dinner, the way he often did. She had tried to remember the dinner, the conversation, what she had said, what tone she might have used. She could have been more enthusiastic, perhaps, could have shown more interest, could have made sure it was all soft and coaxing. Perhaps she should have lit the candles.

But it had just been a normal family dinner. The boys had argued over the last potato, and been full of a toy that the boy down the road had, some kind of new water-pistol that could squirt the water all the way from his front gate to theirs.

It had not seemed especially terrible.

In any case, in the weeks after the event, she had come to see, with a fresh sickness at the heart, that he had been planning the pulleys, the weights, for days. Perhaps for weeks. He had lain beside her in the bed, knowing that he had bought the rope, tested the counterweights. If she had to reproach herself, it was for much more than just one day.

If they thought she had taken her own life, Douglas Cheeseman would live the rest of his life the way she had lived hers for so long, with a hole in his life where the dark knowledge lived: that he was guilty. He was already a man of apologies. It would never let him go. He would reproach himself for making all that dust, for meekly accepting that she did not want a lift, for not finding words that would have made her change her mind. He would go over and over the words, would toss and turn at night with the *what if* of it.

In the end, the reproach would simply boil down to being the person he was, and not some other, better, person.

She would be the only one who could tell him it was not true, and it was already too late to do that, even too late to leave him a note. *Dear Douglas, comma.*

All at once she saw that when someone *took their own life*, they *took* other people's lives, too. They knew that, but they went ahead and planned it, and then did it anyway. They were condemning the ones they left behind to a life sentence of self-reproach.

There was cruelty in that. It was even more than cruelty, it was a kind of sadism. The worse the death, the greater the cruelty.

She had only seen the cruelty Philip had done to himself, and taken it as proof of how bad she must be. As a doctor, he could have chosen a hundred painless ways to die, but had been so desperate he had punished himself in the worst way he could think of.

She had taken it, the savagery of what he had chosen, as the final proof of her own guilt. No clearer statement could be given to her of what a terrible person she must be. She had judged herself, and put herself away in the cage marked *dangerous*.

Thinking of Douglas Cheeseman suffering the same guilt, she saw it differently. His crimes did not deserve such a punishment. Perhaps hers had not either.

What had they been, those crimes of hers? A fear of revealing herself that could look like indifference, a coldness in the face of declarations, a malicious turn of phrase, and all the usual ones: dishonesty, selfishness, envy and greed. None of it was anything special. She was not a monster, so *dangerous* that she had to hide herself away for fear of the damage she might inflict. She was only that most ordinary of criminals, a human being.

She saw it all in a twist of revulsion as if a muscle was turning itself inside out. It was a kind of cramp, except there was no pain, only grief like a knife.

Douglas! she thought, seeing his face, flinching from her last words. *No!*

Move, she told her legs, and felt them wave feebly through the viscous water. *Pull*, she urgently instructed her arms. Feebly, clumsily, the blunt flippers of hands pushed vaguely at the coldness. Slowly, uncertainly, she felt herself rising against the deep numbing pull of the water.

Her first breath felt as if it was the first breath ever. She sucked it into her chest with a long wavering effort like a sob.

She could see the dog now, standing near the basket, shaking itself in a spray of silver drops.

Hoy, she called.

She gathered breath and tried again.

Hoy there!

It heard her and came over the stones, right out into the water, until it was standing chest-deep, looking out towards her eagerly.

Hoy, she called again, and it answered her with one short *yip*. She could see its tail, going backwards and forwards, brushing the surface of the water like a flag cheerfully signalling.

Slowly, effortfully, she swam towards the bank. She kept her chin up, straining away from the water, keeping her eyes on the dog, and when she reached the bank she lay across the warm stones, feeling the hardness of them, their kindly solid shapes under her body.

Walking along the track to the road, her skin felt silky and smooth, as if a layer had been washed off. The heat pressed in around her, but her skin moved through it sweetly. Flies circled and zoomed, but at a distance.

It was a relief to leave behind the hissing of the casuarinas. The noise the wind made here, scraping the stiff leaves of the gumtrees together, was a harder, drier, more straightforward sort of noise.

When she got to the road she stood looking up and down it. The dog stood panting beside her, looking up and down too.

She listened, drawing a half-circle with the toe of her sandal. The dust was as fine and dry as face-powder, stirring in a little cloud under her foot as it left its sign.

She looked, and listened, and so did the dog, but nothing appeared around the bend in either direction. She began to walk. Ahead of her, her shadow lay black on the road so that she trod into herself at each step. She kept stopping, mistaking the sound of the blood in her ears, or the rush of wind in the leaves, for the drone of an engine. Every time she stopped to listen, the wind smudged all the sounds. She took a few more steps, the dog bobbing along in front, stopped to listen again. Even a dog would not be able to hear, if a vehicle – a white ute, just as an example – was approaching, above this constant whispering of the leaves.

She stood for a long time, looking back down the road, listening for the drone that could not quite be heard above the noise of the wind. She stood until the dog pushed at her leg with its nose, but the road remained obstinately empty.

CHAPTER 31

GORGEOUS! WONDERFUL! TERRIFIC!

Freddy's voice was soothing, calling from the darkness. The skin that was, but at the same time was not, Felicity Porcelline, was shadowless under the lights. It was arranged on the tapestry chair with its chin on its hands and a playful little smile on its lips. The hair hung naughtily over one eye, and one leg was stretched out, the toe pointed like a ballet-dancer's.

She glanced down at it, warmly golden in the lights. The way the light fell around the thigh, the gleam along the surface, was lovely. You could lose yourself in the sheen of it, the lovely taut silkiness.

There was a kind of rumble from over in the blackness near the camera. *Thunder*, she thought, and did a different pose, with one leg up over the arm of the chair and a hand behind her head, so her breasts were nice and pointy. She thought about white lilies, four of them in a tall conical vase, their petals cool, smooth, unblemished, and felt her face go cool, smooth, unblemished as well. They had only just started the *poses*. There was all the time in the world.

The thunder rumbled again, and she realised that it was not thunder. It was a voice, a male voice, and it was not

Freddy's voice saying *That's gorgeous! That's perfect!* Freddy had stopped saying anything at all.

It was like the pain of tearing yourself out of a dream, back into daylight and your own flesh, to pay attention. Something was happening, out there in the darkness beyond the lights. She could not see properly, but there was movement, pieces of darkness moving against the deeper darkness.

She narrowed her eyes to try to penetrate the glare. There was a watching silence now from the breathing bulk of the shadows. She remembered not to screw up her eyes because it gave you wrinkles, and shielded her eyes with her hand instead. The lights still concealed whatever was behind them, but there seemed to be more than one shape with shoulders out there, more than one solid mass of something moving.

William's hurt himself at school, the rumble was saying.

It had been words before, too, but she had not been prepared to understand them.

Blood everywhere, but he's all right.

The skin went on sitting in the chair with one leg over the arm, while Felicity withdrew behind it again. It was possible to concentrate quite hard on the small crescent of shadow cast by the knee that belonged to the skin, and to examine just how the light and shade fell on the cloth of the chair. The fabric appeared to be darker in the crescent of shadow, which was just what you would expect, of course. There was nothing actually surprising or unusual about it, but it seemed quite important to go on watching it and thinking about it. For example, you could think about the fact that, if the skin stayed exactly where it was, for a year or so, there would be a little crescent where the fabric would not fade, while the lights would fade the rest of the fabric, and when the shadow was finally taken away, by the mechanism of the knee being moved, as a result of the leg contracting one set of muscles and elongating another, there would always, forever after, be a small piece of unfaded fabric just there.

They had to call me at work.

The words were becoming clearer, not a rumble at all any more, but definitely words, and at any moment the skin was going to have to recognise the voice as well as the words, and would have to go back to being *Felicity Porcelline*.

She wasn't at home. So they called me, you see.

There was a movement in the darkness beyond the lights, and there he was stepping out from the edge of the shadow. *Hugh Gordon Porcelline*. Hugh. Her husband, in his good charcoal suit he always wore, that went with being the Manager of the Branch: Hugh, that familiar stranger.

William told me. Where she'd be. You know. Where she was.

He was taking pains to explain exactly how it had all happened. He was almost apologising.

She stood up, and suddenly she was naked. Posing in the chair she had been simply innocent skin. Now she was naked: worse than naked. She was *nude*. She was bald, ugly, as if plucked. The lights went on pouring down but they were no longer friends. They were like acid: hot, dangerous, stripping her.

She could feel the air going in and out of her mouth harshly and hear the ugly panting noises she was making. She took an unsteady step, although there was nowhere to go, and had to hang on to the chair-arm to balance herself.

The lights were sickening her, inexorable, implacable, unflinching. The silence was staring at her.

She looked down at her foot. Between the pale shape of each toe was a little crooked frill of shadow. It looked as though she had stepped in something black that was oozing up slowly between the toes. But, of course, it was just the lights, and that was just her foot.

Freddy was suddenly there beside her, picking up her blouse from the chair and pulling it around her shoulders. He stood in front of her, between Hugh and herself, pulling the edges together.

It's all right, he kept saying, hopelessly pulling at the little blouse, trying to cover her nakedness for her. She stood passively, her arms pinned to her sides under the blouse.

Eventually Hugh came out of the shadows, taking off his jacket, swinging it around with a wide gesture like a bullfighter with his cape. It fell around her shoulders and covered her up completely. He did not bother with the blouse at all, but let it fall to the floor.

Come on, he said. Come on now.

It was the same voice he used with William.

Come on now.

Look, she heard Freddy start. Mr Porcelline. Listen.

No, Hugh said. There's no need. Really, there's no call for anything.

His voice was mild, uncomplaining.

He led her past Freddy, out of the circle of light. She watched her feet, down there at the end of her body, pushing themselves forward one by one. The stairs were too narrow for both of them, and he went first, holding her arm and guiding her down from below, as if she was blind.

When they came outside she was dazzled by the sunlight, covered her face against it with both hands. But she did not have to go far because he had the car waiting in the lane outside the gateway.

In you go, he said, holding the back door open, steering her in. In you hop.

Then she was in the car, looking out at another, different, Karakarook, the one muted by the tinted glass, and Hugh was driving slowly, as if with an invalid in the back, up the hill towards the house.

CHAPTER 32

HE WOKE UP early from a bad dream about heights. There were cantilevers rearing unfinished into the sky, like the Sydney Harbour Bridge in all the famous paintings. He was up there, and people were calling for him to come down. He could see them, tiny little figures, waving their arms about. When he woke up he could still feel the gritty coldness of the metal bar he had gripped in the dream.

The southern approach had been finished yesterday. Work on the northern approach and the bridge itself could not be delayed any longer.

He had reached the inescapable moment when something had to be done. You did not need to be a psychiatrist to know that was what the dream was about.

Mr Denning, he would have to say, but he could not imagine what might come next. *I've been thinking about the bridge, Mr Denning.* Mr Denning was a busy man. *What bridge, Cheeseman?* he would snap. He might even make a joke. *We don't pay you to think, Cheeseman.*

Head Office would not be impressed by the petition, would laugh at the threat of Thermoses. He would never be able to get them to listen for long enough to be convinced of his idea of the modules. *Nodules?* Mr Denning would ask.

What do you mean, Cheeseman, nodules? He would have to explain carefully about the way casting them upside-down would give them additional strength.

Mr Denning would lose patience with so much detail. *Get out there with the dozer, Cheeseman,* he would say. *Just get on with it.* If he refused, Head Office would simply recall him and send another engineer out, one who was tougher.

Getting on the blower to Head Office had to be done, but he dreaded the way it was not going to solve anything.

It was hopeless trying to get back to sleep. He got up and went over to the window. It was still early. He could hear the rooster, already going strong: *Cock-a-doo! Cock-a-doo!* He supposed it would be possible to get used to it eventually, and stop waiting for it to go *doodle-do*.

A kookaburra was cackling just outside the window. There was a fresh eucalyptus dawn coolness in the air, and the sky was pale and benign now, although it would be harsh with heat later in the day.

The kookaburra was perched on the top of the facade of the shop next door, and when he leaned out it caught his eye and stopped laughing. They stared at each other across the space of air, man and bird.

Karakarook looked picturesque under the early light. Long soft shadows lay mauve everywhere and where the sunlight fell it was syrupy: thick and golden. The sky was artless, empty, bland, pale with newness.

Boldly, he leaned out further and looked down Parnassus Road. Not a soul. Country folk were supposed to get up early, but perhaps that was just another country myth, like the one that had everyone wearing Akubras.

His eye was caught by a movement in the laneway that

ran along behind the shops. They did get up early after all, it was just that they stayed out of sight. Here, for example, was a young boy hurrying along on some early-morning country errand or other, almost running, late for the egg-collecting or the calf-feeding or whatever task it was that a young boy would be hastening to at this hour.

Sunlight was coming in over the shoulder of the Caledonian behind him, lying bent in a narrow band across the window opposite, slanting in on the floor. The bright patchwork was gone from under the camera: now it was something else the same size and shape, only darker. He took a good grip of the frame and leaned forward, and saw that it was the patchwork he had seen Harley Savage making. He recognised it by the squares and rectangles of light and dark, and the border that ran around the edge.

Then he noticed a little cloud of smoke coming up from behind the shop. It had a small cheerful look, as if someone had got the barbecue going. He could not see into the little yard, but listened for voices, although it seemed a funny time of day for a barbecue. The smoke simply puffed up in silence.

He turned back into the room, looked at his bed, the chenille bedspread that had slipped to the floor in the throes of his nightmare, the elastic-sided boots that still pinched, lined up neatly under the chair, the wardrobe door that would not close, swinging open to show his shirts. He was starting to hate Room 8, but it was still too early to go down to breakfast. In any case, having breakfast in the Dining Room, with the woman nodding and smiling at him in approval, was no better than being on his own in Room 8.

He had not spoken to Harley Savage since the day of the

hot dry wind, when she had made it so clear that she would rather walk. He sat uncomfortably on the side of the bed in his checked pyjamas, holding the *Engineering Digest*, thinking about her so hard his thumb made a large damp smudge on the word *hydroscopic*. He had nearly killed her with dust from the ute. And he wished he had not smiled. He had seen the bumper stickers out here in the bush: *No Root No Ride*. She must have seen them too, and perhaps misunderstood his offer.

He turned back to the window: the big pale sky and the balmy movement of air made the room seem stuffier than ever. A few streets away another rooster had joined the first, greeting the day with long tragic crows that ended with a wistful dying fall.

The little cloud of smoke was thicker and blacker now, billowing up strongly.

He thought he could actually hear a crackle, as of fire blazing up around dry wood. He held his breath, listening. Definitely, crackling. As he watched he thought he saw a finger of yellow flame dart up suddenly from behind the roof.

This did not seem to be a barbecue.

Suddenly Karakarook was the emptiest place in the world. He leaned out as far as he dared to look along Parnassus Road. He was actually out of the window almost as far as his waist. He craned around, but nothing moved.

He went to his door, opened it on the dark stairway. *Excuse me*, he called. He heard his voice piping feebly into the heavy beer-smelling silence. *Oh, excuse me?* He peered into the gloom of the stairs above, hung on to the banister to look down to the ground floor. *Anyone there?*

It seemed that no one was.

He went back to the window. The smoke was pouring up from behind the next-door roof in a steady thick stream now.

His mind was going very fast, skimming along through thoughts lined up neatly. There was a fire at the back of the shop. The fire was getting bigger. It would spread to the top of the shop. In the top of the shop was the patchwork that Harley Savage had made. If the fire was not stopped, the patchwork that Harley Savage had made would be destroyed. The fire would only stop if someone came to put it out. No one was coming to put it out yet. When they did, it would be too late.

There was a certain racy pleasure in the logic of it. His mind moved along the tops of the thoughts like a sheepdog over the backs of sheep, not stopping and slipping into the cracks between them. He clung to the windowsill, watching the smoke, with the thoughts tearing along towards their conclusion.

That was the trouble. At the end of this exhilarating rush of thoughts was one that he did not want to arrive at. It was waiting for him, and in the end he was afraid he would have to allow himself to think it.

It was like not looking down. It was possible to choose not to do it. It was possible to choose not to permit the thought that was waiting at the end of the other thoughts.

It was possible to choose not to hear the words, *I must climb into the window and rescue the patchwork.*

He did not think.

He did not look down either, but felt the muscles in his shoulders take the weight as he hauled his body up, on to the windowsill – *Do not look down* – and out on to the metal grid of the fire-escape landing. The structure trembled under his weight, and he heard someone gasp. Hearing it, he felt fright pour through him like a fluid.

Everything went colourless: the brown-painted bricks of the wall of the Caledonian, inches away from him, were eerily crisp but in black-and-white. He could see the shape of every individual flake of paint, where it had cracked. He could see just how it happened, and his mind got to work telling himself the story. The bricks and the paint had heated and cooled with differential rates of expansion and contraction, you see. The paint would have had a certain fixed *modulus of elasticity* but beyond that, at the *modulus of rupture* in fact, it would have cracked. In technical terms it was called *crazing*. Along the cracks, or *crazings*, it would pull away back into itself and form small patches.

He realised he had never really seen paint until now. He had definitely not given it the thought he should have. That had been an oversight, because it was really tremendously interesting.

He gripped the flimsy rail with both hands. The *crazings* in the paint felt like old friends now. He was going to keep watching them, while he lowered himself on to the step. He was not going to look away from them. Looking away would be a bad idea, because it might lead to looking down, and he must not look down. He was just going to go on watching his old friends, the bits of paint. It was lucky that there were so many of them.

Remarkable, how similar it was to his dream. He wondered if this was still part of the dream. That was a steadying thought to have, because in dreams he knew no one ever actually fell.

With the toes of his bare foot he found the first step. He found a particular little fragment of paint and kept watching it while his body followed his foot down on to the step, and then did it again for the next one, and the next. *Modulus of Elasticity*, he told himself. *Modulus of Rupture*. He attached his thoughts very firmly to the words. *Modulus of Elasticity*. They were like poetry, really.

When he got to the next landing he became aware that he was not actually breathing, and told himself to do so. *In. Out. In. Out.* Then he turned his head, very slowly and carefully, sideways. *Do not look down.*

He reached out and dabbed the windowsill with a finger. It was not an optical illusion, it was as close as it looked. Now he could see inside quite clearly. The things he had taken for music-stands were in fact lamp-stands, of course, and he could see the camera now, a big serious-looking black box attached with a lot of G-clamps to a framework so it pointed down at the floor. And there was the patchwork.

It was ridiculous, really, having to do anything as primitively physical as climb in the window and pick it up. If you came right down to it, the patchwork was actually just a lot of molecules, and molecules were just a lot of electrical energy. It was only a matter of time before someone worked out how to transfer matter by molecular means. One of these days someone would work out how to contain that energy and move it to another place, and then let it out. It would put jumbo jets out of business, and it would mean that a brown patchwork could be safely moved out of a burning butcher's shop without anyone having to do anything dramatic.

He waited a long time, but no one arrived to do a molecular transfer.

There was quite a strong smell of smoke now. Surely someone beside himself would smell it, or see it? The Fire Brigade would arrive any minute with hoses, ladders, extinguishers, and save him the trouble.

From where he now was he could only see a small slice of Parnassus Road. It was still obstinately empty. A kookaburra, perhaps the same one that had eyed him earlier, swooped across and perched on the facade of the Mini-Mart.

There was no one to hear, but he tried anyway.

Fire! he called out. Fire!

As he called, the kookaburra began a long robust laugh. Against it, his voice was tiny and smothered. He waited for the kookaburra to pause, and tried again.

Fire!

But the bird seemed to be waiting for him. As soon as he started, it started too.

He had been to dinner-parties like that.

Help!

It was a terrible, tiny, quavery voice. It could not possibly be his own. Nor could it possibly be he himself who was here on a rickety fire escape, preparing to climb over the railing and into a window a long way off the ground.

Do not look down.

So it was not Douglas Cheeseman, and all the history of that man, who gripped the railing and, somehow, scrambled over. Now he was clinging to the outside of the fire-escape railing. It was some other man entirely who looked over his shoulder, and reached across with an uncertain hand to grip the windowsill of the shop.

It was someone acting at a great, vast distance who was actually spread out now, both hands clamped desperately to the windowsill, feet behind him on the fire escape, making a kind of bridge across the alley.

Whoever he was, he was not looking down. He was looking into the room, keeping his eyes firmly on the brown patchwork. He could see the squares and rectangles quite clearly now. He took a moment to consider counting them. *One, two, three.* He heard something creak, some joint in that other man's knees, as he got a foot up and wedged it into the window frame, and now he had to pull himself right across. There was no choice involved, and certainly no courage.

His fingers gripped the frame, his face was jammed right up sideways against the wood of the sill. The paint on this window, colour white, was not crazed. *It is protected from the afternoon sun, you see,* he explained patiently, quietly, calmly, to the man who was hanging by his fingertips. *It is not subject to the same extremes of heat and cold, and thereby of expansion and contraction. Simple, isn't it?*

And now he was in the room – he himself – somehow having squeezed under the sash. He could feel a pain where his spine must have scraped something, and another where his elbow must have hit the window-frame. He was standing unsteadily, like a man on the deck of a boat. He seemed to have lost all sensation in his extremities, but he was in the room, and the patchwork was right beside him.

The first time he stooped for it, to snatch up a corner, he was too quick and missed, his hand scooping air, his nails scratching over the fabric without catching. The second time he got the corner but it was heavier than he had expected and he came up too quickly, and lost his grip. Finally he squatted down and gathered it into his chest, wrapping his arms right around it, and got it over to the window in a big lump, and clumsily shoved it out. He watched it fall, turning over, opening, flying, a corner streaming upward. Then it had spread itself out over the paving of the alley-way and lay still, and he was left hanging on to the window-frame, with the patchwork below swaying and spinning, and only his hands hanging on to the wood keeping him from falling.

CHAPTER 33

DONNA HAD ORGANISED the tennis ladies into a working bee to stitch up a big red and black banner that stretched across the front of the Mechanics' Institute: *Karakarook Pioneer Heritage Museum.* Mr Cutcliffe had got all the children into period clothes: the boys in their fathers' waistcoats, and the girls in bonnets made out of cardboard and crepe paper. Music was provided by the young man from the garage and a few others, playing bottle-tops and washboards and saws. They were in period clothes too. Under home-made cabbage-tree hats, their faces were straight out of Freddy Chang's old photos. On the patch of grass next to the Mechanics' Institute, Chook had a demonstration of Bush Crafts going: a man with a big thick pioneer beard was turning chair-legs on a foot-operated bush lathe, and Chook himself had an array of axes and adzes and was making crude chairs and tables out of buttery new logs.

At the gate of the Mechanics' Institute, Harley glanced around as if she had heard someone calling her, but no one had.

She had missed all the excitement: must have slept through the sirens, too far away in her peaceful sunroom. But

Coralie had told her all about the fire, when she had driven over with the quilt, because Chook was the Fire Chief, and had been the one to go up the ladder to get Douglas Cheeseman down from the window.

She had not asked how it had been done.

There had been a picture in the paper of Chang's shop with the back all burned away into a ragged hole, the curls of roofing-iron hanging down, the gaping window where Douglas had got the quilt out, and a big headline: *HERO!*

Not such a heroic thing really, Coralie said. The fire escape's that close to the window, you can just about walk straight in.

It would take more than that for Coralie to forgive Douglas Cheeseman.

Bloody Main Roads, she grumbled. Who needs heroes like that?

But Harley remembered what he had told her about having to be sedated, up on some bridge or other. He had laughed that embarrassed laugh. She wished she had not laughed, and then had to pretend to be coughing, when he had got to the bit about the stretcher.

She had thought of telling Coralie about all that, but decided against it. In telling her, he had given her a weapon that she could use against him if she wanted to. But she did not want to.

Out the front of the Mechanics' Institute, where the colonnades had been before they filled them in with fibro, she could see the urn rumbling away on a trestle, sending up wisps of steam. Beside it Mrs Fowler was making salad sandwiches, plying the tongs in and out of shiny metal bowls as if playing on some complicated musical instrument. Next to her Merle – or possibly it was Helen, she had never really got them sorted out, but they seemed not to mind when she mixed them up – was dealing saucers on to another trestle like a hand of cards, talking to Mrs Fowler. When she turned her head Harley heard her exclaim: *But I said to her, Mrs Davey always does the pumpkin scones!* Leith, with a serious expression, pressed a pink plastic food cover against her big soft bosom and made it unpop like a little umbrella. Beside her Helen – or perhaps it was Merle – picked up a knife and sliced across a big pink cake with a grand gesture.

Donna was sitting behind the table in the entrance selling the raffle tickets. The patchwork hung from a stand behind her. In the crowd of bright fresh clothes it looked drab and shabby, and Harley's heart went out to it, hanging lonely from its rod, being stared at by eyes that were used to *Log Cabin* and *Bow Ties*. She loved it in a particular, protective way, the way you might love a homely child. She had called it *Under the Bridge*, to help people get the idea, but she did not think it would help much.

Inside the hall, the crowd was so thick no one could move and there was a high excited buzz of talking like at a party. She had begun to think she knew everyone in Karakarook, and now she was astonished at how the seemingly empty landscape had produced all these other people she had never seen before. There were men in tee-shirts and baseball caps. There were older women in flowered dresses, and young ones in shorts, and children running around everyone's legs. There seemed to be a lot of men in hats. Big beefy ones, little skinny ones, ones with little pea-heads and big beer-guts that strained the front of their shirts, tall ones with smiling brown faces.

Not a single one of them was Douglas Cheeseman.

She stood looking into the crowded hall. Each time she saw a flat hat she started a smile and a movement of her hand, but each time it turned out not to be Douglas Cheeseman's face underneath, and she closed down the smile.

After the day at the river, she'd assumed that she'd simply bump into him, though perhaps not literally this time. He would be coming out of the Caledonian, or picking up the paper at the Acropolis, or the brown Datsun and the white ute would pass each other on Parnassus Road and they would stop, the way people did here, to have a conversation through their wound-down windows in the middle of the street.

But in spite of Karakarook being such a small place, it was amazing how you could not find someone you were looking for. After the first couple of days, when she had kept her face prepared for him as she went about her day and gone to bed with her prepared face still unused, she had finally gone to the Caledonian. She had blushed ridiculously, leaning over the bar to ask for him, with all the drinkers turning to stare, and the publican shaking his head. She could see how it looked. She had wanted to say, *It's not what you're thinking*.

But of course, when you came right down to it, it was.

She had not thought beyond the moment when they would be face to face. Words would have to be produced, and smiles would have to be created, that said what you wanted them to say. That part would probably bring all the usual difficulties.

But first, she had to find him.

She tried to push through the crowd, but did not get far before her way was blocked by a group of women staring at the mangles and galvanised washing tubs in the WASHDAY exhibit.

Blue bags, one of them said in the resonant authoritative voice of a deaf person. A small tight perm sat on her head like a tidy brown animal. Without actually pushing at her large flowered bottom, Harley could not get past.

Fancy that, Olive, remember the old blue bags. And look, Empire Starch. Remember starching?

Harley stood on tiptoes and looked over the heads in front of her. All over the hall, flat-topped felt hats were moving slowly around.

The woman with the perm had moved on now to the kitchen behind its red rope, and Harley let herself shuffle along behind. She looked in as if she had never seen it before. The basket of kindling was very life-like, even though there seemed to be more aprons hanging from nails than an average kitchen might be expected to have, and rather more tea-cosies than tea-pots.

Oh look, Olive, the old range. Takes you back, doesn't it?

It was interesting being a stranger in the crowd again. It was like a rehearsal for being back in the city. It would seem odd to be where no one knew you, and no car would ever stop in the middle of the street so the person inside could talk to you.

Lot of old rubbish if you ask me, a man just behind her said sideways to the woman with him.

He leaned in, right over the red rope, and picked up a toasting fork from the kitchen table. She knew without needing to look what the card said: *Toasting Fork Made from Fencing Wire, about 1910.*

Bloody rubbish, the man said.

He was talking out of the corner of his mouth, but loudly. He was only pretending that he did not want to be heard.

Used to have one just like it at home, the woman said.

She laughed in a snort.

Chucked it out, soon as we got the power on.

She took it from him and ran a finger along one of the bent tines.

Rusty. Can you believe it, putting this in a museum?

In her hands, the fork had a pathetic home-made look. Harley watched as she flexed it carelessly. The red rope and the labels were supposed to stop people doing that. It was supposed to *re-contextualise* things – that was the term for it at the Museum in Sydney.

The woman put the fork back on the table next to its card.

Heritage!

Somehow, she made the word sound ridiculous.

Peering around above the heads of shorter people, Harley was pleased to see that the cadet from the *Livingstone & Shire Weekly Clarion* was there, with a camera around his neck and a spiral notebook in his hand. He was Coralie and Donna's brother's brother-in-law on the Fielding side, or some such connection. There would be a nice big splash on the front page. Coralie was there, standing in front of AND SO TO BED, getting ready for him to take her photo.

Freddy Chang had come up with the idea of putting a window frame on the wall and he had supplied a big glossy coloured photo of a view of paddocks and rather overly green trees, which he had cut up and carefully glued into the window-panes. The effect was quite realistic. Under the peaceful scene, Coralie's old wagga looked endearing. It was easy to imagine getting in under it, feeling the warmth of all those old socks and woolly singlets.

Anything that was wool you never threw away, Coralie was telling the cadet, scribbling into his notebook.

It was like a crime to throw away wool.

She was getting herself ready for the photo, making sure the wagga was visible behind her, getting her smile ready, but she suddenly held out a hand.

Stop! Chook's got to be in it with me! Come on, love!

Chook was there then, huge beside her, still in his singlet from the woodcraft demonstration. He put his arm around her shoulders, squeezing her so tight Harley could see the breath was pushed out of her. Harley could see how embarrassed he was, out there with everyone staring at him and Coralie and the wagga, but she could see he was proud too, looking down at his wife with a sort of grimace of tenderness. Coralie looked up into his face with a shy, pleased look, a look just between the two of them, in the moment that the camera flashed.

They were looking deep into each other's eyes, but Harley saw that what they were doing was not the same as *looking deep into each other's eyes*. The fraction of a second that the camera had captured was a fraction of a second of simple love. Their love for each other was at least as complicated as most people's, but just for that moment, it was the simplest thing in the world. That ought to be enough. It did not have to be simple for every single minute of every single day.

She went back out to the porch and sat down behind the table with Donna. There was quite a crowd, pushing around to look at the patchwork. Not everyone liked it.

Oh, she heard someone say, on a surprised and disappointed downward note. It's very original, isn't it?

Harley kept her head down.

Don't know that you'd want it on the bed, though, would you?

She opened the little tin box the money was in and rattled around, pretending to count it.

I wonder if they washed the old suits first. And look, the seams don't line up properly.

It was one thing to know that people thought it, but it was nicer not to have to hear them saying it.

She looked up, and there he was, Douglas Cheeseman, right in front of her, holding a handful of change and saying *One, please.*

When he saw that it was her, he dropped all the money. It bounced and rolled under the table, around the feet of people waiting to come in.

Sorry, he said. Sorry.

He was awkward, stooping and kneeling for the coins. She could see the top of his head, bobbing around on a level with the table. He was not wearing his hat, after all.

Sorry, he kept saying from underneath the table.

When he stood up, she could see that the knees of his pants were picked out in a brown circle of dust. He was red in the face, flapping at the dust on his knees, and his ears had never looked so big.

His mouth was forming words, but as if by remote control. The words did not seem to match the look on his face.

Oh! he was exclaiming. Hello again! Fancy bumping into you here! Terrific!

He laughed, but he did not sound happy.

I've been looking for you, she said.

It seemed important to say it all straight away, while he was here, but everyone was watching.

To say thank you.

A listening silence had fallen around them, as if they were on stage.

Oh, that was nothing! he cried. That was easy!

He choked on the word, and had to cough, and that made him redder in the face than ever.

No, she said, it wasn't nothing.

She wanted to say, *I remember about the vertigo*, but could not go on, with all the silent people watching.

They had to carry me down on a stretcher. It was a vivid picture in her mind, Douglas Cheeseman injected full of valium, strapped on to a stretcher, his eyes staring upwards at nothing.

Yes! he cried loudly and quickly, as if thinking the same thing, and not wanting her to say it. No worries! No big deal!

They sounded like another man's words in his mouth. He glanced around at the people waiting behind him, everyone looking from him to her and back again like people at a tennis match.

Look, I'll have ten, he said.

Suddenly he was a man in a hurry.

How much is that?

Harley could not seem to get her brain to do the arithmetic of it, but Donna had the answer.

A dollar a ticket, or six for five dollars. Take the dozen, pet, and that'll be the ten.

Involved with the change in his hand, he glanced up, startled, at that *pet* and met Harley's eye. Her mouth jumped into a smile, all by itself, and he looked away as if he thought she was laughing at him. She bowed her head to the little book of raffle tickets, smoothing out the dog-eared corners, ironing them flat. She felt herself frowning down at them as if it was important, watching her fingers flatten the corners over and over again.

Then she remembered she could start writing on the tickets.

The Caledonian, isn't it? she asked, as if she did not know.

Caledonian Cheeseman. Caledonian Cheeseman. Caledonian Cheeseman, she wrote on ticket after ticket. No one had bought so many before.

Oh, I never win anything in raffles! he said, watching her write.

He laughed, although it was not actually funny. She glanced up and he stopped laughing, as if she had accused him of lying.

Well, once a set of pewter mugs, he admitted.

He looked at her helplessly. She smiled, and nodded encouragingly, but could not think of anything to say that would rescue him. He floundered on.

They made everything taste funny.

But now there was a family, all in check shirts, that had just come in and not seen that there was something being watched. They were pushing up behind him, with a child nudging at the back of his legs, and the edge of a stroller knocking into his knee, so that he was more or less propelled away from the table.

She took the money from the man in the check shirt, and tried to write down the name he was spelling out. It seemed to have too many *m*s in it, and he was determined that she get it right. *Oh, forget it,* she wanted to say. *Who cares how you spell it?*

Suddenly she realised that Douglas had forgotten his tickets. She jumped up so quickly she knocked against the stand where the patchwork hung, making it tremble and nearly fall.

Whoops! she heard someone call out and laugh, as if this was the best bit of the show.

Douglas! Douglas! Come back!

She had not used his name before. It sounded terribly intimate, although she tried to make it casual. He turned, and suddenly the space between them was empty, and she felt as if she was shouting his name across it. She thrust the tickets at him.

Look, she started, I was –

But he interrupted.

Listen, he said, urgently, and she listened.

I've been thinking about the bridge, he said.

Then he seemed to lose heart.

She tried to help.

How do you mean, exactly, the bridge?

Well, he started, but suddenly another lot of new arrivals was coming in the doorway between them, saying *Hello, Harley!* and *How are you, Harley?* and *Congratulations, Harley!* and crowding around, blocking her off from him.

I said, tomorrow, he said loudly, around the heads. After lunch. At the bridge. I'll show you.

A woman buying raffle tickets heard and looked over at him, smiling as if amused, looking from him to Harley.

Harley stared back into her face. Yes, he was arranging a rendezvous.

And that was perfectly all right, because she was going to say *yes*.

*

CHAPTER 34

IT WAS TRUE that *after lunch* left a fair bit of latitude, but it was now quite a long way *after lunch*. The afternoon was cooler than it had been, the sun sinking towards a mass of little tufted clouds. Long shadows were beginning to stretch out across the paddocks.

Douglas stared out at feathery stalks of long grass haloed with the late sun, and two horses head-to-head over a fence. From his own feet a long thin shadow went out along the roadway of the bridge and bent over the side.

He thought about how she had been at the Museum opening. It had seemed to him then that she had been quite warm. Definitely cordial. Perhaps even something more than cordial. He had gone over it in his mind, the look she had given him, the way she had said his name. He replayed it again and again.

It had not been anything as straightforward as a smile. But there had been something around the mouth, and something round the corners of the eyes too. You could call it a *twinkle*. There had been a *twinkle in her eye*.

Put that way, it did not sound quite right.

He looked up into the bush where the orange ribbons around the doomed trees flickered.

Mr Denning had been surprised to hear from him.

Surprised, too, it seemed, at some change in the way he spoke.

Cheeseman, he had said warily. Everything all right, Cheeseman?

In the moment of hearing his voice, feeling the little clutch of fear, Douglas had realised that talking to Mr Denning had always been like the Legacy teas. Those tough old blokes expecting him to be a hero like his father. The way they turned away, contemptuous, when they found out he was not.

He was still no *hero*. That was never going to be the right word for what he was. But you did not necessarily have to be a *hero*, to do what had to be done.

He had noticed that Harley Savage had a way of squaring her shoulders back before she spoke and he had tried it, right there in the stuffy phonebox at the foot of the stairs in the Caledonian.

It's about the bridge, Mr Denning, he said.

Getting your shoulders back definitely helped. Or perhaps it was thinking about Harley Savage that helped.

I think we can save it.

We, meaning whom, exactly? *We*: Douglas Cheeseman and the Supervising Engineer from Head Office? Douglas Cheeseman and the concerned citizens of Karakarook, NSW?

He knew who he meant. He could pretend to himself if he liked, but he knew that he knew. There was a picture in his mind, of himself and Harley Savage. He could see them, the two of them, side by side. Shoulder to shoulder. Being *we*.

He glanced over the side of the bridge, at his own footprints in the sand down there. When he glanced back along the road that led to town, he saw a little figure coming towards him. It was too far to see, but he knew who it was.

Suddenly he was not so sure about that look she had given him, and the sound of his name in her mouth. Now that she was upon him, he had an impulse to hide. She would never find him if he ran down to his burrow under the bridge. He would hear her walking on top of him, but she would not know he was there. If he was that kind of man, he could even look up through the cracks, up her dress. If she was that kind of woman, the kind who wore that kind of dress.

She was tall and solid striding through the landscape. He was prepared to admit that she frightened him, and the way she walked was one of the things that frightened him the most. It excited him, too. She held her shoulders back hard and took long strides. It was a kind of swagger. Her feet came down hard. She was like an army marching. Nothing would stop her. She could forge on right over you, not seeing you, bearing herself along on those pulled-back shoulders.

It made the fur along his spine stand up.

He did not think she had seen him yet, dim, pale, probably invisible in his *neutrals*. Hiding was not out of the question.

But hiding was not a realistic option. It was a disgrace even to have thought of it. He got his shoulders squared back.

We can save the bridge, he would say. He would not beat around the bush.

Getting his shoulders squared back did not seem to be helping as much this time.

He could see the smile on her face, and it looked as though she might be humming. She still had not seen him. The dog was there beside her but it was having to trot to keep up. It looked alertly from side to side. Soon it would smell the invisible fawn-coloured man who had had shameful thoughts about hiding.

He took a meaningless step forward, snatched his hat off and used it to wave away a fly that was not there, so that she would see him. He did not want her to think he was trying to hide.

The dog saw him first, and then she saw him too. She did not stop coming on but each step was slower than the last. Her smile went through some kind of small metamorphosis.

He told himself not to rush in. Let her set the tone.

I was hoping you'd come, he blurted, as she came closer.

He blundered on, trying to remember what he had rehearsed. She was wearing a blue shirt of some coarse sort of fabric today. It definitely *did something* for her.

To have a chat. About the bridge.

In a bush beside the road a bird was scolding on and on. *Peep peep a cheep a parp par, parp parp parp a chick chick pir-rup.* Another answered: *Eep eep*, then again *eep eep*.

There's no need to knock it down, you see.

Oh?

Under the hat, her face was noncommittal.

He felt things were already getting away from him. Perhaps he should have written it all down, done a list.

The trees will still have to go, but we can use them for the corbels. Chook can work the timber. Then we'll bolt concrete on top to keep it all dry. In modules. We'll cast them upside-down, in sections, you see, to allow for movement.

He had a nasty feeling he was gabbling.

Because really, it's only the corbels.

He could not remember if he had already explained to her about corbels.

As well as the lines going out from her eyes, there were curves cut into her face, like brackets, on either side of her mouth. It must be where her face creased when she smiled. He imagined it. Years and years of smiles. Hundreds and thousands of them.

She was not exactly smiling at the moment. But she was not exactly frowning, either.

The what?

He wished he was better at explaining.

They're sort of joiners, he started.

He put one hand out, palm down, and jabbed the other up against it.

They kind of join where two beams meet on top of a pier.

He jabbed away desperately.

Look, he said suddenly, I'll show you.

He found he had put his hand behind her upper arm. He did not know he had it in him to be so bold. The coarse blue fabric was surprisingly soft to touch. He guided her over towards the fence, surprised, too, at how she allowed him. He folded himself in half to get through the fence, hurrying so he could hold the strands apart for her, and his shirt snagged on the barbed wire, pulling free with a musical twang. It sounded ridiculous and their eyes met for a moment but neither of them smiled.

On the narrow strip of sand beside the water, they had to stand close to each other. Together they looked up into the private underparts of the bridge.

Really, it's as strong as anything.

He slapped at one of the piers.

Not going to move any more.

He wished she would say something.

Look, he said, too loud.

He tried again, softer.

See up there? See the corbels?

He crouched and pointed up into the darkest corner.

Completely rotten. See?

Actually it was hard to see in the heavy shadow, and the flickering reflected light was confusing.

She crouched beside him and stared up at the wrong place.

He leaned in towards her so she could follow the line of his pointing arm.

See?

When he turned too quickly, with another thought about corbels, he knocked against her in the tight space so that she lost her balance and had to save herself with a hand down on the mud.

Oh! Sorry!

She ignored this.

So why are they so important? she said. These corbels.

He glanced at her, to see if she was being hostile, but she was simply waiting to hear what he would say, her face blank with concentration. She was shoulder-to-shoulder with him, their faces almost touching. He could smell something exotic coming off the coarse blue shirt. This close, he could see things he had never noticed about her before. He had a good view of her neck as she looked up. It was not young and smooth, and where the neck of the shirt was open the skin of her upper chest was crepey and spotted with brown freckles. But as he watched her staring up at the underneath of the bridge, strangely lit with rippling light, he longed to put his face into that corner where neck met chest, to feel the warmth of her, the large powerful strength of her, the way the blood moved with such eagerness in her veins.

Well, he started.

He had managed it with Mr Denning, he reminded himself. He would manage it with her, too.

They distribute the load. That's why they're important.

He bunched up his fingers and jabbed them against the pile beside him.

See, when you do that, well, it's quite a load. It's all going into that, um, small, um, area of the headstock.

He jabbed away at the pile. Little flakes of old bark drifted down.

But if you do it like this—

He opened his hand out and laid the palm flat against the wood.

Well, you've got more, um, surface area to distribute the load. The weight. That's what the corbel does, takes the load and distributes it and sends it down into the piers.

He was making broad distributing-and-sending-down gestures with his hand when he became aware of her watching him. He stopped in the middle of a sending-down movement.

Sorry, he said. I'm a bit, um, obsessed.

He looked at his boots, sinking slowly into the mud.

My wife was always telling me I was a bridge bore.

She stood up, a bit at a time, cautiously, between the beams. He heard her joints cracking. She wiped her muddy hand on a pier.

Yes, she said dryly. You already said.

He bit his lip. Not only *a bridge bore*, but a bore about being *a bridge bore*.

Sorry, he muttered.

He could feel the water seeping in over the top of one of his boots.

Well, she said.

She looked up again, at where the light stippled the timbers with light and dark.

That's okay, she said, and laughed abruptly. I interest easily.

She turned her face to him. He had not noticed before how her hazel eyes were flecked with amber when you looked closely. In fact, when you looked closely, there were many colours in her eyes, tiny flecks of a great many different kinds of brown.

The timber's right there, he said.

He spoke straight into those flecked hazel eyes.

Plenty of timber.

His mouth was moving, but he was not really thinking about the words.

It's only the corbels, you see.

He could not remember if he was repeating himself.

She had got closer to him. Or he had got closer to her. Either way, he was close enough now to see the pale line of the old scar on her chin, and the fan of wrinkles raying out from the corner of each eye.

The corners of her mouth were amazingly expressive. The muscular precision was remarkable. The human face. The human mouth. That little muscle, just there, that was quirking up the corner of her lips as she turned towards him.

They were looking at each other, but for once Harley did not feel as if it was a performance. *There they are, looking deep into each other's eyes.* And then the next bit of the script: *They must be in love.*

This was simpler than that, and there did not seem to be a running commentary on it. A conversation was going on, but one that did not involve words of any kind. He was looking at her, at Harley Savage her very self, and she was looking at him. *Douglas Cheeseman.*

It was a joke of a name, but that was just something his parents had done to him. He himself was not a joke.

Look, she said.

There was something that had to be done, now before the wordless conversation became *looking deep into each other's eyes* and was just one more thing to hide behind.

I must warn you, she said. I've got a dangerous streak.

He laughed. There was relief in it, as if he thought she was going to say something worse.

That's okay, he said.

He thought for a moment.

Me too.

It was a good joke, but now it was getting close to being a performance again. Harley Savage, known for her *dry wit*, making someone laugh.

No, she said, the thing is.

She stopped. She had never put into words, aloud, just exactly what *the thing* was. She was dizzy with the fear of it, the palms of her hands suddenly sweaty. She steadied herself with a hand against one of the piers, feeling the wood silky under her palm.

I had a husband.

The words seemed large and foreign in her mouth.

He was nodding.

Yes, I had a wife.

As far as he was concerned, it just meant they had something in common.

No, she said, and it came out sharp. He stopped smiling.

The thing is, he.

She had always hidden behind the tidiness of *took his own life*. Behind it, you could pretend to think it had nothing to do with you.

He killed himself with his circular saw. In the shed.

She took a big quavery breath.

And he.

But she could not find the words for the letter. *Dear Harley comma.* She stopped. A big wad of some kind of thick woolliness was filling her throat, stopping any more words getting out. The whole of the space behind her face had swollen with this thing and was bursting through the apertures. The face could not keep it all out of sight any more.

Yes, he said, and after a moment she felt his arm around her shoulders. Yes.

He did not seem to be disgusted or frightened. He did not even seem especially surprised. *Yes*, he said, as if it was normal, a husband cutting his head off out in the shed. His arm around her shoulder was not *being terribly sorry* or *offering my deepest sympathy*. It was just a matter of geometry: an equal and opposite force. It was what a person needed when they could not balance by themselves any more.

Yes. Yes.

And now the dog was pushing against her leg. She could feel its tail beating steadily, backwards and forwards. It stayed pressed up hard, a big warm shape stuck to her, keeping her company while she went about the business of allowing her face to open up, letting out everything that was behind it.

*

CHAPTER 35

IN SPITE OF his cuts and grazes, William insisted on going to school in the morning, and when he said he would go on his own, Felicity did not argue. As soon as she had the house to herself, she got to work. She did all the washing in the basket and stripped the beds and washed all the bedding. She did the blankets today as well as the sheets and got them all out on the line without needing to tilt her head up. It took a long time, but my word it was satisfying to see them all out purifying in the sun.

Then she got down on her hands and knees to scrub the kitchen floor. It was amazing how much dirt could come off even the cleanest-looking floor when you got down and scrubbed at it. It was the corners especially, of course, and the little cracks where the cupboards joined the floor. She got an old toothbrush – well, it was Hugh's, but she would get him a new one – and got into all the cracks with it, using lots of cleaner, smelling the lemon in it, watching the foam go brown.

What a good feeling it was, sponging off the dirt, pouring the water away down the sink! Just to make sure, she filled the bucket again with clean water to sponge it all over again. Even the second time she thought a bit more dirt came off, so she did it again. So much dirt, hiding in her kitchen, all along, when she thought it was clean!

It was awful, really.

Hugh had not said anything. William had gone to bed early, and so had she. It was not that she was sick, exactly, but it was easier to agree with Hugh that she *needed a rest*. When things got *awkward*, it was always useful to *need a rest*. He brought her a plate of soup and they had quite a conversation about whether it was hot enough, but they had not talked about what had happened. They had never talked about it the other times, either. There was no point. You just *put it behind you*.

But this time he had sat on the end of the bed while she toyed with the soup. *Not in front of William*, he said at last. She could see how hard it was for him to bring each word out. *Just not in front of William, darling.*

Seeing how hard it was for him, she was shocked by a sudden piercing X-ray picture of exactly what she was doing. Just for one moment, holding the plate of soup and the spoon, she saw it, naked, without the veil of not-really-knowing, and was stricken. For a sharp instant she recognised the world that Hugh inhabited as he watched her, seeing and trying not to see. Just for that moment – the space of a breath – she knew how unbearable it was for him, how smiling and ticking things off on his fingers was the only way he could manage. She saw that she was inflict-ing this pain on him by the choices she was making. Just for one puncturing moment she saw herself: a cruel smiling child.

Then she had picked up the spoon, sipped at the soup, and the moment passed.

She decided to make something a bit special for dinner tonight. It would be a pleasure to cook in a kitchen she knew for sure did not harbour so much as a particle of dirt in any hidden little crack or crevice. When Hugh opened the door, coming home this afternoon, he would be greeted with lovely smells. Her special pasta sauce, perhaps, that he liked so much. It filled the house nicely with the smell of oregano. After lunch she would pop into Livingstone to get some mince for it, and something for the rest of the week, that she could put in the freezer.

Before he turned into the gate she would have all the lamps switched on to fill the house with light. It would still be sunny outside, but there were a few spots in the house that tended to be shadowy, even on the brightest day. Everything would be fresh and clean. There would be no dirt, and no shadows, and the only smell would be the oregano. She would be at the centre of it, crisp and clean in the little blue top he had always liked, that showed off her bust, although not in a tarty way, naturally.

She would give him a lovely smile as he came in the door, and another one when he told her how *flavoursome* the dinner was. *Very flavoursome*, he would say, the way he always did.

If she did not smile between now and when he came home, she could afford to give him two smiles tonight. And after each smile she could just pop into the bathroom for a moment to undo the damage by smoothing a little dab of moisturiser around the corners of the mouth.

She would listen very attentively as he told her about his day, and after the second smile there would probably be no need to smile again for the rest of the evening.

CHAPTER 36

HARLEY SAT ON the back step, watching the dog. The early morning sky was luminous, the sun not yet risen, only a big simple radiance behind the horizon. A line of pink clouds above the distant hills formed and re-formed, melting from shape to shape like thoughts.

Whispering together, the leaves of the big gum at the bottom of the yard moved softly in a slight breeze. The pigeons lined up on the top of the garage next door cooed on and on, soothing each other.

She had left Douglas sleeping in the daybed, the tuft of hair sticking straight up on the pillow, and tiptoed out. He had turned over and muttered something in his sleep, but had not woken up.

With him behind her in the house, the view from the back step was somehow different. She knew it all now: the way the shade of the gumtree was as soft as hair when you sat under it, the way the sky out here in the country was always paler at the bottom than the top, the way the birds came right up to the back step if you fed them. Just as she was leaving, she felt as if Lorraine Smart's house was a code she had finally cracked.

But having Douglas Cheeseman asleep in the daybed was

a new part of the code. She did not know what it might turn out to mean. Since the previous day, out at the bridge, things had taken on a different look. Things that had seemed complicated had become simple, but certainties that had seemed set hard had turned more fluid. The solid little block that had been *Harley Savage, the one with the dangerous streak*, had broken open, and it seemed possible that the parts might rearrange themselves, although into what new shapes she could not imagine.

The dog came over to the dish of water at the bottom of the steps, lapped up a lot of water and sneezed twice. It was enough to set the parrot off. *Johnny! Come here, Johnny! Come here!* She could see it sticking its head out between the bars of its cage, peering sideways at the dog as if waiting for an encore. The dog scratched behind its ear, then went and lay down on the grass with a stick, holding one end down with a paw while it gnawed at the other.

The dog was another of the certainties that seemed to have turned fluid. Until today she had never entertained the idea of taking it back with her to Sydney. Now it appeared as a possibility. There was room in her backyard, and she was at home often enough to keep it company.

It was amazing, the way a part of her mind seemed to have worked out all the details.

But even as she pictured it, she drew back. Taking the dog back with her to Sydney would be a *declaration*. It was too soon for that. She did not feel ready to put aside, at a stroke, all those years of avoiding *declarations*.

It had seemed simple enough: you just left the dog here

where you had found it, in Karakarook. You just turned your back and drove away. But she could see now that that simplicity contained layers of complication within itself. The dog would not understand. Whatever her own views on the matter, it had no doubts about their relationship. If she tried to drive away, it would race after the car, barking through the quiet streets. It would think it was all a misunderstanding, or a joke. At worst, it would think it had been overlooked.

It would never occur to this dog that it was being abandoned.

She saw now that she would have to tie it up to stop it chasing the car. But not here, of course, in the backyard, where it would starve to death before Lorraine Smart came home. She would have to take it down to the town and tie it up somewhere, the railing of the War Memorial perhaps. She could imagine the scene as she drove away. It would bark and strain at the rope till its eyes bulged. It would whimper and grieve. Finally it would droop. But it would keep watching the corner of Parnassus Road where it had had its last glimpse of the brown car. It would keep watching that corner until someone untied the rope and forcibly dragged it off.

When he came out to join her on the step, one of Douglas's cheeks was flushed from the pillow, and the little tuft of hair made him look surprised.

There had been moments last night when Harley had felt that things could go wrong in all the old ways, or even in some completely new way. There had been a moment or two when it had been a close thing. But he had seemed to know how much damage the wrong word could do, and had not said much.

She sat a little tense now. The *night before* was one thing, but in her experience the *morning after* was often where it all came unstuck.

She did not want any speeches.

But Douglas Cheeseman was not the man for speeches. He sat with her, saying nothing, but it did not feel like a special, significant *saying nothing*. The possibility of things going wrong, and having to prevent that by working too hard at making them go right, did not seem to be troubling him.

Down on the grass, the dog worried away at the stick. When it split a long piece off the end, the little splintering sound seemed loud in the still morning. Then it set to, crunching up the end with its back teeth as if it was a bone.

It's the wolf in them, Douglas said at last. It's in the blood.

The dog let go of the stick and gave him a look. It was just an accident of the angle of its ears and the way its mouth was, but it looked a little reproachful.

Well, way back, I mean, Douglas said. Stone age, caveman. Not you personally.

Harley found that she had forgotten to worry about how things were, or the way they could go wrong, and without planning any particular, correct sort of laugh, she had simply laughed. She felt him move closer to her on the step. He was jammed up against her hip: warm, solid, not going anywhere.

There was a silence that was nothing more complicated than two people together who did not need to say anything.

Against the pale sky, the leaves of the gumtree swept softly backwards and forwards over each other, providing all the conversation that the moment called for.

The thing about the dog was, whatever she did, whether she left it behind or took it with her, it would be a *declaration*. She had always thought that it was possible to avoid them, but that was silly. Life itself was a *declaration*. You might as well get used to the idea.

What would most likely happen was that she would open the car door, and the dog would jump into the back seat and rest its chin on the back of her seat, the way they had both got used to, for the drive back to Sydney. Douglas would be there, waving them off, and then he would go out to the bridge and start the business with the modules. She had only partly understood it, but she knew it was a kind of gift. *See you*, she would say, and wave. *See you later*.

Later, when he came to see her in Sydney, he would take it for granted that the dog would be there, under the kitchen table or lying in front of the fireplace. *Hi, feller*, he would say, and tickle it behind the ears the way he did.

By then, she might have stopped thinking of it as *it*. She might even have given it a name.

That far she could visualise: sitting at her table with him across from her, his hands rearranging the things between them, the dog on the floor.

Beyond that she could not imagine.

The dawn air was cool and sweet. Up in the sky a flock of birds heeled sideways. The sun had not reached the earth yet but up there the wings were catching the first high rays. They went on turning and wheeling, catching and sending the light through the air, the sky with the dipping and turning birds in it a great bowl of light above the waiting earth.

Dark Places

Albion Gidley Singer inhabits the shell of an entirely proper man of the world: husband, father, pillar of the community. But within him are frightened and frightening dark places from which spring fear and loathing of the flesh of females. And, finally, the kind of violence that might call itself love.

'Grenville's best novel yet . . . very carefully considered, dense and blackly humorous . . .'
THE BULLETIN

'Grenville brilliantly, if chillingly, captures the voice of the smug, self-hating businessman who despises others as he despises himself . . . This is an eloquent, angry and humane novel . . .'
THE IRISH TIMES

'. . . disturbing and darkly funny'
TELEGRAPH MIRROR

'The extreme emotional reaction Grenville gets from her reader is testament alone to her writing abilities . . . Grenville is truly a magician . . .'
BOSTON SUNDAY GLOBE

'Grenville . . . has not just confronted a taboo, but entered into it, and this makes *Dark Places* as disturbing as it is impressive'
TIMES LITERARY SUPPLEMENT

'Carefully thought-through and passionately imagined'
THE INDEPENDENT

Winner of the 1995 Victorian Premier's Award (the Vance Palmer Prize for Fiction)

Crossing Ebenezer Creek

★ "Poetic in tone and savage in its depictions of the tortures slaves endured, *Crossing Ebenezer Creek* grants dignity and depth to its characters and considers the difficult and vulnerable position of African Americans as they adapted to freedom among whites who did not always view them as human beings. Readers will fall in love with Bolden's gentle lyricism as she unflinchingly unfolds a difficult story." —Shelf Awareness, starred review

★ "Bolden bravely concludes this concise, moving story with a historically accurate and horrifying ending." —*Publishers Weekly*, starred review

★ "The well-executed premise, a compelling love story, and unique historical details will appeal to fans of Ruta Sepetys's *Salt to the Sea*. This moving and engrossing portrayal of a little-known historical tragedy belongs on all YA shelves." —*SLJ*, starred review

★ "Mariah and Caleb's unforgettable story is everything historical fiction should be: informative, engrossing, and unflinching. . . . A poetic, raw, and extraordinary imagining of a little-known, shameful chapter in American history." —*Kirkus Reviews*, starred review

★ "Bolden's trenchant, powerful novel is a strong testament to the many lost lives that certainly did—and still do—matter." —*Booklist*, starred review

Inventing Victoria

★ "Seamlessly weaves aspects of black history into the detailed narrative. . . . Victoria . . . emerges as a fully realized character, a product of all her experiences. The depiction of Washington, D.C.'s African-American elite is rich and complex. . . . A compelling and significant novel." —*Kirkus Reviews*, starred review

★ "Poetic, breathtaking, descriptive and fast-paced." —*SLJ*, starred review

Books by Tonya Bolden

Finding Family

Crossing Ebenezer Creek

Inventing Victoria

Saving Savannah

Dark Sky Rising: Reconstruction and the Dawn of Jim Crow
(with Henry Louis Gates Jr.)

Facing Frederick: The Life of Frederick Douglass,
A Monumental American Man

No Small Potatoes

Pathfinders: The Journeys of Sixteen
Extraordinary Black Souls

Capital Days: Michael Shiner's Journal and the
Growth of Our Nation's Capital

Beautiful Moon: A Child's Prayer

Searching for Sarah Rector: The Richest Black Girl in America

Emancipation Proclamation: Lincoln and
the Dawn of Liberty

George Washington Carver

M.L.K.: Journey of a King

Maritcha: A Nineteenth-Century American Girl

Cause: Reconstruction America, 1863–1877

The Champ: The Story of Muhammad Ali

Portraits of African-American Heroes

With Carol Anderson

One Person, No Vote: How Not All Voters Are Treated Equally

We Are Not Yet Equal: Understanding Our Racial Divide

Tonya Bolden

Crossing Ebenezer Creek

BLOOMSBURY

NEW YORK LONDON OXFORD NEW DELHI SYDNEY

BLOOMSBURY YA
Bloomsbury Publishing Inc., part of Bloomsbury Publishing Plc
1385 Broadway, New York, NY 10018

BLOOMSBURY and the Diana logo are trademarks of Bloomsbury Publishing Plc

First published in the United States of America in May 2017 by Bloomsbury Children's Books
Paperback edition published in May 2018 by Bloomsbury YA

Bloomsbury books may be purchased for business or promotional use. For information on bulk
purchases please contact Macmillan Corporate and Premium Sales Department at
specialmarkets@macmillan.com

ISBN 978-1-68119-699-2 (paperback)

The Library of Congress has cataloged the hardcover edition as follows:
Names: Bolden, Tonya, author.
Title: Crossing Ebenezer Creek / by Tonya Bolden.
Description: New York : Bloomsbury, 2017.
Summary: Freed from slavery, Mariah and her young brother, Zeke, join Sherman's
march through Georgia, where Mariah meets a free black named Caleb and
dares to imagine the possibility of true love, but hope can come at a cost.
Identifiers: LCCN 2016037742 (print) • LCCN 2016050232 (e-book)
ISBN 978-1-59990-319-4 (hardcover) • ISBN 978-1-61963-055-0 (e-book)
Subjects: LCSH: African Americans—Juvenile fiction. | CYAC: African Americans—Fiction. |
Freedmen—Fiction. | Sherman's March to the Sea—Fiction. | United States—History—Civil War,
1861–1865—Fiction. | Brothers and sisters—Fiction. | Love—Fiction. | BISAC: JUVENILE
FICTION / Historical / United States / Civil War Period (1850–1877). | JUVENILE FICTION /
People & Places / United States / African American. | JUVENILE FICTION / Family / Siblings.
Classification: LCC PZ7.B635855 Cr 2017 (print) | LCC PZ7.B635855 (e-book) | DDC [Fic]—dc23
LC record available at https://lccn.loc.gov/2016037742

Book design by Colleen Andrews
Typeset by Westchester Publishing Services
Printed and bound in the U.S.A. by Sheridan, Chelsea, Michigan
4 6 8 10 9 7 5 3

All papers used by Bloomsbury Publishing Plc are natural, recyclable products
made from wood grown in well-managed forests. The manufacturing processes
conform to the environmental regulations of the country of origin.

To find out more about our authors and books visit www.bloomsbury.com and sign up for our newsletters.

In memory of those sturdy black bridges,
male and female, I was blessed to have as family.

Crossing Ebenezer Creek

PROLOGUE

In a southeast Georgia swamp, when a driving rain drenches an early December day, bald cypresses seem to screech, tupelos to shriek, Ebenezer Creek to moan.

Science minds try to explain it away with talk of air flow, wind waves, and such, but others shake their heads. *Not so.* They say it's the ghosts of Ebenezer Creek rising, reeling, wrestling with the wind. Remembering.

Remembering desperate pleas, heartrending screams.

Remembering hope after hope, dream after dream, and—

Mariah, who had dreamed of a long life with Caleb and at least one acre, she first remembers that twelve days before she reached Ebenezer Creek, a hungry hush sent a shiver down her spine.

THEN SHE HEARD THE THUNDER

She dropped the scrub brush, sprang to her feet, peered through the cookhouse window. Sudden quiet too queer.

Yonder in a sweet gum tree, a crowd of crows rose up. They hung in midair for three heartbeats, then swept east.

Something was coming. Good or evil the girl couldn't tell, but she knew it best to bolt.

Lithe and long-legged, she bounded through the back door, raced to a little boy picking up pecans from the ground.

On the outskirts of her mind, she heard a bell tolling frantic, glimpsed others dashing, scattering.

"Come on!" She grabbed the boy's hand. Their hiding place was in the root cellar. A dugout beneath a pile of croker sacks.

Amid the musty smell of red clay, sacks of onions and potatoes, bushels of beets, rutabagas, parsnips, and carrots, she listened for sounds in the distance, for gunfire, for—

Then she heard the thunder—pictured a thousand horses, full gallop.

Hands went quick over the boy's ears when the Big House front door was kicked in.

Next she heard Callie Chaney screaming bloody murder.

Then a thud.

The sound of dust settling ensued, followed by the crash-and-shatter of china and glass.

Voices low, muffled. No way to tell. Outlaws on the prowl? Or was it—

Then came flashbacks of Callie Chaney's scare talk.

"Yankees are monsters!" the woman used to shriek. "Devils! Pure devils!" Wagging a bony finger in her face, Callie Chaney had warned, "You go traipsing off after bluecoat brutes, you won't reach nowhere but dead."

Cellar doors creaked. She clamped a hand over the boy's mouth.

A pistol clicked.

"Anybody down there? Come out now if you know what's good for you!"

The voice was hard, quick. Not one word had a curl or dragged out long. It had to be a Yankee!

Praise God!

The girl had never believed the scare talk. She had prayed for Yankees to come her way ever since the war broke out forty-one months ago. Forty-one long months of huddled, quivering hope.

Battle of Fort Sumter . . . First Manassas . . . Second Manassas . . . Sharpsburg . . . Lincoln's great and mighty Emancipation Proclamation . . . Gettysburg . . . Cold Harbor.

With the others she had been stitching things together from news overheard while tending guests or spied during stolen glances at a *Macon Telegraph* meant for trash.

Days ago word came of Atlanta licked up in flames and how on the heels of the hurt he put on that city, a Union general named Sherman had his army marching southeast.

Let them come by here! the girl prayed every day. Atlanta was more than one hundred miles away from where she was held. When she heard that Yankees had stormed Milledgeville, some thirty miles away, she prayed harder. *Lord, let the Yankees come by here.*

And in the last two days, there was gunfire and smoke from Sandersville. And now—

"Anybody down there? Come out now if you know what's good for you!"

Trusting her gut, she shouted from beneath that pile of croker sacks, "Don't shoot! We coming out!"

RIDDLEVILLE ROAD

When Caleb turned off Riddleville Road and headed for the Big House, he heard a woman's screams and the breaking of things.

Under a canopy of oaks he rode down the long driveway thinking about where he'd start loading first. A half mile back the squad had come across an old colored man who told them what they'd likely find.

At first the man had just stared at Caleb and the thirty or so mounted white men. "Y'all what's left of Sherman's army?" the old man asked, utterly dejected.

Captain Galloway instructed him on how to catch up with a larger force. He also told him that when the squad was done scouting out provisions, it would head for this same force. The man was welcome to travel with them.

The old man, now smiling, eased over to Caleb. "How many in what he call the larger force?" he whispered.

"Thousands," Caleb whispered back.

The old man decided to make tracks for the larger force right then and there. Before he did, he told them about the Chaney place up ahead. "Not what it once was, but she still is wukked and got a top tanner." He then sketched out the place, Big House to barn.

"Is the place for the Union or the Rebellion?" Captain Galloway asked.

"Secesh!" the old man replied. "Two hundred percent and higher. Not a place around here for the Union."

"How many white men on the place up ahead?" Captain Galloway also asked.

"Nary a one I know of now," was the old man's response.

Caleb knew that news of a pro-Rebel place with no white men about ginned up some of the Yankees to go in hog wild, no matter what Captain Galloway said. Not wanting to get caught up in that, as they got closer to the Chaney place Caleb put a little distance between his wagon and the rest of the forage squad, slowing his horses to a trot.

Captain Galloway kept his horse at a canter, shouting out to his men, "Order! Remember, all in order!"

Caleb was almost at the end of the driveway when he brought the buckboard to a stop. He took off his duster, balled it up behind his toolbox, took up the reins again.

"Giddyap!"

Smokehouse . . . corncrib . . . root cellar. Caleb played a guessing game of how many sacks of this and bushels of that he could fit in his wagon. Then he reminded himself to leave room for a person or two. After all, the old man said the Chaney place was still being worked. If any of the colored were of a mind to take their leave, like always Caleb would gladly give them a ride.

GREEN EYES

Two scruffy, scraggly bearded soldiers in sky-blue trousers and dark-blue sack coats flanked the root cellar doors. Musket rifles at the ready.

From astride a bay steed, a third white man—crisp, clean-shaven, long, lean—looked down on her and the boy.

"Captain Abel Galloway, United States Army," he boomed, holstering his pistol. "Is the owner of this place for the Union or for the Rebellion?"

From the tone of his voice, the girl sensed the man knew the answer. She took him to be the orderly type. Sounded to her like he was exampling for the scruffy ones.

"Rebellion, sir." She kept her sharp, dark eyes trained on the ground, the boy tight by her side.

"And you have been held in slavery?"

"Yes, sir." The jackknife in her apron pocket got a nervous pat.

"No more!" announced the captain. "No more slavery for you. You now own yourselves."

Something in his voice made her chance a glance up.

The keen-faced captain was smiling. Jet-black hair gleaming. Green eyes sparkling. He could have been singing "Joy to the World" on Christmas Day.

She lowered her eyes as the man continued his say. "By proclamation of President Abraham Lincoln, on the first of January in the year of our Lord 1863, you are free!" He cleared his throat. "And as a member of the United States Army I am obliged to maintain your freedom."

"Thank you, sir." She curtsied, as she had been trained to do not long after learning to walk.

"Always curtsy, no matter their station," said her ma one day while at the loom. "And never look whitefolks in the eye."

"Never let 'em know what you think," her pa had told her on another day while planing pine wood. "Better still, don't even let on you *can* think."

When the girl saw the boy peek out from behind her skirt, she remembered another lesson on survival. Scared stiff that he'd speak, she clamped a hand over his mouth. She was looking past Green Eyes now, wondering about Josie, Jonah, Mordecai, the rest.

"Anyone else in the cellar?" the man asked.

She lowered her eyes again. "No, sir."

"Much food in there?"

"Fair amount." She glanced up, saw him wave the two scruffy ones down into the cellar.

"Remember, Private Sykes, Private Dolan, don't take it all," he said. "Rebel-she though she be, it's not for us to make her starve." With that, off he galloped.

A split second later, little boy in tow, the girl took off for one of the dismal mud-daubed log cabins that bordered the woods. Heart pounding and the words from Green Eyes a song to her soul, she outright wanted to fly. *No more! . . . No more slavery for you . . . You now own yourselves . . . You are free!* At last she was getting away from the Chaney place! At last she was—

But she had a fright when she entered her cabin.

Ladder-back chair overturned. Water jug in pieces on the floor. Cedar trunk lid thrown back.

Thank goodness, the trunk had only been rifled through. Nothing taken. Not her second dress, not the boy's second britches, not other bits of clothing, her sewing things. Safe, too, the pouch of keepsakes.

From a nail on the wall, she grabbed a sling sack and stuffed it with the contents of the trunk. She tried not to tremble.

Just hurry! Hurry! Hurry!

After praying for this day, after planning how she'd pack up quick—she wasn't prepared for the rush-and-roll of emotions, for the trembling.

On she packed while the boy spun in circles smack in the middle of their one small room. Smiling, he flapped his arms every turn or so.

With one sack filled and another begun, the girl let the boy be.

Tin cups. Wooden bowls. Quilt from their bed. Candles from the crate beside it. Bucket by the hearth that *ka-lanked* with fishhooks, weights, a deadfall trap, snares. Last in, the calabash canteens that hung by the door near her cloak.

"We settin' off." She helped the boy into his wool jacket a size too small. "We leavin'." She had told him that this day might come, told him they'd have to move cottontail fast, but she never knew how much he understood.

"Freedoms?" The boy jumped up, yanked his cap from his jacket pocket, and put it cockeyed on his head.

She looked into his big brown eyes, as round as his chestnut face. "That's right, freedoms." She straightened his cap, pulled it down tight on his head. And just then the porch steps creaked. Heart in her mouth, the girl froze.

She didn't breathe easy till she saw who was at the door.

It was freckle-faced Josie, like a big sister. Josie's baby girl, Sarah, was against her bosom and her son, Little Jack, hung on to her skirt. No bundles, no sacks. The girl knew what that meant.

They'd talked about Josie's rock and a hard place many times after her husband, Big Jack, got the hire-out.

"Can't do it." Josie's tears flowed. "Jack's comin' through this. He'll head back here, I know. If we go, he won't never find us. Never."

"But, Josie, are you—"

"Sure. And sure we'll be fine. Will stay in prayer and keep a machete by my side."

Josie's mind was made up, the girl knew. "Till we meet again," she said, trying not to cry as she hugged Josie, kissed baby Sarah, patted Little Jack's cheek.

"Till we meet again," Josie sniffled.

The sling sacks dug into the girl's shoulders as she headed out. She looked around, back into the woods, called out, "Jonah . . . Mordecai . . . Dulcina . . ."

Yankees laughed, cussed, sent up whoops and hollers. Yankees grew louder with her every step.

Stuffing hams into sacks.

Stringing squawking chickens to saddle-flaps.

Corralling horses.

Bringing hogs to a halt with bullets and bayonets.

She stopped at the root cellar, now ringed with sacks, bushel baskets. Tightening her grip on the little boy's hand, the girl searched the faces of Yankees tramping, galloping by. She was sizing them up, waiting for one it felt safe to ask, "What now?"

Rag-and-Bones Belongings

He was drawn to her, like a river to the sea, the minute he saw her emerge from the root cellar.

Caleb was out of earshot but close enough to see how she avoided Captain Galloway's eyes, kept her words few. She was cloaking her strength, just pretending to be simple, he knew. And so protective of the boy, must be her—

Was her man on the place too?

When she spirited away, Caleb had an impulse to go after her, let her know that he would give her a ride. But what if she had hurried to the quarters to get her husband? Besides, he couldn't come up with an excuse for following her. Nothing to load up back there. Anybody who wanted to escape with the Yankees didn't have to be sought out or called for.

Only once had Caleb gone into the quarters to fetch somebody. Back in Sand Town, on that rainy afternoon, when a half-naked little chocolate girl ran to him crying her heart out. Her granny couldn't walk.

Caleb pulled off his jacket, put it on the child, then had her take him to her cabin.

What a wretched hut. Roof leaking. Holes in the walls stuffed with rags. The room reeked of misery.

The girl's granny lay on a pallet. Mouth twisted. Left hand like a claw. Holding his breath against the stench, Caleb lifted her up, bedding and all, carried her to his wagon. Once he got her positioned safely and a blanket over her body, he helped in the little girl with her rag-and-bones belongings.

"You give your granny some water," he said, handing her his canteen. "And you have some, too, if you want." From his pocket he brought out a biscuit from that morning's breakfast, gave her that too. Wide-eyed and willowy, the little girl reminded him of his sister, Lily.

"I'm Caleb. What's your name?"

"Cora Lee," the girl whispered.

About an hour later, when Caleb reached the campground, he discovered that Cora Lee's granny was dead.

"She went up to be with God," said Caleb to Cora Lee. He closed the woman's eyes, pulled the blanket up over her face.

Cora Lee was a fountain of tears, clinging to Caleb with all her might.

"But just think, Cora Lee, up in heaven your granny will be able to walk again, move about free all she wants."

Caleb held Cora Lee until she quieted down to sniffles,

then reached for an empty sack, filled it with some of the day's forage—salt meat, sweet potatoes, corn. He scanned the crowd of colored people already camped. With Cora Lee by the hand and that sack over his shoulder, Caleb headed for the first two young women who struck him as capable. He explained the situation, asked them to take in the girl.

Cora Lee latched onto Caleb again. "Please don't leave me!" she cried out.

"Now, now," said Caleb. "These young ladies are two of the finest in the land. They will take good, good care of you."

"Come here, darlin'," said one of the women, holding out an apple to Cora Lee.

Once the little girl was in the woman's arms, Caleb took his leave and dealt with the corpse. That done, he thought about going back to where those two young women had camped, make sure Cora Lee was settled and all right. In the end Caleb decided against it. No attachments, he told himself.

No attachments, he reminded himself on the Chaney place, after loading some hay from the barn, finding the smoke-house almost empty, and heading for whatever Privates Sykes and Dolan had brought up from the root cellar.

MOON IN THE MIDDLE
OF THE DAY

A two-horse buckboard pulled up. Fella at the reins not one bit
familiar. She tried to make sense of him from the moment he
leapt from the wagon till he reached whispering distance.
He brought to mind sightings of the moon in the middle of
the day.

Almost ebony. High cheekbones. Narrow, slanted eyes.

"Your everything?" the stranger asked.

The girl nodded.

He returned to the wagon, rearranged some sacks, stuffed
empty ones in a corner of the wagon. He motioned for her and
the boy.

She hesitated. Then, sensing no menace, she led the boy
over. If she was going to chance it with anyone, who better
than one of her own?

He planted the boy in the cushioned-up corner of the wagon.

"You Yank?" the child asked.

The young man smiled. "No, son, I'm no Yank, but my name's Caleb." After a pause, he asked, "And you?"

The boy stared at the air.

"Name's Zeke," said the girl, then added, "Me, I'm Mariah."

Caleb relieved her of her sling sacks. "Well, Mariah, I'll need every inch in the wagon. You sit up front."

"Not yet. Somebody I gotta find. We got a minute, right?"

"Got more than one," Caleb replied.

Mariah took off, then spun around. "Zeke, you stay put, you hear me?"

The others could take care of themselves, bound to come out any minute now. But Dulcina, she might not understand what was going on.

"That's not a bad-looking filly," said a soldier as Mariah dashed by, heading for the quarters.

Running faster, she cupped her hands around her mouth. "Dulcina! Dulcina!" she shouted, hoping to be heard above all the Yankee racket.

Where to look?

Mariah ran to Josie's cabin. "Seen Dulcina?"

Josie shook her head. "But you go on, Mariah, go on to freedom. I'll take care of Dulcina as best I can."

Mariah raced into the woods, looked this way, that. "Dulcina! Dulcina!" In a small clearing she saw a bit of cloth fluttering behind a red cedar.

Mariah tiptoed over. "Dulcina? It's me, Mariah."

Dulcina peeked out from behind the tree. Clearly something about the commotion had registered, for the woman clutched a grimy bundle to her chest. Gently, Mariah took her by the hand.

When Mariah returned to the wagon, she saw that Caleb had it all loaded up. Also that he couldn't contain his shock at the sight of Dulcina. So used to her, Mariah had forgotten that to a stranger Dulcina looked a fright. Red-rimmed, darting eyes. Hair a witchy-wild, silver-streaked mane. And so scrawny.

"Texas?" Dulcina's voice was a scratchy meow. There was so much pleading in her eyes.

"Texas?" she meowed again.

Mariah nodded. If telling the poor thing they were bound for Texas would get her into the wagon . . . "Yes, Dulcina, Texas."

But the wagon was full and up front couldn't hold three. Mariah looked at Caleb. Now her eyes pleaded.

She watched the frown fall from Caleb's face, watched him glance around, grab a couple of sacks, step double quick to the root cellar. He took another look around, dropped the sacks into the hole. In under a minute Dulcina was in the wagon, squeezed between a bushel of rutabagas atop a bushel of carrots and sacks of sweet potatoes. Mariah smiled as Zeke brought out a pecan from his pants pocket and handed it to Dulcina.

*   *   *

When the wagon got going, Mariah's heart began pounding again in jubilee of escaping the Chaney place—but not yet. They had just moved over to wait. Caleb brought the horses to a halt a stone's throw away from the Big House.

Before it two soldiers chewing tobacco were in a lazy lean against a wagon with a helter-skelter of stuff: barrel of whiskey, hogshead of molasses, crates of home-canned peaches and peas, bedding, books, tablecloths, piano stool, chair, small table. Spotting some of her dead master's clothes, Mariah knew they'd even rambled the attic. She figured Jonah had been their guide when he loped through the front door behind another soldier. This one had a small chest under one arm, brass spittoon under the other. After he added his spoils to the helter-skelter wagon, Mariah watched as brawny, barrel-chested Jonah led the soldier over to the camellia bushes.

Must be one of the places Miss Callie had him bury silver, Mariah thought just as Jonah smiled at her like she was a sight for sore eyes, then scowled. Mariah read his mind. To ease it, she nodded at Caleb, cupped the fingers on one hand into an *O*, then rearranged them into a *K* that quickly collapsed.

Jonah jerked his head at the camellia bush, winked, tapped his hawk nose. Mariah knew he was signaling something. But what? Before she could signal him to be clear, Jonah dashed back inside the Big House.

Captain Galloway rode up, eyed the soldiers by the helter-skelter wagon, at the one digging up silver candlesticks, tureens, platters. "No fear of God or man," he muttered.

Mariah tensed up when his eyes moved from the camellias to her.

He smiled.

She stiffened. No white man's smile had ever led to anything good. She was relieved when Green Eyes clip-clopped to the other side of the wagon, whispered something to Caleb, who nodded in reply.

"You Yank?" Zeke piped up.

Mariah looked back. Zeke was staring so hard—too hard—at the white man. "Hush up, Zeke!" she scolded. To the captain, polite as pie, she said, "He meant no disrespect, sir."

"None taken," replied the captain. Then to Zeke, "Yes, son, I'm a Yankee."

"Ma say Yanks gives freedoms!"

Mariah trembled as she watched Zeke's eyes scurry over the white man's pockets then stop. "Where freedoms at?" Again he was looking the captain dead in the face.

"Zeke!" Mariah snapped, then to Captain Galloway, "He means no rudeness, sir. Slow-witted." Mariah forgot to breathe.

"But no less precious in God's sight," said Captain Galloway. He reached into his saddlebag, pulled out a pouch, handed it to Zeke. The boy looked inside, beamed. "Look, Ma!" He pulled out two peppermint sticks. "Freedoms!"

The captain chuckled, Caleb chuckled, Mariah exhaled, and out onto the second-story veranda flew Callie Chaney.

The woman's thin white hair was in disarray, like the rest

of her. Stumbling around, she looked this way and that. "Y'all git back here!"

Mariah faced front, clenched fists pressed in her lap, bile at the back of her throat.

"Mariah!"

No more. No more.

"Mariah!"

No more!

No more head shoved into a chamber pot. No more slaps, kicks. No more brooch pinpricks to her arms. For taking too long to get a fire blazing. For scorching a tablecloth. For being two feet away when Callie Chaney was in a murderous mood.

No more!

No more tongue-lashings taken for Zeke, who left the back door open or tracked in mud. "My fault, Miss Callie," Mariah always said. "Was me."

She wiped her eyes, looked back at Zeke. He was gazing into his bag of peppermint sticks as deeply as Dulcina was staring at her pecan.

"Mordecai! . . . Jonah! . . . Sadie! . . . Sam! . . . Esther! Come back here!" Out of the corner of her eye, Mariah saw Callie Chaney walking in turnarounds now. But at least Mariah knew others had packed up for freedom. In such a state of upset, she was too scared to look around and see for sure.

"Nero!" Callie Chaney called out. "Nero, where you at? Nero, bring the bullwhip!"

More haunting, hellish memories surged up. Mariah

fought back tears. *No!* she told herself. *Only praise God! Only fix your mind on freedom!*

"Mariah! Zeke! Dulcina! Git back here!" Callie Chaney's voice had some trail off to it now. "Y'all only off to perish! To perish, I say!"

Mariah looked up, looked around, saw that she was right. Clutching sacks and bundles, others had gathered around the Yankees.

Then came the sickening sight of a soldier by the helter-skelter wagon mocking Callie Chaney. Sashaying around in a circle, he cried out in a fake falsetto and an exaggerated Southern drawl, "Oh, muh darkies! Where muh darkies? Whatever shall I do without muh darkies! Oh, I *do* declare!"

For Mariah, Callie Chaney's screams were no laughing matter, but hammers at her head. Hard as she tried, she couldn't keep the hounding memories at bay, felt dragged back to that dreadful night when she was twelve and her pa—

No, daughter, git inside . . .

No! Eyes shut tight, Mariah strained to keep her mind on freedom.

And Callie Chaney kept calling out names.

Of people long ago sold, hired out, dead.

Of wily ones who stole off after war broke out.

Of those taking freedom now.

"Mariah!" The old woman wouldn't quit. "I told you . . . them Yanks? Monsters! Pure devils! You'll perish, I say. *Perish!*"

Mariah was about to burst. *May you burn in hell!* she screamed within. *May you burn in hell!*

A bugle brought silence, stillness. Two long minutes later, Mariah heard Caleb giddyup the horses, felt the wagon jostle and bump.

This time it didn't stop after a few yards. It rolled on and on out to Riddleville Road with Mariah yearning for nothing but freedom on her mind.

BITTER

Caleb studied Mariah while her eyes were shut tight against the old crone's shrieks.

Burn scar on her neck.

Tiny gash above her left eye.

He cataloged details that hadn't registered before. Faded but clean russet head wrap. Black cloak and gray homespun dress patched in places with burlap. Half apron frayed. Beat-up brogans too big for her feet. He imagined the toes stuffed with rags.

What happened to her man?

Dead?

Sold?

Did he escape—leaving her and the boy behind?

Seeing Mariah in such a terrible state while they waited to move out cut Caleb to the quick. But he didn't think she'd break. If she had held up this long . . .

Mariah. Strong, proud-sounding name. But then he remembered that passage in Exodus about a place named Marah. "A place of bitter water," Caleb said to himself.

How bitter her days? Caleb speculated on how much hell Mariah had endured, especially with her being such a pretty one. Mahogany. Her dark eyes had a shine like diamonds. Lips a bit pouty. Button nose.

If only they were in a different time, a different place. Far away from war, from hate. She would not be in torment, and he would not be a bystander to her pain. Instead . . .

Sighting Mariah, sizing her up, was prodding Caleb to own up to his loneliness. That frightened him. He didn't understand it. It was all so quick.

Caleb had known plenty of girls. Conveniences, ways to pass the time. He had never put effort into anything close to courting. Whether it was easy ones like Clara or Maggie or husband-hunters like Kate, Caleb never formed attachments. Those girls were around his life but never in it. But now his mind was moored on Mariah.

Pretty girls, smart girls, strong girls. Caleb had known a few who were all three like Mariah. But he had never met anyone like her. The way she was with the boy, the madwoman, such a deep goodness, a goodness he had never really cared about until after that bad business a few months ago when he went out of control.

After he came to his senses and changed his ways, he poured all his energy into helping Yankees help his people and thinking about how he could help them more after the war. To do that he needed to keep away from entanglements, attachments. Mariah had him a bit muddled up. Caleb feared the march was addling his brain.

WINGS AS EAGLES

Yard after yard, the farther away the wagon rolled, the more Mariah's pain and anger ebbed.

Not until they were a long holler from the Chaney place did she open her eyes. She found herself on a narrow road. It snaked between a gully and a field of broom sedge. Afternoon sun had it all aglow as far as she could see.

Mariah looked back to check on Zeke.

Asleep.

Dulcina too.

In a wagon behind, Mordecai. Next to him Jonah, hugging one sack like it was life. A little farther back rode Sadie and her youngest. Walking alongside them, her oldest and her husband, Sam, a large leather bag over his shoulder. Heavy, Mariah knew, with scrapers, awls, lasters, and other tanner's tools. Farther back still was Hannah and Esther with their sprouts.

Jonah was smiling. Mordecai was smiling. So were Sadie and Sam. Esther too.

Eyes skyward, Mariah spotted a golden eagle gliding high. Its wingspan had to be over eight feet.

All creation seemed a new sight.

She followed that golden eagle's flight, remembering her ma's frequent whisper at the end of a hard day of carding wool, spinning, reeling, and still with supper to fix. "Shall renew their strength," Patience would say, getting her second wind. "Shall mount up with wings as eagles."

Now Mariah believed that she could run and run, run a thousand miles and not be weary, that she could walk along roads, up mountains, walk forever and a day—not faint.

She took a deep breath, let herself dream.

Still waters, green pastures, peaceful, merciful place. Even if they had to live in a cave, they'd survive. She knew how to fish and trap. Yes, she and Zeke would be just fine, Mariah decided, as the caravan came to a halt.

At the crossroads up ahead, row after row, four abreast, blue-coats marched by. Row after row after row. After them rolled wagons. Steady on came more rows of soldiers.

The men stepped lively to a peppy drum-and-bugle tune as if their gear—haversack, knapsack, bed roll, poncho, ammunition, and rifles slung over their shoulders—was featherweight.

"My goodness!" Mariah gasped. Couldn't tear her eyes away from all the Yankees marching by. "What a power!" She turned to Caleb. "This the rest of Sherman's army?"

"Some of the rest."

"Some?"

"Lots more, whole lot more." Caleb smiled, pointing west. "Miles thataway, the right wing." Sherman's army had a left wing and right wing, Caleb explained. And each wing had two corps. And mostly they marched in four columns.

Mariah had no idea what Caleb was talking about.

"Each corps has more than ten thousand soldiers," he continued. "We're with the left wing, marching with the Fourteenth Army Corps. Just shy of fourteen thousand men."

Caleb didn't stop there—his speech caught speed with every item.

Each corps, three to four divisions.

Each division, two to three brigades.

Each brigade, three to seven regiments.

Each regiment, ten companies. "On average, that is. Some might have nine, with roughly a hundred men in each. All told, there's more than fifty-five thousand infantrymen and artillerymen."

Mariah frowned. "Infant men?"

"In-fan-tree-men. Foot soldiers. Artillery, they handle the big guns. Each corps also has an artillery brigade."

Mariah's mind was stuck on the number.

"More than *fifty-five thousand*?" That sounded like a world. "Some sight that must be." Mariah ached to be, for a slice of time, that golden eagle gliding high. What she'd give for a sky-high view of General William Tecumseh Sherman's mighty march. Like others, she'd learned his complete name, whispering it sometimes like a prayer. She'd heard others call him Moses.

"And there's General Kilpatrick's cavalrymen—the ones who fight on horseback."

Was there anything about the march that Caleb didn't know?

"Five thousand of them, give or take. Cavalry is there to protect both wings, switching back and forth depending where Rebels harass."

So that makes it about sixty thousand, Mariah thought. *A world indeed!* And she envied Caleb's knowledge. She only had bits and pieces, scraps and rags. He had whole cloth.

"Rebels harass much?"

"In spots. Mostly they sabotage, trying to make the march harder than it needs to be."

Mariah didn't know what sabotage meant, but she guessed it was some kind of devilment. "How do Rebels make the march harder?"

"Chop down trees to clutter up a road. Burn bridges."

"Yankees then have to find another way?"

"Usually the pioneers just get to work."

"Pioneers?"

"Soldiers always near the head of the line of march who are skilled at repairing bridges, clearing roads, cutting side roads through forests. Sometimes there's quicksand, mud, marsh. In those cases, pioneers lay down corduroy roads. Most of the able-bodied colored men who join the march wind up with the pioneers. Some help out the pontoniers."

"The what?"

"I'm sorry. Pontoniers are another class of soldier. In charge of floating bridges called pontoons."

Mariah had never met anybody so talkative with a stranger. And by the time Caleb finished telling her about the twenty-five-hundred wagons, the five-thousand cattle, and what all else Sherman left Atlanta with, Mariah's head was spinning. She eyed him suspiciously. "How you know so much?"

"Captain Galloway mostly."

"One with the green eyes, who gave Zeke the sweets?"

Caleb nodded. "We're waiting to fall in with the second division—"

Mariah chuckled. "You truly have a head for all this soldier business. And numbers."

Caleb looked at her, smiled.

"It's how I keep my mind from becoming mush. Learn and think. Think and learn."

His smile was nice, warming.

And they continued to wait. But not Sadie and Sam, not Hannah, not Esther. Hurrying up to the crossroads with their children in tow, they gesticulated, called out. Mariah couldn't hear their words, but she was pretty sure of their want: the whereabouts of Yankees who passed through Hebron, where they all had kin, kin they were sure had joined Sherman's March.

Mariah soon saw that Sadie and the others met with satisfaction. Smiling wide, they waved good-bye.

Bittersweet.

She couldn't begrudge them seeking family, but as Mariah waved back, a sadness crept over her. Snatches of times past hovered up.

Sharing food.

Doing each other's hair.

Turning castoff clothes into quilts.

Dulcina. They had all chipped in some of their rations and side food after Judge Chaney told Nero to cut Dulcina off. "No use feedin' the wretch. Can't work. Can't be sold. Useless."

And whenever Dulcina went off into the woods for too long, someone was bound to notice, and one or more of them scouted her out, fetched her back. Mariah could see Sadie coaxing Dulcina to eat, Esther struggling to get her to wash, and Sadie trying to pass a comb through her hair. No matter how Dulcina lashed out—pushed the food away, overturned the wash tub, slapped them in the face—Sadie and Esther never gave up on her.

Mariah had a sudden urge to call out to them, jump down from the wagon, rouse Zeke and Dulcina, grab their things, and take off after Sadie and Sam, Hannah, Esther. But then

Mariah glanced back at Jonah and Mordecai, and she decided to stay put. Familiars enough. Facing front, she snuck a look at Caleb. Not a familiar, but something close. Agreeable, though peculiar.

Mariah marveled at the good state of his denim pants, blue-checked shirt, the mustard duster stashed under the seat. Clearly his master hadn't been mean as a hungry bear.

Intriguing too was the toolbox she'd spotted beneath the seat. It had an odd design on the front: like a stack of spinning whorls, with a ram's horn poised on top. All in all, Caleb seemed safe. Something of a comfort too. More comfort—and joy—swept over Mariah when she looked back and sighted two more familiars, the Doubles, striding strong as always, matching as always: black linsey dresses and turbans made from a goldenrod cloth. Mariah jumped down from the wagon.

By the time she reached the Doubles, Mordecai and Jonah were already beside them.

"Bless God," said Chloe, squeezing the breath out of Mariah.

Zoe hugged Mariah hard too.

Mariah filled the Doubles in on Josie and those who had fanned out to find family.

A heavy silence followed, like a boil about to burst.

"Nero?" asked Chloe.

"Hide nor hair," replied Mordecai, ramrod straight. "Not since I saw him scoot up under the Big House."

Mariah sent up a silent hallelujah. No more Chaney place! And no more Nero! The fiend, always lording his power over the rest of them. Too vile to show Dulcina mercy—tying her to a post or tree, taunting her, pelting her with chicken bones, stones, whipping at the air above her head, at the ground beside her feet. And frightening her even more with his devilish laugh, his devilish grin.

Chloe nudged Mariah. Eyes trained on the back of Caleb's head, she asked, "And him?"

"Was with the Yankees who came our way," replied Mariah. "Name's Caleb."

"Y'all sure was talkin' a lot," muttered Jonah.

"About the march. He told me a heap of things about the march."

"Sumpin' 'bout him don't seem right," sneered Jonah. "Seem shifty, like he hidin' sumpin'."

"Who ain't when whitefolks around?" snapped Mordecai. "Seems to me it's a benefit that this Caleb came our way."

"How so?" asked Jonah.

"There's an ease to him," replied Mordecai. "And Mariah just said he has knowledge about the march. And look."

Mariah and the others turned to see Caleb and Captain Galloway talking.

"That white man's manner," continued Mordecai, "suggest they got some common ground."

"That's Captain Galloway," said Mariah.

Jonah snorted. "Any colored man got common ground with a white man gotta be a hazard to the rest of us."

"Jonah, please," said Mariah, patting his arm. "This here's no time to borrow trouble—not on this glorious day! Let us fix our minds on freedom and ready ourselves for new tomorrows!"

MORE THAN A MISTY MEMORY

When Captain Galloway came over and started talking about an idea he had—what a relief! It took Caleb's mind off Mariah.

He had been thinking about the light in her eyes when he told her about the march. A babbling fool is what he felt like. And he couldn't stop wondering what happened to her man. He was about to ask at one point, then had second thoughts. Talked about General Kilpatrick's cavalrymen instead. He was talking so fast—he hoped he hadn't come off as a know-it-all, hoped he hadn't made her feel bad about all the words she didn't know. But then he remembered how she teased him about having a head for soldier business and numbers. She wouldn't have done that if he'd made her feel bad. And now he couldn't decide what was more delightful. Her smile? Her laugh?

The twin women she ran off to meet. Impressive. Big-boned but slender and with great horned owl eyes. Stately.

Tall. Were they kin? Clearly they meant much to Mariah. The way she and the others crowded around—were they figuring out a way to travel together? Or worse, head for a different part of the march like those others did during the halt at the crossroads?

Any minute they'd be falling in. Any minute Caleb would learn if Mariah would be riding with him a little longer or never again. He tried to convince himself that if she came back to the wagon to get the boy and the madwoman, he'd handle it fine. Told himself that by the time they reached the campground—and surely by the time he blew out the candle in his tent that night—Mariah would be nothing more than a misty memory.

When the signal to fall in came, Caleb looked back, saw Mariah heading for his wagon. His heart sank when she climbed into the back, but then his spirit soared when she pulled a quilt out of one of her sacks and placed it over Zeke and Dulcina.

"Captain Galloway gave you some good news?" Mariah asked as she rejoined Caleb in the buckboard.

"Not really. Why?"

"You look like you won a prize or somethin'."

MOVING WOUND

On the move again and traveling a wider road, along with rows and rows of bluecoats, Mariah beheld a growing crowd of people. All shades. All sizes. All ages.

From behind boulders and trees and across fields they came. Doubled up bareback on lank mules, scrawny nags. Squeezed five, six in oxcarts, belongings pressed to chests. Women in worn-out dresses, bundles atop their heads, babies on hips. Men in patched pants and frayed frock coats toting sacks. Some old folks had churn staffs as walking sticks. A few were crumpled up in wheelbarrows and being pushed.

A host of girls and boys skipped.

Hosannas honeyed the air. Hallelujahs to God, hallelujahs to Yankees. Even while savoring sounds of jubilee Mariah couldn't help but liken this exodus to one great moving wound. Like her, they all had scars.

Mariah saw limps—some from accidents, some from

hamstringings, she guessed. Saw cropped ears, cheeks branded with an *R*. Saw forefingers missing first joints.

The sight of a girl about nine leading a big grown man by a rope tied around his waist was a punch in the gut. The man had a dull, vacant stare, the same as Zeke sometimes lapsed into. Mariah had vowed that if she ever got free she'd hunt up a special kind of doctor, get Zeke some help. Looking over her shoulder, she saw him still asleep, like Dulcina. Maybe in freedom she'd find help for her too.

"Girl, you keep looking back like that, you'll get a crick in your neck," Caleb teased. "Rest easy."

Rest easy?

All her life Mariah had lived on tenterhooks, even in her dreams.

Rest easy?

What a freedom that would be! If only the Yankees would whip the Rebels today, tomorrow—soon—so she could get on with having new tomorrows.

But where would that be?

"Where we headed?" she asked. She figured they were more than a mile away from the Chaney place.

"Goal is to make Davisboro before dark."

Mariah had never been to Davisboro but knew it wasn't that far away. "After that?"

"Louisville."

"Then?"

"On to somewhere farther south."

They had just rounded a bend. Mariah fought the impulse to look back on Zeke. "This somewhere place have a name?"

Caleb nodded. "Bound to, but General Sherman keeps that to himself."

"Why's it a secret?"

"Keep Rebels in a scramble."

This didn't sit right with Mariah. Going deeper south was not what she wanted. Up north where slavery had been done away with a long time ago—that's where she wanted to go.

New York, if Mariah had her pick. That was the only place up north she had ever had a small glimpse of thanks to a stained, tattered print, that looked to be torn from a book. It pictured a proper brick building. "New-York African Free-School, No. 2" was written at the bottom. Below that, "Engraved from a drawing taken by P. Reason, a pupil, aged 13 years."

Was "P." for Peter or Paul? Maybe Pip? Mariah had wondered the first time she laid eyes on the picture. Did P. Reason have a sister who had pretty dresses? Did she get to go to school too?

Mariah kept the print tucked inside the old speller hidden beneath a floorboard in her cabin. Some nights after Zeke fell asleep she brought out the book, gazed at the print.

Daydreaming on freedom, Mariah could never envision the journey once she got away from the Chaney place. Couldn't imagine the world beyond. Kneading dough in the cookhouse, beating a rug out back, staring at P. Reason's school—Mariah sometimes conjured up a flying carpet at the end of Riddleville

Road. A flying carpet that would take her high up and away to New York, where more good fortune would follow: work and a place to stay in one of the buildings on either side of African Free-School No. 2.

But there was no flying carpet, and the march was heading south.

She glanced at Caleb. He looked relaxed. That calmed Mariah's mind. A bit. Had her trying to convince herself that General Sherman's somewhere place would be safe.

Mariah turned to Caleb with a half smile. "We jus' have to trust the Yankees, right?"

"I trust God and my gut. And Captain Galloway, I trust him."

"He's a kind one?"

Caleb nodded. "More than kind. He's good. Been strong against slavery since he was a boy."

"Abolition man."

"Two hundred percent. More than a few of them on the march."

More than a few of them? What an odd thing to say.

"There's General Oliver O. Howard," Caleb continued. "He heads up the right wing. Like Galloway, strong Christian. They call him Old Prayer Book." After a pause, Caleb added, "There's Sergeant Hoffmann in the company we're with. There's—"

"Ain't they all?"

"Ain't they all what?"

"Ain't all Yankees abolition men?"

Caleb shook his head.

Mariah frowned. "But they freein' us."

Caleb had a funny look on his face.

Mariah became more anxious. "I know about Lincoln's proclamation. And I won't ever forget what Captain Galloway said to me, 'No more slavery!'" After a pause, Mariah added, "They really are freein' us, right?"

Caleb faced her. "Freedom is real, Mariah," he replied. "Don't fret yourself."

Mariah sensed that Caleb was taking her measure. She also sensed that he was holding something back. "What is it, Caleb?"

"I hate to be the bearer of bad news, but the thing is . . ."

"What?"

"Truth is, lots of Yankees don't really care what happens to us."

Mariah's eyes narrowed.

"Many look on colored the way they do cattle. Freeing colored is the same as hauling off Rebel livestock and crops, same as tearing up Rebel railroad tracks, burning down Rebel buildings. Whatever means hell and a mess for Rebels, whatever makes them cry mercy, that's what the Yankees will do."

Mercy. The word triggered another horrible memory, picked at a scab.

Mercy. She'd known precious little of that.

Mercy! She saw herself at the feet of a figure head to toe in black, beginning with a veil. Saw herself a bundle of snot and tears, pleading for mercy.

No more, no more! Mariah pushed back against that memory. She looked up, took a deep breath, fixed her mind on freedom and the mercy at hand. Maybe all Yankees weren't abolition men, maybe many saw colored as cattle. Right then, right there, that didn't matter none to her. Prayer had been answered! Yankees had come her way! Being in that wagon *free*—that was a mercy for the ages! And anybody out to make the likes of Callie Chaney cry mercy was all right with Mariah.

"We heard how they burned Atlanta to the ground."

"Not the whole city, but plenty," said Caleb, suddenly solemn. "Railroad tracks, locomotives, train cars, round-houses, bridges, machine shops, mills. Some blown up. Some burned." Caleb tightened his grip on the reins. "Pillars of fire everywhere."

Mariah felt a chill. She rubbed her arms. "Learned all that from Captain Galloway?"

Eyes on the road, Caleb shook his head. "Lived it."

Caleb's jaw tightened. Mariah wondered what else he was holding back.

Dulcina stirred, mumbled. Not "Texas," just gibberish.

Caleb glanced over his shoulder. "Her name again?"

"Dulcina."

"Always like this?"

Mariah shook her head. "Not before Judge Chaney sold her husband and their boys."

"Judge Chaney?"

"Who owned us."

"I saw only the old woman."

"His wife, Miss Callie. Judge died a few years back." Again Mariah pushed back against memory. After a swallow, she unwrapped the rest of Dulcina's story.

She explained that the judge sold Dulcina's husband, Joe, and sons, Fred and Bunny, to clear up gambling debts. "Not his, but the son, Master Robert." Mariah paused. "Had they been sold to somebody near . . . but they were carried off far."

"Texas?" Caleb asked.

Mariah nodded. "So we heard. And Dulcina, she couldn't bear up. Mind went loose."

Wagon wheels and horses' hooves did the only talking for a while.

"Master Robert reformed himself for a time. But after the judge died, he went back to his mess." Mariah's eyes latched onto a stand of dogwoods, bare to the bone, branches uplifted in worship, fingertips bearing shiny red drupes. "More got sold," Mariah continued. "Didn't stop till Master Robert got killed last summer."

"In a battle?"

"No, in a street in Milledgeville. Shot over some woman."

Gingerly, Caleb asked, "Your husband, he was among the sold?"

Mariah shook her head.

"Hired out?"

Again, Mariah shook her head.

"Did he—?"

"Never had no husband." Mariah was bewildered until she caught Caleb's drift. "Zeke ain't my son."

Caleb rubbed his chin, frowned. "But I heard him call you Ma."

"He's not yet mastered my name. Zeke's my brother."

By then, Caleb was pulling into a meadow bordered by a grove of longleaf pine.

STROKING THE SCRUB OAK

Hordes of Yankees had already made camp. Arms stacked. Tents pitched. A thousand campfires crackled.

The wagon rolled on, horses in a four-beat gait.

Caleb looked out over all the people, in small and large clusters, making camps in the meadow some distance from the soldiers. Familiar scene. Day after day he'd seen families and flung-together folks, without much talk, with no ado, fall into timeworn routines. Certain ones minded little ones. Others headed for the stream with pots and buckets or into the woods with hatchets and machetes.

Caleb brought the horses to halt by a scrub oak. "This looks a good spot."

By the time Caleb reached the other side of the wagon to help Mariah down, her feet were already on the ground and she was heading for Zeke.

"I'll tend to him," said Caleb. "You take care of Dulcina."

He picked up Zeke and planted him by the scrub oak, then watched as Mariah gave Dulcina a gentle shake.

Dulcina sat bolt upright, looking like her brain was in bedlam. She hauled off and slapped Mariah.

"What in the—" Caleb headed over.

Mariah waved him off. "No! It's fine. I'm fine." She rubbed the left side of her face. "Just one of her upsets."

"Better let me see to her."

"No, Caleb, really, I can handle her."

Caleb wasn't about to leave Mariah's side. He looked from her to Dulcina, saw a calm come over both. He walked with Mariah as she led Dulcina over to Zeke, who was rolling a peppermint stick between two fingers. Not until Dulcina was seated on the ground did Caleb return to the wagon to get their things, even Dulcina's grimy bundle.

"Much obliged," said Mariah.

"Not at all." Caleb was still worried about Mariah. "She in need of restraints?"

"No, she'll be fine."

"You can handle her and the boy by yourself?"

"Won't be by myself," replied Mariah. "Here come my people."

Caleb turned around and saw the old man, the young man, and bringing up the rear, the twin women, heading their way.

Caleb tipped his hat. "I best be on my way now, but—"

"You leavin' for good?"

Not if I can help it, thought Caleb.

"Just wanted to know if . . . if you leavin' . . . for good, for if so—want to give a proper thanks. For the ride, all the aid."

One horse nickered, the other neighed as Caleb watched Mariah fidget. "Need to parcel out some things then take the remainder to the commissary officer," he explained. "I'll be back."

SAVORING THE SIGHT

Mariah had no idea what a commissary officer was, and she didn't care. Caleb was coming back. Nice. Warming like his smile. As she watched him walk away, she found herself savoring the sight of his shoulders. And the way he walked. Like he knew how to make his way in the world. She wondered—

No, woolgathering wouldn't do. She needed to get her bearings.

Mariah reckoned the time by the sky. Took in the height of longleaf pines. Her mouth watered as the aroma of beef stewed, roasted, of pork being fried, wafted her way from where soldiers camped. Her stomach growled. During the ride she'd felt peckish, but now it was as if she hadn't eaten a morsel in days.

Mariah saw herself in their cabin after sundown, slicing fatback to flavor a pot of greens, heating the skillet to a sizzle for corn pone. Big dinners at the Big House before the war came to mind next. Sadie in commotion, fussing over the feast. Baked ham with brown sugar glaze, spiked with cloves. Turkey oozing oyster dressing. Corn soufflé, potato soufflé, creamed peas, candied carrots. Mariah smiled at memories of Sadie slipping her a bit of berry cobbler or sweet potato pie for Zeke.

The cracklin' bread she'd packed—how long would she have to make it last, Mariah wondered as she went to help the Doubles bring their sacks and bundles over to the scrub oak tree. One of Miss Chloe's was bound to hold hyssop, pennyroyal, dandelion, and bundles of other roots and herbs. Bark too. And Mariah was pretty sure that Miss Zoe wouldn't have come away without at least one cast-iron pot, skillet, and some cooking utensils.

"I'll go for water," said Mariah after everybody got settled, then to Jonah, "You'll see to firewood?"

"Yup," Jonah replied.

"I'll get to work on a couple of lean-tos," said Mordecai.

"Zoe packed some ham, biscuits," said Chloe.

"You'll find some cracklin' bread in one of my sacks," said Mariah as she headed for the stream, a bucket in each hand and a calabash canteen around her neck.

Along the way Mariah found herself smiling. Smiling at the people she passed. Smiling at the trees. At freedom. Smiling, too, at the thought of Caleb coming back.

LEARN THEIR STORIES

"One chicken per dozen or so, one sweet potato each."

That's what Caleb heard Captain Galloway tell Privates Sykes and Dolan as he drew near.

"Colored people are not the only ones in need," the captain had said earlier. "My men are needy too. In need of seeing how the world should be. In need of seeing how much they don't see . . . the family of man."

Captain Galloway was the most unusual white man Caleb had ever met. He was leery at first, suspected the captain's kindness was a cover for a coming trick. After traveling with him for thirty miles, Caleb was convinced that the captain was genuine.

Days back, while they supped together, before he knew what came over him Caleb told Captain Galloway about his life in Atlanta. About what a rascal he had been. About those days of hosting evil. How close he came to murder. Then about his turnaround.

"Appreciate it, sir, if you keep it all to yourself," Caleb had asked.

"You have my word," Captain Galloway pledged, stirring his three-legged cast-iron pot. Then he shared his own journey to faith. He also told Caleb about his mother's side of the family. "Two plantations on Maryland's Eastern Shore. At the start of the war, they had over a hundred slaves."

"Your father from the South too?"

"No. New York born and bred." After a pause, Captain Galloway said, "I'm sorry, Caleb. So very sorry."

"You can't help what your mother's people did."

Captain ladled a helping of beef stew into Caleb's mucket. "Not talking about just them."

Caleb thought he saw tears in his eyes.

"I thought I knew how evil slavery was," the captain continued. "Reading about it doesn't tell the half. Hearing Douglass or Brown or some other soul fortunate to have escaped, even that doesn't truly capture it, because when such people are giving lectures and writing their books, they've had some time to heal. But on this march I see hundreds, thousands who aren't even at the start of that." After a pause the captain said again, "I'm sorry, Caleb, so sorry."

That was the first time Caleb ever heard a white person apologize to a colored for anything. When the stagecoach ran over Keziah Turner's lad, there had been no sorry. When

Jeremiah Auld falsely accused Mac Purdy of stealing horses—and got him whipped—there had been no sorry. For all that Caleb's father had endured—no sorry. And when Caleb went after the man who destroyed his sister, he knew there'd be no sorry from him. By then Caleb hated them all. Since then, he had worked hard to conquer hate, but there were moments on the march when bitterness got the best of him. Captain Galloway's sorry helped. That and the man's efforts to make a mission field of the march, aiming to convert as many of his men as he could to see the world as he did. To see colored people as he did.

A time or two Caleb sat in on one of the captain's talks where he handed out tracts about slavery. And now he watched him put another plan into action, starting with Privates Sykes and Dolan. "They say they are Christians. I want to help them prove it."

Captain Galloway had the privates load a wagon with food, then said, "Twelve. Get them in groups of twelve or so. They might be one family, might be two, possibly more. If there's any bunching up to do, let them know it's only for purposes of provisions. Once the meal is done they can belong as they wish."

Private Dolan, slack jawed and rangy, ran a hand through his tousled blond hair. "I should get our rifles?"

Galloway peered at him. "Rifles?"

"To round them up?"

"Round up who?"

"The nig—the colored people."

Caleb could see the captain struggling not to lose his temper. That was one of their bonds. Both had worked hard to tame their tempers.

"Private Dolan, there is no rounding up!" said the captain. "You simply move out across the field, call them over, and explain things in a Christian but firm way." He looked from Dolan to Sykes. "Understood?"

"Yes, sir!" said the privates in unison.

"Then you hand out the food," Galloway continued. "As I said, one chicken per dozen or so, one sweet potato each."

Caleb had seen the captain hand out more than chickens and potatoes. He guessed he wanted to keep Sykes and Dolan's first time simple.

Sykes, stout and ruddy, scratched his head.

"Is there a problem, Private Sykes?" asked Captain Galloway.

"No, sir. Well, sir, I was just—it sounds like we'll be serving the . . . them."

Caleb looked down, tried not to laugh.

"You will be serving your Lord and Savior," said Captain Galloway.

When Caleb looked up, he saw the two young men heading off on their mission.

"And one more thing," Captain Galloway called out.

The privates about-faced.

"Talk to them," said the captain.

"About what, sir?" asked Private Dolan.

"About anything that will allow you to learn their stories." The captain pushed his slouch hat over his eyes as he watched the privates cross the field, park, and wave people over.

The people just looked at them. The privates waved again.

"Food, we bring you food," hollered Private Dolan. "In the name of our Lord and Savior, Jesus Christ!"

Caleb drew up beside Captain Galloway. "Good work, sir."

"There's hope for them yet," said the captain.

"Looks like it."

"Sup with me tonight?"

"No, sir. Some business I need to tend to."

Copper-Skinned Boy Was Ben

Mariah returned with another two buckets of water and another full calabash canteen around her neck. During her first trip back she saw Zoe getting food from the two scruffy ones, and so she knew they could save her cracklin' bread and Zoe's ham and biscuits for tomorrow. And it wouldn't be long before her hunger was gone.

Zoe was about through dressing the chicken, Mordecai about done building one lean-to. Zeke and Dulcina still sat by the scrub oak, behind a fortress of sacks and bundles. Both looked like they had not a care in the world. And to Mariah's eyes, that was a good thing.

She set the buckets down, stretched her back, took the calabash canteen from around her neck, then headed for Zeke and Dulcina. As she gave them sips of water, Mariah tried to get a read on the folks they wound up with for supper.

Old man, olive-skinned, rigging up a spit.

Old woman, nutmeg, impish eyes, keeping the fire.

A brown-skinned girl, younger than Mariah and shy-looking, just sat there fumbling with her fingers.

About Josie's age, Mariah reckoned of the short, dark-skinned, bowlegged woman in the family way. The rail-thin pop-eyed girl on her lap was maybe three.

"I'll make her some sage tea," Mariah heard Chloe tell the woman after checking the child's glands.

Before long the chicken was on the spit, the sweet potatoes in the ashes. While they all readied for supper—brought out tin plates, cups, gourd dippers—there was soft talk, acquaintance making.

Mariah learned that the old man was Hosea and the old woman his wife, Hagar. She told everybody that the timid one was Miriam and that they'd taken her in after they saw her join the march by herself. The way Miriam shied away from her gaze, Mariah wondered if the girl was mute. Or had her mind gone loose like Dulcina's?

"Name's Rachel," said the pregnant woman. "And this my daughter, Rose."

"Like Miriam," said Hagar, "when we seen Rachel and Rose with only theyselves, we welcome them in, too. A few miles later he come along on a wall-eyed pony." Hagar pointed at the copper-skinned boy who had helped Jonah fetch firewood. The copper-skinned boy was Ben.

More than once during supper, with the children given mostly the stray parts—liver, gizzard, heart, neck, feet—Mariah saw Zeke stare at Ben's right hand, at the forefinger with the first joint gone. Each time Mariah steered her brother's attention to something else, like sucking the chicken neck clean.

Every now and then Mariah glanced around the campground.

Was Caleb really coming back?

GENERAL REB

Caleb came back with a dinted coffee pot, a couple of large tin cups, canned peaches, hardtack, a bar of soap, blankets, bedsheets, brocade draperies, a wedge tent.

He nodded, said "Pleased to meet you" as Mariah introduced him to Mordecai, the Doubles, Jonah. After he put the basket of goods on the ground he took out something wrapped in a coarse linen towel, handed it to Mariah.

Caleb watched her unwrap the package and light up over an almost new pair of lace-up boots.

In no time at all Mariah had her beat-up brogans off and her new shoes on.

A fine fit, Caleb could see.

"Mighty grateful," said Mariah.

It did Caleb's heart good to see Mariah happy for at least a moment in time. And he pretended not to notice Jonah's dirty looks. Instead Caleb turned his attention to Zoe inspecting the hardtack. She sniffed it, gave it a titmouse taste, arched an eyebrow.

"For emergency," Caleb explained. "In case there's no time to cook or weather won't permit. Kept dry, hardtack will last a hundred years."

Now that he got a long look at them Caleb was convinced that the only way to tell the Doubles apart was by their duties and dispositions. One not prone to much chit-chat, the other sunnier. The way the silent one took charge of the peaches and the hardtack, Caleb figured she was a cook. The way the other one was grinding up some bark and herbs with a mortar and pestle—a healer. *But clearly no miracle worker*, he thought as he glanced at Zeke sitting in Mariah's lap staring into another world and Dulcina picking lint that wasn't there from her grimy bundle.

Watching Mordecai and Jonah floor two lean-tos with pine boughs, Caleb guessed from their bearings that one had been a butler or coachman, the other a field worker—and Jonah seemed to be spoiling for a fight. *Let it not come to that*, Caleb said to himself, then went to work on the tent. A tight fit for the women and Zeke, but surely they'd rest better.

"There are pickets posted around the campground, on guard all night," Caleb explained. He told them about the bugle call for lights out, the bugle call for rise.

Caleb saw Mariah watching his every move. How he laid out the canvas, where he drove the stakes, joined the poles, assembled them. When done, he handed her the mallet. "Come morning I'll show you the quickest way to strike."

Caleb sat down on his haunches, lowered his voice. "I'm sure I don't have to tell y'all about the need to keep alert and watchful. All along the march we've run into Rebel sharpshooters. Mostly if they ambush they go after Yankees. But still . . ." He paused as Zoe arched an eyebrow and Chloe, Mordecai, and Mariah leaned in. Jonah tossed pine knots on the fire.

"Rebels ain't the only ones you need to watch out for," continued Caleb. "You especially need to keep top eye open for the commander of the corps we're with. He hates us and got not one quarrel with slavery. Believes it's what we fit for. Some soldiers call him General Reb—but only behind his back."

Caleb paused to let it all sink in.

"I told them what you said about us bein' like cattle to some Yankees," whispered Mariah. "Now you say some Yankees favor slavery?"

Caleb nodded, then told them about one of General Reb's recent orders. "He complained about there being too many what he called 'useless negroes' on the march, that our people eat food much needed by the troops and take up too much space in the wagons."

"'Useless negroes'?" Mordecai frowned, rubbed his bald pate.

Caleb nodded. "And what General Reb decreed is that no wagons are to carry colored people or their belongings. Except for ones serving certain officers, no colored are allowed to ride on horse or mule."

"How will we know this, this General Reb?" asked Mariah.

"First off, generals have stars on their shoulder boards, and General—"

"Shoulder boards?" asked Mariah.

Caleb tapped one of his shoulders. "Patches on each," he explained. "General Reb, he has two stars. His face fits his spirit. On the ghoulish side. Bushy mustache and beard. Hangdog pasty face. Cold blue eyes. Right deadly."

"What kind of horse he ride?" asked Mariah.

"I've seen him on a dark bay, a sorrel, but mostly on a dapple gray." Caleb looked over his shoulder, then back at the group. "Adding salt to the wound is his real name. You'll never guess." When no one did, Caleb said, "Jefferson Davis."

"What that cuss have to do with General Reb?" asked Mordecai.

"No, that *is* General Reb's name. Jefferson Davis."

"You joshin'!" Mariah gasped.

"Not one bit," said Caleb.

"Jefferson . . . Davis." Mariah frowned, shaking her head in consternation that this hateful Union general had the same name as the president of the Confederacy.

Caleb rose, looked at Hagar and Hosea's band making their campsite some ten yards away. Didn't recall seeing them before. "Put it on the grapevine for everybody to be on the

lookout for General Reb. Don't let him catch any colored riding in a wagon or on a horse or mule. I also advise not letting
him catch sight of any of us receiving kindness from a Yankee." With that, Caleb bid them all good night. Even Jonah.

At the Cusp of Dawn

A part of her walked with him until Caleb was out of sight, the outline of his body blended into the night.

Then duty called.

Mariah had to get Zeke and Dulcina settled in the tent and off to sleep. Zeke under a blanket, Dulcina under the drapes. That done, she joined the others around the fire, only half-listening to their talk. She reckoned Caleb was two, maybe three years older than her, and she wondered what manner of man he was.

She remained around that fire after the Doubles said their good night, after Mordecai stretched out his long bones in his lean-to. The last thing Mariah wanted to do was sleep. And she knew that if she stayed up, Jonah wouldn't head for his lean-to anytime soon.

Mariah tightened her cloak around her.

"Warm enough?" asked Jonah.

Eyes on the fire, she nodded, knowing Jonah would lay on more firewood anyway, which he did.

In the distance somebody blew a few notes on a harmonica, eased into a lilting, yet mildly mournful tune.

"Sure is a fine night," said Jonah.

Mariah gave him a quick smile.

Jonah cleared his throat. "Our long wait is over."

"Moments I can't believe it's true, fear I'm in a long dream." Mariah looked around at the night.

Couples cuddled up.

Mothers rocked babies.

She imagined bobwhite quail and timberdoodles nestled in the woods.

Jonah leaned in. "What you thinkin'?"

Mariah pictured whitetail deer padding close by. "About freedom."

"But you seem so . . . solemnlike. Ain't you gladhappy?" Jonah pulled his cap down tighter on his head.

"Gladhappy?" Mariah stretched her arms, her back. "Gladhappy is . . . a hambone to flavor soup, new cloth at Christmas. Those the sort of things that make for gladhappy." She saw Jonah turn glum. Had she accidentally given him the look?

"It's a look that tells me you think I'm thick," he had once grumbled. "Like when you got on me about lessons."

How well Mariah remembered that argument. Her pushing Jonah to learn his letters. Him saying there was no need for both of them to be able to read and write. Her pretending she didn't catch his drift.

Jonah had called it quits after learning the alphabet and how to spell a few simple words like dog, cat, and okay. "Can't see how readin' come in handy if you hungry or freezin' to death."

Mariah knew that if Jonah had to choose between hunger and cold, he'd choose hunger. So great was his fear of the cold, a fear that came on him after that day they were helping Sadie in the cookhouse. Sadie sent Jonah to the Big House with a tray of groundnut brittle, meant for white children soon to come caroling. After he laid the tray on the front hall table, even though Sadie had said she had set some aside for him, Jonah couldn't resist temptation. He snuck a piece of brittle into his pocket, and Judge Chaney saw him.

No shoes, no stockings. No coat, no cap. In just his tow cloth shirt Jonah was made to stand out back for what seemed like hours, shivering so on that cold and windy Christmas Eve. Little Mariah had wondered if his tears would freeze.

Jonah added sticks to the fire.

"This is beyond gladhappy, Jonah," Mariah said. "Bein' here right now, breathin' in freedom . . . Gladhappy don't strike me as a big enough word." Then she rose.

"Turnin' in?"

Mariah shook her head, tightened her cloak around her.

"Well, where you off to?" Jonah rose too.

"To myself." Mariah smiled, patting Jonah's arm. "Don't worry. Not far."

By the scattering of campfires Mariah stepped gingerly to a clear stretch of ground. Stars, numberless, were beginning to shine.

Gazing up, Mariah whispered, "Thank you, Lord."

For Jonah—always a help. Skinning rabbits and possums she trapped. In the winter daubing chinks in the cabins along with collecting cow chips and kindling overmuch so all in the quarter could keep warm.

She thanked the Almighty for Mordecai too. *So wise.* He'd picked up where her ma and pa had left off on how to read people and such. *And so kind.* Warning her when Miss Callie was in a tempest. Sparing her from having to carry things up to Master Roberts's room when the miscreant was in it. "I'll take it up," he'd say if Miss Callie wasn't about.

As for the Doubles—*like mothers to me.* When Chloe was called to the sick room on the Chaney place, she could make a sweat seem a fever, a sprain a break, so a body got more time off work. Some Sundays Zoe came with a basket of ginger cakes or other treats. Hidden under the treats, now and then, was an item a member of the Melrose family had tossed aside. Blue-back speller. A reader. Half-used copy book. Cracked slate. Lump of chalk. That print of the African Free-School No. 2 in New York.

Mariah eased down onto the ground, pulled her knees up, and draped her arms around her legs. She rubbed a hand over the top of her boots.

And Caleb. She added him to her list of blessings.

Mariah went misty-eyed thinking about her brother. Zeke's simple cheer had been her only real joy these last few years. Then she saw herself over the years, praying as she polished the parlor floor, lit fires, made beds, cleaned grates, washed chamber pots, milked cows, churned butter. Saw herself praying as she stood, paced, knelt, rocked before her hearth. All those days, weeks, months, years of pleading. For a weakening of the Chaney wrath. All those days, weeks, months, years of pleading. For strength of body. For her mind not to go loose.

Not now. On this night so divine, Mariah did no pleading. The only thing on her heart was gratitude.

But she did have one request.

She wanted to stay awake, wanted to see what freedom looked like, felt like at midnight, then at the cusp of dawn.

CAMPED AT DAVISBORO

"Sun., Nov. 27th, 1864," Caleb wrote in the upper right-hand corner of the page. He chided himself for failing to write for the last few days, wanted to play catch-up.

"Milledgeville is behind us. It is a bit simple for a capital. The governor and other high-ups were gone by the time Yankees marched in." Caleb wrote of the burning of the depot, the hotel. The looting of stores. "Even ransacked the library, tossed a passel of documents & books out into the muddy street." And there was the white lady who chased two soldiers from her establishment with a shotgun. "You dirty thieves!" she screamed. "You dirty thieves!"

More Yankees were running amok. It worried Caleb. He understood that Sherman planned for his men to live off the land. He understood wrecking railroads and whatever else could be used against Union troops. He understood that along the way Yankees had need of fresh horses and mules. But the senseless destruction, the heedless, needless stealing—with some even robbing colored folks of their few possessions. Caleb feared that some Yankees would get more reckless with his people. General Reb wasn't the only one who grumbled about the thousands of coloreds on the march.

The thought of General Reb called up Caleb's rage. Beyond dangerous, the man was evil. How many minds had he poisoned with his "useless negro" decree? A lot of hogwash that was. Soldiers had more food than they could eat. Private Sykes had told Caleb that meals on the march were better than what could be made of regular army rations. And what harm did it do to let folks ride in a wagon or on a mule?

Night and day, from the way Captain Galloway saw things. "They have more than paid for any clothing, food, and whatnot that comes their way." That was his position when Caleb collected things his people needed.

Back to his diary.

"Capt. G. spoke with Col. L. about the rampages. Was told to think of it as letting off steam. The most Capt. G. can do is ride with foragers & set an example for the likes of Pvts. S. and D."

Caleb put his pencil down. His zeal to make a record of the march had suddenly petered out. But not his thoughts about Mariah.

"Met a young woman today. She came away with us down below Sandersville. Her name is Mariah. She is—"

The march was no place for feelings. Too much danger. Better he put down the diary and pick up the Bible, read from Lamentations or another book with a lot of destruction, affliction, plagues, and the like. The book of Job with that poor man's boils head to toe and ten lifetimes of sorrows—that story would definitely take Caleb's mind off Mariah.

Before Caleb closed his diary, he ended the entry as he always did. With location.

"Camped at Davisboro."

SPILLING MEMORIES

Many roads were sandy, hard on the feet.

They slogged through swampland with towering cypress trees veiled in ghostly Spanish moss. Mariah almost lost her footing when she saw a silver-gray crane staring at her as if privy to some great mystery.

Now and then they heard rifles firing or cannon booming in the distance. Just as unnerving were the pillars of smoke. And there'd been that long halt yesterday after a handful of miles thanks to Rebel devilment—bridge at Black Rock Creek burned. Nearly nightfall by the time the laying down of a pontoon bridge was complete and they finally marched on into Louisville. And it already in flames.

But none of it dampened Mariah's spirits. Struggle in freedom was nothing like struggle in slavery. Before she struggled to stay alive and in her right mind. Now the struggles of the march were hitched to striving for a new life.

And last night had a sweet ending. When Caleb came to their campsite with socks, waistcoats, shirts, bandanas, clothespins, tin canteens, bacon, and other random things—and a small wagon—he came early enough to sup with them. Then this morning he came with good news.

"Division won't march today," Caleb told them before he headed out with a forage squad.

"Why?" Mariah had asked. "Some trouble?"

Caleb shook his head. "Soldiers deserve a rest is what I heard."

As the day wore on Mariah saw soldiers do more of what they usually did during a long halt. Fill canteens. Nap. Get up games of chuck-a-luck or whiskey poker. She also saw her people chopping wood for Yankees, currying their horses, blacking their boots.

"Useless negroes." Nobody wanted to be seen as that.

Mariah made herself useful for a while in a mess tent with Zoe, chopping, dicing, slicing for a big batch of Hunger Stew. Mariah also took charge of the coffee, lard, and salt soldiers chipped in as thanks, along with the bucket of liver, chitlins, kidneys, shanks, and bones the regimental butcher let them have.

Later Mariah worked alongside Chloe. She turned bedsheets into bandages, prepared a poultice, and boiled cow feet for a compress. She and Chloe got sugar, a penny or two, sometimes a dime, depending on a soldier's rank, for treating snakebites, sores, or sprains, and for balms to treat blistered feet.

"Ointment and aid!" Chloe called out as she walked among

the soldiers during long halts and on this stay-put day. Mariah walked behind her. Over one shoulder was a beat-up saddlebag with scissors, needles, lance, boiled rags, and gauze. Over the other a sack with bundles of herbs and blended teas, like red oak for stomach miseries and boneset for fevers and other things. As she looked out over the sea of soldiers, Mariah knew that after dark some young women would make themselves useful to Yankees in other ways.

"It ain't so bad," said a slender, doe-eyed girl Mariah figured to be her age.

It was going on dusk. Mariah was riverside, wringing out a pair of socks.

Hagar and a couple of other women had sucked their teeth, snatched up their clothes, and huffed off up the bank when the girl came near.

"You not gonna flounce off like them witches?" asked the girl.

Mariah glanced up. The girl had her mouth poked out, her hands on her hips. "Beg pardon?" Mariah dropped the socks into her basket.

"Ain't you gon' flee too?"

She looked now, not at the girl but at the dirty petticoat over her shoulder. "I got no cause to flee," Mariah said drily. She lifted a pair of britches from the water, reached for a stone slightly larger than her hand.

"Not ashamed to be seen with a fancy girl?"

Mariah commenced scrubbing Zeke's britches. "Happy girl, sad girl, fancy girl," she said without looking up. "It's nothin' to me what kind of girl you are." She rinsed the britches, started wringing them out.

The girl stepped closer to the water's edge, dunked her petticoat. "Name's Praline."

"Mariah."

She got an earful about Praline's life back in Louisville. Like Mariah, mostly Big House labor. Only Praline's white-folks had five young children. "Little hellions. Their mama an idiot. And Master, he—"

One of the huffed-off women cried out. Mariah looked up the bank and saw her sloshing into the river with a long stick to recover a piece of her washing the current sent adrift.

"Anyhow," Praline continued, "when Master John used to hand me around to his men friends, I didn't get nothin' but sore."

By now Mariah was washing a head wrap.

"But these Yanks," Praline continued, "one give me a tent all to myself. Nother a little bottle of scent. It ain't so bad."

With washing done, supper done, Praline, thank goodness, nowhere in sight, and Zeke and Dulcina tucked in, Mariah again found a clear patch not far from the others, again went to herself. Third night of freedom. Third night and still in the dark about the somewhere place. And sad that Caleb hadn't supped with them. Hadn't come after supper either. Mariah tried not to worry.

By now she knew not all foragers came back whistling happy tunes and with plenty of plunder. Hagar had heard of one getting a back full of buckshot and of another found in a ditch, throat cut ear to ear. If Rebels did that to Sherman's soldiers, Mariah knew they'd do worse to a colored man.

"Mind some company?"

Mariah almost jumped out of her skin. So lost in thought, she hadn't heard his footsteps. "Not at all."

What a relief. Caleb had gotten back in one piece.

Mariah fumbled for something else to say as he joined her on the ground. "You took supper with Captain Galloway?"

"Ate on the run. Was helping out at the forge. Shoeing horses, repairing some limber chests."

Mariah couldn't think of anything else to say. Or ask.

Caleb got a small fire going.

As the minutes went by Mariah still couldn't think of anything to say, kept hoping Caleb would come up with conversation. When he didn't she wondered why he came to be with her if he didn't—

Caleb gently tapped the burn scar on her neck.

She flinched.

"What happened here?"

There was a breeze, bearing the scent of pine.

Mariah pursed her lips, looked up at the sky. "Miss Callie

and the tip of a hot poker . . . candle wax on the parlor carpet. I was nearest to blame."

Next, Caleb's finger swept gently across the tiny gash above
her left eyebrow.

"Judge Chaney backhanded me. Wore a locket ring on the
hand he used."

Another question, then another—before Mariah knew it,
she was spilling a host of pent-up memories. The slaps, the
kicks, the pinpricks. Then she told him about her pa.

She never knew what her pa did to get the dungeon: a hole in the
ground big enough for a body to fit sitting up but too small for a
body to move. A piece of board weighed down by a stone covered
the pit. A few crude holes allowed just enough air to live.

The man was stuck in the dungeon for one day, two days.
At eventide on day three, the dungeon cover, stone and all,
blew off in a hurricane rain.

Mariah saw her ma, Patience, fly to the Big House. "Master
Chaney, he'll drown!" she screamed. "Master Chaney, please,
have mercy!"

Little Mariah grabbed a kettle from their hearth, raced to
the dungeon, bailed out water as fast as she could, soon sop-
ping wet herself as she tried to save her pa—and he tried to
be heard above the storm's roar.

"No, daughter, git inside 'fore you catch sick. Daughter,
git inside."

She kept on with the kettle despite the pain in her thin arms, despite the hard, heavy rain beating her down.

"Love you, daughter," her pa panted, the water at his chin.

Behind a blind of tears, Mariah bailed and bailed and bailed—until Nero descended upon her, snatched the kettle from her hands, dragged her away.

"No!" she screamed, trying in vain to kick and bite free of the hazel-eyed beast. "No!"

Years later Mariah overheard Mordecai tell Esther about that night. "For all of Patience's pleading, Judge Chaney just grunted, 'He be all right,' then knocked back another whiskey."

When done telling Caleb about her pa, it dawned on Mariah that this was the first time she'd ever told anybody about it, the first time she recalled it out loud. Never had a need to. Everybody on the Chaney place knew. The Doubles knew. Others miles around knew. There had never been anybody new to tell. And hardly anybody went in for recollecting nightmares out loud. Or asking. Comfort mostly came in code. A basket of ginger cakes, the soft-singing of "There Is a Balm in Gilead," or whispering "God's watchin'."

For the first time in her life Mariah knew the benefit, the balm of not keeping blistering memories padlocked in her mind.

She wiped her eyes with her sleeve, took a deep breath, managed a half smile.

Caleb handed her a handkerchief. "Didn't mean to cause distress. I don't know what came over me. I just—"

"You caused no distress. Did me a favor. Been a long time since I had a good cry."

"Would you rather be left alone now?"

"No, no." She looked into his eyes. "Stay."

Caleb reached into his coat pocket, brought out a paper packet, and handed it to her.

"What's this?"

"Rock candy."

Mariah undid the packet, popped a few blue crystals into her mouth. "From Captain Galloway?"

Caleb nodded. "I've never known a grown man with such a love for candy."

They burst out laughing. When they settled down into another silence, Mariah longed to tell Caleb more, longed for more relief. She told him about her ma.

About a month after her pa died in the dungeon, Judge Chaney gave up the ghost. Cause of death was a mystery. Miss Callie, bedeviled by the notion that Patience had put a hex on him, ordered Nero to give her fifty lashes.

"Please, Miss Callie, please have mercy!" Mariah threw herself at the woman's feet. They were behind the Big House. Callie Chaney, head to toe in black, beginning with a veil.

"Please, Miss Callie, please don't whip my mama!"

Mariah watched in horror as Nero stripped her mother naked to just below her big belly, tied her up to a rough red oak.

"She ain't put no hex on him!" Mariah clamped her hands over her ears, muffling her mother's screams after Nero laid on the first lash.

"Please! Please!" Mariah sobbed. "I beg you, Miss Callie!"

Nero, in a sweat and grunting, cracked that bullwhip again, again, again.

"My mama believe in Jesus, only in Jesus! She ain't no conjure woman! Please, Miss Callie!"

The whipping continued as did a woman's screams, a little girl's pleas.

At lash thirty-three, Mariah saw Callie Chaney raise a hand, signaling Nero to stop. Mariah, a trembling mass of snot and tears, kissed the woman's feet. "Thank you, ma'am," she whispered.

Miss Callie looked down on her. Voice candy-coated, she said, "She'll get fifty on top of fifty if you don't hush up that hollerin'."

Mariah clamped her hands over her mouth.

Callie Chaney lowered her hand.

Nero resumed his bullwhipping work.

In spilling that memory Mariah also told Caleb about her ma's piercing cries when, after the scourging, Nero doused her back with brine, about how with Josie's help she got her ma to their cabin. But Mariah couldn't bring herself to tell Caleb how she covered her mother's nakedness with her apron, how her stomach churned, how she gagged at the sight of the bloody, shredded back. But she did tell him how Josie ran to Miss Callie, begged her to let Jonah go get Miss Chloe because the baby was coming.

How it seemed a lifetime before Miss Chloe came.

"Then came my mama's last breath, glassy eyes. All I felt was . . . hollow. Too hollow to shed another tear. Life seemed a sorrow without end. I think that day was the last time I cried. Five years ago."

Caleb rubbed her shoulder.

Mariah tensed up, then quickly relaxed. Caleb's hand felt good. "When I finally looked around me, that's when I first laid eyes on the baby boy Miss Chloe was swaddlin'." Mariah took a deep breath. "She said it was for me to name him, so I did. Ezekiel, after our pa."

Mariah heard twigs snap, footsteps.

Jonah. "Everything okay?"

Mariah looked up, saw Jonah standing a few feet away. The fire flickered, flared up, casting long shadows on the pine trees towering above their heads.

Secesh

"Tues., Nov. 29th, 1864."

Caleb paused, stuck on Mariah's story. Such cruelty, brutality was hardly news to him, hardly shocking, but it ate at him in a way that no other story had. Hatred was trying to claim him again.

Best not to dwell on it. Best to focus on the fact that she came through it all sound, didn't wind up like Dulcina. For his own soul's sake, Caleb needed to change the subject.

"Col. L. and his entire staff are stinking drunk, after making 'war' on a distillery," he wrote.

The candle went out. Caleb reached for his brass match safe. With the candle flickering again, he went back and forth on what to write next.

He thought about the waves of people who poured into the march mile after mile. "They come with hopeful hearts.

Every evening somebody brings roasted groundnuts, persimmons, or some other gift to Capt. G.'s tent."

Caleb remembered the bright-looking young men who approached Captain Galloway yesterday. They stood at attention, gave the sharpest salutes. They wanted to join the army.

"Want to help you lick the Rebels!" said one.

Another: "Do our part for freedom!"

Caleb could still see their downcast faces when the captain explained that there were no colored soldiers in Sherman's army. "It's outright lunatic that Sherman won't let hale & hearty colored men join the ranks, but he will only take our labor. To his credit, at least he pays us."

Caleb sharpened his pencil.

"When out foraging today Pvt. D. asked, 'What is secesh?'" In talking with some colored people he got lost every time they spoke of 'secesh.' I explained that it meant Rebel, that it came from 'secessionist.' I then had to explain 'secessionist.' Capt. G. has gotten him and Pvt. S. to give up those beards & use shaving kits every day. He told me this a.m. that they have sworn off cards."

Caleb's mind meandered to Mariah, to how it took every ounce of self-control not to take her in his arms as she talked about what happened to her pa, her ma. How he wished that he could hold her now.

"Camped near Bostwick."

BEHOLD A PALE HORSE

He came out of nowhere like a hound from hell. Mariah was about twenty yards from her campsite, lugging two buckets of water, when he charged toward her.

"You!"

She froze, turned. "Yes, sir?"

Astride a pale horse, he looked Mariah up and down, pointed at his horse. "Water."

Trying not to tremble, she set a bucket before the horse, watched it dip its head down, looked away when it slobbered. Raising her head slightly, she saw the man looking out over the colored section of the camp. Everybody had stopped what they were doing. Mariah saw Chloe hugging Zeke and Dulcina to her bosom. She saw Zoe, Mordecai, and Jonah shrink back into the woods.

"Girl!" the white man barked.

Mariah swallowed. "Yes, sir?"

"Look at me, girl!"

Mariah obeyed but kept her head to the side.

The man was a winter wind, his gaze chilling her to the bone. Spittle in his beard. Face unworldly white. Heavy-lidded blue eyes. Steel blue. Icy. Caleb was right. Deadly.

General Reb.

"Remove the bucket!" he commanded.

Mariah obeyed, holding her breath as he spurred his horse, charged off, then cantered up and down knots of cringing colored people. All eyes lowered as he passed by. A time or two he stopped before a group. His horse reared up, grunted, squealed.

And behold a pale horse! streaked through Mariah's mind, taking her back to that jackleg preacher, Archibald Dyuvil, who came to the Chaney place at Christmastime. The man always took his text from the Book of Revelation, had a hard fascination with the Four Horsemen of the Apocalypse. The word "apocalypse" terrified little Mariah. More so after she asked her pa what it meant.

"End of days."

Mariah could see, could hear that preacher reading one passage again and again. About the opening of seals, the noise of thunder, and four beasts saying, "Come and see . . . Come and see . . . Come and see . . ."

A white horse, a red horse, a black horse—then the preacher paused. Rising to his full height, he bellowed, "And I looked, and behold a pale horse and his name that sat on him was Death, and Hell followed with him."

Bible slammed shut, he shouted, "The Four Horsemen of the Apocalypse be War, Famine, Disease, and Death!"

While General Reb taunted her people, Mariah remained motionless. She didn't move a muscle until a trail of dust was all that remained of the pale horse and its pale-eyed rider.

The man left evil in the air and Mariah sick to her stomach. A cup of red cedar bark tea didn't help much.

"Did he hurt anybody?" asked Caleb later that evening.

"No," replied Mariah. "Just seemed out to terrify."

"But thank the Lord, we had wagons hid like you told us," said Chloe. "Nobody had to scatter and scramble."

Mariah wished Caleb didn't have to go to the forge, wished he could stay longer than the time it took for him to hand out goods.

And behold a pale horse! Those words haunted Mariah as she lay in the tent later that night, praying for sleep, for General Reb's face to be wiped from memory. No sooner than it began to fade her mind was flooded with frightening news on the day's grapevine. Rachel had heard of soldiers in another part of the march finding colored people tiresome. "Cast them out from their camp. Cast them out without so much as a kernel of corn. Sent them to their death or to a maulin' for sure when Rebels come upon those poor souls."

Hagar had heard about a man who didn't move fast enough when some soldiers ordered him to groom their horses. "Whipped the fella with their belts to get the name and place of his owner, then hog tied him and hauled him two miles back to the plantation, dumped him at his owner's front door." She had also heard that days back a couple of Yankees had snatched a young girl, dragged her into some woods, and—

Rest easy.

If only Caleb was there to repeat those words himself.

Rest easy.

In slavery Mariah had never known what it was to feel safe. And now she didn't feel safe on the march.

She remembered Caleb's calmness during that first wagon ride. How sure he was of things. Mariah fixed her mind on that to banish the storm clouds in her mind.

Many Thousand Gone

Caleb had pulled a muscle in his back in the forge the night before. Captain Galloway spared him forage duty. "Rest up. Heal quick," he said.

Caleb was sure he would with the comfrey poultice Chloe was applying to his back. As he sat there on a carbine crate, he saw his injury as a blessing in disguise. It meant a whole day with Mariah, who looked like a new penny.

With the poultice in place and his back bound, Caleb harnessed and hitched the horses.

"I'll load," said Mariah.

"Let me help with some things."

"I insist."

Caleb didn't argue. He stepped over to the cook spot for another cup of coffee. He was impressed with the orderly way Mariah got Dulcina and Zeke in the wagon, then the provisions and belongings.

Things were a little more chaotic with the wagon Morde-cai was set to drive carrying Hagar, Hosea, Rachel, Miriam, the Doubles.

Ben placed little Rose on his pony.

"Where's Jonah?" Caleb asked.

"Captain Galloway asked him last night to report early to run messages," replied Mariah.

Another blessing, thought Caleb.

Then a shock.

Wagon loaded, Mariah was climbing into the driver's seat.

Caleb poured the rest of his coffee onto the ground.

"What do you think you're doing, young lady?" He had reached the wagon.

"What it look like?"

"I ain't crippled."

"But one wrong move and you could go from bad to worse."

"You can truly handle horses?" Caleb teased Mariah. "You sure I can trust you with my life? How I know you won't drive us off a cliff or into a gully?"

"Caleb, you can trust me. With your life. With anything else."

Caleb reached into his back pocket for his buckskin gloves, and handed them to Mariah.

"Who taught you to drive?" They were about a half mile along.

"My pa."

Behind them some distance, people riding on mules, in oxcarts and wagons, along with ones walking had been singing "Didn't My Lord Deliver Daniel." Now they switched to "Many Thousand Gone."

No more auction block for me.
No more, no more.
No more auction block for me . . .

On they sang of terrors, of toil. No more peck of corn, driver's lash, pint of salt, hundred lash, mistress call, children stole.

No more slavery chains for me.

The refrain was a shout.

Many thousand gone!

"Yes, thank God." Mariah sighed. "Thank God, many thousand gone."

"Come on," said Caleb. "Let's hear you sing."

"Oh no, you don't want that."

"I bet you're a regular little songbird. Bet you have a lovely voice."

Mariah looked at him out of the corner of her eye. "Caleb, I can't carry a tune to save my life."

He had never met a girl so guileless. It made her all the more adorable. "What else did your pa teach you?"

"Swim, fish, trap."

Mariah's hands were practically swimming in his gloves, but the girl was more than making do. Caleb had to admit it. Mariah could drive. Right amount of give and take on the reins. Knew how to take a curve. Not once did she crack the whip.

Caleb found it hard to keep his eyes on the road or on anything else other than Mariah. He was trying to occupy his mind with the silky, swirling bands of clouds when Mariah asked, "When you go out with a forage team, do you bust into homes and stores like we heard soldiers do?"

"I stay clear of all that. Just load what I'm told to load."

"So how is it that you're able to bring us things? Seen you give things to Hagar and others too."

"On occasion I find things lying in the street, on the side of a road. Banjo, jackets, hats, parasols, trousers. Cases where soldiers weren't in a mood to take, just ransack. Something in particular you need?"

"No. Just curious."

"Other times I put it out there some of the things people could use. Pay for it with favors. Shoe a horse and things like that, or trade with something a soldier asked me to be on the lookout for."

"That's how you got my boots. Put it out that there was a need?"

"Uh-huh. Lately, most of what I come by is thanks to Privates Sykes and Dolan. They keep an eye out. Oftentimes soldiers just grab and dash. Don't really know what they got till they camp and start sorting."

"The first time those two handed out food they looked at us like . . . creatures from the moon."

Caleb laughed. "Most of them have no idea, no custom with being person to person, white with colored. But Private Sykes and Private Dolan they are trying. One of the blacksmiths with the Fourteenth is an uncle of Private Sykes. So I help the uncle out at his forge sometimes. And Sykes helps me out."

"Blacksmith, that's your trade?"

"Uh-huh."

"Trained up from young?"

"Yup."

Caleb felt uneasy about this turn in the conversation. He was fast thinking about how he could turn it back to the march.

"Can I ask you something, Caleb?"

"Go ahead."

"Your speech has a—you talk with a little more polish than I've ever heard from colored. Did your master let you learn openly?"

Caleb looked away, rubbed his chin. "I guess you could say I was allowed to learn openly."

"So your whitefolks wasn't all-out crazy?"

Caleb shrugged.

"Your ma and pa, they were on the same place?"

Caleb started to tell her the truth, then thought better of it. Now wasn't the right time. He just wanted to enjoy her. "Yeah, my folks they lived together," he finally said.

"Were they—"

Thank goodness—a bugle call came. *Halt!*

As soon as Mariah brought the horses to a stop, Caleb eased down from the wagon. "Want to find out why he stopped. Won't be long."

"Another bridge Rebels burned," Caleb explained when he returned.

"Any idea how long before the pion—I mean, the pontoniers be finished?"

Caleb smiled. What a head she was developing for all this soldier business in just a few days. "Not long," he replied. And now that the conversation had moved from him to the march, Caleb was determined to keep it that way.

"They say Rebels in all kinds of confusion. Can't make out if Uncle Billy's boys are aiming for Macon or Augusta. Some predict he will cut east and storm South Carolina."

"Wait now, who's Uncle Billy?"

"General Sherman. Troops call him Uncle Billy," Caleb explained. "Loyal to the death. Anyhow, soldiers sent on destruction raids are going above and beyond. When wrecking railroad track, bending rails into hairpins and neckties not enough for some. They aim for something more insulting to Southern soil, like twisting rails into a giant US."

"Us?"

"No, short for United States."

"Why all the destruction? Why don't Sherman simply hunt down as many Rebel soldiers as he can?"

"Rebel soldiers not his main concern."

"Who is?"

"Sherman's out to terrify civilians—the everyday people. Figures if he makes their lives hell, they'll clamor for Georgia to quit the Confederacy. Surrender."

Mariah looked worried. "But what if it don't work, what if—?"

"With or without Georgia, Confederacy is on its last legs. Lost cause."

Mariah didn't look like she believed him. She had gone from the picture of delight to the picture of worry.

"Really?" she asked.

"Last summer, in July, y'all heard about Gettysburg and Vicksburg?"

"The battles?"

Caleb nodded. "Gettysburg made Rebels abandon hope of invading the North. After Vicksburg the Union was on the way to getting back control of the Mississippi." Caleb saw Mariah still looked worried. "And by smashing up Atlanta, Sherman destroyed a chief source of weapons and other supplies."

"Caleb, couldn't there be some battle up ahead that the Union could lose?"

"Could be, but the Union will win the war."

"But what if they don't? What if—if the Union lose . . . will the Captain Galloways of the world have to—"

Now Mariah looked downright terrified.

"Have to do what?"

"Give us back?"

"No one's giving you back, Mariah. Nobody's giving anybody back."

Ten minutes later, they were on the move again. When they reached a wide stretch Caleb saw Mordecai's wagon gaining on them.

"Mordecai and Chloe?" Caleb asked. "I notice most nights he cozies to her the most. Was there a time when they were, you know—"

"Coupled up?"

"Uh-huh."

Mariah shook her head. "Looks to me like Mordecai out to make up for lost time."

"Lost time?"

"Yep." Mariah turned to Caleb. "I reckon about . . . thirty years."

Caleb asked God to let him grow old with Mariah.

"The way I heard it, they had eyes for each other, but as a

boy Mordecai vowed to never marry so long as he was in bond-age. Didn't want to ever see his wife or children abused."

"That's some sacrifice—and Chloe strikes me as one of the finest women God ever made."

"A saint."

Caleb noticed that Mariah was squinting. He removed his hat, plopped it on her head, and tipped the brim down.

"Thanks much." She smiled. "Anyhow, Miss Chloe, she tried to get Mordecai to budge by tellin' him that her white-folks wasn't all-out vicious. And that was true. Never struck any of their slaves. Never had anybody whipped. Never had that many slaves to begin with. I think five at most. The Doubles, their butler, Jim, who died last year, and the house-keeper, Gertie, who decided to stay. But back to Miss Chloe. See, she argued that if her whitefolks ever gave her a cussin', he would not be there to hear it. She said them bein' on two different places was good. Would make their Sundays together much sweeter."

"Thirty years, that's a long time to hold out on love. Think they'll marry now?"

"I hope so. They long overdue for some happiness."

In a different time and place Caleb would have inched closer and slipped his arm around Mariah's waist.

"If you don't mind me asking, you and Jonah. You two ever—?"

"No."

Caleb loved the quick response. So definite.

"Jonah's another brother to me. Nothing more."

"Seems to me Jonah would like to be more than a brother."

Mariah pursed her lips. "Can we talk about somethin' else?"

Caleb gave her a salute. "Yes, Captain Mariah!"

"Captain?" she said. "Can't I be your general?"

Caleb melted under Mariah's sly and frisky smile.

Sweetest day of my life, Caleb thought later that night, a night bearing easy breezes and calm. Just about everybody seemed in a light mood.

Hosea on the banjo he'd found for him. Ben playing the spoons. One gaggle of youngsters did the cakewalk. Another was patting juba.

Jonah was the exception. Sour all through supper and afterward he stomped off. Caleb was glad he did. But he hoped Jonah would cool off, recognize that he wasn't the one at fault. A man can't keep what he never had.

Caleb was grateful to Mordecai and the Doubles for once again giving him and Mariah private time. After supper, with oversight of Dulcina, they passed the time with Hosea and Hagar's band.

Caleb didn't mind sharing Mariah with Zeke at all. He enjoyed watching her tickle him, make funny faces.

When Mariah settled Zeke down and began darning a sock, Caleb went to work on the timberdoodle he'd started the other day. As she talked, Caleb whittled away.

"Cabbages big as moons!" Mariah exclaimed, recalling her ma's garden.

When she fell silent, Caleb feared bad memories were creeping up. But then she jumped up, smiled. "I want to show you some things."

She returned with a pouch. In it, a tin. In the tin, wrapped in a handkerchief, twelve blue glass beads. "Was a Christmas gift from Pa to Ma. Wore them in her hair most Sundays."

"She must have looked lovely." Caleb imagined Mariah on a sunny Sunday with blue glass beads in her hair.

Caleb's conscience took him to task for sharing so little about himself, as Mariah recalled her pa making her ma a new spinning wheel, taking delight in carving tiny flowers on the whorl.

And there was the cedar trunk he made. And a fiddle for her one Christmas. "Like his, only smaller, made of a gourd and groundhog hide. Bow from bamboo and horsehair."

"And I'm guessing your pa taught you to play."

Mariah nodded. "His fiddle was his peace at the end of a day. Not much for fast tunes. Windin' down kind mostly."

"You still got your fiddle?"

Mariah shook her head. "Wore that thing out." From the pouch she brought out a chisel and a small wooden mallet. "These my main keepsakes of my pa." From her apron pocket she brought out the jackknife. "This was his too."

"Whoa!" Caleb laughed. "I'll be sure not to rile you. You could do some real harm with that thing."

Mariah looked on edge.

"What, did I hit a nerve, Mariah?" he asked, looking down at the bone-handled knife in her hand. A six-inch blade, he reckoned. "Mariah, tell me you've only had to use that knife for cutting twine, bark, and such."

"Yeah, twine, bark, and such." She smiled.

Caleb didn't believe her. It was a put-on smile, but he wasn't going to push it.

Caleb was almost finished with the timberdoodle's long, needle-thin beak when Mariah told him about times her pa blacked out the windows, brought out a speller from beneath a floorboard in the back of their cabin, then had her and her ma gather around the hearth.

Caleb handed Zeke the timberdoodle.

"My bird?"

"Yes, your bird, my boy," replied Caleb with a tug on Zeke's cap.

"That's precious," said Mariah.

You're precious, thought Caleb.

"Thanky," said Zeke.

"Most welcome," said Caleb.

As Mariah delighted in Zeke zigging and zagging his timberdoodle, Caleb imagined her lips upon his, his hand—

Once again her joy was gone. Her eyes were no longer on her brother, but on something—or someone—behind him.

Caleb turned around. In the distance stood Jonah gawping, looking vexed.

Goodness Like Mint

Onward Mariah marched to the somewhere place, feeling the strain by day six. A little more jittery when a bobcat yowled or cannon boomed. A little more anguished by scenes along the way bringing to mind the end of days.

Chimneys the only things left standing in some towns.

The stench from the burning—homes, buildings, gin houses, bales of cotton.

Pillars of smoke, pillars of fire.

Women wailing, children's hoarse cries. But silent as the grave was the white girl Mariah spotted spearing a pocket gopher on this day.

Stringy blond hair. Stick-skinny legs a mass of scabs and bruises. Bruises on her face, neck. And welts. The girl's dress, crusty-looking and tattered, was a burlap sack and never bleached. "Flour" was stamped across the girl's back. She moved like it hurt to walk.

The girl picked up the gopher, put it behind her back as they passed by. Mariah gave her a slight smile.

"What you lookin' at, you filthy nigra?"

Mariah felt pity more than anything else. If goodness was like mint . . . She sighed, thinking of a bright March day long ago and making a mental note to tell Caleb about it when she saw him that evening.

"Whatcha gon' do with all them stones?" she asked her ma.

They were behind their cabin. Mariah dangled on the post and plank fence around their patch. All winter they'd been feeding it ashes, eggshells, bones, fish heads, other scraps. Now planting time was on the horizon. Her ma had already turned the soil. Her pa had just brought over a wheelbarrow full of stones.

"Stones are for the mint," Patience explained. "Putting in mint this year."

"But can't nothin' grow in stones," Mariah puzzled, crinkling her nose.

Patience beckoned her over, pointed to the back corner of the garden patch, told her that's where the mint would live. "It'll spread if it ain't hedged," her ma explained, then told her how mint roots roam under the soil and send up shoots inches, feet away, making more roots, and those roots then roam, send up shoots, making new roots. "And up comes more mint. If I don't wall it off, mint will take over the garden. We'll wind up with no corn and cabbages, no beans and tomatoes, no peppers, no goosefoot, no squash, no okra."

Mariah asked if the mint could spread all the way out to Riddleville Road if there were no stones in its way.

"Possible," said Patience.

"Could the roots roam and shoot up, roam and shoot up, over all of Georgia—over the whole Southland?"

"Wouldn't that be a sight!" Patience replied. "And just imagine what a fine world this would be if goodness was like mint."

"And nobody troubled it with stones."

Her ma's mint left Mariah's mind during a halt before a row of dilapidated double-pen cabins. Two boys, one cream, one caramel, stood in the door of one. Big heads. Large, empty eyes. Matted hair. Spindly. No shoes. One, about Zeke's age, was sucking his thumb.

Mariah waved. "Come on!" she called out. "Tell your people to come on! Come to freedom!" She was about to fetch the boys when a rheumy-eyed, rickety man, bent almost in two, came to the door. "Git inside!" he growled. After the little boys obeyed, the old man shut the door.

What would keep that old man from taking freedom? Too broke-down to care anymore? Was he like Josie? Staying because someone he loved got hired out? His son? Was he the little boys' pa? Where was their ma?

Josie, baby Sarah, Little Jack. How were they faring? Had Nero taken off? If he didn't, Mariah hoped he got the hire-out and was put to hard labor building barricades, digging trenches, and whatever else Rebels needed doing to free up a white man to fight. Serve Nero right. Mordecai had told Mariah that hire-outs died like flies, something they kept from Josie. If Nero didn't take off and didn't get hired out, Mariah prayed to God he wasn't giving Josie torment.

Of all the men to be on guard against—pattyrollers, Judge Chaney's brother with his thick, fleshy fingers, tarrying a fortnight most times, Master Robert—Nero was the worst.

First time was in the barn when she was milking a cow. Nero crept up behind her, mumbled something about her growing so pretty, laid a hand on her back. "You mine," he slurred.

All on fire, Mariah grabbed an empty pail, swung it with all her might, left Nero clutching his side when she fled.

Weeks later Nero tried to shove her into the corncrib. By then Mariah went nowhere without her jackknife. She whipped it out in time to ward off Nero.

"Second time you refuse me," Nero had barked. "Ain't gon' give you but so many chances. Six, thas all. You don't be mine six time I come for you, I will tell Miss Callie you due a whippin'."

Along with Miss Callie's madness, Mariah had to deal with Nero's cat-and-mouse.

Him looking about to charge on her when she was getting a wash pot going, then steering clear and snickering.

Him peeping at her through the cookhouse door, making nasty gestures.

Him trying to sneak up on her when she headed to the chicken coop.

Him once just staring at her, mumbling about extra dresses, more food, and how she was to respect the white in him.

Her shoving the cedar trunk against her cabin door. Nightly.

The day before Yankees descended on the Chaney place, Nero had preyed on Mariah for the sixth time. In the barn again. She didn't use a pail to fend him off this time or her jackknife. She used her knee.

"Yo' time up!" Nero raged, clutching his groin. "You fool heifer, yo' time up!"

Mariah knew the only reason she didn't get whipped was because, what with all the commotion coming from Sandersville, Callie Chaney kept Jonah and Nero busy hiding silver and other valuables.

More than once Mariah was tempted to tell Jonah about Nero's dirty ways—tempted to even turn it into a tale of all-out outrage. She knew Jonah would hurt Nero, maybe even—

She couldn't. Couldn't set Jonah up for hard trouble. Hitting a slave driver was second to hitting a white man. If Jonah hurt or even killed Nero, he could be made to suffer a hundred different ways.

Just as Mariah prayed that no outlaws came to the Chaney place, so she prayed that Nero had gone away. She chided herself for not trying harder to talk Josie out of staying. But then she remembered Josie's resolve, reminded herself that she could no more have talked Josie out of staying than Josie could have talked her out of leaving.

Mariah had to leave, doubly so for Zeke's sake. Her brother would never be strapping-strong like Jonah. With the way Zeke's mind came and went, there'd be a limit to the work that he could do. The older he got, the harder Callie Chaney would be on him. Maybe even label him useless.

No more. That worry was behind her now. All the wickedness too. That thought alone helped Mariah soldier on.

No more, she reminded herself as her feet burned, stomach griped, temples throbbed.

No more, she thought when a wagon wheel got stuck in a rut and she had to help with the unloading, the pushing, the lifting, the loading up again.

No more, Mariah thought when reminding herself that it was only right that she and Miriam walk the most. And now Ben. His pony died during the night.

On this day, like other days, Dulcina and Zeke always rode in the wagon. Mariah learned early on that if on two feet Zeke was apt to stop and spin, Dulcina to wander off, like she sometimes did when they camped. Just last night, Mariah heard stirring in the tent, then saw Dulcina poking her head through the flaps. As Mariah got her settled back down, she saw the strangest look in her eyes. Delight.

"Texas." Meowed, caterwauled, whispered—that was still the only word Dulcina uttered. But now Dulcina sometimes fell into lapses of silent talking. No sound, only lips moving. Mariah feared things were getting worse, feared there was nothing she or others could do except keep close watch.

Dulcina was beyond repair, Mariah had concluded, but she held out hope for Zeke, growing more curious by the day—sometimes by the hour.

"Big worm have feet?" He pointed at a red-black-yellow-ringed creature slithering at the base of a tree.

"Ma, when you gon' learn me to fly?" Mariah followed his gaze. She shared in his delight at the sight of a bluebird on the wing.

Though feeling poorly, with the brutal sun helping none, Mariah wanted her brother to keep asking questions.

Of the red-black-yellow-ringed slithering thing, "No, Zeke, it don't have feet and it ain't a worm. It's a king snake."

"Keen snake."

"King snake," she repeated. "And as some snakes do awful harm, you steer clear of all. You hear me?"

Zeke nodded rapidly as Mariah had done years ago. It was during one of what her pa called their Sunday "excursions."

If they set out for the river, her pa didn't just help her perfect how to bait, how to wait, when to slack. He also had a lesson on something else, like how to tell sweet from brackish water.

Fond memories flowed of her pa teaching her how to trap a possum versus rabbit.

Names of trees—hawthorne, spruce, buckeye, sweet gum.

How to tell a deer's disposition by the bleat.

And birds—coot, grackle, meadowlark, mourning dove, timberdoodle, bobwhite, quail—Mariah's pa taught her their names and had her listen closely to their songs.

"Learn all you can," he always said. "Never know what will come in handy."

Just as he had given her the gift of curiosity, so now on the march Mariah encouraged the same in her little brother—though she had never asked her pa to teach her to fly.

"No, Zeke, I won't be teaching you to fly."

"But . . ."

Mariah saw Zeke strain to string a thought together. "You learned me to swim like fishies," he finally said.

"That's different." Mariah laughed.

"Why?"

"People can swim. People can't fly." She waited for Zeke to ask "Why?" stumped as to how she'd answer.

But she didn't have to. Her brother's mind had moved on, to a chipmunk at the edge of the road. It twitched its nose, reared up on its hind legs, and twitched its nose again. Zeke twitched his nose, then gave the critter a salute.

Watching her brother in his new bliss, Mariah tried to reclaim that joy she felt when she joined the march, tried to get back that feeling that she could run, run, run, not faint. Now . . .

Hazards, hardships—nothing new. But now hourly, daily, the ground beneath her feet was always shifting. Not a minute passed that Mariah wasn't grateful for the journey, but she was tired of the march.

Tired of still being trapped.

But the march was her only hope. Couldn't take off and make her way to a place of her choosing, not that she had any place to choose. New York was a fantasy. Milledgeville was the only place she'd ever been. When she learned that they were camped at Louisville or Bostwick—they were just words. Mariah had no idea where she was. And only one certainty: clinging to Yankees was clinging to freedom.

As they neared the campground, Mariah thought about her ma and her mint, Zeke and his peppermint sticks—mostly shards by now. By day the pouch was tied around his rope belt. At night, looped around a wrist. Again and again Mariah urged her brother to eat his sweets. "After a while all you gon' have is a bag of dust."

Again and again Zeke shook his head, then said, "My freedoms!"

Again and again Mariah thought, *If only freedom came with wings.* She wouldn't be on a march to another's somewhere place, but high in the sky soaring on wings like that golden eagle's, scouting out her own somewhere place, a place where goodness grew like mint.

SO BEAT DOWN

When Caleb checked in on them that morning Mariah looked so beat down. What a shame after their glorious yesterday together. Fitful sleep, he guessed. When he learned about Ben's pony, he knew that didn't help.

Before he headed out, Caleb made a mental note to be on the lookout for something that might cheer Mariah up. Dress? Straw hat? Cloth for a head wrap? Taffy? Then he remembered that he already had something that would lift her spirits.

Earlier that morning, Captain Galloway showed him on a map the line of march for the next few days. As Caleb studied the route, he had a hunch about the final destination. When the captain revealed that one division, with General Kilpatrick's cavalry, would form a flying column, striking out toward Augusta "to convince Rebels that we are gunning for

Augusta"—Caleb's hunch was even stronger. It was a place he was eager to see, a fine place to make a new beginning. At least it was before the war.

Caleb started doing rough figures in his head. Printing press. Ink. Paper. Printer. Rent. Days ago, when he told Captain Galloway about his dream, he learned the captain had a cousin in the business, knew a thing or two.

Caleb tallied up the figures the captain had given him, thought about the sum he'd left Atlanta with, Sherman's pay. Not bad. The enterprise was doable.

But there was something he forgot to factor in, something that wasn't on his mind when he latched onto his dream. Till now he was the only one in the picture. Figured he could make the shop double as home till he got the business built up. But now he wanted Mariah in the picture. He'd need to do more figuring, taking into account Mariah and Zeke. And when the war ended, he'd probably have to get supplies from the North with so much of the South in wreck and ruin. Everything would be more expensive. "Where there's a will, there's a way," Caleb whispered to himself, when the squad reached a farm. He decided to scratch the printing press and heed Captain Galloway's advice to contract with a printer at the start. That would save him about a thousand dollars.

Seeing Mariah in the picture made Caleb remember the moment in the wagon when he had an urge to tell her about himself. Skirting her questions wasn't far from lying. Caleb felt bad about that.

Caleb, you can trust me. With your life. With anything else.

Of course he wanted to trust her. If he didn't, how could he love her?

Tonight. Tonight will be the night, he decided, as he loaded sacks of rice into his wagon. Tonight he'd tell Mariah his story. If he paired it with news of the likely somewhere place it would all go down easier.

LASHING FURY

Lonesome and pale was the late afternoon moon. Mariah was so grateful to be out from under the broiling sun.

Thankful, too, that Mordecai and Chloe had volunteered to haul water.

The tent. She was strong enough to tackle that after getting Zeke and Dulcina settled. Maybe once she had the tent up she'd crawl inside, grab a quick nap before supper. Just a few winks. Just a little quiet near the end of a day that started off with trouble. And there was more to it than her waking up tired and Ben's tears over his pony.

At daybreak, Hagar had lashed out at Miriam for spilling water on their fire. "You clumsy fool, you!"

Minutes later two other women got into a shouting match over clothespins.

About an hour after Caleb headed out to forage, two men

Mariah only knew by sight got into a shoving match over a can of beans. One pulled out a razor.

"Saddlebag!" Chloe had called out.

Mariah helped Chloe tend to the one got his cheek slashed, while Mordecai talked the other man down.

Mariah was nearly done with the tent when Jonah came over loaded with firewood.

"Need a word," he said.

Mariah looked up, troubled by his tone. "Say on."

"Private."

Jonah put the firewood down, took the mallet from her hand, helped her up. "Miss Zoe?" He nodded at Zeke and Dulcina, then dropped the mallet on the ground.

Zoe, stirring a pot, nodded back.

"You stay put, Zeke," said Mariah.

"Yeah, Ma," replied Zeke, zigzagging his timberdoodle.

Dulcina was crouched beside him, caught up in silent talking. But Mariah didn't worry. Dulcina never wandered off when engaged in that.

Mariah didn't appreciate the tight grip Jonah had on her arm. With his strides so wide, she had to practically skip to keep up.

"Jonah, what's happened?"

He stopped between two live oaks dripping Spanish moss.

Had Jonah found out where the march would end? Did he have news of a battle? But why would he take her aside for that? He'd want the rest to know too.

Jonah looked so betwixt and between. Was he bearing good news or bad?

He shoved his hands into his pockets, paced. "You said in freedom you would . . ."

Mariah smelled ashes in the air. "Would what?"

"Get on with life . . . like men and women do."

She had been dreading this moment, had fretted over what to say. Be direct, no beating around the bush—that's what she had decided. But now, face to face with Jonah, in the clear light of day, Mariah lost her nerve. "We only on the road, Jonah. Don't know how many more miles till we reach a place permanent, a place safe—"

"We been free six days now. And you said in freedom me and you—"

"I said . . . maybe, Jonah. Maybe."

"Wasn't no maybe." Jonah paced again. "I remember how you looked at me, so tender that day, like I matter to you."

"That's not how it was," Mariah snapped, then regretted that. She didn't want to bruise Jonah.

Mariah tempered her tone. "Jonah, you always have, always will matter to me." Now Mariah paced. "And naturally I was lookin' at you tender that day. Your ma wasn't in the ground two weeks." She swallowed. "You were all jumbled up inside."

Jonah took Mariah by the shoulders, his touch gentle. "Never been jumbled up when it come to you."

Those had been days of confusion for Mariah too. Even then, when her life was so cramped, so bitter and Jonah so thoughtful . . . She had worried that maybe something was wrong with her. Maybe she was unnatural. After all, Jonah was a good man. Why didn't she love him? But she knew she didn't. And she thought it more unnatural, downright wrong, to take up with a man she did not love.

When her ma told her a day would come when big boys and even men would notice her, Mariah had taken to heart some strong advice.

"Don't let just any man have your grace." Patience was spinning flax. "Mariah, you keep yourself for a good man." Mariah could hear the wheel rattle and whirl, rattle and whirl. "A good man. Like your pa. On top of him being good, he needs to be a true love."

"How to know a true love?"

"When you get beyond the moonstruck stage and you hit a rough patch, but find you can't stay mad at him for long."

Mariah had never been moonstruck over Jonah. But back when his ma passed, she couldn't bring herself to tell him the truth. Then Mordecai's vow came to mind.

"Not until I'm free," she had told Jonah so as not to hurt his feelings. "Not unless I'm free will I take a man or bring a child into this world." When Jonah asked if he would be that man if freedom came, Mariah had said, "Maybe." She hoped Jonah would lose interest, get impatient, go court one of the girls on the Ramsey or Rucker place. Like then, so now, Mariah couldn't tell Jonah the truth.

She wriggled out of his grasp, took a step back, folded her arms across her chest. "Jonah, we not fully free."

"What you mean we ain't fully free?"

"True, we out from under Callie Chaney, but—"

"We free, Mariah, we free!"

"Not fully, Jonah!" Mariah paced again. "The way I see it, the way it sometimes feels, it's like Yankees are our masters now. We wake, eat, march, halt, sleep all on their say. Ever at their mercy." Mariah stopped, looked up at Jonah. "How you know we won't get split up, you sent to be with a different regiment, brigade, or—"

"Captain Galloway won't let that happen."

"Captain Galloway got ones above him."

Jonah shoved his hands back into his pockets. "I feel it in my bones, Mariah, we'll get to full freedom . . . have a . . . have new tomorrows. Won't be beggarly, neither." Jonah stepped toward Mariah. "I looked out for us."

What on earth was he talking about?

"It's what I signaled right before we left the Chaney place. I didn't tell Yanks all where Miss Callie had me hide things."

Jonah smiled wide. "I snuck away some. Small things. Spoons, forks, match safe, little box like a casket, case for her visit cards, one of the judge's flasks, things like that . . . Judge's gold watch. Got that too."

Mariah was shocked. She never expected such cunning from Jonah.

"That ain't all." He reached into his vest pocket, brought out a twenty-dollar gold piece.

"Where'd you get that?"

"From where Miss Callie had me hide it in the henhouse."

Mariah knew the price of some things from being Miss Callie's pack animal during her spur-of-the-moment trips to Milledgeville to visit with kin and spend big at the clothing store, tailor, confectionary, dry goods store, and the shops where she bought liquor and bitters. Mariah knew the price of clocks, tinware, and sundry other items from the peddlers who called at the back door. She imagined the food, the clothes— the land—that one gold coin could buy.

"Got five more like it."

There was something weaselly about the look on Jonah's face. Something unsavory. Like a soldier sidling up to a fancy girl. Mariah took a step back.

"There's things I lack, Mariah. Never learnt to read. Not good with words in speech. But one thing I know, I can take care of you—and Zeke. Was y'all I had my mind on when I took the silver, the gold."

"Mighty sweet of you, Jonah, but—"

From another pocket Jonah brought a gold spray of posies, a diamond at the center of each flower. He held the brooch out to Mariah. "For you."

"I don't want that!" Mariah backed away, remembering the pinpricks.

"What's wrong?"

"I want *nothing* that belonged to that woman."

Jonah pushed his hat back on his head, ran a hand across his brow. He laughed.

Was he mocking her? "What's so funny?"

"You." Jonah put the brooch back into his pocket. "You say you want *nothing* that belong to that woman?"

"Still don't see cause for laughter."

"Mariah, *you* belonged to that woman. *I* belonged to that woman. Your *brother* belonged to that woman."

"Your point?"

"If we don't belong to her no more, then what I carried off don't neither."

Mariah's arms were folded across her chest again. She knew what was coming when Jonah's eyes lingered on her lace-up boots.

"You know what else?" he sneered. "Them boots didn't drop down from heaven. They once belonged to somebody. Somebody like Miss Callie, I reckon, yet you was mighty pleased to—"

"That's different!" Mariah snapped.

"How?"

"They didn't belong to Miss Callie!" Mariah looked away. If only she could make Jonah go away. "And I had need of better shoes."

"Wasn't the gift. Was the giver!" Jonah yelled.

"You sound crazy." For the first time in her life Mariah was afraid of Jonah.

Nostrils flared. His footsteps were heavy as he paced, eyes lashing fury. "I see how you look at him!" Jonah muttered. "Always talkin' to him!"

Mariah turned her back on Jonah, stepped away.

"Look at me, Mariah!"

A few steps on she looked over her shoulder. Jonah was charging.

Mariah spun around. "I *know* you not about to lay a hand on me!" Now she was breathing hard. Now her eyes were lashing fury. "You don't rule me, Jonah! You have no say in how I look at anybody, who I talk to, what I put on my own two feet!"

"No, Mariah, no! Not tryna rule you," Jonah said softly. "It's jus' that you, me, we come up together. Know each other. Have the same story. Caleb's different. He's—"

"Don't start that again!"

"Mark my word, sumpin' ain't right." Jonah snorted. "He hidin' sumpin'. Got an air about him like he had some rule. You ask me, I say Caleb was a driver."

"That's foolishness, Jonah!" Mariah was fit to be tied. And so tired.

Tired of doing her business and helping Zeke do his in the woods.

Tired of the contortions she had to go through to keep herself and him halfway clean.

Tired of the smell of old folks who couldn't help wetting themselves and the folks, young and old, who came down with the flux.

Tired of colicky, mewling babies.

Tired of the stench of burning timber, steel, cotton.

Tired of bracing for cannon boom, rifle fire.

Tired of seeing turkey buzzards circling carcasses of hogs and cattle Yankee butchers left behind.

Tired of worrying about being seen as useless.

And now so tired of Jonah. "All Caleb's done for us day in, day out, and *you* run him down?" Now Mariah was angry enough to tell Jonah the truth. "Jonah, I can't see gettin' on with life like men and women with you. I don't love you, Jonah."

Mariah headed for their campsite. She didn't get far before Jonah caught up with her, grabbed her by the arm.

"Get off me!" Mariah shouted, loud enough for others to hear. She strode on faster. As she did, she saw Mordecai and Chloe rise from an ammunition crate, Zoe shake her head.

She was a few yards away from them when Caleb pulled up to their campsite.

He jumped down from the buckboard. "Mariah, what happened?"

Mariah shook her head. "Nothin'." She sniffled. "Jonah—we just had a—a little mix-up."

Zeke looked up, scrambled over. "Ma cry?" He hugged Mariah around the waist.

Mariah patted her brother's head. "I'm not cryin', Zeke," she cooed.

Zeke handed her his timberdoodle.

"Thank you, Zeke." Mariah gave the bird a halfhearted zigzag, then stopped when she looked up.

Jonah was charging.

And eyeballing Caleb hard.

DRIVER!

Caleb looked up, too, saw Jonah in a rage, a rage rising with his every heavy step. In a few wide strides, Jonah was within a few feet of him, shaking his hat in his face. "Say what kind you were!"

Caleb took a step back. "Whoa now, Jonah. Don't know what you mean."

Jonah got within a foot of Caleb.

Mordecai stepped in between them. Facing Jonah, he extended a hand, palm out. "Son, you best go somewhere and cool off."

Caleb looked around, saw Zoe stop stirring a pot, saw Chloe frowning, saw Mariah take Zeke by the hand. "Come now, let's have us a little excursion."

"No, Mariah!" yelled Jonah. "You stay and hear this thing out."

Mariah stopped in her tracks but kept her back to Jonah.

"I ask you one more time!" Jonah was breathing hard. "Say what kind you were!"

"I think I'll be saying good night." Caleb headed for the wagon.

"You stand and answer me!" Jonah shoved Mordecai aside, grabbed Caleb by the collar, then punched him in the face. Caleb's hat went flying. His body crashed into the wagon.

Mariah spun around. "Jonah, what in the world is wrong with you?"

Balance back, Caleb snatched up one of the fence rails in the wagon, raised it, then let it drop. He put his hand to his left cheek, winced, picked up his hat from the ground.

Mordecai again stepped between Jonah and Caleb. Zoe and Chloe rushed over. Hagar and others camped nearby gathered around.

"Nothin' wrong with me," shouted Jonah. "It's him!" He pointed at Caleb, then jabbed at the air with each word. "I say he was a driver!"

Hagar gasped. "Driver? He was a driver?"

Caleb backed away as others within earshot came over. He guessed that most in the crowd had never known of a driver who wasn't a low-down, dirty dog, a traitor to his people. Short-changed people on rations. Lied on people so they'd get the lash.

Hagar scurried over to the wagon, grabbed a fence rail meant for firewood, made it a menace. She thumped the ground. "Driver!"

Others reached for fence rails, thumped the ground too.

"Driver! Driver! Driver!" they chanted. Some just stamped their feet. "Driver! Driver! Driver!" The crowd swelled.

Caleb looked around, confounded, as the people closed in.

Hagar in the dress he'd provided.

Hosea holding the banjo he'd found for him.

Even Ben in the pants and waistcoat he'd provided.

Rachel, Jedidiah, Effie, John, Leah, Elisha, Carrie, Tom, Bill, Emmanuel, Emmaline, and a host whose names he didn't know—Caleb had done most all of them good turns along the way. But none of it meant anything now. Worst of all was the look on Mariah's face.

Caleb saw a flicker of heartbreak, a flash of sorrow. *Does she truly think I was a driver?*

"Have y'all lost your minds?" Caleb shouted.

"Driver! Driver! Driver!"

"I wasn't no driver! I swear!"

Mordecai stepped in. "Hagar, Hosea, everybody, just calm down now. Go about your business."

"I don't believe him!" fumed Jonah.

"Jonah! That's enough!" cried Chloe.

"I swear, Jonah," said Caleb calmly. "I wasn't no driver. Don't know how you ever got such a notion."

"You got bossman ways about you!" Jonah yelled.

"No driver, Jonah."

Jonah turned to the crowd. "Y'all notice he got a quality of clothing not like the rest of us?"

"Amen to that!" somebody called out.

"Y'all see how he friendly with Yankees?" Jonah was shouting now.

"Seen it!" somebody else called out.

"Driver! Driver! Driver!"

The crowd had grown larger.

Caleb feared for his life—he had to put the fire out now. "I couldn't have been a driver, people!" he shouted. "I wasn't a slave. I was born free."

"Order!" Captain Galloway roared. "Order!" He was on his bay steed. Privates Sykes and Dolan, both clean-shaven, trotted behind him.

"Order!" Captain Galloway shouted again. He pointed at Jonah. "Take that man away. Put him in the stocks!" Then to the crowd: "We have trouble enough with the Rebels," he said. "We need no trouble from the colored."

Caleb watched Hagar and the others hurry back to their campsites. Mordecai and the Doubles only stepped back. Mariah didn't move. Now it wasn't heartbreak and sorrow that Caleb saw on Mariah's face, but shock. Anger too.

Caleb stepped over to Captain Galloway. "A word, sir?"

Captain Galloway nodded.

"No harm was really done here."

"Really?" said Captain Galloway, inspecting Caleb's eye.

"Just a small misunderstanding."

"Small misunderstanding?"

"Yes, sir," Caleb replied, looking Galloway eye to eye. "My fault."

Up jumped Zeke. He hurried over, pulled on the captain's coat. All smiles, he offered a salute.

Caleb knew Captain Galloway didn't want to put Jonah in the stocks. He had done it once to a colored man outside Atlanta, punishment for trying to steal a rifle. "Made me feel like a filthy slaveholder," the captain later told Caleb. And now Caleb could see that the captain was looking to maintain order and save face.

"Privates Sykes, Private Dolan," said Captain Galloway, "first take him to my tent for interrogation."

"Thank you, sir," Caleb whispered.

When Galloway rode away, Caleb looked around and saw people stealing glances at him, guilty looks on their faces.

And Mariah was gone.

TIGHTROPE WALKER

"Did you know Caleb was always free?" asked Chloe over supper.

"No," Mariah replied, head down, embarrassed.

"I'm sure he kept it from you for a good reason," said Mordecai.

But what possible reason could he have had? Mariah asked herself. She couldn't help but feel betrayed, made a fool of, even.

After supper Chloe handed her a sliced-up potato in a bandana and Zoe a small kettle filled with soup.

"You should go see about him," said Chloe.

"I'm sure he's fine," replied Mariah.

"What did I say?" Chloe had her hands on her hips now.

Mariah relented, realizing that a small part of her did

wonder how Caleb was faring. But more than that, she wanted answers.

She walked from group to group, bandana in one hand, kettle in the other.

"Up thataway," somebody said.

"Cross yonder," another told her.

The wind was at her back when she found Caleb sitting outside his tent. Like every night before, a thousand campfires were crackling.

"Why you never told me?"

His shrug hurt.

"Captain Galloway know?"

Caleb nodded.

That hurt worse. After all she'd shared with him. She handed Caleb the kettle, the bandana, and got furious when he barely looked up.

"The less they know about me, the more I learn. If they think I was a slave, I'm invisible, I'm—"

"Like cattle? Like me?"

"That's not what I meant."

Somewhere in the darkness, a man sang "Go Down, Moses."

"Caleb, I thought we were . . ."

He looked up. "What?"

Mariah looked away. "Well, friends. But now it's like I don't even know you."

"Some soldiers likely to think a free man uppity. Could make me a target."

"But *me*? I'm no Yankee soldier."

"Didn't want it to get out. After I told Galloway I regretted it."

"But *me*? You didn't trust *me*, Caleb? You trusted that white man more than me?"

"It wasn't so much that I was trusting him. It just slipped out."

A saw-whet owl *hoot-hoot*ed.

"I was planning to tell you."

"When?"

"Was waiting for the right time."

"Why wasn't it the right time when I told you about my pa, my ma? Why wasn't it the right time when—"

"Nothing's changed, Mariah. I'm still the same man. Whether I was a slave or always free, what's changed?" He unwrapped the bandana, put a potato slice to his left cheek.

"We from different places, different worlds."

"We both colored. We both Southern born. Besides, you're free now."

Mariah waited for him to go on, explain himself, but all he gave her was silence.

Along with being angry, Mariah now also felt a tinge of guilt. Back when people were about to mob Caleb, for a split second she had wavered, remembering what Jonah had said the day they left the Chaney place. *Any colored man got common ground with a white man gotta be a hazard to the rest of us.* Yes, for an instant she had doubted Caleb, thinking if he had been a driver that explained why he talked more about the march than himself.

And perhaps Caleb had seen her doubt.

Mariah sat down across from him. "What was it like?" She had never met a free colored person.

Now someone was playing a ditty on a reed pipe.

"Ever been to the circus?" Caleb asked.

"Once." Mariah thought about that one precious day she saw a talking horse, a jester, tiny people juggling. "Years ago. With money ma made from her garden."

"Was there a tightrope walker?"

Mariah stared into the fire as Caleb told her about white guardians to vouch for free colored, about free papers, kidnappings. "Over us hung a fear that if we were ever caught without our papers, we'd wind up on an auction block in New Orleans. Never let our guard down when not among just our own."

"Your own bein' other free colored?" All this time what she thought was care—was it all just pity? When he looked at her, did he only see damage?

"Our own being colored people, free and slave. Like I said, Mariah, we both colored, both Southern born, and now both free."

"Soup's goin' cold."

"Will heat it up in the morning, have it for breakfast."

An awkward silence followed.

Caleb was the first to speak. "Look, Mariah, my pa spent twenty-six years in slavery. Most colored in and around Atlanta was in slavery, some of them kin. So it's not like I lived in ignorance before I met you."

That stung and surprised her too. Mariah had assumed that . . . "How did your pa get free?"

"His skills and good fortune."

Mariah thought for a bit. "A blacksmith?"

Caleb nodded. "His fences, gates, railings—all of such fine quality, patterns of charm, grace—he never had trouble getting work. Most of his customers were big planters."

"This after he got free?"

"Before and after. When a slave, he was allowed to hire himself out. Had to give his owner fifty dollars a month. All above that was his to keep. This was in Decatur."

Mariah saw pride rising in Caleb when he told her how his father scrimped and saved for freedom. "Cost him eighteen hundred dollars, and he had enough left over to buy a few acres right outside Atlanta. Built a nice-sized house, workshop out back."

"Why didn't he go North?"

Caleb stared at Mariah for a while, then said, "Because a fine young lady named Rebecca Baker wasn't North."

Mariah smiled. She knew where the story was going. "Your ma?"

Caleb nodded. "She and her family were freed years earlier. Owner got true religion. Anyhow, her family ran a secondhand clothing shop in Atlanta. That's where Pa first laid eyes on her. Knew at first sight that she was the one. After he got himself set, he went about courting the apple of his eye."

"And was he the apple of her eye?"

Caleb leaned back on his elbow. His eyes danced. "Ma always said Pa had been coming around the shop for weeks before she paid him a wisp of attention. Then Pa, he'd stroke her face and say, 'Becky, you know you loved me right off,' and she'd say, 'Jacob Drew, you stop being so full of yourself.' Then they'd laugh and let the story lie."

"Did your pa really love your ma from the moment he first saw her?"

"That's what he said. And Pa wasn't one to trifle."

"And your ma, you think it took her a while?"

"I tend to think not."

Mariah found herself lingering a little too long in Caleb's eyes. When she looked away, she scratched a spot on her neck that didn't itch.

"Could be your ma took to your pa at first sight, just like

he did her, but she just wanted to wait a bit. Make sure he was a good man."

Caleb sat up and tossed a pine knot on the fire, looked directly into Mariah's eyes. "You think my ma wasn't smart enough to know a good man when she saw one?"

Mariah scratched a place on her forearm that didn't itch. "I'm sure your ma was plenty smart, Caleb," she finally said. "Most likely she just wanted to make sure. Have some extra guarantee. Maybe she didn't want to let on at first how she felt for fear he'd change his mind."

"My pa wasn't the changeable type."

"But your ma didn't know that."

Caleb laughed. "You got a point there." He rubbed his hands before the fire. "Whatever was holding Ma back, it didn't last long. They married two weeks after he gave her a gold double locket on a neck chain."

"What was in the locket?"

"Nothing. Both sides empty. He asked her if she could ever see the locket with a portrait of him on one side and her on the other. As husband and wife."

"And she said yes?"

"What do you think?"

Mariah looked down sheepishly, feeling a bit silly. Some-what giddy too.

Caleb undid the top buttons of his shirt, took from around his neck a locket on a chain, and handed it to Mariah.

She hesitated.

"Go on," he urged.

Mariah wiped her hands on her dress before taking it. Carefully, she opened the locket, stared in awe at the two photographs. Woman on the left. Man on the right. Both in fancy black.

Mariah saw that Caleb had his father's cheekbones and jaw. Same broad shoulders.

Caleb's eyes and his full lips were like his ma's.

Fine color came from both. Pa like velvet midnight. Ma only a tad lighter.

"They look so prosperous and so happy." She closed the locket, handed it back to Caleb. "You fortunate to have a keepsake like that. Only likenesses I got of my folks is what I hold in my head."

Just then Mariah realized that she had failed to stay mad at Caleb. The anger, the hurt, it had all drifted away like dry leaves whisked away by a breeze. Even more unsettling—and scary—was that Mariah found herself wondering what it would be like to give Caleb her grace, and she found herself knowing that he was her somewhere place.

But she thought it best to shift her mind to something else. Mariah puzzled for a bit. If Caleb was on the march, his folks must be dead. No matter how wrecked Atlanta was, if they were still alive, she couldn't see him leaving them behind.

"Your folks? Both gone?"

He nodded. "Pa right before the war broke out, passed in his sleep. Ma went earlier this year."

Mariah saw that Caleb no longer wanted to talk about his folks.

"You the only child?"

"Yep." After a pause Caleb said, "Only one to survive. Some died as babies and—"

Caleb's jaw tightened.

"And what?"

"Had a sister, Lily. She died earlier this year too. Was only thirteen."

Caleb's whole mood had changed. He looked in pain.

Had his sister and mother been taken by consumption? Winter fever?

Now was not the time to ask, she decided. "I should turn in," she said.

She didn't want to leave, hoped Caleb would ask her to stay a little longer.

Those words never came.

Offered Him a Chocolate

For Friday, December 2, 1864, Caleb jotted down that the division had moved out at daybreak, that the march had been zigzagging.

What a jangled day it had been. "Pvt. L. who went missing 2 days ago was found dead. More things are breaking. Wheels. Wagons. Tent poles. Limber chests. Men." Caleb wrote about the picket guard who took leave of his senses in the middle of the night. The Irishman had ripped off all his clothes and jabbered about Judgment Day.

"J. attacked me this evening & tried to loose others on me, claiming I was a driver. I had to let out that I was born free so as not to be killed." Caleb admitted that for a split second he relished the thought of Jonah in the stocks, but then he realized that if he didn't intercede on Jonah's behalf then he really was no better than a driver. "Capt. G. said when he had J. in his tent, he looked very sorry and said as much. For that,

Capt. G. offered him a chocolate. When J. asked a favor, Capt. G. obliged him."

Caleb wished he had had some chocolate or other treat to offer Mariah when she came to his tent. The hurt and anger in her eyes grieved him. "At one point I thought she might throw the soup in my face. But she gentled down, went back to her sweet self. And now she knows how I came to be free, some things about my folks. I told her of Lily, but only that she was dead. Camped near Waynesboro."

Till We Meet Again

"You don't need to do this, Jonah."

"Yeah, Mariah, I do."

"But where will you go?" asked Chloe.

"Asked Captain Galloway to get me on to the pioneers."

Chloe shook her head. "We'll hardly ever see you."

"I'll keep in touch through the grapevine." Jonah lifted a sack from the ground, slung it across a shoulder. Eyes on the ground, he said, "I'm real sorry for the strife."

Mordecai rose from a half barrel, patted Jonah on the shoulder. "None of us perfect. Owning up is a giant step."

Mariah's stomach was in knots from the guilt. Had she never told Jonah "maybe" back when they were on the Chaney place, none of this would have happened. "Jonah, I'm sorry I—"

"No, Mariah, you did nothin' wrong. Only told the truth."

"But there's no cause for you to go." Mariah fought back tears. "Things will smooth over."

"As I see it," said Jonah, "I'll be gettin' myself ready for full freedom. Learnin' to build roads, bridges. Skills should put me in good stead wherever we—wherever I settle."

Zeke sat cross-legged beside Mordecai. "Jonah go?"

Dulcina, sitting beside Zeke, looked up. "Texas?"

"No, Miss Dulcina, not Texas, not that far." Jonah squatted down next to Zeke. "That's right, little man, Jonah go." He removed his muffler from around his neck, put it around the boy's, then said to Mordecai, "That other sack, will you mind it for me, please?"

"Will do," replied Mordecai.

"And if . . . if we get lost to each other, y'all split it up fairly."

"We won't lose each other!" Mariah insisted. "There's the grapevine, like you said."

Zoe handed Jonah some breakfast wrapped in a bandana. Johnnycake and cracklins.

Jonah nodded his thanks. "I thank all y'all for your goodness to me over the years." Jonah reached into his breast pocket and handed Mordecai, then the Doubles, then Mariah a twenty-dollar gold piece.

Zoe arched an eyebrow, Chloe gasped, Mordecai ran a hand over his head.

"I'll explain later," said Mariah.

"Y'all the only family I got left." Jonah wiped his eyes. "Tell Caleb I hope he can forgive." Jonah put his hat on his head. "Till we meet again," he said.

"Till we meet again," said Chloe, Zoe, and Mordecai.

Mariah closed her hand around the gold coin out of regard for the giver. She tippy-toed up, gave Jonah a kiss on the cheek. "Till we meet again."

FAMILY

Caleb was of two minds about Jonah joining the pioneers. On the one hand, it put an end to the friction. It would, he hoped, also ease Jonah's pining for Mariah. Caleb knew how he would feel if he couldn't have her heart. And last night he knew he did. There was something in the way she looked at him when they talked about his folks' courtship.

But Mariah had known Jonah all her life. In time would she come to resent Caleb for the separation—even though it hadn't been his fault? Every time she looked at him would she be reminded of losing Jonah?

Only temporary, Caleb told himself. At the end of the march there'd be a reuniting. *Lord*, he said to himself, *don't let Jonah get hurt—or worse—while a pioneer.*

Caleb was on his way to see Jonah that morning, to tell him no hard feelings and urge him not to go. When he saw Mariah and the others huddled around Jonah, he stopped in his tracks.

He was too far away to hear what they were saying, but he could see anew how very much they were family. A family forced and forged under slavery's brutal reign, but a family nonetheless.

What he'd give to have a family again. What he'd give to be part of this family. Husband to Mariah. Father to Zeke. Maybe even work into a bygones-be-bygones brotherhood with Jonah. Keep Mordecai and the Doubles close for fatherly and motherly advice. Keep Dulcina close, too, because it was the right thing to do.

When Caleb saw Mariah give Jonah a kiss on the cheek, he felt he had no right to approach, interrupt their sad and tender parting. Caleb also thought it best if he kept his distance that evening.

NIGHT BECAME A WISHING WELL

Mariah stayed on the lookout for Caleb that evening. When they camped. When they supped. When she got the tent up. She could understand why he made himself scarce what with the way folks had ganged up against him on Jonah's wild say, but didn't he want to see her? She had only laid eyes on him once that day, at the Buckhead Creek crossing. But he said not a word to her. Just helped.

With Zeke in the tent, tucked in with his pouch of peppermint sticks and his timberdoodle, Mariah sat alone by the fire. Missing Caleb. Jonah too.

She wondered, hoped, second-guessed. None of it did a bit of good. She finally gave up and joined a gathering around a bonfire.

Mordecai beside Chloe. Between her and Zoe, Dulcina curled up in a ball. Effie, who had joined the march outside Louisville, made room for Mariah between herself and Zoe.

Hagar was telling of what she called her "all-time scariest meet-up with a haint." The ghost was swooping down, she said, when her brother cried out, "'Quick, turn your pockets inside out!' Quick, I did, and that haint wizened into vapor!"

Some in the gathering seemed frightened. Others not much.

"Dead can't do us no harm," said Effie. "Seen plenty o' haints in my time. All on the playful side. None never done me harm. All my hurts and pains come from the livin'."

"Amen," said Hosea, after a puff on his pipe.

Mariah felt a growing tension in the air. *Like me, they all have scars*, she thought. *Like me, they all have terrors to tell.*

"My whitefolks was both devils," testified Dessa from Davisboro. "Come Christmas warn't no use chillun scamper to the Big House shoutin' 'Christmas gif'! Christmas gif'!' Git they ears boxed is all."

Mariah recalled Christmases past, days when the Chaneys had everybody head to the Big House back door for bounty. Dried Fruits. Fresh meat. New shoes. Cloth. As a child, Christmas after Christmas, she believed that the Chaneys' gifts were a sign of a softening of their hearts.

She remembered, too, Christmas merriment in the quarters. Her pa playing his fiddle—fast-time tunes during these days. Her ma shake, shake, shaking her gourd rattle. Others strumming banjos, blowing the quills. And ancient Aunt Minda patting her feet, bobbing her head, ancient Aunt Minda who beguiled her, Jonah, and the other children with tales of a village far, far away in a land called Guinea, tales she'd been told as a child and told to pass on. Along with the stories of frisky spiders and big cats getting spots, Aunt Minda sometimes taught little Mariah and other children words from Guinea.

Aban—Strength! *Akoben*—Devotion! *Akofena*—Courage! *Sankofa*—Remember!

Mariah remembered boundless cheer at Christmastide until they were made to gather outside and listen to that preacher with a fire-and-brimstone mind. "The Four Horsemen of the Apocalypse be War, Famine, Disease, and Death!"

"We call it the killin' stone." Those words wrenched Mariah back from memories. Effie again. "We call it the killin' stone," she repeated, rocking slowly, eyes on the fire.

Effie told of a rock outcrop on the edge of her town, of white women snatching light-skinned babies from black women's arms. "Them white women cuss up the colored women somethin' awful. Scratch, kick, slap. Act like the colored women had a power to keep massas off 'em." Effie wiped her eyes. "Them white women bash colored babies' brains out on the killin' stone. Sometime they hurl the little bodies into the bush, sometime just drop 'em right there by the stone. Howsoever us could, us sneak and bury. Warn't right to leave 'em for varmints to devour."

Across from Mariah, a woman new to the march began sobbing. "Was sold from place to place when young on account of I couldn't bear no children. Each time farther away from my folks."

"Take your time, take your time," said Mordecai softly as Miriam struggled to tell about the bloodhounds unleashed on her brother. The boy had been caught sneaking a ham from the smokehouse, then he fought back when the driver tried to whip him. "D-d-d-dawgs t-t-t-tow the flesh fr-fr-fr-from m-m-m-mah br-br-br-brutha buh-buh-bones."

Copper-skinned Ben held up his right hand with its forefinger missing the first joint.

"Tried to learn your letters?" asked Mariah.

Ben nodded.

"Beastly people." Rachel sighed, circling one arm around her little Rose, one hand spread on her big belly.

A nighthawk cawed. Mordecai rose, tossed a few fence rails onto the fire, returned to Chloe's side.

"We was born in Virginia." She sniffled.

Mariah turned, saw Chloe with her head lowered, saw Mordecai patting her hand, saw Zoe swallow.

"Was six years old when Doc Melrose's father paid a visit. His wife took a shine to us. Given they important folk, our master—" Chloe took a deep breath, stroked Dulcina's arm. "Night before we was to go, our mama fixed on our memories." Chloe paused again. "Mama said, 'You Zoe and Chloe from Richmond, Virginia.' Then she had us say it back to her three times."

From off a ways came a squeal. Like a rabbit in an owl's talons.

"Next, Mama said, 'You born on James Carter place.' We repeated that three times."

Zoe sniffled.

"Then she said, 'Your mama named Ruth. She second cook on the Carter place.'"

Zoe reached over Dulcina, took her sister's other hand.

"Your daddy named—" Chloe began to sob.

Zoe, fighting back tears, picked up where her sister left off. "Your daddy named William. He a wheelwright and cooper on the Carter place."

Chloe spoke on. "You got five brothers and sisters—"

Zoe spoke on. "Hannah, Daniel, Phoebe, Cyrus, Peter."

"Come morning," continued Chloe, "after Mama and Daddy hugged us hard, Mama asked if we remember the lesson. We was too crying to speak, so we nod. She pat our heads, hold us tight one last time, then told us to keep remembering because"—Chloe took a deep breath—"because every good-bye ain't gone." After another pause, she added through tears, "That was nearly—"

"Fifty years ago," Zoe finished up, wiping her eyes.

Mariah was stunned. She had never heard their story, never seen the Doubles cry, never known them to put an ounce of pain on display. And now there was a glistening in Mordecai's eyes.

"At ten I was made playmate to Miss Callie's brother, taught to groom the boy's pony, groom the boy." Mordecai paused. "Was a cruel boy. Used to saddle me with a collar, leash, make me walk on all fours." Mordecai paused again. "Time and again my pa looked on in pain when he was out there trimming hedges, pruning roses, weeding, swinging the scythe across the lawn. For Pa's sake I tried to keep my tears inside."

Mariah saw Chloe squeeze Mordecai's hand.

"There were times he couldn't do the same when the boy was abusing me. Also when he heard Miss Callie's mother or father cuss my mama, smack her around. Was a horrible thing to see my pa cry."

Mariah saw Chloe rub Mordecai's back.

"One night I found my pa in the garden, weeping a river. 'I ain't a man. I ain't a man,' he kept saying." Mordecai swallowed. "I helped him to our cabin, cheered him up some with a hand-shadow show, went to bed plum proud that I'd saved Pa from a consuming sorrow."

Mariah was by now on the verge of tears herself.

"Turns out all I'd done was fool myself." Mordecai's voice quivered. "In the middle of the night, Pa slipped from the cabin and hanged himself in the livery."

Rachel shook her head. "Poor man."

Mordecai took a deep breath. "On that day I made a pledge. Never take a wife. Never sire a child, not so long as I'm bound.

Kept the pledge when a young valet. Kept the pledge when Miss Callie, off and married, wrote to her father begging for me, saying none of the judge's colored men had the quality to be a butler."

Chloe wrapped her arms around Mordecai. Mariah heard him whisper, "Now you know why."

"And to think," said Della, "some of them shocked to see us take off with the Yanks." Della, a high yalla, angular woman with a patch over her right eye, had joined the march only a few hours before. With her was a grizzled, old, humpbacked man, her father, Gus.

Mariah soon learned that Callie Chaney was hardly the only one to give out scare talk about the Yanks.

A woman named Nannie recalled her owner telling her that before the Yanks set fire to buildings in Atlanta, they locked up hundreds of colored people inside them.

"We was told self-same story," whispered Rachel.

Ben cleared his throat. "Massa told me Yanks drowned all the colored women and children in the Chattahoochee."

"Them devils say anything to keep us bound," muttered Mordecai.

"And the Bible say the devil is a liar!" Hagar roared.

"So many Yanks been mighty kind," said Rachel.

With that, talk turned to individual bluecoats. Thoughts, observations, news picked up while cooking, herding, laundering, blacking boots. There was talk of the ones who tickled them, like the burly sergeant who went about slapping younger soldiers on the back and exclaiming, "Prave boys! Such prave boys!"

"That's Sergeant Hoffmann," said Mariah.

"Ones like him," said Mordecai. "They from Germany."

"That near New York?" someone asked.

"No, across an ocean. In Europe."

"They have slavery over there?" asked Ben.

"No, they do not," Mordecai replied.

Hosea recalled Sergeant Hoffmann handing out pants and caps. Hagar spoke about Private Sykes handing out socks. Rachel remembered Private Dolan bringing baskets for laundry.

"You know it's Captain Galloway behind their goodness," said Chloe.

"Captain Galloway, he's the king of kindness," added Mariah.

The captain had supped with them that night. It had been a one-pot meal of cowpeas, rice, and pork.

"Most delicious!" he said after his first forkful. "What flavor!" he exclaimed. "I taste the . . . hot pepper . . . onion, and . . . ?" He looked at Zoe.

A tightlipped smile was all he got back by way of a reply.

"Go on." Captain Galloway smiled back. "Aren't you going to tell me the rest of the ingredients?"

"Well, sir, if I tell you, sir, all the fine flavor will fade away."

Captain Galloway wagged his finger. "I've heard how you cooks guard your recipes," he said. "But you know, you might want to give up some of your secrets. There's money to be made in a cookbook. An uncle of mine has a small publishing company. I could make an introduction after, well, you know, when we get through all this."

Mariah was stunned to see the captain acting like he was with his own. Was something wrong with him? He didn't smell like he'd been drinking.

"And your cookbook," Captain Galloway continued after another forkful, "it might just become a calling card for a catering business. You might even open a restaurant. I have some friends who might back such an endeavor."

Is he crazy? Mariah couldn't recall a white person having a conversation with a colored person. She remembered plenty of talk—

Fetch me a sherry, then draw my bath!

Yes, ma'am.

Can't churn faster than that?

Yes, ma'am.

Have Jack butcher that hog Friday next!

Yes, sir.

Put the kettle on!

Yes, ma'am.

Send for Reuben!

Yes, ma'am.

That silver better have a mirror shine!

Yes, ma'am.

Where the blazes is Reuben?

Don't know, ma'am.

Talk. Never conversation, like Captain Galloway was making, being more than kind, being friendly.

They had just sat down to eat when the captain came over. When they stopped, stood up, he bid them take their seats.

Awkward smile on his face, hands clasped behind his back, he rocked on his heels.

"Something we can do for you, sir?" Mordecai had asked.

"Oh no. I just, just came to see how you all are faring."

"Right fine," replied Mordecai.

"Having supper?" The captain rubbed his hands.

"Yes, sir."

"Looks good."

"Would you like some, sir?" asked Mariah.

"Yes, I would—if you have some to spare."

Mariah rose. "Zeke, give me your cup."

The captain tensed. Was he afraid to eat behind colored? No, she soon found out. It wasn't that.

"I wouldn't dare take the child's food!" he said.

"Don't trouble yourself, sir," said Mariah. "I can put his in my cup—he can eat from mine. I'll just give his cup a little wash up for your portion." Mariah lifted the lid from the pot. "See, there's plenty more."

Mariah watched Galloway peer into the pot, then get a fix

on the beat-up tin half skillet Mordecai ate from, the Doubles' dented dipper cups, her and Zeke's tin cups. Dulcina, her back to the group, wasn't eating at all.

"No need," said Galloway. "Please, Mariah, sit back down. Let your brother keep his cup. I'll be *right* back," which Mariah knew would be true, for this night, the captain camped closer to the colored than to his comrades.

"Well, I never," said Chloe when the captain was out of range.

"That is one peculiar man," added Mordecai.

When Captain Galloway returned, Mariah eyed his tin plate, a strange long mahogany case with a brass shield and a silver cap. She had seen other soldiers' eating ware, what Caleb had told her were called mess kits, but she'd never seen any as marvelous as the captain's. Inside the case was a fork, spoon, and knife with fancy black handles. There was also a corkscrew and a strange little contraption. The case's silver cap she realized doubled as a cup.

"Salt and pepper anyone?" asked the captain, unscrewing the little contraption and revealing two shakers.

As he supped, Captain Galloway seemed to be enjoying every forkful.

"And what is this dish called?" he asked at one point.

"Hoppin' John," replied Zoe.

"Hahpin—"

"Think of a boy named John, sir," said Mordecai. "Then see that boy hop."

"Oh," said Galloway. "Hopping John."

"Yes, sir," said Mordecai.

"And why, pray tell, is it called hopping John?"

"No idea, sir."

Before Captain Galloway left he gave Mordecai his tin plate and mess kit.

"Oh no, sir, I couldn't possibly take your things," Mordecai protested, but the captain insisted.

"Captain Galloway, he's the king of kindness," Mariah said again, later that night during the bonfire gathering. She looked over at the captain bundled up in his overcoat, warming his hands by a small campfire.

"Captain Galloway, sir!" Mordecai called out. "You should know a host of us pray you up every day!" Standing at his full height, Mordecai gave the captain a salute.

Captain Galloway returned the salute.

"We pray for all the good Yanks!" Effie hollered out. "Sherman on down."

"I heard Sherman insane," whispered Hagar.

"Aw, stop that now," said Mordecai, shaking his head.

Nannie looked over one shoulder, then the other. "Is odd how he go about more like vagabond than ginral. Black hat half-covering his face, ratty brown overcoat like—"

"Ever get a close look at his face?" interrupted Hagar.

"Not close," someone replied.

"Red hair tussled up," said Hagar. "Pale eyes jump all over. Face like a skirmish."

"That's the truth," said Mariah. The few times she'd laid eyes on Sherman his face was a scowl.

"Don't much sleep, I hear," added Lovie. "Deep in the night, up a-walkin' an' a-walkin'."

"Sound like he haunted," said Hagar.

"Ghost of his son." That was Hosea's guess. "Heard it only been about a year since the little fella died."

"Boy must be comin' to him in his sleep," insisted Hagar. "That's why he walk the night."

"Could be the son's death is what made Sherman crazy," offered Ben.

"Crazy or not," Mordecai weighed in, "if not for Sherman we wouldn't be on the freedom road right now. I say if crazy make a man bring wreck and ruin to secesh and freedom to us, we all need to pray every hour for a hundred more crazy General Shermans."

"And no more General Rebs!" declared Mariah. She knew that if some thought Sherman was crazy, they all saw Jefferson Davis in Union blue as a son of ole slewfoot, evil shot-through. "Put nothin' past that man," she said. "Not after what he did today."

"What happened?" asked Gus.

"Before we all could get across," explained Hagar, "soldiers pulled up that newfangled bridge they got."

"It's called a pontoon," said Mariah. "Pontoon bridge."

"Did it on General Reb's say is what we heard."

"And who is General Reb?" the newcomer asked.

"Evilest Yank in the world," replied Hosea. "Was him, they say, ordered the bridge pulled up. Left us to slosh our way across."

"If anybody deserve a hauntin', it's Ginral Reb," said Hagar. "And I don't mean no playful haints."

"They say five or six of our people drowned," added Mariah.

"Some turned back," said Hosea.

Hagar frowned. "Lord knows what they up against now."

Mariah could see that Mordecai didn't like things going gloomy again. "People, let us cease from talk of evil," he said. "I say it's time to speak of our dreams, our new tomorrows."

Mariah looked around. Everyone seemed adrift.

Caws of a nighthawk came and went.

Mariah wondered if anyone would dare speak of dreams, of a new tomorrow, what with nothing certain. After a few more nighthawks cawed away, to Mariah's surprise, the night became a wishing well.

Sleep in a proper bed . . . Sleep till noon for just one day . . . Find my sister . . . Find my daughters . . . Get my little ones some learnin' . . . Learn my letters . . . Weeklong barbecue! . . . Get my picture took . . . Shoes that fit my feet . . . Be lazy one whole day . . . Fair money for my labor . . . Go to a real church . . . Brick house . . . Become a soldier . . . Go to Europe . . .

"Have shops side by side," said Zoe. "Eating house. Healing house."

Mordecai squeezed Chloe's hand.

"What about you, Mariah?" asked Hagar.

Mariah looked up. "I hope to get my brother some help."

"But for you, what you want for you?" asked Ben.

Caleb. Mariah didn't dare say that out loud. But there was one thing she'd always wanted whenever she fixed her mind on freedom. She fingered the tiny sling sack she'd made for the gold coin from Jonah, a sack tacked in her apron pocket.

"My own ground," she said sheepishly. "Don't need to be a lot. I'd be content with one acre. One acre with good soil for growing our food. One acre near a fine fishing spot. One acre to call my own. My own ground."

RELISH IN DESTRUCTION

"Division moved at 7. Made 10 miles," began Caleb's entry for Saturday, December 3, 1864. "We passed through Millen."

The more Caleb thought about what he wanted to do after the war, the more he thought of his diary becoming a book. He doubted that many of his people on the march could write, and he was certain that a load of Yankees would write articles or books about the march. He'd bet money that most would give colored short shrift.

"Did Jack tell you about those monkey-like pickaninnies?" That's what he'd heard one private tell another when he returned from Social Circle.

It sickened Caleb the way some soldiers mocked his people, making them sound so ignorant. Like the lieutenant who told of happening upon a toothless old man, shouting, "I is off to Glory!"

Back when they marched through Milledgeville there was

the colonel who had several soldiers in stitches with his tale of encountering a group of "greasy black wenches" living in boxcars.

The darkies this. The darkies that. Caleb couldn't count the times when, while repairing a wheel, shoeing a horse, or packing a wagon he had to bite his tongue, keep his head down, pretend to be nothing but a simple darkie himself.

If Captain Galloway, Sergeant Hoffmann, or a few other Yankees who treated him like a man wrote about the march, Caleb knew his people wouldn't be presented as beasts and buffoons. But if they didn't, the world would never know how much the colored on the march endured, never know the brains and brawn they gave to the march—all their labors, all the intelligence on treasure hiding places, Rebel militiamen, geography. The more Caleb thought about it, the more he truly wanted to make his diary the basis of a book. For that, he'd need to write in more detail about everything.

On the night of December 3, he wrote about the shock the Yankees got when they reached Camp Lawton, right outside Millen. "Yankees hoped to liberate about 8,000 Union men from that prison camp. When they got there they found the place deserted. Sgt. H. said there were corpses strewn about aboveground and hundreds buried in a mass grave. The hovels prisoners were forced to live in weren't fit for a dog, he said. Gen. W.T.S. ordered Gen. F.B. to make Millen a wasteland. Sgt. H. said all that is left of Millen, from its depot to its hotel, are ashes. Yankees also burned Camp Lawton.

Capt. G. told me he fears that too many Union soldiers are taking too lusty a relish in destruction."

Caleb gave his pencil a shaving. Then he recorded what happened at Buckhead Creek.

He had crossed earlier in the day to be on hand for repairs as wagons reached the other side. When he heard about the bridge being pulled up before all the colored crossed, he hurried to their rescue. "About a dozen Yanks, Pvts. S. & D. among them, also helped. Miss C. lost some of her herbs. Z. his cap. Mord. his hat. After I helped at the crossing I kept clear of M. and the rest. Camped at Lumpkin Station."

TEXAS

Mariah awoke in a sweat, breathing hard. Scraps of a nightmare drifted around her mind. When she came clear—saw she wasn't back at the Chaney place but in the tent—she breathed a sigh of relief. A few seconds later—panic.

"What happened?" Chloe rubbed sleep from her eyes.

Mariah had a dress on, was reaching for her shoes. "Dulcina! She's gone!"

"Good Lord!" Chloe gasped.

When Mariah saw Chloe moving to get dressed, she said, "No, you stay here! Mind Zeke."

"Zoe can do that." Chloe stirred her sister. "You can't be going about on your own."

"I'll get Mordecai."

"Three heads are better than two."

* * *

If only she hadn't slept so hard, Mariah chided herself as they searched for five minutes, ten minutes, fifteen, around a host of other campsites, in the woods, near a stream.

In the predawn light they finally found her in the brambles, up on a knoll near a copse of loblolly trees.

Neck broken. Dress, torn in places, up about her waist. A Union blue cap stuffed in her mouth. Cold eyes stared into gone tomorrows. Before heading back with the grim news, Mariah pulled down Dulcina's dress. Chloe closed her eyes.

Mariah was hollowed out, couldn't cry.

Digging the shallow grave.

Caleb making a cross from a fence rail.

Mordecai saying a few words, then leading them in prayer.

Still Mariah didn't cry.

When she looked up from prayer, she saw Captain Galloway approaching.

"I will launch an investigation," he said, his face so solemn.

"Thank you, sir," said Mariah. Still she had not cried.

Back at their campsite, Mariah declined the bit of breakfast Hagar and Rachel had put together for them. No taste even for a cup of coffee.

What should she tell Zeke, who was sitting in Rachel's lap nibbling a biscuit.

If only Caleb didn't have to ride out. She didn't just want him. She needed him. But all that morning he hardly said a word to anybody, including her. And why did he look so . . . it was more than sorrow. It was the same look that came over him when he told her about his sister, Lily, being dead.

As Mariah watched Caleb head off with Captain Galloway, her mind wound back to that first big meet-up in the quarters when the war began. With Nero out cold from corn liquor, they had gathered in Aunt Minda's cabin. They whispered what they heard, thought, hoped.

Aunt Minda, blind and with her joints locked up from rheumatism, just listened, bundled up in her bed.

After Jack, Josie, Sadie, Esther, Maceo, Upson, Paul, Flora, Reuben, Nate, Mordecai, Jonah, and everybody else had their say, only then did Aunt Minda speak. Whatever she foresaw, they would believe.

A candle in the middle of the floor flickered.

"Git ready . . . ," Aunt Minda said, voice raspy, rattly. "Freedom dawnin'." She raised a gnarled finger. "Southland will reap a whirlwind."

The joy, the hope, people making plans for hiding places if trouble came—sheds, stable, barn—and how to pack up quick if Yankees came their way. Mariah couldn't remember why she settled on the root cellar, just her worry about Dulcina. *How will she know to hide?*

* * *

Mariah marched in silence, in a fog most of the day. None of the others had much to say. Only Zeke bore a smile.

Mariah envied him his cheerfulness. In a way he was blessed. Didn't know how ugly the world could be, how much evil worked its will even in the days of jubilee. And for him, freedom was a pouch of peppermint sticks.

No large gathering around a bonfire that night. But when night took over from day, Hosea brought out his banjo. "Swing Low, Sweet Chariot," down tempo, start to finish.

Mariah was glad that Caleb didn't make himself scarce that night, but it bothered her that he was so distant. He had pitched his tent close to the one she now shared with just Zeke and the Doubles, but he didn't sup with them. Said he wasn't hungry.

"May we all sleep like Zeke tonight," said Chloe, taking a whiff of what she called nerve tea.

Like always, Mariah had tucked Zeke in early.

"Cups up." Chloe raised the dented coffee pot from the fire, began to pour into Mordecai's cup, her sister's, Mariah's.

Mariah tasted lemon balm and lavender.

Chloe handed her another cup. "Caleb could use some, I'm sure."

The tea was a brace against a howling wind. But Caleb was so silent, time so still.

Mariah tried to come up with light talk. "Is a brigade in a

regiment or is it the other way around?" she was about to ask but didn't. She knew the answer, and Caleb knew she knew.

Why is he taking Dulcina's death so hard?

When Mariah saw his fire getting low, she rose. "I'll get you some pine knots."

"Never mind," he said. "Turning in soon."

She so badly wanted to be with him, to hug him, for him to hold her. And how badly she wanted to soon be someplace safe. Safe from Rebels, Yankees, safe from another wound.

"How much longer, you reckon?" she asked.

"The march?"

"Uh-huh."

"A matter of days."

"The somewhere place still a secret?"

For the first time Caleb looked up. He shook his head. "No longer a secret."

Mariah waited, worried about Caleb getting back inside himself, shutting her out.

"Caleb?" She rubbed his arm. "What's wrong?"

"Nothing."

When eyes met eyes, Mariah held on for dear life. She saw a change come over him. She continued to stare into his eyes, continued to rub his arm. "So tell me, Caleb, where is the somewhere place?"

Caleb almost smiled. "Savannah."

"Savannah?" All Mariah knew was that Savannah was a city by the sea. "Do you know what Savannah's like?"

"Fine city, I hear," said Caleb. "Palm trees and parks, fountains, statues. Laid out orderly, in twenty-four squares. Mansions in peach and other soft colors, with porticoes, balconies. The ironwork—fences, gates, stairways, railings—some of the most magnificent in the world, they say."

Mariah knew that Caleb was coming into a better mood. He was talking whole cloth. She was overjoyed as Caleb talked on about having people there. "Well, before the war they were still there. A cousin named Isaac is a carpenter. His wife, Jane, has been running a secret school for our people for years."

"They free?"

Caleb nodded. "Quite a few in Savannah. Some you might even call prosperous."

Mariah couldn't wait! And she was so glad for some good news.

Savannah.

Sounded restful, easy, brought to mind a sweet breeze.

Mariah smiled at the sound of Savannah.

No Longer with Us

Caleb was hard pressed to take up his diary after Mariah left his tent. He lingered on the long look into her eyes. Her hand on his arm. The joy that came over her as he talked about Savannah. But as the minutes passed he could feel himself growing grim again.

The more I write now, the less I'll have to write later, he told himself. He reached for his diary, his pencil, and wrote, "Sun., Dec. 4th, 1864" at the upper right-hand corner of the page. He started with terrain.

"Sandier by the day. More clogged roads, burned bridges, thick woods. We are deep into the river-road region, mad tangle of swamps and creeks, large and small. Not many shallow. Pontoons laid down all hours. If we are not trudging through a swamp, we are up to our ankles in sand. Foraging thin. Fewer farms. We return with very little. A few sacks of sweet potatoes, a pig or 2, some chickens. Rice the only thing in abundance."

Rice and more danger.

"Reports of more than 50 deaths in Gen. Kil's cavalry in the Waynesboro battle. Rebels lost about 5 times more."

Caleb thought about the danger Mariah and other colored women on the march faced—from the men who were obliged to protect their freedom. Even though her tent was not that far away from his, Caleb had insisted on walking her to it when she decided to turn in.

Now, about an hour later, he stared at his lantern candle. For more than a minute. More than five. It was going on fifteen when Caleb felt ready to record the incident that had him all torn up.

"Dulcina is no longer with us. Same as happened to Lily. When M. came to my tent tonight I started to tell her about Lily, tell her everything, but stayed clamped up. Talked about Savannah instead. Camped near a bend in the Ogeechee River."

Dear Lord!

"Miss Chloe! Need your services!"

Mariah was sitting on a weather-beaten green cartridge crate patching a pair of Zeke's britches when Caleb called out.

Wagon load on the light side. Only a few sacks. Rice, she guessed.

And a body under a blanket.

What now?

Mariah saw Chloe roll her eyes, take a deep breath. So worn out. Mariah had spotted her trying to rub away a hitch in her hip now and then as they tended to Rachel's awful cough, prepared a compress for Hosea's back, set a soldier's broken arm. She knew Chloe had been in quite a bit of pain all day. That's why, though she herself had been feeling feverish since midday, Mariah had insisted on gathering the birch bark and leaves for a brew to treat two other soldiers suffering from the flux.

Chloe rose from the white pine crate across from Mariah. "Where's the saddlebag?" She patted her right hip.

"I'll get it," said Mariah.

She hoped it wasn't another man with a shotgun wound to the head or some part of him cut off. They had found more than a few like that. Left for dead, and Chloe unable to save them. Mariah could only speculate that the men, in one case a boy with an iron collar around his neck, had been chased down by their owners or random Rebels bound and determined to keep them from freedom.

"Found him a mile or so back," Mariah heard Caleb say as she emerged from the tent and Chloe reached the wagon. "Seems the worst of it is his—"

"Dear Lord!" Chloe gasped, stepped back.

"What's wrong?" asked Mariah. She picked up her pace, saddlebag slung over her shoulder.

Zeke scrambled up. "Mariah! Mariah!"

Mariah shooed him back. "Miss Zoe, take hold of him, please."

When Mariah reached the wagon, like Chloe, she gasped, and like Chloe, she stepped back.

CRY MERCY?

"What is it?" asked Caleb.

By then Mordecai was beside the wagon. Hagar too.

"What is it?" Caleb asked again. Mariah looked like she'd seen a ghost.

"Nero," Mordecai spat. "Mariah's no doubt told you about Nero."

"But who is he, this Nero?" asked Hagar.

"Was our driver." Mariah was trembling.

Caleb moved to her side and put an arm around her, then watched Hagar broadcast the news.

A crowd formed soon. The stamp of feet began.

"Driver! Driver! Driver!"

"String him up!" somebody shouted.

"You ain't gon' see to him, are you?" Hagar asked Chloe.

Caleb could see Chloe was in a dilemma, knew she was the

type who couldn't turn her back on a dog. "Zoe," she yelled, "boil water!"

Caleb lifted the saddlebag from Mariah's shoulder, handed it to Chloe, watched her with a rag, clearing blood from around the side of Nero's face, taking stock of the wound. He had a shoulder out of joint. A busted-up ankle too.

Mariah, arms at her sides, fists clenched, was frozen.

"How bad was he?" Hosea asked Mordecai.

Mordecai rubbed his chin, shook his head.

"The way Mariah look," said Hagar, "seems he done her a heap of harm." Hagar reached down, picked up a rock, held it out to Mariah. "Only right for you to cast the first stone."

Others reached for stones.

"Now, people!" Caleb cried out. "Let's all just calm down!" He scanned the crowd. Most in it hadn't been able to look him in the eye since they almost lynched him. Especially Hagar. "The other day," Caleb continued, "y'all came close to—"

"But we know for a fact this here man really *was* a driver!" someone shouted.

And none of them knew the half of it. Caleb imagined what was going through Mariah's mind. Reliving her father's last words—*Love you, daughter*—with the water at his chin. Remembering her mother's bloody back. Part of Caleb wished to God that he'd never come across the fiend in a ravine, never got him to come around, never practically carried him to the wagon. Part of Caleb wanted to beat the man's brains out.

"Help me!" mumbled Nero.

Mariah still hadn't moved a muscle. She only stared at Nero. Her sharp, dark eyes like knives.

Tears ran down Nero's face. "Mercy," he pleaded. "Mercy."

Mariah snapped out of her trance. "Mercy?" she shouted. "*Mercy?* You got the *nerve* to cry mercy?"

Snot dripped onto Nero's lips. "Don't let 'em do me in," he wept. "Please, Mariah. 'Member all them times I coulda, coulda had you . . . lashed?"

"I remember, Nero. I remember everything you did." Mariah pulled out her jackknife, lunged forward.

"No!" Caleb grabbed her, took the knife from her hand.

The crowd pressed closer in.

"You can't hold us all back, Caleb!" Hagar called out. "We act on Mariah's say."

"What all did he do?" needled Hagar. "Fifty stripes for every wrong!"

"You'd be whippin' till kingdom come," said Mariah.

"Jus' say the word, Mariah," Hagar intoned. "Jus' say the word!"

Caleb couldn't bear the sight of Mariah. What he saw on her face was beyond agony and rage.

She was hosting evil.

POWER

Days, weeks, months, years of misery, of terror. Days, weeks, months, years of doing other people's bidding. Days, weeks, months, years of being bypassed by mercy.

All those tears and lamentations.

For the first time in her life Mariah had power. She didn't have to contain her rage, stifle her will. For once in her life, she could do more than weep and pray.

"Look at me!" she yelled at Nero.

Nero obeyed.

Mariah relished the sight of his tear- and slobber-stained face, of his battered body. She could smell his fear and savored that.

Nero lifted a hand. It shook like he had the palsy. He raised an index finger, seeking permission to speak.

Mariah nodded.

"I done you some good turns." He swallowed. "That

night—the dungeon. Drug you away when I seen he already . . . spare you the sight of that."

"Spare me? You wretched, filthy—"

Two questions asked but never answered. Everyone on the Chaney place, the Doubles—all had pleaded ignorance, turned her mind to something else when she raised her suspicion that Nero was at the root of it all.

"Nero," Mariah said slowly. "Gonna ask you some things. You tell me the truth or I'll loose these people on you."

Nero nodded.

"What did my pa do to get the dungeon? And was it you who told Callie Chaney my ma was a conjure woman?"

Nero swallowed.

"The truth, Nero. The God's honest truth."

"I loved your mama, Mariah." Nero sighed. "After Joe pass and Judge Chaney made me head man, I thought fo' sure yo' mama be mine. Tole her as wife of a driver she get *three* dresses a year and eat mo' better."

"None of this answers my questions, Nero." The idea of her mother and Nero made Mariah sick to her stomach.

"Then yo' pa was brought to the Chaney place . . ."

"The dungeon, Nero?"

Tears streamed down his face. "I, I tole Judge Chaney he broke tools on purpose an' disrespec' me."

Mariah's hate grew hungrier by the second.

"Jus' to punish him some fo' my pain . . . Didn't know a storm was comin'."

All over again, Mariah saw herself bailing water as fast as she could.

"And did you tell Miss Callie my ma put a hex on Judge Chaney?"

"Wasn't me, I swear."

"But you're a liar, Nero. Everybody knows that." Mariah thought she now knew what it felt like to be a general. She was in charge, in command. Hagar and the others were her troops.

"I swear, Mariah, it warn't me," Nero blubbered. "Back then Miss Callie was makin' visits to that sayons woman, tryna talk wid Judge Chaney's spirit. Was sayons woman who tell Miss Callie there be evil in her house." Nero paused, took a deep breath. "I never say yo' ma did conjure. I swear to God, Mariah. I swear to God."

"What do you know of God?" Mariah yelled. She saw her young self at Miss Callie's feet, begging for mercy.

"It warn't fity," said Nero. "Times when Miss Callie had eyes on you, tree was all I whip. Didn't lay on the full fity."

The wind, whispers from the crowd, trills of birds, the crackle of campfire—all of it ceased. There was only her and Nero. And her power.

"But she died, Nero, my mama died!" Each word a gouge, a chisel. "And my—" Mariah struggled not to cry. "My brother was marked for life!"

"Miss Callie fault!" Nero whimpered. "I only done as tole!"

Mariah could no longer contain her tears. "But *you*, Nero, *you*, you set it all in motion!"

When Caleb took Mariah in his arms the tears didn't cease. When he whispered, "Don't do this—you can't do this," she sobbed harder. When Caleb tried to walk her away from the wagon, Mariah stood her ground, jerked free.

"I can do whatever I want!"

"Jus' say the word!" goaded Hagar.

Savoring her power, Mariah leaned over the wagon, got within inches of Nero's face. "You hear that, Nero? 'Jus' say the word.' All I need do is say the word, and these folks will do as told. Tear you apart."

"Tomorrow." She faced the crowd. "You'll have my decision tomorrow." Mariah wanted Nero to twist in the wind, spend the night in terror.

Monsters

Caleb followed her. Past her campsite, up an embankment.

"Mariah!"

He broke into a run. When he finally reached her, he took her in his arms, stroked her neck, and rubbed her back.

The more she cried, the tighter he held her.

"He don't deserve to live!"

Caleb held her still tighter, pulled out a handkerchief, wiped tears from her face. "Awful man, it's true."

"Awful man. That all you can say? I never told you all, Caleb. How I lived in fear of him, all the times he tried to— Caleb, he tried to take me, have his way with me! He's a monster!"

Caleb rubbed her neck, her back. "Believe me, I know what you feeling, know how much you—"

He was stunned, hurt, frightened when she pulled away. "You don't know, Caleb! Can't know! Jonah was right. You

not like us. Every *second* of my life been a tightrope! A mountain of misery was Nero's doing. He don't deserve to live! No
justice in that!"

"No, it ain't justice, not as humans see it." Caleb reached
out to her. "But you're wrong about Nero, he—"

Mariah gave him a look that cut him to the quick.

"What?" Mariah shouted, taking a giant stride away from
Caleb. "I'm wrong about Nero? Have you lost your mind?"

"What I mean is, Nero ain't the *root*. He's a branch. Say
he's killed. Then what? Go back to Callie Chaney? Kill her
too? Then travel back in time? How many people would need
to be killed to reach the root?"

"You sayin' it ain't Nero's fault?"

"I'm—"

"He had a choice! Didn't have to—didn't have to do what
he did. Because of him I lost my pa, my ma. And Zeke—if it
wasn't for the bullwhip he woulda . . . been born normal. I
just know it."

"What I'm saying is for your own sake, Mariah. You need
to tell those people to just go about their business. Or if you
want, I can tell them you said—"

The sight of her stopped him again. It was as if she wanted
to scratch his eyes out. But he couldn't give up on her. Caleb
walked over to Mariah, grabbed her firmly by the shoulders.
"Mariah, please listen to me. For your own soul's sake, you
need to tell those people to—"

It looked like her mind was going loose.

Caleb stepped back. "Do what's right—otherwise you'll never know peace of mind, of spirit."

"Peace? We in the mouth of war! Peace? Beginnin' to think it ain't possible in this world. And don't try to tell me that demon Nero don't deserve to die! It ain't right for him to go unwhipped of justice."

Caleb had an urge to tell Mariah that he knew about monsters. Monsters in others. The monster in him. He wanted to tell her about Lily, the family joy.

Tell her about seeing his sister busted up. How a simple errand in town took her across the path of a monster. Wanted to tell of the knock on the door, of Lily found in an alley, left for dead, not living long, but long enough to say who did it. A local white man Caleb knew by sight.

Yes, Caleb thought, as he watched Mariah pace and rage, he knew what it was like to burn to be the justice. He remembered that queer taste in his mouth, the fire in his belly as he bided his time, learned the man's patterns. Where he worked. Where he gambled, drank. Remembered the searing pain when his mother passed from grief. Rage became Caleb's daily bread all the more. And then came his chance for revenge.

The culprit stumbled from a tavern.

Caleb ran over, played the darkie, told him he knew where he could have a good time if he had a taste for colored girls. "Young ones," he said.

The man took the bait, followed Caleb to a bawdy street, where noise, day and night, didn't cease. Steered him to an alley, rained down blow after blow—for his sister, for his mother, for all the wrongs done to his people. Then he grabbed a brick.

Caleb wanted to tell Mariah how much he understood, then thought maybe his story wouldn't help.

Would fear?

"Mariah, Yankees won't tolerate a lynching. If you head it up, there'll be a price to pay."

"Look what happened to Dulcina. Nobody paid. Can't see Yankees bothered over a slave driver. Colored lives don't matter. And so what if I pay a price? So what?"

Caleb had one last hope. "If you loose people on Nero, and if the Yankees show them no mercy, show you no mercy . . ." Caleb stepped closer, put a hand on Mariah's shoulder.

Mariah shrugged it off. "Then what?"

"Where will that leave Zeke?"

No More!

She took off for the woods, ran blind, shattered in mind. Ran until she all but collapsed beneath a giant live oak dripping thick with Spanish moss.

Mariah sat there, behind a veil of Spanish moss, soul in civil war, fighting for some purchase on peace, but unable to cool the burning to see Nero dead.

Dusk descended.

Daylight faded.

The cloak of darkness came.

Still, Mariah sat listless, drained of tears.

On the outskirts of her mind, she heard footsteps, rustling. Soon, a crackling. Before long, warmth wafted her way.

She heard voices.

We call it the killin' stone . . . I only done as tole! . . . Jus' say the word! . . . And behold a pale horse! . . . My whitefolks was both devils . . . For your own soul's sake . . . You mine . . . Nero

ain't the root . . . *What you lookin' at, you filthy nigra? . . . Jus'*
say the word! . . . Peace of mind, of spirit . . . Where will that
leave Zeke?

Then she heard herself—*What do you know of God?*

She battled to believe.

"By and by all will be put right. God's watchin'." That's
what her ma had murmured the day after the dungeon.

But by and by her ma was dead too. Nothing had been put
right.

There was cannon boom, rifle fire, yet Mariah didn't flinch.
Muffled and muted too was the crackle of the fire, the squeak
of bats clustered above her head.

"Watch," Mariah muttered, coming to a cruel conclusion.
"That's all God does," she whispered. "Watch."

No more! She shook her head. *No more! No more! No more!*
Done with praying, done with hoping, with believing. Done
with God.

"Useless," she mumbled. "Nothing but useless."

But then she heard another voice.

Mariah! Mariah!

WELL?

Caleb awoke to drifting mist. In the hollow of a giant tupelo. Mariah in his arms.

He pulled his overcoat tighter around her.

She stirred.

He kissed her forehead, pressed her against his chest.

When Mariah woke up a few minutes later, Caleb saw the startle in her eyes, saw her do a double-take when she realized she was in his arms.

Caleb said nothing. Just loosed his arms. Watched her sit up, wipe away leaves, dirt, rise on wobbly legs, get her bearings, then make for camp.

Caleb followed a few feet behind.

He hung back when he saw Chloe meet Mariah halfway, hug her, and lead her over to a campfire, where Mordecai and Zoe sipped coffee and chewed on hardtack.

"Where Zeke?" asked Mariah.

"Still asleep," said Mordecai as Zoe handed Mariah a cup of coffee.

When Mariah waved it off Caleb saw her eyes were fixed on the wagon bearing Nero. Still in the same spot.

Caleb could see Nero's head bandaged. Figured Chloe had his shoulder in a sling, a splint on the bad ankle.

"Can you take me to Captain Galloway?" Mariah asked Caleb.

"What for?"

"You'll see."

As they made tracks for Captain Galloway, Caleb spotted others rising, stretching, getting their bearings, starting fires. Some eating breakfast, others staring at the dawn.

He heard scraps of conversation. About a nightmare. About the witch riding all night long. About cold in the bones.

When they reached Captain Galloway's tent, Caleb called out for him. "Captain, sir, a moment."

Captain Galloway emerged from his tent wearing his dark-blue trousers but up top only his long johns and suspenders. He had a razor in one hand and shaving cream on one side of his face. "What is it?" he asked.

Caleb looked at Mariah. She seemed tongue-tied.

"Well?" asked Captain Galloway, looking at Caleb for a clue.

Again Caleb looked at Mariah. Now he saw her strength.

Looking the captain in the eye, she asked, "Favor, sir?"

Blue Glass Beads

Mariah told Captain Galloway about the bad blood between the man ailing in the wagon and her and some others. She asked if he could get the man removed for the sake of peace.

"Not callin' for him to be cast out," she said, "but sent to colored in another part of the march."

Inside of an hour, Mariah watched Caleb driving the wagon away, with Privates Sykes and Dolan on either side, riding chestnut bays.

When the wagon was out of sight, Mariah readied herself and Zeke for the march. When they camped that evening, she was prepared to face Caleb.

"Awfully sorry for the way I acted yesterday. Sorry for yellin' at you, bein' so ugly." Instead of waiting for him to come sup with them, Mariah had brought two helpings of rice and gravy to his tent.

"No need for sorry, Mariah. Just wasn't yourself."

"But now you must think me—" She lowered her head.

"I don't think any worse of you."

Mariah looked up. "Truly?" Mariah prayed to God that Caleb was like his father. Not the changeable type.

Caleb stroked her cheek. "Really. I'm in no position to judge. Remember I told you I understood? This is why. You see . . ."

For the longest while, Mariah asked no questions, made not a sound. She just listened as Caleb told her about Lily.

"You killed that man?" Mariah interrupted when Caleb told of picking up a brick.

"Was about to when something came over me. It wasn't like I heard some still, small voice. More like I saw myself becoming a worse evil, knew if I murdered the man, his blood . . . never enough. Me, I'd never be right. I'd only soil my soul."

Mariah couldn't imagine Caleb killing a fly, let alone coming close to murder.

"Before that I used to frequent saloons, gamble, do a host of things that woulda broke my ma's heart had she known. Bad enough she couldn't get me inside a church. But after I was kept from killing that man, I put all that foolishness behind me. Set my sights on becoming a better man."

"What happened to that white man?"

"Cleaned him up. Got him into a hack. Never saw him again."

They finished their rice and gravy in silence.

Caleb was dipping their tin cups in a bucket of water when he asked, "What turned you around?"

Mariah bit her bottom lip. "I guess you could say it *was* a still, small voice."

She could see Caleb couldn't tell if she was joking or not. "Still, small voice of Zeke."

"Zeke?"

Mariah bobbed her head. "Yesterday when I went to take Miss Chloe the saddlebag, Zeke jumped up, called out to me." Tears on the rise, Mariah paused, swallowed. "He didn't call out 'Ma.' He called out 'Mariah! Mariah!'"

And the tears flowed. "Caleb, he's mastered my name." Mariah paused again to collect herself. "With all the commotion I didn't take it in. Not till later. Last night when I was drifting off." She sniffled, wiped her eyes. "Made me think maybe peace and resting easy are possible after all. Made me believe again in new tomorrows. Couldn't begin my new life with blood on my hands."

Mariah stretched her back. She wanted no more talk about the past, about pain. She wanted to talk about Savannah. "Caleb?"

"Yes?"

"What you told me the other day about your kinfolk and others in Savannah, how you know all that? How you keep in touch?"

They were still outside Caleb's tent. He'd just put more pine knots on the fire.

"By post, mostly."

"Wasn't afraid whitefolks would open your letters?"

"If they did, they wouldn't have found anything alarming. Say my cousin wrote that his wife had four new chicks, we knew Jane had four new pupils. Nothing too weighty ever went into a letter though. For that we used—mind if we continue inside?"

Mariah hesitated, then said, "Fine."

Once inside the tent, Mariah waited for Caleb to get back to the conversation. Waited while he reached for a fold-up candle lantern, a match safe, got the candle lit. Waited for him to close the tent flap. Waited for him to brush debris off his pallet. Waited for him to bid her sit down.

"For deep things we used the Kobe."

Mariah sat cross-legged on his pallet, he on the ground.

"The Kobe?" she asked. Mariah felt a tug at a memory, dismissed it.

"The Kobe is a group, but not like one with bylaws and a meeting place. Nothing like that. A secret society. Get up funds for buying folks out of slavery. Hide people who stole off. Keep our ears to the ground."

"Those in this society, they all over Georgia?"

"All over the Southland," Caleb replied. "Some free, some in slavery. Blacksmiths, carpenters, tanners, and like that." Caleb paused, then recounted his fourteenth birthday when his father told him about the Kobe. "I asked him what kind of word is that, what it meant. He said it meant to be on duty for our people."

Mariah was confused. "How did you find each other? How would you know who was a member?"

"All members have somewhere outside their house, inside their house, on their clothing, gear, or tools, a mark." He reached for his toolbox, pointed to what had always looked to Mariah like a stack of spinning whorls with a ram's horn on top.

Mariah fingered the mark. "The Kobe." She sighed, then her face lit up. "Caleb?"

"What is it?"

Mariah told him about Aunt Minda's tales and lessons. "She taught us *aban* meant strength. Her people's word for devotion was *akoben*."

"Did she now? How interesting." After a pause Caleb asked, "Did this Aunt Minda ever tell you her people's word for love?"

Mariah paused, but not because she didn't know or had forgotten. The question had her flustered. "*Eban*," she said, avoiding Caleb's gaze. Aunt Minda said it also meant safety, protection.

The candle flickered. Mariah sat silently, wondering what Caleb would ask next.

"Speaking of devotion," he finally said, "my cousin belongs to First African Baptist—can't wait to see that church."

Mariah knew Caleb was moving into whole cloth knowledge. "Say on?" she teased. "So I can think and learn, learn and think."

Caleb smiled. "Used to be a white church and a wooden

structure. Colored bought it for fifteen hundred dollars. After a while, with the building falling apart and the congregation growing, they made up their minds to tear down the old, build anew, something to last for ages. Took four years, finally finished in '59."

"Four years to build it?"

Caleb nodded.

"Why so long?"

"Most of the work was done by bonfire and moonlight, from the bricks made down by the river to the walls made four bricks deep. Most all the ironwork, carpentry too."

"Why was so much work done at night?"

"Most of the congregation in slavery. Only allowed to work on their church in their spare time."

"Where'd the money come from in the first place?"

"Many had been saving to buy freedom. That's where the first thousand came from. The rest from a new surge of scrimping and side work."

A matter of days. That's what Caleb had said. Soon the march would be over. Even still, Mariah wished again that freedom came with wings.

"It's the church floor I can't wait to see," said Caleb.

"Fancy like marble?"

Caleb shook his head. "Wood. Here and there holes in it. In a pattern. Diamond with a cross in the center." Caleb moved the candle lantern to the side. "Never learned the meaning of the pattern, but I know the purpose of the holes."

Mariah leaned in.

"Crawlspace beneath the floor. Holes so that folks down below could breathe."

Mariah felt a shiver down her spine. "Folks who slipped off?"

Caleb nodded.

Savannah was a miracle place! Churches of their own out in the open! When he first told her about prosperous colored folks she could hardly believe it. Now she wanted to know more.

"The Pettigrews have a big brick and brownstone house. He keeps an oyster house. His wife is a top seamstress."

And there was Georgiana Kelly. "Miss Chloe will enjoy meeting her. She's a nurse."

William Cleghorn, he explained, owned a bakery on Liberty and Habersham.

"And there's Garrison Frazier. Story is he got up a thousand dollars in gold and silver to buy himself and his wife. Another minister."

"How many colored churches are there?"

"Last I knew, three, four," Caleb replied.

"I do hope your people are still there." Mariah daydreamed about stepping foot in the city by the sea.

She noticed Caleb lower his eyes. "Me too. If they are—or any of their friends—they will surely help us get our bearings, do all they can for us."

The way Caleb said "us"—Mariah wanted to hear it again. And again. "You planning to stay South?" she asked sheepishly.

"Think so."

"Wouldn't you rather head up North when the war is done?"

Caleb shook his head. "Most of our people are in the South. When the war's over and this slavery business is crushed, multitudes will need help. I want to stay and do my part."

"Let me guess." Mariah smiled. "With all that thinkin' and learnin' I bet you aim to be a teacher."

"Indirectly, you might say. Newspaper. Want to start a newspaper." After a pause, he asked, "What do you want?"

Mariah hung her head. "Nothing so grand as having a newspaper."

"A thing don't have to be grand to be good."

"There was a time I daydreamed of New York," Mariah said. She told him about her print of the African Free-School. "Had no idea how far New York was, or what I'd do once I got there." She laughed. "Now I got a hope I think I can make happen. Like I said, it's not grand." Mariah looked him in the eye. "Promise you won't laugh?"

"Promise."

"One acre. I want one acre of land somewhere safe. I want me and Zeke to be able to live off my one acre."

Mariah told Caleb about Jonah's twenty-dollar gold pieces.

"I can imagine how much you must miss him," said Caleb.

"I do, but it's all for the better. Besides, you said it's only a matter of days. How far are we from Savannah?"

"As the crow flies, twenty, twenty-five miles. Surely this terrain and Rebel devilment will slow us down some. Likely to be some Rebel resistance once we get there."

"Strong forces?"

"Captain Galloway says no."

"Any colored doctors in Savannah?"

"Don't know, but—"

"Not for me," Mariah said, seeing the alarm on his face. "I wonder if there's some special kind of doctor who might be able to make Zeke better, even if only a little."

"Well, if there's no special doctor," Caleb replied, "I promise you this. I will help you take care of Zeke." When Caleb reached for her hand, Mariah didn't flinch. "Be whatever you want me to be to him." Caleb brought her hand to his lips. "Friend." He kissed her hand. "Father. Whatever you want."

Mariah's heart raced when Caleb joined her on the pallet. She felt a quivering, a quickening, became aware of breathing heavier, of how warm his lips felt, of how good his hands felt on her face, her neck, her—

Mariah pulled away. "I should leave."

"No, you shouldn't."

"But I, I—"

"Stay."

She couldn't tear her eyes away from his. He was magnificent. "I, I, Zeke'll be—"

"The Doubles will see to him." Caleb began stroking her face again.

"I, uh—"

"Stay."

Oh God did she want to stay, but—

"All I'm asking you to do, Mariah, is stay. Nothing more." Caleb removed his hand from her face, leaned back. "This march has done wonders for my self-discipline." He laughed. Mariah burst out laughing. Both were soon laughing so hard their eyes were gleaming with tears—happy tears, love-of-life tears, love-for-the-ages tears.

When their laughter died down, Caleb took Mariah's hand. "Girl, we ain't wild dogs. You merit better than a tent on the edge of swampland. You merit a warm room, fireplace, fine clean sheets on a proper bed. And blue glass beads in your hair."

STONE OF HELP

For Wednesday, December 7, 1864, Caleb didn't start off writing about the march.

"Hardly saw M. at all today. Spent a little time with them for breakfast. In the evening I brought her a dress, a shawl, and a few other things. Also brought a high-crowned black hat to replace the one Mord. lost in crossing Buckhead Creek. Spent most of the evening at the forge."

Caleb looked at his nub of a pencil. No shaving left to do. He reached into his toolbox for a new pencil. But he didn't return to his diary. His thoughts rested on Mariah.

He dreamed of making her happy, doing all in his power to see that she never knew another hurt, another pain. He was sure she'd like Savannah. And if she didn't, they'd move to wherever suited her. If she wanted to live in New York, he'd make that happen. That's right—that's where Captain

Galloway was from. Surely he'd help them make their way in New York. And Zeke, Caleb thought. Most likely there were better doctors up North anyway.

Beside himself with anticipation, Caleb felt like the happiest man on earth!

Calm down, he told himself. *Let's first get to Savannah and see what's what.* He then returned to his diary to stabilize his mind. By writing about the march.

"Division moved at 6½. Made 7 miles. At our rear 3 skirmishes today with Rebel horsemen. 13 Yankees lost. They say Rebel soldiers have been dispatched from Augusta. All is getting worse. More fallen trees. More swamps. Sometimes 2 or 3 men needed to push wagons along. Rain this morning did not help. Nerves fraying with every mile."

And the glum and gloomy surroundings. This was an uneasy place to be.

"We have been marching among giants these days. Giant bald cypresses. Some wade in the waters, some stand on dry land, all with some of their roots jutting up. Otherwordly. Same with the giant tupelos. You could sleep three in the hollows of some trunks. And so much sound. Flying squirrels. Tree frogs. Owls. Nighthawks. Right now the wind is wailing, and this night feels too alive. Cannons in the distance."

It was past midnight, and Caleb knew he was hardly the only one still awake. He knew the pioneers were hard at work. A couple hours after they camped, a scout reported that a few miles ahead the bridge across Ebenezer Creek had been destroyed, so yet another pontoon had to be laid down. "Capt. G. has ordered me to cross with the first group in the morning to be on hand for repairs to the wagons when they reach the south bank."

Tree frogs and other creatures were getting louder. The night became a scream.

Earlier in the day, when out foraging, Sergeant Hoffmann told Caleb about the history of this desolate place. Of a town started long ago by folks from Germany fleeing some kind of hell. They named the settlement Ebenezer.

"Stone of help," Caleb wrote. "That's what Sgt. H. said Ebenezer means. The town did not prosper & folks moved to higher ground. All that's left of their first try are ruins of a redbrick church. It's across Ebenezer Creek."

Ever since the sergeant's history lesson, Caleb hadn't been able to get the hymn "Come Thou Fount of Every Blessing" out of his head.

Come, Thou fount of every blessing,
Tune my heart to sing Thy grace;
Streams of mercy, never ceasing . . .

Here I raise my Ebenezer;
Here by Thy great help I've come;
And I hope, by Thy good pleasure,
Safely to arrive at home . . .

With the night so alive Caleb figured he might not get much sleep, but given his early rise, he thought the least he could do was rest his eyes. He scribbled one last thing.

"Camped at Old Ebenezer."

FREEDOMS

Mud.

Swamp.

Tripping over tree roots.

Sloshing through streams.

Roads so snaky, narrow.

Mariah had never experienced so much stop and start on the march as she had the last two days. Stopping while wagons got righted. Stopping because of roads cluttered with slashed-down cypress trees.

And now Mariah, Zeke, and the rest, they all would have to walk today. Just as they made it to the campground last night, their wagon's front axle snapped and the front wheels fell off. Mariah knew Caleb couldn't come to the rescue. He had sent word that he needed to be at the head of the column the next morning and had camped up there overnight.

Mariah was grateful that at least her shoes were holding

up. Could be worse. So many others trudged on bare feet. She couldn't count the times she'd seen blistered feet, swollen feet, and toenails torn off. Shoes. They were the one thing Caleb always tried to rustle up. The pairs he parceled out didn't make a dent in the need.

Mariah reckoned it high noon when word spread that the work on a pontoon bridge started in the middle of the night was finally done. There was chatter, too, of skirmishes with Rebels in the rear.

"Thank God we'll be crossing soon." Mariah sighed as she summoned up the strength for another day on the march, got her sling sacks on her shoulders, her calabash canteen around her neck, then Zeke on his feet, cap tight on his head. She figured with Rebel horsemen in the rear, everybody— colored and Yankee—would move double-time as best they could. She took comfort in knowing that once they got across the creek, there'd be less to fear from the Rebels because Yankees would pull up the pontoon.

But Mariah and the others had only gotten themselves ready for another wait.

"Step aside! Step aside!" a soldier commanded.

Row after row of bluecoats marched by.

"Step aside! Step aside!"

Row after row, wagon after wagon, cattle, more bluecoats, row after row.

Cannon boom from somewhere left made everybody more anxious. Mariah guessed it was coming from the Savannah River. Gunboats.

Bluecoats. Wagons. Cattle. More cannon boom.

As Yankees passed by, the only colored marching with them were strapping-strong young men. Pioneers.

"Step aside! Step aside!"

Mariah began to panic. Never before had all the other colored been made to wait until this many Yankees marched by. Never before had they been stopped from marching behind the Yankees who had found them useful.

In vain Mariah had searched for Jonah. She had even searched for Captain Galloway, Private Sykes, Private Dolan, and Sergeant Hoffmann—any kind face.

An hour passed, another. Still waiting.

"What in creation is going on?" asked Mordecai.

"Maybe part of the bridge broke?" Chloe wondered.

"Could be Rebels ambushin' on the other side of the creek," suggested Ben.

"But then we'd hear gunfire," Mordecai pointed out.

"Maybe they makin' sneak attacks with sabers." That was Ben again.

"No," said Mariah, trying to clear the panic from her voice. "I think they makin' us wait for the whole Fourteenth Corps to cross." She racked her brains. How many soldiers did Caleb tell her were in the Fourteenth? "If I remember correctly, that's about fourteen thousand men." Now that number sounded like a world.

"I reckon we'll be here awhile." Mordecai took a deep breath and let out a loud sigh.

Dusk. Still waiting.

Just hardtack for supper in case the wait would soon be over.

It was a dry supper too. With no fresh water nearby, they only put their canteens to their lips for small sips. Mariah barely drank any water at all because Zeke was strangely thirsty, along with being fidgety, whiny. He was also spinning a lot. Mariah prayed that he wasn't coming down with whatever had Rachel's little girl in fever on and off the last two days, whatever had Miss Zoe coughing and sneezing. And Miss Chloe out of pennyroyal.

Mariah also hoped that Rachel didn't come due before they crossed. The night before Miss Chloe had said it was a matter of days, maybe hours. Rachel could barely walk, and her back was killing her.

And chilling Mariah was the sight of an old woman about to camp by herself, someone Mariah had never seen before.

Stooped but strong and the color of sweet corn, the old woman had a snakeskin around her neck. Cracked and creased leather pouches dangled from a rope around her waist. One gnarled hand gripped a walking stick fashioned from a long bone. Dimes with a hole bored through were tied around her ankles.

The woman was staring at Mariah, just like that silver-gray crane the other day. The bird looking like it was privy to a mystery.

Mariah had a bad feeling that something was wrong, or something was about to go wrong.

Under moonshine and stars. Still waiting. They took catnaps, two or three at a time.

Then came the break of dawn.

Mariah peered ahead, saw the last of the soldiers about to cross. "Get ready to move out, everybody," she said.

Gathering her things, she looked behind. For as far as she could see, hundreds, maybe thousands, of colored people, most asleep on the ground or up against a cypress or tupelo tree. Cannon boom startled them awake.

This ragtag colored regiment was soon on its feet with sacks over shoulders, bundles on heads, and maybe a walking stick—or nothing—in their hands. It brought tears to Mariah's eyes.

She looked around for the strange old lady with the long bone walking stick she'd seen the night before, but there was no sign of her.

But there was more cannon boom. A shell whizzed through the air.

Mariah looked ahead, saw Yankees moving faster across the bridge.

Another boom.

Mariah looked back, saw people rushing forward.

Something was coming. Good or—

Evil.

Mariah knew it in her bones.

Hand tight on Zeke's she prayed for wings as eagles as she, Ben, Rachel, Rose, Miriam, Mordecai, and the Doubles neared the water's edge. She felt a tightness in her chest when she saw the tramp of troops coming to an end. Only about a hundred left to cross. From the back of the last covered wagon, a pair of eyes peeked out. Praline.

Mariah looked back, saw colored crammed against each other. The air reeked of fear.

Mariah's group was within a few yards of the planked way leading to the bridge when she—they all—got a fright.

"Stand where you are!" shouted a soldier, his musket rifle at the ready. One, two, three other soldiers raised their rifles too.

Mariah stared at the soldiers in disbelief. They can't be . . .

Rachel cried out, "They gon' do what they did at Buckhead Creek! Gon' take up the bridge!"

Hagar screamed, "Good God, they can't do that!"

Mordecai shouted, "Buckhead wasn't nowhere deep as this one!"

Mariah stood there in frozen fear, staring at the black water, reckoning it to be more than a hundred feet wide, terrified at the thought of how deep.

Mariah stood there in frozen fear as the bluecoats walking backward began to pull up the bridge, with the four rifle-ready soldiers behind them, guns still trained on the people on the north bank.

"Please, no!"

"Stop!"

"Don't leave us!"

"Have mercy!"

Mariah stood with her arms around Zeke, tears streaming down her face, staring at the nothing. The nothing between Ebenezer Creek's north and south banks but water. It looked icy cold.

Then she heard the thunder—pictured a thousand horses, full gallop.

From behind more shouts and cries. One word over and over, first too faint for Mariah to make out, but it was soon a roar as people shouted it up the line.

"Secesh!"

"*Secesh!*"

"SECESH!"

Then a chorus of bloodcurdling screams.

"Help us!"

"For the love of God!"

More thunder. Could only be Rebel horsemen.

They were trapped. With no hope for Rebel mercy there was only one thing to do.

The crowd from behind surged forward, became a shove.

Bullets cracked the air.

Mariah saw Rachel grab her stomach, collapse on top of little Rose.

Saw Hosea, eyes heavenward, tears streaking down his wrinkled face. Saw Hagar drop to her knees and wail.

Saw Ben jump in.

Miriam jump in.

"Swim, Zeke, swim!"

Hand in hand with her brother, Mariah plunged into Ebenezer Creek.

Before they hit the water, she heard Zoe cry out, "We can't swim! We can't swim!"

The thunder was louder, muting the cries for help.

"Swim, Zeke, swim!"

Muted, too, the angry shouts and curses on the other side of Ebenezer Creek.

"Swim!"

Mariah caught sight of men, colored and white, hurling logs into the water, lashing branches fast together for rafts.

She heard Zeke calling out, "Mariah! Mariah!"

"Swim, Zeke, swim!"

She spotted a log, reached it, reached Zeke. "Hold on tight!"

More bullets whizzed.

She ducked. Up again she saw a pouch bobbing in the water, floating away.

"My freedoms! My freedoms!" Zeke cried out.

Then she saw him—

"No!"

Let go of the log.

"No! No, God, no!"

More rifle shots shattered the air.

She saw Zeke flailing, thrashing.

Another bullet whizzed, sent her ducking.

Up again. "Zeke!"

Down again. Couldn't see.

Up again. Couldn't see.

"Ze—"

ON THE EDEN ROAD

Slumped in his tent, cup of coffee gone cold, Caleb stared at the pages of his diary. He flipped back to the entry he made the day he left Atlanta. He skimmed other pages at random. Then, for a while, he just listened to the pouring rain.

Thirty minutes had passed since he wrote in the upper right-hand corner of a new page, "Fri., Dec. 9th, 1864," then put his pencil down.

What time the division moved, how many miles marched— none of that was worth writing about. Not today. And he couldn't muster the strength to write about the crossing at Ebenezer Creek.

If only he hadn't been so far ahead.

When word reached him, Caleb had leapt onto the first available horse he saw, rode hard. But by the time he reached Ebenezer Creek all that lay upon its waters were cloaks, caps, shoes, kerchiefs, walking sticks, shawls, leather pouches, calabash canteens.

He searched among the survivors, many in huddles before fires bundled up in Yankee blankets and coats.

No Hagar.

"Mariah!"

No Hosea.

"Mariah!"

No Ben.

"Mariah!"

No Rachel, no Rose, no Miriam.

"Mariah!" Caleb called out as he stumbled from cypress tree to cypress tree, from tupelo to tupelo. "Mariah!"

"Mordecai!"

"Chloe!"

"Zoe!"

"Zeke!"

Caleb cried out until he went hoarse.

"Mariah! *Mariah!* MARIAH!"

Soon he knew that somewhere upon the waters blue glass beads floated too.

"How'd it happen?" Caleb, in a daze, asked Captain Galloway long minutes later as they sat on the banks of Ebenezer Creek.

Captain Galloway looked away, hung his head.

Caleb shook with rage. "General Reb?"

Captain Galloway nodded. "He swore a select few to secrecy, told them—" The captain swallowed.

"Told them what?"

"Told them other than pioneers to not let any colored cross."

Caleb looked up at the sky, peered at massive anvil-shaped clouds, figured there'd be rainfall soon. "Captain, can you do me a favor?"

"Anything."

"Get me attached to a man like you in the right wing. I can't ride with the Fourteenth Corps, with the left wing, no more."

"Yes, of course. I'll do that."

"Can't say what I'll do if I cross paths with General Reb."

"I understand."

Captain Galloway also vowed to write General Grant, President Lincoln, Secretary of War Stanton, and every newspaperman he knew to tell them about General Reb's infamous order.

Colored lives don't matter.

It was dusk and there Caleb sat, hollowed out and alone in his tent, when he remembered Mariah uttering those words. A tear made tracks down his cheek. And steady on was the downpour. As Caleb listened to the rain, he longed to hear her voice once more. But then he saw her. Saw her emerge from the root cellar, saw her leading Dulcina over to the scrub oak, saw her jubilant over those lace-up boots, saw her hands swimming in his buckskin gloves, saw the love in her eyes right before they kissed. His everything was gone.

Caleb did something he had not done since Lily, then his mother, died.

He wept, knowing the rainfall would drown out his sobs.

When spent, Caleb wiped his eyes, took a sip of that cold coffee, and picked up his pencil again, willing himself to write about Ebenezer Creek, telling himself that he *had* to get it all down while it was still fresh in his mind. But, in the end, all he could manage was a few words.

"Camped on the Eden Road."

Epilogue

Many hundred gone? Many thousand?

Not a soul would ever know nor untangle tales about what Rebel horsemen did to those who did not plunge into Ebenezer Creek.

Rife were the rumors of folks hacked to death.

Shot.

Bludgeoned.

Rampant were reports of Rebels hauling scores back into slavery.

And onward went the march.

Two more days, three, four—twelve days after Ebenezer Creek, Uncle Billy's boys took the city by the sea. And owing to the march, more than twenty thousand of Georgia's colored men and women, girls and boys, who trooped with Sherman's four corps made their great escape.

When, a few weeks later, Sherman's army quit Savannah to plunder the Carolinas, steady on a multitude marched. A host of those folks attached themselves to Captain Abel Galloway, stuck with him through the end of the war that had split America asunder, an end that came four months after Ebenezer Creek. An end with true freedom—and great hope—in its wake.

Some of those hopeful souls even followed Captain Galloway to Washington, DC, and became a part of his new mission field: a school named after a founding father and Galloway friend, General Oliver Otis Howard, "Old Prayer Book." Among the Galloway loyalists were some survivors of Ebenezer Creek.

And Jonah.

Other survivors put down roots in Savannah and surroundings, made their livings as barbers, bakers, cooks, coopers, farmers, fishermen, milliners, masons. They celebrated freedom with fish fries, barbecues, picnics. They laughed, loved, married, had children.

Caleb dropped his dream of being a newspaperman, never wrote that book, never married. He built a smithy and a home some miles shy of Savannah. Though he could have afforded one, his wasn't a large spread. Just one acre. On the Eden Road. And he called his homestead Mariah.

Year after year, on December 9, even in the pouring rain, Caleb rode out to Ebenezer Creek and tossed flowers upon the waters. Standing there alone, he saw Mariah's profile in a cloud, heard her laughter in the wind. On bright days her smile was in the sun. And year after year he recounted what happened at Ebenezer Creek to whoever would listen, whoever he thought, hoped, prayed would remember to pass the story on.

And that's how it came to be said that in a southeast Georgia swamp, when a driving rain drenches an early December day, bald cypresses seem to screech, tupelos to shriek, Ebenezer Creek to moan.

Down through the years, when science minds tried to explain it away with talk of air flow, wind waves, and such, others shook their heads. *Not so.* They said it was the ghosts of Ebenezer Creek rising, reeling, wrestling with the wind. Remembering.

Remembering desperate pleas, heartrending screams.

Remembering hope after hope, dream after dream, and body after body flowing downstream.

Mariah, who had dreamed of a long life with Caleb and at least one acre, she first remembers that twelve days before she reached Ebenezer Creek, a hungry hush sent a shiver down her spine.

Author's Note

Years ago I was invited to do a presentation in Pocantico Hills, New York. Before it, I and other authors were treated to a lovely dinner. Most of the conversation was about history. At one point, my book on Martin Luther King Jr. came up.

One host, Robert Balog, asked if King's ancestral church in Atlanta, Georgia, and other black churches carried in their name "Ebenezer" because of what happened at Ebenezer Creek.

"What happened at Ebenezer Creek?" I asked this Civil War history buff.

I knew about Sherman's March to the Sea. I knew about his vow to "make Georgia howl," and that he made good on that vow to the tune of a hundred million dollars' worth of damage.

But I had never heard about the tragedy, the betrayal at Ebenezer Creek.

During the rest of dinner, after the program, and days

later I couldn't shake the story. I wondered about the lives of those who perished in Ebenezer Creek and about the lives of those who didn't plunge in. Who did the world lose? What did the world lose?

I did a little digging. One of my first finds was an article, Edward M. Churchill's "Betrayal at Ebenezer Creek." Then in late 2010, I discovered that in the spring of that year, the Georgia Historical Society placed a marker about a mile south of Ebenezer Creek, at the end of Effingham County's Ebenezer Road. It reads:

March to the Sea: Ebenezer Creek

One mile north, on December 9, 1864, during the American Civil War, U.S. Gen. Jeff. C. Davis crossed Ebenezer Creek with his 14th Army Corps as it advanced toward Savannah during Gen. William T. Sherman's March to the Sea. Davis hastily removed the pontoon bridges over the creek, and hundreds of freed slaves following his army drowned trying to swim the swollen waters to escape the pursuing Confederates. Following a public outcry, Sec. of War Edwin Stanton met with Sherman and local black leaders in Savannah on January 12, 1865. Four days later, President Lincoln approved Sherman's Special Field Orders No. 15, confiscating over 400,000 acres

of coastal property and redistributing it to former
slaves in 40-acre tracts.

A marker can only say so much. There was no room to note
that it was from Sherman's Special Field Orders No. 15 that
the myth arose that all black people—or all once-enslaved
people—in the United States had been promised forty acres
and a mule.

There was also no room to note another betrayal: in the
fall of 1865, President Lincoln's successor, Andrew Johnson,
revoked that special order. Almost all those four hundred
thousand acres on which thousands of black people had begun
to build new tomorrows in self-governing communities went
back into the hands of ex-Confederates.

As for Secretary of War Stanton's visit to Savannah in
January 1865, before he met with General Sherman and those
black leaders—Garrison Frazier among them—he had a talk
with Sherman about Ebenezer Creek.

Stated Sherman in his memoirs: "He talked to me a great
deal about the negroes, the former slaves, and I told him of
many interesting incidents, illustrating their simple character and faith in our arms and progress."

When the conversation turned to his general Jefferson
Davis, Sherman assured Stanton that he was a fine soldier and
that he put no credence in talk that he hated black people.

Stanton didn't let it go. He showed Sherman a newspaper

article about the incident at Ebenezer Creek. Sherman admitted only to having heard rumors about Davis taking up a bridge and leaving some black people behind. He then suggested that Stanton speak with Davis himself. When Stanton did, General Davis explained that the closer they got to Savannah the more creek-ridden the terrain, thus requiring constant use of the pontoon bridges—and Rebel cavalrymen were in hot pursuit. Yes, Davis told Stanton, at Ebenezer Creek, the bridge was taken up before all the black people crossed. But they were ones who had fallen asleep, he claimed.

And yes, said Davis, some were picked up by Confederate cavalrymen. As for Confederates killing blacks in cold blood, like Sherman, Davis dismissed that as claptrap. In a later defense of Davis, Sherman told someone that his general "took up his pontoon bridge, not because he wanted to leave them [the colored people], but because he wanted his bridge."

Jefferson Davis in Union blue survived the brief investigation into the incident at Ebenezer Creek, survived the march through the Carolinas, survived the war. He died in Chicago on November 30, 1879, at the age of fifty-one. The *New York Times* reported that he breathed his last "after being confined to his bed for five days with pneumonia." The article was titled "Gen. Jefferson C. Davis Dead. The Honorable Career of a Soldier Who Began in the Ranks—Incidents of His Life."

*   *   *

Jefferson C. Davis came to me out of history, as did the black people in Savannah Caleb tells Mariah about. Mariah, Caleb, Zeke, Dulcina, the Doubles, Mordecai, Jonah, and the rest, they feel to me like messengers from history. They are fictional but based on real people I have read about in books and heard of as a child during firefly nights on Southern porches and around cozy Northern kitchen tables when family lore was being served up and consumed. My characters are also based on what history tells me was possible.

Of course the journey was real.

So it is my hope that through these characters, through this book future generations will not lose sight of what happened at Ebenezer Creek, that they will remember.

And pass the story on.

RESEARCH AND SOURCES

Many sources played a key role in helping me write about the people and the places in *Crossing Ebenezer Creek*: books, diaries, and articles, which allowed me to put myself—and thus my characters—on Sherman's march and enabled me to visit the lives of black Georgians during the Civil War as well as those of Union soldiers and white Georgians. The following are chief among the sources on which I relied.

"Betrayal at Ebenezer Creek" by Edward M. Churchill (accessed from www.historynet.com).

Black Savannah, 1788–1864 by Whittington B. Johnson (Fayetteville: University of Arkansas Press, 1996).

"The Civil War Diary of James Laughlin Orr" (accessed from http://freepages.genealogy.rootsweb.ancestry.com/~jonnic /People/zUnknownConnections/Churchyard/civwdiar.html).

Cornelius C. Platter Civil War Diary, 1864–1865 (accessed from the Digital Library of Georgia, http://dlg.galileo.usg .edu/hargrett/platter/001.php).

History of the Fifty-Eighth Regiment of Indiana Volunteer Infantry based on the manuscript of Chaplain John J. Hight, compiled by Gilbert R. Storming (Princeton, IN: Press of the Clarion, 1895).

"An Indiana Doctor Marches with Sherman: The Diary of James Comfort Patten," by Robert G. Athearn, *Indiana Magazine of History* (December 1953): 405–422.

Jefferson Davis in Blue: The Life of Sherman's Relentless Warrior by Nathaniel Cheairs Hughes Jr. and Gordon D. Whitney (Baton Rouge: Louisiana State University, 2002).

Memoirs of General William T. Sherman, vol. 2 (New York: D. Appleton and Company, 1866).

Saving Savannah: The City and the Civil War by Jacqueline Jones (New York: Vintage, 2009).

Slave Life in Georgia: A Narrative of the Life, Sufferings, and Escape of John Brown edited by Louis Alexis Chamerovzow (London: n.p., 1855).

Slave Narratives: A Folk History of Slavery in the United States, produced by the Federal Writers' Project, 1936–1938, sponsored and assembled by the Library of Congress (Washington: n.p., 1941; accessed from Project Gutenberg, www.gutenberg.org).

Southern Storm: Sherman's March to the Sea by Noah Andre Trudeau (New York: HarperCollins, 2009).

The Story of the Great March: From the Diary of a Staff Officer by Brevet Major George Ward Nichols (New York: Harper & Brothers, 1865).

Three Years in the Army of the Cumberland: The Letters and Diary of Major James A. Connolly edited by Paul M. Angle (Bloomington: Indiana University Press, 1987).

"'We have Surely done a Big Work': The Diary of a Hoosier Soldier on Sherman's 'March to the Sea'" by Jeffrey L. Patrick and Robert Willey, *Indiana Magazine of History* (September 1998): 214–239.

I also drew upon knowledge acquired in writing two of my nonfiction books: *Cause: Reconstruction America, 1863–1877* (New York: Knopf, 2005) and *Emancipation Proclamation: Lincoln and the Dawn of Liberty* (New York: Abrams, 2013).

ACKNOWLEDGMENTS

Ever grateful to my first editor, Michelle Nagler, for believing that this was a story that needed to be told. And oh so grateful to my second editor, Mary Kate Castellani, who thoroughly and utterly embraced the project. Mary Kate's enthusiasm along with her wise and wondrous direction opened me up to discover things in my mind and on my heart that I didn't know were there. Thanks is also due to others in the Bloomsbury "crew": Jill Amack, Colleen Andrews, Diane Aronson, Erica Barmash, Beth Eller, Courtney Griffin, Melissa Kavonic, Linette Kim, Donna Mark, Lizzy Mason, Shaelyn McDaniel, Patricia McHugh, Emily Ritter, and Claire Stetzer. I thank you all for all your fine and so excellent work. You did so much for the book and thus did so much for me. As does my agent, Jennifer Lyons.

And, bless you, my fellow writers Joyce Hansen and Sharon

Flake. I can't thank you enough for giving the manuscript a close read and for giving me such useful feedback.

Thank you, Joseph McGill, Civil War reenactor and founder of the Slave Dwelling Project, for your read and feedback too!

Thank you, Jim Prichard, professional researcher, for reading a chunk of an early draft and for telling me about the killing stone.

Thank you, Robert Balog, for telling me about what happened at Ebenezer Creek.